C000094439

HAPPY ENDINGS AT MERMAIDS POINT

SARAH BENNETT

Boldwood

First published in Great Britain in 2022 by Boldwood Books Ltd.

Copyright © Sarah Bennett, 2022

Cover Design by Alice Moore Design

Cover Photography: Shutterstock

The moral right of Sarah Bennett to be identified as the author of this work has been asserted in accordance with the Copyright, Designs and Patents Act 1988.

All rights reserved. No part of this book may be reproduced in any form or by any electronic or mechanical means, including information storage and retrieval systems, without written permission from the author, except for the use of brief quotations in a book review.

This book is a work of fiction and, except in the case of historical fact, any resemblance to actual persons, living or dead, is purely coincidental.

Every effort has been made to obtain the necessary permissions with reference to copyright material, both illustrative and quoted. We apologise for any omissions in this respect and will be pleased to make the appropriate acknowledgements in any future edition.

A CIP catalogue record for this book is available from the British Library.

Paperback ISBN 978-1-83889-969-1

Large Print ISBN 978-1-83889-970-7

Hardback ISBN 978-1-80483-978-2

Ebook ISBN 978-1-83889-971-4

Kindle ISBN 978-1-83889-972-1

Audio CD ISBN 978-1-83889-964-6

MP3 CD ISBN 978-1-83889-965-3

Digital audio download ISBN 978-1-83889-966-0

Boldwood Books Ltd
23 Bowerdean Street
London SW6 3TN
www.boldwoodbooks.com

This book is for my editor, Sarah Ritherdon, who has helped me rediscover my writing mojo x

MERMAIDS POINT CHARACTER LIST

Alex Nelson. Tom's half-brother, Emily and Max's uncle, son of Archie and Philippa Nelson. Former accountant, now runs Mermaid Tails and Treasures, the village bookshop. Author of the bestselling novel *The Marriage Roller Coaster*. Hero of *Love Blooms at Mermaids Point*.
Ali Mackey. Runs the late-night diner at Cleopatra's hotel in Las Vegas with her husband, Gus.
Alun Wise. Local estate agent.
Andrew Morgan. Married to Sylvia, Laurie and Nick' father. Owner of The Mermaids Cave, a large gift shop on the seafront.
Anna Nelson. Tom's late wife and mother to Emily and Max.
Archie Nelson. Tom and Alex's father. Married to Philippa, grandfather of Emily and Max. Known in the family as 'Pop'.
Audrey. A nosy neighbour of Aurora's parents.
Augustus 'Gus' Mackey. Runs the late-night diner at Cleopatra's hotel in Las Vegas with his wife, Ali.
Aurora Storm. Pop star who staged a number of mermaid sightings around the Point as part of a viral campaign for her comeback album. Had a very brief fling with Nick Morgan while she was in the village. Heroine of *Happy Endings at Mermaids Point*.

Barbara Mitchell. Part of the local knitting circle. Lives with Malcolm Gadd.

Bev. Part of the local knitting circle, known to have a sharp tongue.

Blaze Reynolds. Founder of ATG (All the Goss). A scurrilous gossip website.

Bud Callaghan. On honeymoon in Las Vegas with his wife, Helen.

Carly King. Tabloid showbiz reporter.

Carlotta. Barbara Mitchell's cat.

Chad Logan. Hollywood legend. Married to Melissa Howard.

Damian. A young boy who lives in Mermaids Point.

Dennis Rouse. Head of DR Talent Agency. Aurora Storm's agent. Married to Hetty.

Emily Nelson. Tom and Anna's teenage daughter.

Gabriel. A cairn terrier.

Gareth Beckett. Nerissa's late fiancé. Died in a road accident whilst on a military deployment twenty-five years before the books are set.

Helen Callaghan. On honeymoon in Las Vegas with her husband, Bud.

Hetty Rouse. Married to Dennis, helps him run DR Talent Agency.

Ivy Fisher. Runs her own design, repair and alterations service which is located within the village bookshop. Laurie's best friend. Heroine of *Love Blooms at Mermaids Point*.

Jake Smith. Investigative journalist currently working on a non-fiction book about county lines drug smuggling. Hero of *Summer Kisses at Mermaids Point*.

Janey. Mermaids Point resident. Talented singer.

Jen Fisher. Ivy's mother, passed away in January after a long illness.

Julian Knox-Cavendish. Ex-boyfriend of Aurora Storm.

Kayleigh. Backstage assistant for the Divas show in Las Vegas.

Kim Powell. Aurora Storm's mother. Married to Ross.

Kitty Duke. Part of the local knitting circle. A darling.

Leonard Cavendish. Former owner of the local bookshop which now belongs to Alex and Ivy.

Liam. Local architect who works with Nick Morgan.

Linda Smith. Jake's mother and a close friend of Nerissa's.

Lorelai 'Laurie' Morgan. Runs a café next door to her parent's gift shop. Heroine of *Summer Kisses at Mermaids Point*.

Louise. A resident of Mermaids Point. She and her husband are in the process of purchasing one of the warehouse apartments recently redeveloped by Nick Morgan.

Luca. Owns and runs the local delicatessen. Married to Maria.

Lucifer. Alex and Ivy's black cat.

Mac. Newspaper editor. Jake Smith's former boss.

Malcolm Gadd. Mermaids Point former doctor, known to everyone as 'Doc'. Mostly retired. Lives with Barbara Mitchell.

Marcy Johnson. Singing superstar and the headline act of the Divas show in Las Vegas.

Margot Beckett. Gareth's mother.

Maria. Runs the local delicatessen with her husband, Luca.

Max Nelson. Tom and Anna's teenage son.

Melissa Howard. Former Hollywood actor, now a celebrity talk show host. Married to Chad Logan.

Mrs Bailey. A regular customer at the bookshop.

Nerissa Morgan. Andrew's younger sister, paternal aunt of Laurie and Nick. Manages the doctor's surgery. Heroine of *Second Chances at Mermaids Point*.

Nick Morgan. Runs a tourist boat business from the Point's commercial harbour with his and Laurie's uncle, Tony. Still pining after a brief fling with Aurora Storm. Hero of *Happy Endings at Mermaids Point*.

Nicholas. A miserable toddler at a service station motel.

Pete Bray. Landlord of The Sailor's Rest, a popular pub on the seafront. Owns the Penny Arcade a few doors down from the pub.

Philippa Nelson. Archie's wife, Alex's mother and Tom's stepmother. Step-grandmother to Emily and Max. Known in the family as 'Mimi'.

Reverend Steele. Mermaids Point's vicar.

Rob. Local contractor who works for Nick Morgan.

Ross Powell. Aurora Storm's father. Married to Kim.

Ruby. A school friend of Emily Nelson.

Sophia. A young girl who lives in Mermaids Point.

Sylvia Morgan. Married to Andrew, Laurie and Nick's mother. Runs The

Mermaids Cave with her husband as well as working part-time at the village school as classroom assistant.

Toby. Tom and Nerissa's golden retriever.

Tom Nelson. Widower of Anna, and father to Emily and Max. The village doctor. Hero of *Second Chances at Mermaids Point*.

Tony Evans. Sylvia's brother and maternal uncle of Laurie and Nick. Owner of Mermaid Boat Tours, a pleasure boat business which takes tourists on trips around the area and out to the Seven Sisters, a group of nearby islands.

Wendy Hancock. Ex-girlfriend of Ivy's estranged father. Works in the local greengrocer's.

PROLOGUE

'Grab that end, will you?' Nick's father, Andrew Morgan, gestured to the opposite end of the brightly striped windbreak he was wrestling with. It wasn't that breezy, but the taut piece of fabric would help their ever-expanding family group to stake a claim on the beach and provide a visual guide back to the right spot as the narrow stretch of sand filled up. There was plenty of space on the pebbles behind them, but it was one of the few days over the summer when no one was working, and his father was determined to grab a prime spot, which was why the two of them were out on the beach before 7.30 a.m. setting up. With the late August bank holiday weekend behind them, the Point was rapidly emptying of tourists and the Morgans and the Nelsons wouldn't be the only local families taking advantage of the glorious weather before they fell back into the routines of school and work.

Nick held the wooden pole in place while his father hammered it into the sand with a rubber mallet and tried not to think about the million and one tasks waiting for him back at the warehouse. His parents didn't ask much of him so when they'd gone to all the effort of coordinating a family day, it was the least he could do to show up with a smile on his face. Apart from his aunt, Nerissa, who worked at the local doctor's surgery supporting her partner, Tom Nelson, who'd arrived just about a year ago to take over the practice, their entire extended family relied on the tourist season to keep their heads above water. Everyone had worked flat-out through what had been an incredibly successful season thanks to a prolonged period of high pressure over the UK, which had led to a particularly warm summer. His parents ran a gift shop on the seafront, his sister the adjoining café. Alex, Tom's brother and a good friend of Nick's, had taken over the village bookshop in the spring. Although everyone still referred to it as the bookshop, it had grown into so much more thanks to Ivy's innovative fashion and homeware designs which occupied one half of the shop. Nick himself helped his uncle run a pleasure boat business out of the old harbour. Juggling his commitment to Uncle Tony while trying to project manage his new venture to turn an old warehouse into four modern apartments had been a struggle. Nick had leaned heavily on Rob, his lead contractor, to keep things running smoothly. From the enthusiastic way Rob had greeted the prospect of a day off site, Nick fully expected he would see him, his wife and their three small children making the most of the sunshine. Hopefully it would earn Nick some goodwill when things got down to the wire with the warehouse conversion and the inevitable late nights needed to get things done on time. Now summer was almost done, Nick would have more free time away from the boats, and he intended to throw every hour he could into getting the flats completed before the weather turned.

Leaving his father to roll out the straw mats that would keep the worst of the sand off their towels, Nick raised a hand to shield his eyes and stared out across the calm expanse of blue ocean. Mornings like this made it easy to believe they would enjoy sunshine forever, but like all residents of the Point, he knew better. Come the winter, that blue blanket would be a seething mass of dark grey topped with white rollers crashing in to swallow the sand and halfway up the pebbles too.

'We couldn't have asked for a better start to the day,' his father observed as he came to stand beside Nick. 'I know there's as many hard times as there are good, but I wouldn't want to be anywhere else.'

Nick swallowed a frustrated sigh. Though his dad probably thought his comment was the height of subtlety, it was one of many similar observations various members of the family had made to him in the past few months. They sensed the restlessness inside him, and he knew they were worried about it. *He* was worried about it. His project to convert the old warehouse overlooking the harbour into four apartments was supposed to have given him a new focus, as well as providing him with a home of his own because he was too damn old to still be holed up in the back bedroom at his parents' house. As he'd started looking at the sample books, he'd found himself choosing the same neutral kitchen units and bathroom tiles for all four of the flats, rather than his original plan of designing one to his own specific tastes. Best to keep his options open, the small voice in the back of his head had said, in case he decided to rent, or even sell the place at a later date. He should've been brimming with excitement at the prospect of finally having a home of his own; instead, he just felt... flat.

A group of bobbing pink swimming caps caught his eye, evidence of the local open-water swimming club making the most of the peace and quiet before the body boarders and pleasure bathers took over the water. Grabbing at the chance to steer his father away from any more well-intentioned pep talks, Nick pointed them out. 'I wonder which one is Linda.' After a shy start while she'd found her feet, Linda had thrown herself into all sorts of surprising activities since she'd followed her son, Jake, to the Point. They were both such a part of the family, it felt like much more than a year since Jake had come to the village to investigate a rash of mermaid sightings that had gone viral and fallen in love with Nick's younger sister, Laurie.

'Probably the one near the back who's waving at us,' his dad said with a laugh as he raised his hand to return the greeting. Soon half the swimmers were waving and calling out 'good morning' as they breast-stroked past. There were a few in the group who took things more seriously and were ploughing through the gently rolling waves like one of the Brownlee brothers trying to win Olympic gold in the triathlon, but most were happy to go at a pace where they could chat as well as keep an eye on each other. Nick's gaze wandered beyond the swimmers to the scattered islands on the horizon, known locally as the Seven Sisters. After his years taking tourists and bird-watchers out to view them, he knew all the secret landing spots... Nick turned away, cursing himself for thinking about Linda, which had led to thinking about Jake, those stupid mermaid stunts and therefore... *No*.

He would not let his brain spiral around that hopeless loop yet again. Shaking himself like a dog emerging from the ocean, as though *she* could be shaken off as easily as droplets of salt water, Nick marched back up to the spot they'd staked out and began laying out towels over the mats. The others would be here soon – Laurie had promised them bacon rolls in return for their early morning efforts – and Nick would not let anything spoil the day. Even his pathetic yearning for what could never be.

* * *

Nick's mum, Sylvia, arrived a little over half an hour later with Laurie and Jake in tow. His sister waved when she spotted them, holding up an insulated bag that Nick fervently hoped carried the promised bacon rolls. Jake trailed a few steps behind, his brow creased from the effort of lugging a pair of enormous cold boxes, which were no doubt packed with other tasty treats Laurie had prepared to sustain them. With the cold boxes tucked deep in the shade of an oversized sun umbrella, Nick settled on his towel and began to unwrap the silver foil that was keeping his roll warm. The smell of crispy bacon made his mouth water and he half-closed his eyes in anticipation of the first bite as he raised it to his lips... *Splat!* A dollop of something cold hit him on the back of the neck and he ducked reflexively from the shock of the unexpected sensation. He turned his head, only for his mother to grasp it from behind and force him to face the front. 'Keep still while I rub this in,' she scolded him as her fingers began to rub at the sun cream she'd squirted from a large bottle.

'I can do it myself,' Nick grumbled, trying to shift away so he could eat his breakfast. 'I'm twenty-eight, not eight.'

'Oh hush, you big baby, I'll be done in a minute,' his mum admonished before leaning around to plant a kiss on his cheek that made Nick want to roll his eyes and smile at the same time. Sylvia Morgan was a force of nature and it was pointless trying to change her – not that Nick wanted to, for all her fussing.

Nick shot an imploring look towards his father, who was grinning around his own half-eaten roll. 'Best do as your mum says, lad, you know she'll get her way in the end.'

So much for moral support! Nick stared glumly at his roll for a moment before wrapping it up with a sigh and setting it on the towel beside him. Leaning back slightly, he let his mother finish rubbing in the sun cream, only protesting when she yanked at the neck of his T-shirt to reach down inside the neckline and almost cut off his air supply in the process. 'Enough, Mum, seriously.' With a click of her tongue, Sylvia Morgan shuffled on her knees towards her husband, who only let his grin slip for a second when he realised he was next in line for the same treatment. Letting his own smug smile stretch his lips, Nick retrieved his breakfast and wolfed it down before anything else could spoil his enjoyment.

He'd just finished the last bite and handed his scrunched-up bit of silver foil to Laurie, when a chorus of greetings – including an enthusiastic bark – announced the arrival of the Nelson family group. As well as Tom, Nerissa and Tom's two teenage children, Emily and Max, the party included Alex and his girlfriend and business partner, Ivy, and his parents, Archie and Philippa. Last but by no means least was Linda, rosy-cheeked from her swimming exertions. She'd moved into the upstairs flat at the surgery on a temporary basis back in the spring, but no one seemed in a hurry for her to move out.

Although they still lived in London, Archie and Philippa were currently staying with their eldest son while Archie recuperated from a broken leg after an ill-advised attempt to prune the wisteria without someone to hold his ladder. Nick noticed he was having to use a stick to negotiate his way over the slippery pebbles, but at least he was up and about, which would be a relief to everyone. Alex had told him he was avoiding the surgery because his father's temper seemed to grow shorter as his convalescence continued. The scowl Archie cast at his eldest son when Tom dared to offer him a hand spoke volumes. Oblivious to any tensions in the new arrivals, Toby, the family's boisterous golden retriever, was beside himself with excitement as to who he should greet first. Nick managed to fend off an enthusiastic lick, but his dad wasn't so lucky and received a full face-washing. Toby had belonged to the previous doctor and somehow wound up staying on at the surgery after he retired. It had worked out all around as Max had bonded with the soft-hearted dog and it was plain for all to see the pair were now inseparable. Doc had moved in with his long-term partner, Barbara, who not only lived in a cottage too small to comfortably contain a large dog, but also owned a very fussy cat named Carlotta. Carlotta had a lot to answer for when it came to people adopting unexpected pets, as Alex and Ivy had ended up being caretakers for an enormous black cat – aptly named Lucifer. Barbara had promised to take Lucifer in when old Mr Cavendish had sold up his bookshop and moved to Cornwall. Carlotta, however, had other ideas so Lucifer had kept showing up at the bookshop until the new owners had caved in and let him stay. Alex and Lucifer shared something of a tolerate-hate relationship, although the old bruiser was starting to soften towards his new owner and only clawed him every other day.

As he scrambled up to help the Nelsons get all their stuff sorted out, Nick couldn't help but laugh as absolute chaos descended. Tom and Archie were giving entirely contradictory instructions about what should go where, while Max tried without much success to stop Toby from poking his inquisitive nose into the bag where Laurie had stashed their rubbish from the bacon rolls. The women were all ignoring the men as they exchanged hugs and kisses as though they hadn't all seen each other the day before. Nick glanced around at his dad, who was wisely sprawled on his towel with a paperback shielding his face from both the sun and the mayhem around him and thought yet again that he could do worse than follow the example his father so often set. As the noise around him reached a crescendo, Nick struggled to imagine what life must be like at the surgery with everyone on top of each other. His parents' place was much quieter since Laurie had moved into a cottage Jake was renting up near the top of the large outcrop of land that gave the village its name, but even so Nick was itching for some solitude. As soon as the basics were done, he intended to move into the warehouse, even if he had to manage with little more than a sleeping bag on the floor for the next couple of months.

Spotting a football in amongst the jumble of bags, towels and other paraphernalia, Nick snatched it up. The only way things stood a chance of settling down was to thin out the group a bit. 'Fancy a kickabout?' he asked Max, who was still wrestling to get the dog under control. Toby wasn't a badly behaved dog for the most part, but like all retrievers he thought more with his stomach than his brain.

'I'm in!' Jake said, catching on to Nick's plan as well as the dog's lead. 'Enough of that,' he told the dog in a low, firm tone, which Toby instantly responded to. Jake was a quiet man, but there was a presence about him that was impossible to ignore. Max shot Jake a grateful grin and the three of them moved a few steps away from the rest of the group.

'Anyone else joining us?' Nick called out.

'As long as you don't mind another thrashing,' Alex said with a laugh, toeing out of his trainers and jogging over to join them. He raised a palm to his nephew, who slapped it with his own. 'Dream team united, hey, Max?'

The teenager whooped. 'We kicked their ass—' Max swallowed the word as both Nerissa and his grandmother whipped their heads around to shoot him a warning look. '—bottoms,' he finished in a chastened tone.

'If you give me five minutes,' Tom said, sounding harassed as he wrestled with a large reclining garden chair. 'Here all right?' he asked Archie.

'A bit more in the sun, I think,' Archie replied.

'It's fine where it is,' Philippa, Archie's wife cut across him. 'You know what the doctor said about that mole on your arm.'

There was a brief moment of tension between the two before Archie's frown relaxed into a fond smile. 'Where would I be without you looking after me?' He allowed his wife and Tom to ease him into the chair, his leg obviously still quite stiff.

As soon as he was settled, Philippa turned to Tom. 'You go on with the rest of the boys and we'll sort everything else out.'

Nick couldn't hide a grin as Tom glanced around at the sea of female faces all wearing the same expectant expression. For a man used to the responsibility of being the village doctor, it must be something of a blow to the ego to be dismissed so readily as being surplus to requirements.

Nick's dad tossed aside his book and stood. 'Come on, Tom, let's leave the ladies to it and show these youngsters a thing or two about how to play football.' His dad could always be relied upon to smooth things over. Too many people were fooled by his easy-going nature and readiness to laugh, but Nick didn't think there was anyone with a better insight into people

8 SARAH BENNETT

than Andrew Morgan. Still wearing something of a distracted expression, Tom allowed Andrew to sling a friendly arm around his shoulder and steer him over to where the rest of them had gathered.

'Morgans versus Nelsons?' Alex suggested, taking advantage of Nick's distraction to snatch the ball from his grip and start jogging down the beach to a quiet spot where they wouldn't risk annoying anyone.

'You really are desperate to lose, aren't you?' Jake bantered back as he made his own feint for the ball and almost knocked the two of them into the surf in the process. After twenty minutes of a raucous combination of blatant cheating, hastily invented on-the-spot rules and the unrestrained enthusiasm of the dog, which both teams claimed to be on their side, everyone was soaked to the skin from multiple tumbles into the water. Tossing his too-long curls out of his eyes with a shake of his head, Nick sent a deliberate spray of saltwater towards Alex, who had just finished trying to dry his face with his saturated T-shirt.

'Cheers,' Alex said, wiping his cheek and throwing Nick a mock-glare.

'Any time!' Nick responded in his most cheerfully annoying tone. Even with Max's creative scoring method, Team Morgan had emerged victorious. 'Beers are on you tonight, then.' He pointed out to his friend.

Alex grimaced before he broke into a grin that made him even more impossibly handsome than usual. It really wasn't fair for one man to look as good as he did and be such a nice bloke. No wonder Ivy had fallen for him hook, line and sinker. Nick pushed the thought away, still not quite ready to come to terms with the reality of the two of them being together. Even though they'd never dated, there'd been an expectation growing up that Nick and Ivy would somehow end up together. Their mothers had been best friends since their school days, a relationship that Ivy and Laurie had echoed, apart from a brief period of estrangement. Nick had seen Ivy as another little sister when they were younger, but he'd be lying to himself if he said he'd not noticed the way she'd grown into a beautiful, caring woman. Even though there'd never been much of a spark between them, he'd found himself wondering more than once whether their friendship might one day lead to something more. Which all sounded a lot more calculating than it was – he cared deeply about her, respected her and knew they'd have been able to build something lasting between them if they'd both been willing to put in the effort. Not every relationship started with fireworks and skipped heartbeats. He knew better than most that scorching chemistry wasn't enough to hold on to someone. Especially when that person had the whole world at their feet and all he had to offer was a part-share in a tourist boat business in a backwater village clinging to the far reaches of the west coast. For all his restlessness, Nick still thought the Point was the most beautiful place on earth, but a penny arcade on the seafront didn't exactly make it comparable to Las Vegas. And gigging in the backroom of The Sailor's Rest sure as hell wasn't a three-month residency in the showroom of Cleopatra's, one of the largest hotel and casino complexes in Sin City. It was such a ridiculous comparison, Nick couldn't help laughing out loud.

'Hey, my cooking's not that bad,' Alex protested, proving that Nick had been lost inside his own head once again and not paying attention.

'Sorry, I was thinking about... something else.' The sympathetic look his friend shot him as he clapped him on the shoulder did little to lift Nick's mood. Turning his attention away from what could never be, Nick slung a friendly arm around Alex's waist as they strolled back along the beach. 'I'm listening, I promise. Tell me what's on the menu for this evening.'

* * *

It didn't take long for the heat of the day to dry off their clothes and soon everyone was lazing around in the sun or the shade, reading books or listening to music. Nick had removed his T-shirt to make the most of the glorious sunshine and was contentedly listening to a cricket podcast when a shadow passed over him and he raised a hand to shade his face as he opened his eyes. It was only Aunt Nerissa and Tom taking the chance to steal away for a bit of quiet time. There was a bit of a kerfuffle behind him when it looked like Max might be trying to join them but he was quickly dissuaded by Sylvia, who caught the lad by the wrist and tugged him down to whisper in his ear. Whatever she said made the boy's eyes widen before a huge smile broke out across his face. He settled happily at Sylvia's side to tackle a puzzle in the thick book on her lap. Amazed as ever at his mother's persuasion skills, Nick turned back to watch the couple strolling along hand in hand at the edge of the water and smiled quietly to himself before settling back down on his towel. He was pleased Nerissa had found someone who adored her in the way she deserved after so many years of being alone. Maybe he should take a leaf out of her book and learn a little patience. To be fair to Nerissa, her first big love affair had ended in tragedy rather than a mildly dismissive text message, so it wasn't any wonder she'd found it hard to move on. All Nick had done was fall in love with someone who was unobtainable. He'd gone into it with his eyes wide open, and they'd been apart for more days than the cumulative hours they'd spent together – so why couldn't he put her out of his mind? Realising he'd missed the last five minutes of his podcast, Nick rewound it and tried to recapture the chilled-out mood he'd been enjoying.

It almost worked.

His podcast ended and Nick tugged out his earphone with a sigh. It had gone in one ear and out the other. Before he had the chance to open his app and find something else, his mum leapt to her feet and raised a hand to shade her eyes as she stared at something down the beach.

'Is that them?' Sylvia asked, before adding in a more excited tone: 'Yes! He's waving, Andrew, that's the signal!' Turning, she gestured impatiently at Laurie. 'What did you do with the keys? Hurry now!'

'I've got them here.' Laurie tossed the keys to the café towards her dad, who was scrambling up from his towel. 'Do you want Jake to give you a hand?' She didn't need to ask as Jake was already up and shoving his feet into a pair of battered trainers.

Confused at the sudden commotion, Nick watched the two of them depart at a jog. 'What's that all about?'

'You'll see,' was all his mother would say with an infuriatingly smug smile as she hurriedly resumed her seat. 'Act natural, everyone!'

Nick cast a bemused look towards Alex and Ivy, who shrugged. Turning to glance in the direction his mother had been looking, Nick received a swat on the back of his head with her puzzle book. 'Don't stare, you'll spoil the surprise.'

'I can hardly spoil something when I don't have a bloody clue what's going on,' Nick grumbled, but he snatched up his father's discarded paperback and pretended to read it while casting the odd furtive glance down the beach.

Moments later, Jake and his father returned, the latter somewhat more out of breath than the former. They stowed what looked like an insulated bag and a large cardboard box in the shade behind Archie's deckchair, then flopped down on their towels. Nick handed the book back to his dad but Andrew didn't have a chance to open it before Tom and Nerissa arrived back from their walk. They were both beaming from ear to ear and Nerissa had tears in her eyes. The moment she thrust her left hand towards them to display a simple diamond solitaire on a gold band, everything fell into place. As the congratulations rained down on the happy couple, Nick leant towards his father and nudged his arm. 'This is why you wanted us all together today, isn't it?'

His dad grinned as he threw an arm around Nick and tugged him close to smack a kiss on his cheek. 'It might have been one of the reasons, yes, but not the only one.' As he pulled back, Nick noticed Nerissa wasn't the only one with tears glistening in their eyes. For all his size, Andrew Morgan had a heart as soft as a marshmallow. Nick found he was also having to swallow around a sudden lump in his throat.

'I'm so, *so* happy for you both,' Sylvia cried as she hugged first Nerissa then Tom. 'We must drink a toast to your future happiness!'

Jake and his father's mad dash made sense when they retrieved a couple of bottles of champagne from the insulated bag together with a stack of disposable plastic glasses. As Sylvia handed a plastic flute full of the golden sparkling wine to Nerissa and a second to Tom, he raised an eyebrow at her presence of mind. 'I never doubted you for a second,' she said, giving his cheek a quick pat. 'Or you,' she added, grasping Nerissa's free hand and giving it a squeeze. 'If ever there was a couple who were made for each other...' She turned away with a laugh, fanning a hand in front of her face to ward off her own tears. 'Give me a glass of that before I start blubbing, for goodness' sake!'

With their glasses charged, they formed a circle around Tom and Nerissa. 'To the happy couple,' Nick's father said, raising his glass. 'May you bring comfort and joy to each other every day.'

'To the happy couple!' they all chorused, then sipped their champagne.

Max and Emily crowded in, one either side of Tom and Nerissa, for a hug. 'Can I be a bridesmaid?' Emily asked, all big eyes and excited smiles as she leaned into Nerissa's side.

'Of course you can, darling,' Nerissa replied. 'I can't think of anything I'd like more.'

'Can I *not* be a page boy?' Max asked in a wry voice that made them all laugh.

'I thought you might be my best man,' Tom said to his son, with a quick, almost apologetic look towards his brother.

'Fabulous idea,' Alex said, showing no signs at all of feeling slighted at Tom's choice. 'Nick, Jake and I can be ushers.'

'Can we?' Nick poked his friend in the ribs. 'Maybe ask before you volunteer me for stuff.' He'd been joking, of course, but when he caught a shadow pass over his aunt's face, he hurried over to reassure her. 'Whatever you need me to do, I'll be there. Just let me know the date when you are ready.'

Nerissa exchanged a quick glance with Tom. 'We haven't had time to discuss the practicalities.'

Tom curled an arm around her waist. 'I don't want to wait too long; perhaps we could do it sometime over Christmas?'

His suggestion was greeted with another flurry of excitement, mostly from the women, who immediately launched into a discussion about dresses and capes and the like, which Nick quickly extricated himself from.

Moving back to Alex's side, he clicked their glasses together. 'Good call about the usher thing,' he said before taking a sip.

Alex shrugged as though it was no big deal. 'I could see Tom was worried, but there's no need for him to be. I think it's only right that they involve Max and Emily right in the heart of everything – Nerissa's not just marrying Tom, she's making a permanent commitment to them too.'

'Good point.' Nick glanced back at his aunt. He'd always wondered what people meant when they said someone was glowing – but no longer. Happiness seemed to shine from Nerissa's very core. He was delighted for her – delighted for all four of them for building a family after so much heartbreak. 'Christmas, eh?' he muttered, staring at the bubbles in his glass. 'That gives me a few months to sort out a date, I suppose.'

Jake had wandered over to join them. 'What was that about a date?'

'I was just saying I've got a few months to sort myself out so I'm not the only sad singleton at the wedding.' Nick paused, a sly grin forming. 'Unless your mum is in the market for a toy boy, that is?'

Perhaps he shouldn't have said that just as his friend was taking a sip of his champagne, Nick thought as he thumped a choking Jake on the back. 'No chance,' Jake wheezed when he finally caught his breath.

'Hey, I'm not that bad!' Nick held his hands up in protest. 'I'd be the perfect gentleman. It's not like we're likely to feature on one of those morning scandal shows – "My new dad is also my brother-in-law".' Nick and Alex both burst out laughing.

'You're so funny, you're almost a comedian,' Jake said with a roll of his eyes before he joined in. 'Even if the idea of you dating my mum wasn't completely abhorrent, I'm afraid you're too late.'

'Linda's got herself a boyfriend, has she?' Alex gave Jake a none-too-gentle nudge in the ribs. 'I bet you're thrilled about that.'

Jake mock-punched Alex in the arm, almost spilling his champagne in the process. 'Keep your voice down,' he hissed. 'I'm not sure she's ready to go public with him yet.' They all looked over towards Linda, but she seemed oblivious to their conversation, her head full of plans for the wedding. 'Don't tell anyone, but she's been on a couple of dates with Pete Bray. She's playing it casual, but I think she likes him.' Jake sighed. 'It's about time she had someone treat her right; I hope he doesn't let her down.'

'Pete's got a heart of gold,' Nick reassured him. The landlord of The Sailor's Rest had been divorced for a while now, and he and his ex-wife got on fine, which said a lot about the man's decent nature. Jake's father had died the previous year and, well, the less said about him the better. 'I hope they make a go of it, I think they could be really good together.'

'I do too.' Jake sighed again. 'It's a bloody weird thing worrying about my mother's love life, I have to say.'

Nick found his gaze wandering over to his own parents, who were snuggled up against each other. They'd been sweethearts since school and

were still clearly smitten with each other. Which was great and all that, but
not a topic he liked to dwell upon. 'Best not to think about it too much.'

Jake gave a shudder. 'Get me another drink and let's change the
subject.'

* * *

The impromptu celebration wound down and everyone settled on their
towels and in their deckchairs to enjoy the sun. Nick had only been half-
joking about finding himself a date for the wedding but as he looked
around at his friends and family, it struck him anew that life was passing
him by. His thoughts strayed once more to the woman who'd stolen his
heart with one curve of her cupid's bow mouth. Even if he was brave
enough to risk another rejection by reaching out to her, there seemed little
point when she was an ocean away. His gaze strayed to the gentle rolling
waves as though he could see across the Atlantic. From the bits and pieces
he'd seen on social media, she was making a new life for herself. It was
past time he tried to do the same. Hoping some music might distract him
from his melancholy thoughts, Nick decided to do something useful and
start building a playlist for Tom and Nerissa's wedding reception.
Reaching for his phone, he opened his Spotify account, took one look at
the top trending artist the app was pushing and immediately closed it
again.

If fate wanted him to forget about Aurora Storm, it had a funny way of
showing it.

1

'You were great, Aurora, you really knocked it out of the park tonight! You had them eating out of your hand.' Accepting the stage manager's effusive praise together with a bottle of water and a crisp, white towel, Aurora managed a smile of thanks before making her way to a plastic folding chair in the corner of the backstage area. The sweat soaking her short blonde hair was already cooling thanks to the cranked-up air conditioning. She shivered as she hooked the towel around her shoulders. Hands shaking from the adrenaline, she wrestled with the lid of the water bottle before finally managing to unscrew it. She preferred the pop-up style, but unlike some of her co-stars on the rather aptly named Divas tour, she tended not to make a fuss over things like that. The stage crew all had more than enough on their plates and Aurora hadn't fallen for her hype to the point where she had her agent, Dennis, adding a list of demands to her contracts. Though her throat was parched, she forced herself to take small sips of the water. She'd made the mistake once of chugging it down early in her career and vomited the whole lot back up on the suede shoes of a creepy executive from her record company. At least he'd stopped trying to invite her out to dinner after that. Although perhaps that had been down to Dennis. He'd been apoplectic when she'd let it slip that the exec had been hanging around too much. His thinning hair and slightly drooping jawline had always reminded Aurora of a sad-looking bloodhound, but Dennis was pure Rottweiler when it came to protecting his clients. The roster at the agency he ran with his wife, Hetty, had a high proportion of female clients. It was one of the things that had attracted Aurora in the first place, and she had thanked her stars on many occasions over the past ten years that it was his door she'd gone knocking on as a naïve girl with a big voice, bigger dreams and absolutely no clue of the realities of life outside the working-class town she'd grown up in. As she took delicate sips of her water and listened to the glorious tones of Marcy Johnson, the multi-platinum-selling superstar who'd gone onstage after her, Aurora felt a million miles away from that girl. Not for the first time, she found herself missing home. How was it possible to miss somewhere you'd never felt like you fitted into in the first place?

A wave of loneliness swept over her as she looked around the crowded backstage area. She recognised all the faces but hadn't managed to learn everyone's name in the madness of joining the Divas two-week residential concert run at the last minute. One of the original announced line-up had been forced to drop out at the last minute due to a nasty bout of laryngitis, and Aurora had been asked to step in. It was a reflection of how well her breakout tour earlier in the year had been received. These shows were the culmination of a very successful year, which had included her first forays into acting when she'd guest starred in a couple of long-running network TV shows. It had been equal parts fun and terrifying, and she'd found herself bitten by the acting bug. Dennis was always on the hunt for new opportunities for her and he'd taught her that saying 'yes' was nearly always worth the risk. He was the reason she'd had the chance to trip the light fantastic on *Strictly* and spent a wild couple of weeks in the Australian rainforest on *I'm a Celebrity*. She had to admit she'd much preferred learning the tango to enduring some of the eating challenges, but both had been the kind of experiences she'd never dared dream of as a girl. Doors were opening for her left and right, so why was she pining for a tiny back bedroom in the cramped terrace house her parents wouldn't leave even after she'd offered to buy them a lovely new home?

'Can I get you anything, Ms Storm?' A bouncy, sweet-faced girl of about nineteen or twenty was smiling down at her, eager to please in any way she could.

Wracking her brain for the girl's name, Aurora shook her head. It began with a K, she was sure of it. Not Kelly but something similar... 'I'm fine, thank you, Kayleigh.'

Kayleigh's grin made Aurora glad her brain had snatched her name out of the ether at the last minute. 'No problem! I'm around so just give me a wave if you change your mind.' She hesitated, then leaned a little closer. 'I know we're supposed to be professional, but I just have to tell you how much I love 'Home Again'. I must've listened to it a million times!'

'That's so sweet of you, thank you.' Aurora leaned in as well, adding to the conspiratorial nature of their conversation. 'If you want a photo together then catch me tomorrow when I'm fresh out of make-up and not all red-faced and sweaty, okay?'

'Oh, I'd *love* that! Not that you don't look beautiful all the time, of course!'

Aurora laughed at the horrified expression on Kayleigh's face. 'Don't be daft, I always look a fright when I come offstage.' Though she'd ironed a lot of it out, a few of her Northernisms slipped out now and again. She rose from the chair and gave the girl a reassuring pat on the arm. 'You are doing a brilliant job, thank you for looking out for me. Come and find me tomorrow before the show, okay?'

'Okay, I will!' With another beaming smile, Kayleigh dashed off. Onstage, the singer who'd followed Aurora was ripping through the final notes of her most famous hit. The power in her voice sent another shiver through Aurora's spine. Really, it was some kind of miracle that she was surrounded by so much amazing talent. She ran through the rest of the show in her head. There were two more acts before the headliner was on and then there was a mix of duets and trios, one of which she was involved in, before the show wrapped up with everyone onstage to sing 'I'm Every Woman'. Aurora headed towards the dressing room for her costume change and a check over by the make-up team. The stuff they used was pretty much bulletproof, but Aurora never went onstage looking or sounding anything less than perfect – people had paid their hard-earned money to see her perform and they deserved the very best she could give them.

An hour and a half later, she was showered and changed into what her dad would've called a trackie and trainers. If he had any idea of how much the aquamarine ensemble had cost, he'd have been horrified. No, not horrified, just confused and maybe a touch sad about how little the two of them had in common these days. When she'd first started attracting attention, Aurora's instinct had been to hide herself away in baggy clothes and under baseball caps. All that had happened was she'd been photographed anyway and plastered on the showbiz pages looking like a bag lady. Blending in was the key and here in Las Vegas, colourful resort wear made her blend in with the tourists much better. People saw the colour first; a few glances might linger on the shape of her figure, but very few concentrated on her face. Switching out the contact lenses she wore onstage for a pair of black-framed glasses helped a lot. Clark Kent had been onto something with that disguise.

Riding down from her hotel room on the penthouse floor, her hide-in-plain-sight strategy held up when a couple entered the lift a few floors later and barely offered her more than a smile. They were too intent on checking the lift was heading to the casino level, their eyes already full of dollar signs as they discussed their strategy for the blackjack and poker tables. Aurora listened to their conversation with half an ear. The tables had never attracted her, but she'd been tempted by the flashing lights and the frenetic music of the slot machines a couple of times. With a strict budget set, she'd spent a carefree couple of hours winning a bit here, losing a bit there and people-watching to her heart's content. The casino wasn't her destination of choice this evening, though, and she exchanged a polite farewell with the couple as they alighted the lift and carried on down to the street level. The lobby area was heaving with people, busier than she'd ever seen it, even for a Friday night. She guessed many of them were taking advantage before the prices jacked up for the Christmas holiday fortnight.

Instead of making her way to the huge bank of revolving doors that led out onto the bright lights and sleazy shadows of the Las Vegas strip, she headed for a side entrance that opened out into the hotel gardens. As much of a tourist attraction as the casino and show rooms inside, the extensive outside space was a gaudy reimagining of ancient Egypt, complete with pyramids and a sphinx whose eyes changed colours like a pair of giant disco lights. Fountains shot up in all directions, dancing in time to the booming, ostentatious trumpets of Verdi's 'Triumphal March' from *Aida*. Aurora loved the gardens. They were kitsch and cheesy and fun, but they were also a masterpiece of plants, trees and flowers. People might come to be photographed with one of the actors dressed as pharaohs in elaborate headdresses, or temple dancers in diaphanous robes and pencil-straight black wigs, but whoever tended the gardens behind the scenes had the greenest of fingers. Without their hard work the display would be nothing more than a handful of foam models. She'd had a few guilty pangs about how much water it must take to create this lush oasis in the desert climate of Nevada until she'd bumped into one of the gardeners and he'd mentioned during their conversation that the hotel collected the grey water from the hotel showers and sinks and, thanks to a filtration tank hidden in the depths of the giant pyramid, they used it to water the gardens.

She wandered in quiet solitude for a few minutes, needing to decompress after the excitement of the show. It didn't matter if it was the first night or the last, it still took her hours to unwind enough to get to sleep. She paused by one of the dancing fountains, not thinking about anything, just enjoying the clever display when a voice came from just behind her. 'Excuse me, can we have a photo taken?'

Damn. Aurora closed her eyes for a second as she reminded herself that this was part and parcel of doing the job she loved. Fixing a bright smile, she turned to face the woman who'd spoken to her. She was slightly older than the usual fan who sought Aurora out for a selfie, but they were the reason she enjoyed a life of relative privilege, and she wasn't so far removed from her own upbringing to remember what it was like to be a fan. It had taken a huge amount of willpower not to gush like a giddy schoolgirl at Marcy Johnson and all the other Divas when she'd joined the show. Pushing back the hood of her top, Aurora ruffled a quick hand through her short hair in case it had been squashed. 'Sure, it'd be my pleasure.'

'That's so kind of you!' the woman gushed, thrusting her phone towards her. 'Bud and I are on our honeymoon.' The woman smiled indulgently at the greying man at her side. 'We were childhood sweethearts, you know, but both ended up married to other people.'

'Come on now, Helen, this poor young woman doesn't need our life story.'

Slowly it dawned on Aurora that they had no clue who she was, they just wanted a snapshot to commemorate a special moment. With a grin at her own hubris, she studied the phone and quickly located the photo app. 'How about we switch places so you have the fountain behind you?' she suggested.

'Oh, that would be just darling,' Helen said with a beaming smile as she herded poor Bud into place.

'Are you two staying here at the hotel?' Aurora asked while they fiddled around trying to find the perfect position in front of the fountain.

'Yes, it's so beautiful, isn't it, Bud?'

'Should be for what we paid for it,' he grumbled, but there was an indulgent smile that said it was worth every cent for the way Helen was gazing up at him. His smile dimmed a little. 'I chose it because Helen is such a big fan of Marcy Johnson, though I didn't realise the concerts were all sold out when I booked it.'

Helen patted his chest. 'Don't start that again, Bud. I told you it doesn't matter one bit.'

Aurora finally got them to stand still long enough to snap a couple of shots of them, the second of which managed to catch the full effect of the water and lights behind them – a fluke of timing rather than any skill on her part as a photographer – but they were delighted nonetheless. As she handed back the phone to Helen, Aurora offered her hand to Bud. 'Well, it was a pleasure to meet you both and congratulations on your marriage, Mr...?'

'Callaghan,' he replied, as she'd hoped, with the automatic politeness of someone of their generation. 'But you can call me Bud.'

'Well, congratulations, Bud, and to you too, Helen. I hope you enjoy the rest of your honeymoon.' She slipped away into the darkness while they were still admiring the photo she'd taken. As she ducked behind a large bank of cacti, Aurora heard Helen comment on what a nice girl she was. Grinning to herself, Aurora hurried back into the hotel to have a chat with the concierge. Up until now, she hadn't had anyone to gift the handful of VIP tickets she'd been allocated as part of her appearance with the Divas, but that was about to change.

She was still imagining Bud and Helen's reaction as she crossed the lobby and entered the fifties-style diner that was one of half a dozen different restaurants incorporated within the hotel. Even this late in the evening it was still busy with people scoffing down mountainous burgers and slurping on milkshakes so thick it was a struggle to draw the liquid up through a straw. Pleased to see her usual spot at the counter was free, Aurora hopped up onto the low-backed stool covered in vibrant red vinyl and waved at Gus, the night manager.

Flicking the tea towel he'd been using to polish some glasses over his shoulder, Gus wandered over. 'Here's our girl, and looking mightily pleased about something. Show went well?'

Aurora nodded. 'It was great. I can't believe there's only a handful of shows left.' It was the twelfth of December, and the final show was scheduled for the fifteenth. They'd been due to finish on Sunday, but ticket demand had been such that they'd tacked on a couple of extra shows on Monday. They couldn't extend it any further as another show was already booked in. As it was, the crew would be working all night to break down the staging and transform the concert hall into a replica big top show ring.

'Gotta make room for the Holiday Extravaganza. How's your circus skills?'

She laughed. 'Sadly lacking so I'll have to give it a miss, I'm afraid.'

Gus grinned. 'I was thinking about auditioning for the flying trapeze, but I don't think my Ali will be too keen on the idea.' He cast a quick glance towards the pretty woman who was filling a stack of glasses with the soda fountain hose. A good foot shorter than her husband, she ruled the diner with a sharp wit, a ready smile and more energy than a woman half her age.

'Unless they need an extra clown, Augustus Mackey, you'll be staying right where you are.' As dry as her words were, they were softened with a smile of deep affection. She swept up the piled-high tray of drinks and was gone before her husband could say a word.

Aurora tried – and failed – to turn her laugh into a cough when Gus turned wounded eyes towards her. He held the hangdog expression for all of two seconds before he burst out laughing. 'No chance of a man getting too big for his boots with you two around, that's for sure. Now then, honey, what'll it be tonight?' One of the reasons Aurora had started eating regularly in the diner was Gus and Ali's willingness to adjust their menu to suit her needs. She'd had a chicken Caesar salad the first night, not realising the chicken was coated in a thick layer of breadcrumbs or that the salad would be doused with quite so much dressing. When Gus had caught her look of dismay, he'd whipped it away despite her protests and returned a short while later with a steamed chicken breast nestled on a huge mixed salad with a jug of dressing on the side. She'd come back the following evening to find he'd sourced a lovely piece of salmon from the kitchen of the high-end restaurant that was also part of the hotel complex and served it up on a bed of rocket with a baked potato and fat-free sour cream.

She hesitated for a moment, thinking about how delicious the burgers had looked as she'd passed a table near the door. Performing burned a lot of calories so the occasional blowout wasn't a problem, but it was just too late. She'd be prone on her bed nursing a food belly and unable to sleep if she indulged herself too much. 'I'd like a salad, please, and a jacket potato if you've got a smallish one.'

'Absolutely. How about a little grilled steak on top of that salad?'

'Perfect. And a small chocolate shake and a glass of iced water as well, please.'

'Coming right up!' With another flash of his brilliant smile, Gus bustled off to fix her order.

As she waited for her drinks to arrive, Aurora cast an eye around the bright interior of the diner. The combination of shiny chrome, dark polished wood and the bright leather seats made it feel a bit like sitting in one of those huge American classic cars. She'd seen a few of them cruising up and down the strip and couldn't imagine what it would be like trying to drive one. Since living in London she'd given up her car – a tiny little Ford with several careful owners that her parents had saved hard to provide for her when she passed her test. There'd seemed little point when public transport was so much easier than fighting her way around the crowded roads of the city. If she needed to get anywhere now, she was nearly always provided with a driver. The enormous Cadillacs looked more like boats than cars, and if she tried one of the monster trucks that were another popular choice in Vegas she'd probably need a booster cushion to see over the steering wheel. Gus set her drinks in front of her with a quick wink, distracting Aurora from her rambling thoughts.

The first sip of the delicious, creamy shake was so cold it sent a stab of pain to her temple. 'Brain freeze,' she said with a rueful grin to no one in particular as she rubbed her head. The shock of sensation faded as quickly as it had come and she ventured a second, tentative sip. She could almost feel the sugar rushing around her veins so it was just as well she'd shown enough restraint to order a small one or she'd never sleep later.

'So what are your plans for when the shows are finished? Are you sticking around for Christmas?' Gus asked as he buffed the already spot-less counter between them.

Aurora shook her head. 'I'm going back to the UK on Wednesday to stay with some friends.' She was staying with her manager and his wife, actually, but that would sound pathetic. Besides, Dennis and Hetty were her friends and closer to her these days than her parents. She'd let her mum and dad know she was going to be back home for a couple of weeks, but they hadn't called her back with a definitive date for a visit. There'd certainly been no suggestion she should go home and spend Christmas Day with them. It wasn't that they didn't get on, it was more like she'd never fitted in with them. Like a cuckoo who'd been laid in the nest of a pair of meadow pipits, she'd always been too big and loud for a couple like Ross and Kim Powell, who very much favoured a quiet life. She shrugged the thought away; there was no point in feeling sad about a situation that was unlikely to change.

The phone she'd tucked in her hip pocket before leaving her suite vibrated, making her jump. Aurora retrieved it, unsurprised to see Dennis's name on the display. 'Morning, Dennis!'

'Hello, petal, how's tricks?' Though he'd never smoked a day in his life, Dennis Rouse had the raspy tones of a man who lived on cigars and cheap whisky. He sounded more like an East End barrow boy than one of the most successful and well-respected agents in the business.

'Good thanks. You're up early.'

'Like a bloody lark, me,' Dennis quipped. 'Look, I know it's late there, so I'll cut straight to it. I've had an email from Chad Logan's production company and they're interested in you for a part in his next film.'

'Ch—' Remembering where she was at the last moment, Aurora clamped her lips tight to stop herself from blurting out the name of one of Hollywood's biggest stars. 'I'm just grabbing something to eat,' she muttered as she glanced around, suddenly paranoid she would be overheard. The other diners paid her absolutely no attention, their focus on their meals or their own conversations.

'I can call you back, if that's easier?'

'No, no, that's fine, you carry on.' As Dennis began to outline what he knew from the email he'd received, Aurora tried her best to concentrate. It was hard, though, because Chad had been one of her pin-up stars when she'd been a teenager. She'd had a poster of him on her bedroom wall, for goodness' sake! He was also reputed to be one of the nicest people in the business, a fact backed up by the enduring nature of his marriage to one of his earliest co-stars, Melissa Howard. Finding the constant pull of filming a battle after she and Chad had children, Melissa had transitioned from film to television and was the host of one of the most popular daytime talk shows in America. Aurora had been a guest on the show back in the summer when her single, 'Home Again', had hit the top of the Billboard charts. Melissa had been kind and generous, dropping into Aurora's dressing room beforehand to introduce herself and making a point of saying what a fan she was of her music. Perhaps she did that to all her guests, but it had felt genuine enough that Aurora had been able to relax and really enjoy the interview.

Gus approached with her meal and a smile, hesitating when he saw she was on the phone. 'You want this to go, honey?' he asked in a low voice and Aurora's heart lifted at his innate thoughtfulness.

'Yes, please.' Aurora blew him a quick kiss.

'I haven't even finished telling you about it yet,' Dennis said with a laugh.

'Oh, I wasn't talking to you. Gus is boxing my dinner for me. I'll take it upstairs so we can talk properly.'

'Good idea. I'll call you back in five minutes.' He was gone without saying goodbye.

Accepting the styrofoam box, Aurora thanked Gus again before heading swiftly out of the diner and across the foyer to the bank of gleaming lifts. A noisy group of men were waiting, and she hung back instinctively, not wanting to end up stuck in a confined space with them. After her experience with Julian, she never allowed herself to be alone with a man she didn't know and trust. She caught a glimpse of herself in one of the myriad mirrors lining the walls and exchanged a bitter smile with her reflection to acknowledge the flaw in that plan. Julian should've been the person she could trust above and beyond all others. She shook her head to dispel the dark thoughts that lurked at the edge of her awareness. No. She'd shut herself away from the world once because of him; she would not remain his prisoner forever. Luckily the lifts were frequent and she hopped in the next one and pressed the button to close the doors before anyone else had a chance to get in. Not wanting to give the unhappy thoughts the chance to creep back in, she focused all her attention on the floor indicator and silently counted along with the flashing numbers until she reached the penthouse level. In less than five minutes she was safely ensconced behind her double-locked hotel room door, sitting cross-legged on her bed with her dinner resting on her lap and her phone next to her. She flicked it onto speaker mode as soon as it rang. 'Hello again.'

'Right, where were we? Chad bloody Logan, eh? Who'd have believed it.'

Aurora laughed as she forked up some of the fluffy potato. 'It's mad, isn't it? I was thinking just now about when I met Melissa Howard on her talk show, that was crazy enough, but Chad Logan is next level.' She hadn't, of course, she'd been thinking about Julian, but she'd never tell Dennis that.

'His rep mentioned that in the message. Apparently you made quite an impression on her and she's the one who suggested you.'

'Maybe she really was a fan and not just being polite,' Aurora mused before picking up a slice of beef with her fingers and taking a bite. It all but melted in her mouth and she closed her eyes in appreciation. 'God, the food here is so good, I'll have to go on a diet straight after Christmas.'

'Rubbish. Knowing how much energy you burn onstage, I'll be amazed if we won't have to feed you up!'

She'd meant it as a joke but Dennis jumped straight onto the comment. One of the things he'd drilled into her from the start was that there would be pressure from all sides about her looks and most especially her weight. He'd warned her there'd be cruel paparazzi snaps purporting to show her cellulite or pointing out even a hint of muffin top above her jeans. Healthy and happy was his mantra, and it wasn't just lip service. Part of agreeing to be signed with him was to have a handful of sessions with a nutritionist to make sure she understood the difference between a healthy diet and food deprivation. 'I'm taking good care of myself, I promise,' she said in a gentle tone, even as she glanced at herself in one of the many mirrors gracing the hotel room walls. She had lost a few pounds, but that was down to the hectic concert schedule. A few days of Hetty's home cooking would sort that out.

'I should bloody well hope so,' he grumped, making her smile. 'Speaking of food,' he continued. 'Hetty wants to know if you want her to get anything special in.' He said it in such a casual way that Aurora didn't know whether to laugh or cry. Dennis and Hetty didn't have kids of their own and she'd never dug any deeper to discover if that was a choice on their part or not. Though they were always professional with their business transactions, they both had a tendency to treat her as something of a surrogate daughter.

'Honestly, getting to spend a few days with you is all I need.' She had a charity gala concert at the Royal Albert Hall between Christmas and New Year, but other than that she intended to lounge about and let Dennis and Hetty spoil her.

'It'll be good to see you, girl. Hetty misses you something awful.' Dennis didn't do emotions – well, he did, but he always used his wife as a conduit for them.

Aurora found herself swallowing around the lump in her throat. 'I don't know what I did to deserve you two,' she murmured, heart full of love.

Dennis was quiet for a moment before he coughed loudly. 'Right, that's enough of that soppy crap, let's talk about this film. If you're interested, Chad's in Las Vegas at the moment, scouting locations, apparently. It's not a formal audition, he just wants to meet up and have a chat. They've included a couple of scenes and suggested you could run through them together, see how the chemistry is.'

Chemistry? The short hairs at the nape of her neck prickled at the word. Anything that even hinted at intimacy with a man set her nerves on edge these days. Well, that wasn't strictly true. There was one man who'd made her feel safe from the first time he'd offered her his hand as he'd helped her on board his boat. A pair of vivid blue eyes beneath a shock of untidy curls, the corners creased with lines from squinting against the glare of the sun off a crystalline sea, sprang into her mind. She pushed the image away. Now was not the time to think about Nick Morgan. He'd been a mistake – albeit a very pleasant one – a deviation from her self-imposed single life. A blip on the radar, nothing more. She forced herself to concentrate on the matter at hand. 'What exactly is this part, again?'

Dennis snorted. 'It's a typical Chad Logan thing. Lots of running about, flexing his muscles as he saves the world from impending doom. You're the beautiful, clever heroine – an archaeologist who helps him crack an ancient code. Christ, where do they come up with this bollocks? And, of course, you fall for the hero's wise-cracking charms in the process – never mind he's almost old enough to be your father, eh?' Dennis' snort of derision made her laugh. Hollywood still had a blind spot when it came to age gaps. Mind you, with the amount of clever nipping and tucking Chad Logan had undergone over the years, his features had frozen into an approximation of how he'd looked in his late twenties. He had a kind of Ken-doll handsomeness – bland and unremarkable. Though teenage Aurora had thought him the handsomest man in the world, these days she preferred character actors with a bit of quirkiness to their features. There were no wrinkles on Chad's face, no smile lines or freckles from the sun.

'Any idea of the certificate rating?' Aurora wasn't a prude, but she didn't want her big break to be reliant on her taking her clothes off.

'I guess it'll be much like his other stuff. He's firmly in the family-friendly market these days so a couple of kisses and a cut to the morning after would be my guess but we'll have to see the full script before making any commitment.' Dennis went quiet for a long moment. When he spoke again there was no hint of his usual brash and breezy self. 'We'll put hard boundaries in your contract, sweetheart, and one of them intimacy coaches on set with you if that would make you more comfortable. You know I've always got your back.'

Aurora pushed her dinner away, her appetite gone. 'I know.' She took a deep breath. It had been her choice to try something different and go ahead with the small TV parts she'd been offered. She'd been a love interest in one of those, appearing in a couple of episodes before one of the producers decided her gruesome murder would be character-building for one of the show's stars. The cast and crew had treated her with utmost kindness and respect – even when they'd been painting her body with gory wounds – and there was no reason to suspect a movie set would be any different. After a raft of casting-couch scandals and worse over the past few years, Hollywood was desperate to clean up its act. 'This is a once-in-a-lifetime opportunity.'

'It could certainly be a breakout role for you, assuming that's still something you want to pursue?' Dennis kept his voice quiet and careful as though he wanted her to know it was one hundred per cent her decision. He'd always let her go her own way, even when she'd veered away from her usual pop stuff for an edgier one-off collaboration with a rock band she liked.

'I can't be a pop princess forever.' Aurora knew she'd already had more chances than most people. Her decision to disappear after Julian had been a matter of survival and it had kept her name in the press for a while as they speculated over why she'd vanished overnight. But the news cycle moved on and newer, prettier, more talented girls had come onto the scene and replaced her. Making a comeback had been a risk that could well have fallen flat, but she'd still had too much ambition inside her, too much she hadn't achieved. It had also been an act of healing, a way to tell herself that he hadn't won.

The influence of social media had exploded in the two years she'd been away so she and Dennis had devised a viral marketing campaign involving some faked mermaid sightings. Between that and the renewed speculation on where she'd been hiding, Aurora's name had trended everywhere. Wanting to be more than a five-minute novelty, Aurora had worked in partnership with one of the best songwriters in the business and between them they'd created not only the hit of the summer, but a Christmas number one on both sides of the Atlantic and a best-selling album. Writing her own songs had been almost as much fun as performing them and she was keen to stretch herself even further on her next album. She'd been touring non-stop since January so there'd been no time to write any new material beyond a few half-scribbled lines that had gone straight in the bin. She desperately needed a break to recharge her batteries, but the Divas slot had been too good to turn down, and now this Chad Logan thing... Aurora bit back a sigh. 'I should at least meet him. Did they say when?'

'It's a bit short notice, but they've suggested Sunday brunch. Do you want me to handle the arrangements?'

That *was* short notice, but manageable. 'With the difference in time it would probably be easier if I handle it directly. Let them know I'm on for Sunday and include my number and I can finalise a time with his assistant. I'll let you know the details as soon as it's sorted out.'

'I'll send a reply now so she's got the info first thing your time. Are you sure it's not too soon? I can always bump your flight home if you want a few extra days to prepare?'

A wave of homesickness washed over her. She'd been living out of a suitcase for too bloody long and even the thought of another couple of days felt like too much. 'If he's suggested Sunday then let's do that and then I can fly home as planned. Brunch would work best with my schedule as I can still get back for the matinee performance.' Brunch would also mean meeting in a public place in the daylight, which helped settle the lingering nerves in her stomach. After a few more minutes' reassurance from Dennis that it was a good thing that her name was even linked to a project of this size regardless of the outcome, Aurora hung up feeling much better. Even if nothing came from it, Dennis was right – there was no such thing as bad publicity.

2

'I really appreciate you stepping in,' Alex said to Nick as he wheeled out a cart full of books from the storeroom.

'Anything I can do to help, you know that.' Even for a Tuesday, the bookshop, like everywhere else in Mermaids Point, was seeing an influx of customers trying to get themselves sorted before Christmas. He glanced down at the cart. 'So, I just find space on the shelves for these?'

Alex nodded. 'These are for the alphabetical shelves. I've got some more out the back for the display tables and the specific genre sections when you're done, if that's okay?'

'Like I said, I'm happy to do anything – better than sitting at home on my arse.' With the warehouse conversion finished and the weather too grim for anyone in their right mind to want a sightseeing trip, Nick was at a total loose end. Winter was always the worst time of year for him, work-wise, and he scratched around doing whatever needed doing. In the past week he'd done two shifts in his parents' gift shop, three in the café his sister Laurie ran next door to it and three delivery runs for Jim, the local greengrocer. With Christmas only nine days away, the whole village was buzzing so there were plenty of people in need of an extra hand. He was helping out in the bookshop today as a favour to Alex because Ivy was over at his aunt Nerissa's place to carry out some last-minute alterations to

Nerissa's wedding dress. He already had a paying job lined up later, helping out behind the bar at The Sailor's Rest. Once the Christmas and New Year's rush was over, things would be pretty bleak for him on the job front. Even the most generous souls would be tightening their belts and battening down their proverbial hatches to get through the slow months before spring brought the first of the tourists back to the Point.

Alex grinned at him. 'While you're in such a generous mood, what are you doing on Saturday?'

Nick frowned as he worked through his list of odd jobs. 'Let me think. I'll be busy in the afternoon and early evening helping to set up for the RNLI charity fayre on Sunday. Pete hasn't said anything about working that morning, though. Why, what did you have in mind?'

'We've got an activity day for the local kids. Ivy's going to do a load of crafts with them, and we'll be doing story time and a surprise visit from Santa.'

'I'm not gluing on a fake beard and dressing up as bloody Santa, if that's what you're after,' Nick said with a snort. 'I like you, Alex, but there's a limit.'

Alex threw back his head and laughed. 'Don't worry about that, I've already roped Dad in. Not that it took much asking; I just deployed my secret weapon.'

It was Nick's turn to laugh. 'You got Ivy to ask him.' Alex's parents had made no secret of how much they adored their son's girlfriend. Archie especially. He'd confessed after a glass or four of red wine that although he loved both Tom and Alex to the ends of the earth, he'd always hoped to have a daughter as well. Though he hadn't elaborated further, there'd been a misty look in his eye as he'd glanced across to where his wife, Philippa, was chatting with Ivy.

'Of course I did. Anyway, Saturday's a big deal for us, at least I'm hoping it will be, so if you don't mind lending a hand...?'

'No problem.' It was turn and turn about as far as his friends and family were concerned and both Alex and Ivy had given up plenty of the little bit of spare time they had to help him with decorating when he'd asked them.

A customer came to the counter and Nick grabbed the cart and steered it towards the shelves while Alex served them. He was supposed to be there to work, so he'd better get started. As he began transferring the books onto the shelves, Nick found his thoughts straying back to that night when Archie had become sentimental. They'd all been gathered in the big back garden of the surgery the weekend before Hallowe'en to officially welcome Archie and Philippa to the village. After he'd finally recuperated from his broken leg, neither Archie nor Philippa had much enthusiasm to return to their house in London and the hunt had been on for somewhere suitable. They'd found a place in the next village, which conveniently had a links golf course that had once hosted the British Open. Everyone seemed happy with the arrangement – they were close, but not too close as Alex had put it. Archie and Philippa had had more than enough from the sale of their London home to buy their new place and a small flat in the capital, which they used to visit friends once a month. Archie had made it clear that it was available for anyone who wanted to use it. His folks had taken them up on the offer and enjoyed a mid-week break for their anniversary, but Nick had so far declined. It wasn't like he knew anyone up there; well, anyone who would want to see him anyway.

Nick sighed. It had been eighteen months since he'd seen Aurora – nearly twelve since she'd ignored his pathetic attempt at a Christmas greeting, so why on earth was he still thinking about her? She wasn't even in the country, for God's sake. *She will be soon, though*, a very unhelpful part of his brain prompted.

There'd been a full-page spread in several of the Sunday papers his dad always read advertising a one-off concert at the Albert Hall. It wasn't like Nick had gone looking for news of her, he actively avoided the showbiz pages, but it'd been impossible to miss her smiling out at him from the ad. But what the hell was he going to do even if he did have the kind of money to blow on a ticket? Try to get a message to her backstage? Climb on the stage while she was performing and throw himself at her feet? Either option would come across as mad or pathetic – probably both – and result in him being thrown out by security for good measure. No. That bird had well and truly flown the nest of romance and he was just going to have to get the hell over himself – and her.

His phone beeped and he set the book he was holding on the shelf while he scanned the message from Alun Wise, the local estate agent. Pleased with how well the warehouse conversion had gone, Nick had asked for a heads-up on anything else that came onto the agency's books that might be suitable for a similar project. According to Alun's text, the owner of one of the bed and breakfast businesses in the village was looking to retire and no one in his family was interested in taking it on. Nick knew the guy – hell, he knew everyone in the village. Like many of the people Nick's own age, the owner's children had long since moved away – the lack of jobs and suitable housing forcing them to look for better opportunities away from the coast where they'd grown up. He knew the property as well as it was a few doors down from his parents' house. The owner had purchased two adjacent houses long before Nick had been born and knocked them through to create one large property.

He flicked through the photos Alun had helpfully added to his WhatsApp message, trying to look beyond the dated interior and focus on the layout of the building. It wasn't easy; the carpets were the kind of lurid patterns popular in the seventies and eighties. An ugly wooden bar dominated the communal lounge and there were thick lace curtains at every window. So many possibilities hummed in Nick's mind. He could strip everything back, modernise the lot and resell it as a going concern, in and out in a couple of months. If he could get the finances squared away, he might even get it turned around in time for the start of the next tourist season. There was also the option of reinstating the party wall and converting it back to separate large family homes, or he could do as he had done with the warehouse on the dock and convert it into apartments, which he could either sell to locals or rent out as holiday homes. Both of those options would take longer and cost more, but had a higher potential return. He wondered if Liam, the local architect, was free for a viewing...

'Earth to Nick! Customer needs something.' Alex's bellow from across the shop startled Nick so much he almost dropped his phone. Looking around, he felt his face heat as he realised there was a woman standing not two feet away, her features scrunched up in an irritated frown. She was around his mother's age, but he didn't recognise her, which was unusual for this time of year when the Point received very few visitors.

'God, I'm so sorry, I was miles away.'

'Clearly.' Her tone was sniffy, and he wondered how long she'd been standing there.

'Well, I'm all yours now,' Nick said, giving her his most winning smile. 'How can I help you?'

The up and down look she gave him was brutal enough to wither his very soul and he felt his smile falter a little under her glare. 'I just need you to move your trolley so I can get at the shelf.'

Feeling chastened, and more than surplus to requirements, Nick grabbed the handle of his trolley and wheeled it back towards the counter. 'Sorry,' he murmured to Alex, making sure he pitched his voice low enough so only his friend would hear. 'I appear to have pissed her off.'

Alex glanced past him towards where the woman was browsing the shelf, a bemused smile on his face. 'Mrs Bailey? Are you sure, because she's always been an absolute sweetheart.'

Nick shrugged. 'I asked if I could help her, and she looked at me the way you look at Lucifer when he's left a present on the shop floor for you to clean up.'

Alex's smile widened as he leaned closer to Nick. 'Maybe Poldark isn't one of Mrs Bailey's romantic heroes.'

The reference was a swipe at Nick, who'd let his once-hated curls grow out a bit when Aidan Turner had first graced the screen in the BBC adaptation and made curly hair trendy. The show might have had its day, but Nick had got used to the scruffy wildness. A quick trim with the kitchen scissors a couple of times a year was enough to keep his fringe from his eyes and the length manageable. His hand was halfway towards his hair before he caught the self-conscious action and he stuffed it quickly in his pocket with a scowl at his friend. 'What are you on about?'

Alex cast a quick glance over to ensure Mrs Bailey was still absorbed in her browsing. 'She drives over from the next village every couple of weeks and raids our romance section. I've had some fascinating chats with her and ordered stuff it would never have occurred to me to stock. I might have to start paying her commission because everything I've put on the shelves after her recommendation has sold.'

'If she's an expert in romance, perhaps I should ask her for a few tips,' Nick said gloomily.

Alex's expression turned rueful. 'Still pining for your pop star?'

Nick nodded. 'I need to find a way to get her out of my head once and for all.'

'You haven't been on social media today, I take it.' Alex's tone was guarded, his expression suddenly a bland mask.

'What are you talking about?'

'Nothing, forget I said anything.' Alex grimaced. 'Ivy is going to bloody kill me for mentioning it.'

'But you haven't mentioned anything...' Frustrated, Nick moved away from the counter as Mrs Bailey approached with a stack of books so tall she'd had to brace them against her upper body so it didn't topple over.

Steering his cart back to the shelves, Nick tried to pretend he wasn't dying to know what Alex had been hinting at. He managed to slot all of two books away before he yanked his phone out of his pocket with a muttered curse. The fact he didn't even need to type Aurora's name into the search function on Twitter was an immediate red flag as she was trending at number three behind an American movie star and a politician who'd obviously said something stupid on the breakfast TV and radio rounds that morning. Feeling more than a touch queasy, Nick clicked on her name and found himself confronted with a picture of Aurora wrapped in a tight embrace with the movie star who was trending at number one. *Shit*. He couldn't see her face, buried into Chad Logan's neck the way it was, but he recognised her short shock of bright blonde hair, and that black hoodie with its distinctive scatter of sparkling stars on the sleeves and back. She'd all but lived in the thing during those few short weeks she'd spent in the Point the summer before last.

Maybe it isn't what it looks like...

Though he wished he had the willpower to tuck his phone away and not get sucked into whatever the drama was, he found himself clicking on the top trending post. Well, shit, it was *exactly* what it looked like.

'Me and my big bloody mouth, I knew I shouldn't have said anything.' Alex's voice at his shoulder startled Nick enough to tear himself away from doomscrolling through the hideous comments below the main story.

'There could be a hundred reasons for them to be embracing, you know how touchy-feely those Hollywood types are.' God, even when the evidence of it was staring him in the face, he was still grasping at straws. Path. Et. Ic.

'Yeah, maybe.' Alex didn't sound any more convinced than he was. 'Forget about it, mate. She's not your problem now, is she?'

He was right. Aurora had made that abundantly clear. *It's been fun, Nico.* That was the last thing she'd said to him before brushing a kiss on his lips and climbing into her Range Rover with the blacked-out windows. She hadn't even responded to the message he'd sent last Christmas congratulating her on her number-one single. He had been a blip on her radar, an amusing distraction for a couple of weeks, nothing more. His eyes strayed back to his phone once more. Hadn't Chad Logan been married to Melissa Howard for forever? A sour feeling curdled in Nick's gut. If Aurora was the type to mess around with a married man, perhaps he really had been wasting his time all these months longing for even a word from her. With a sorry shake of his head, he locked his phone and stuffed it back in his pocket. 'Definitely not my problem.'

The shop filled with customers and soon there was no time for Nick to brood over Aurora and her escapade with Chad Logan. He dashed from pillar to post, doing his best to help everyone while Alex remained all but pinned down behind the busy till. It seemed like half the village had decided to break the back of their Christmas shopping all at the same time. He was comfortable enough handling the book side of things, but when he found himself standing guard outside the little fitting room Ivy had rigged up in one corner to serve the customers who came to try on her handmade fashions, he couldn't help but sneak a quick glance at his watch and wonder how much longer she was going to be.

'Nick, are you there?' He rolled his eyes as he wondered what was wrong with Kitty now. She'd already tried on half a dozen different dresses, sending him scurrying for a different size a couple of times before handing both garments back with a shake of her head before she returned to the little cubicle with yet another one draped over her arm.

'Everything all right, Kitty?' Regardless of his frustration, he kept his tone polite and even. Kitty Duke was an absolute sweetheart – even if she did find it hard to make a decision – and he'd known her all his life. She was a stalwart of the local knitting circle and was most often found in the corner of Laurie's café, needles flying as she gossiped with her best friend, Barbara.

A long silence followed and Nick straightened up from where he'd been slouched against the wall, suddenly uneasy. Perhaps she was unwell? He had no idea how old Kitty was, only that she must be a good few years older than his mum. It wasn't the sort of question one went around asking, not when you'd been raised right. He edged closer to the curtain and pitched his voice low so as not to draw attention. 'Everything okay in there?'

'What time did you say Ivy would be back?' There was a hint of panic in the question.

'Umm, she didn't, I'm afraid.' Nick cast a quick glance over to where Alex stood behind the till. At least half a dozen people were in the queue to be served. 'I can check with Alex if you like?'

'No!' Oh, that was definitely panic he could hear.

'Kitty, I'm getting worried now.' Nick laid a hand on the curtain, but didn't pull it back, not wanting to invade the poor woman's privacy. 'Please tell me what's wrong.'

There was another long silence and he was just about to whisk the curtain aside when he caught a soft mutter. 'I'm stuck.'

'Stuck?' Nick parroted as he tried to picture the fitting area in his mind's eye. It was a simple space with a mirror, a small backless stool in the corner and a couple of hooks screwed to the wall. How on earth could she be stuck? ... Oh! Swallowing down the urge to laugh, Nick summoned his gentlest voice. 'Do you need me to give you a hand?'

More silence, during which Nick threw a quick glance around the room. The customers not in the queue seemed happy enough browsing for now. He spotted Bev, another member of the knitting circle, and all but sighed with relief. 'Bev's over by the books,' he called through the curtain. 'Shall I fetch her?'

'God, no!' Kitty's wail was even more desperate than before. 'I'll never hear the end of it if she finds out about this!'

Nick could sympathise as, like most of the village at one point or another, he'd been on the end of Bev's sharp tongue. The other ladies in their group liked a chit-chat and it was only natural for people to be in each other's business in a close-knit community like the Point, but Bev had a bit of a mean streak sometimes. If Kitty didn't want to ask her for help, then there was only one thing for it. 'Let me in, Kitty,' he pleaded softly. 'I promise not to look any more than I need to, and I won't say a word to anyone.'

'O...okay.'

After one final check to make sure no one was paying him any attention, Nick slipped behind the curtain and stopped dead at the sight of a rather large pair of beige support knickers. He immediately averted his gaze upwards to discover the top half of Kitty was trapped in a tangle of floaty cream and blue fabric. She had one arm twisted behind her back, scrabbling ineffectually at the inside-out fabric. 'Right then,' he said, keeping his tone matter-of-fact. 'What's the problem, exactly?'

'I couldn't get the zip down properly so I tried to take the whole thing off over my head.' Kitty's plaintive tones came from somewhere in the depths of the mass of fabric. 'But then I felt something pull tight and I'm worried I'll rip it.' She started to wriggle.

'Hold still a sec,' Nick urged. 'Let me have a look.' He was all business now he could see the problem. He studied the layers of the dress, trying to make sense of its construction. It wasn't exactly his area of expertise. 'Can I lift this bit up?' he asked, waiting for her permission before he moved any closer.

'Do whatever you think is necessary to get me out of this blasted thing. It's not like I have any dignity left to hide, is it?' Kitty asked with a resigned sigh.

'Oh, hush,' Nick said with a grin. 'I'm sure you've seen more than your fair share of my dignity over the years.' He'd been something of an escapologist when he'd been little, especially when it had come to things like bath and bedtimes or being made to stand still while his mum or his nan tried to towel him off on the beach.

Kitty laughed, sounding more like her usual self. 'I seem to remember that time you were caught halfway along the street in a Superman T-shirt and not much else.'

'It was Batman, actually.' On that particular occasion he'd clambered out of the cot he'd all but grown out of that his parents kept in the back room of their shop. It had been the middle of summer and the village had been humming with tourists – or so the much-repeated story his father told about the incident had claimed – and they'd been unable to get anyone to babysit. Nick was supposed to have been taking an afternoon nap, which was something he'd always hated, and had made it out of the shop and was making a beeline for the steps that led to the beach when he'd been scooped up by a local who'd spotted him. He had no memory of who it was who'd put paid to his adventure, but he could still remember the sensation of the cold glass of the counter beneath his bare bottom as he'd been plopped down in front of his exasperated father. He'd learned a long time ago that there was no escaping your childhood escapades in a small village, so why waste time being embarrassed about them? He turned his attention from the past back to the problem at hand. 'Right then, let's see about getting you out of this dress.'

'I bet I'm not the first lady you've said that to.'

Kitty's arch comment caught him off guard and Nick barked out a laugh. 'Ah, but few of them have been as lovely as you.'

'Get on with yourself!' Pleased with how much more relaxed their silly exchange had made Kitty, Nick made swift progress. A couple of gentle tugs and he managed to get the inner layer of the dress straight and pulled back down to cover Kitty's body. As the loose upper layer drifted back into place, Nick spotted the cause of all the problems. 'You've got a bit of material trapped inside the zip. Hold on and I'll see if I can get it loose.' With gentle persuasion, Nick tugged and teased the soft, semi-transparent cloth until he'd worked it free from the teeth of the zip. Keeping the material free with the thumb and finger of one hand, he slid the zip a couple of inches to make sure it was moving freely then whizzed it down to the bottom with a quick tug. 'There you go!'

He met Kitty's reflection in the mirror, noting her heated cheeks and the glint of moisture in her eyes. 'You are a good boy,' she said on a laugh that ended with a touch of a sniffle.

Fishing in his pocket for the neatly folded handkerchief he always carried with him, Nick pressed it into her hand then patted her shoulder. 'Batman to the rescue. Take your time; I'll make sure no one disturbs you.' With a quick peek outside to make sure the coast was clear, Nick slipped back out of the dressing area and resumed his casual lean against the wall. A few minutes later, the curtain swept back and a much-composed Kitty came sailing out, the offending dress dangling from the hanger in her hand. 'Any good?' Nick asked her, keeping his face perfectly straight.

'Not really my style,' Kitty said as she pressed the dress into his hands, giving one a quick squeeze as she did, before she swept past him like a queen to greet someone she knew who was waiting in the queue.

'Good on you, Kitty,' he murmured to himself as he watched her chat and laugh like an absolute trooper, not a hint of her earlier embarrassment.

Thankfully, Ivy returned soon after and he was more than grateful to hand back the clothing and crafts section of the shop into her much more capable hands. 'How was everything?' she asked.

Keeping his voice low, Nick briefly outlined Kitty's struggles with the dress, omitting his part in her rescue. 'I left it hanging up in the changing area. I think it's okay, but thought you would want to check.'

'Of course, thank you.' Ivy sighed. 'Not one of my better designs, I'm afraid. Someone else had a similar problem with the zip last week. I think I'd better take them all off display and see if there's something I can do to fix that.' Nick gave her a non-committal nod, his basic knowledge of women's clothing having been stretched far beyond its limits already. He was about to escape to the relative safety of the general fiction shelves when Ivy placed a hand on his arm, her expression full of soft sympathy. 'Alex texted me earlier; are you okay?'

She didn't need to say anything more because even his travails with Kitty hadn't been enough to distract him from that damn photo of Aurora and Chad. 'I'm fine,' he said through a smile that felt forced. 'Water under the bridge and all that.' Ivy gave him a speculative look, but Nick was saved from further scrutiny of his pathetic feelings when his phone started to ring. He fished it out and checked the screen, wondering if it was Pete Bray needing him to do an extra shift in the pub. The number was withheld, likely a spam call about a non-existent problem with the Sky TV package he hadn't actually got around to installing in his apartment as yet. This would normally be grounds to ignore it, but he'd chat happily to someone who was trying to scam him out of his pitiful bit of savings if it got him out from under Ivy's gaze. He tapped the screen and raised the phone to his ear. 'Hello?'

'Nico?'

Everything stopped. The noisy chatter of the bookshop faded into the background as his ears seemed to fill with the sudden pounding of his heart. 'Aurora?' At his elbow, Ivy gave a little gasp but gathered herself swiftly as she all but shoved Nick into the dubious privacy of the fitting room and yanked the curtain shut.

'Oh, Nico, thank God!' Her voice was the same, and yet somehow different, softened with a hint of accent she must've picked up over the past twelve months in the States. 'I was worried for a minute that you might have changed your number!'

If she'd bothered to answer his text, she wouldn't have had to worry, now, would she? It was a petty thought, and not the sort of thing he liked to believe himself capable of. 'What do you want?'

3

Aurora found herself shivering at the coldness in Nick's tone and she wondered for the hundredth time if she was making a terrible mistake. The past thirty-six hours had passed in a blur of disbelief and panic. She'd left the audition with Chad Logan feeling like she was walking on air. He'd been so accommodating and polite – spending ages before and after the actual audition discussing the proposed movie with her, making her feel like he really was interested in her opinion about the character she might be playing. Although she'd been a bit worried about meeting him at a hotel on the strip, his assistant had made it clear to Dennis they'd hired a separate meeting room and the audition had taken place in that bland, corporate space. A couple of chairs had been set up in the centre of the room for them to chat, a table laden with an enormous breakfast buffet that twenty people would've struggled to get through, never mind the two of them. Even when the assistant had excused herself after taking a few photos, which Chad had said could be used as promotional teasers if she got the job, Aurora hadn't felt any kind of premonition that there was anything wrong. Indeed, Chad had been professional throughout, and talked earnestly about how important intimacy coaches were and assured her one would be on the payroll from the very start of filming. It was as if he'd already anticipated her questions and was going out of his way to make her comfortable.

She'd all but floated out of the room, taking him at his word that hers was the last audition of the day, and he'd asked her if she minded walking out with him as he was desperate to stretch his legs after being cooped up in the over-airconditioned room all day. As they'd exited the front of the hotel via the huge revolving door, the Las Vegas heat had slapped her in the face, the change in temperature so extreme it had dizzied her for a moment. When Chad had opened his arms wide for a hug, she hadn't liked to say no given how polite and respectful he'd been. He'd held on for a bit longer than she'd liked, pressing her into his body until a sliver of panic had risen. Stunned, she'd frozen on the spot, her mind screaming at her uncooperative arms and legs to move. A moment later, he'd dropped his hold and stepped away, not a flicker on his face that it had been anything more than a regular goodbye. A sleek limousine arrived at the kerb, the blacked-out rear window lowering to reveal a smiling Melissa waiting for her husband in the back seat. They'd both given Aurora a cheery wave as the car drove off, convincing her that it'd been nothing. That it was her own bad experiences tainting an entirely innocent encounter.

The nightmares had come for her again and she'd spent an exhausting night shivering in the depths of her hotel room's maximum-tog duvet, watching, but not really seeing, an endless round of rom-coms on the TV's streaming service. She hadn't even bothered to pick them, just let the next recommendation start playing until the light outside her wide-open curtains had shifted from black, to pale grey, to a glorious, burnished red. The pollution in Las Vegas might have her reaching for her inhaler any time she ventured outside, but it sure provided some spectacular sunrises and sunsets. And then the phone beside the bed had started ringing, jolting her out of her stupor. She'd fumbled for the handset, assuming it was a call from a member of the hotel staff, because everyone she knew personally used her mobile.

'Hi, Aurora, it's Blaze Reynolds here from ATG.' Her befuddled mind had taken a second to place the name but she'd barely had time to register the owner/operator of All the Goss, the internet's most scurrilous gossip website, before he'd continued speaking in that super-chatty we're-all-just-friends-here way she recognised from the many clips that had trended on social media over the years. 'Care to comment on your affair with Chad Logan? Girl, you must have some special kind of magic because everyone thought he and Melissa were rock solid!'

She'd known she should hang up, had been through umpteen and one media briefings from the PR teams she'd worked with about not engaging with any journalist – and she applied that term to Blaze in the very loosest sense – who approached her without clearance. Unfortunately, after her sleepless night she had been barely firing on one cylinder and she'd reacted on instinct. 'Wh... what are you talking about? I... I barely know Chad; I mean, we met yesterday for an audition—' Her brain had finally engaged and she'd clamped her mouth shut.

'Ah, the old casting couch scenario, eh?' Blaze's slimy voice had all but oozed over the phone connection into her ear.

'No comment!' Aurora had slammed the phone down, missing the cradle the first time because her hand had been shaking so much. A few seconds later, her mobile had started vibrating on the bedside table. She'd snatched it up, pressing the loudspeaker button without saying anything and Blaze's voice had filled the room. 'Come on, Aurora, don't you want to put your side of the story?' She'd stabbed at the 'end call' key, cutting off his ugly laugh. The calls kept coming, until she managed to get through to the hotel switchboard and ask them to block her number and found out they'd been coming to her direct – a quirk of the hotel system that if you had a guest's room number and knew the code, you could direct dial. They'd apologised and blocked all external calls, but it had left Aurora feeling unsafe because it meant someone had given out her room number.

Her mobile had been easier to control; she'd simply put it in 'do not disturb' mode. Venturing onto social media had made her stomach churn. Everywhere she'd looked there'd been a photo of her wrapped in Chad's arms – that awful, creepy hug! Why had she questioned her instincts about it, when she knew, she *bloody* knew from bitter experience when something wasn't right. She'd made a shaky call to Dennis, who'd been at lunch with a prospective client, and he'd been apoplectic. Not at her, never at her. He'd switched immediately into crisis management mode, ordering her to pack an emergency bag and get the hell out of the hotel. She'd done as she was told, not letting anyone at the hotel know she was leaving and using a service elevator that took her to the backstage area of the vast concert arena. It had been deserted, the late nights meaning the crew didn't come in before lunchtime, and she'd been able to slip out of a rear exit. She'd walked half a dozen blocks before flagging down a taxi and getting a ride to the airport. The driver made no show of recognising her, more interested in arguing with the talk radio show he was listening to. The blazing sun had been enough of an excuse for her oversized sunhat and sunglasses, an easy way to shield her face and look like every other tourist who'd been in town for a weekend visit to try their luck at the tables. She'd waited until he'd driven away from the departure zone drop-off before turning away from the terminal building and around to the arrivals area, where she slipped inside, lost herself for an hour just wandering and trying to calm the rising panic. Exiting arrivals at the back of one of the many streams of people, she'd caught another taxi and headed for a chain hotel at the budget end of the spectrum.

And here she was twenty-four hours later, still holed up and counting down the hours until her flight home that evening. Dennis had issued a brief statement yesterday morning on her behalf, denying any wrongdoing and saying she would miss the final night on the Divas tour. That had been with the organiser's blessing; in fact, they'd been so quick to dump her, Aurora wouldn't be surprised if they'd erased all mention of her from the billing.

From Chad Logan, there'd been only silence. He'd been spotted checking in to one of those high-end rehab facilities, which had of course sent the gossip mill spinning all that much faster. His wife's television show had been replaced by an old repeat – something else to send Aurora's anxiety spiralling to sky-high levels. Why were they acting as though there was a problem? Maybe there was and it was unconnected to her. It was a foolish notion, one she dismissed almost as soon as it formed. When Dennis had called to brainstorm possible ideas to rescue the situation, she'd been ready to agree to almost anything and that's how she found herself on the other end of the phone with the one man she'd tried very hard not to think about for the past few months.

'It isn't what you think,' Aurora tried again.

'And how would you know what I think about anything? We hardly know each other.' It wasn't anger she could hear in his voice, more like disappointment. And who could blame him after the way she'd treated him?

'I'm sorry I hurt you.' She didn't try to hedge it, because she hated those non-apology apologies politicians and celebrities always seemed to give. They not only sounded insincere, they were also a subtle form of gaslighting, like it was the wronged person's fault for feeling the way that they did. 'I wanted to reply to you last Christmas, but I knew I was coming over here and I...' *didn't want to risk letting you back into my life because I liked being with you too much.* She trailed off, not sure whether it would be a good idea to put voice to the words that had popped into her head, especially given where she hoped this conversation might go. She swallowed hard. 'Regardless of that, it was rude of me to ignore you and you deserved better from me.'

'What do you want?' The same words as before, but softer now.

'I take it you've seen the news?'

He laughed. 'Kind of hard to miss.'

'You should try being on this end of it.'

'Not a lot of fun, I imagine.'

It was her turn to laugh, and the sound surprised her as she hadn't thought she'd be capable of it, not when everything she'd worked for was crashing down around her ears. She decided to come clean, to explain things to Nick in the simplest terms possible. 'Chad Logan's assistant approached me via my agent to do an audition. I was told he was in town and was happy to set up something locally as they knew I was busy with the show I was involved in. We met, in a meeting room, I hasten to add, in a local hotel in the middle of the day and everything went really well.' She paused for a bitter laugh. 'I honestly thought I'd made a great impression, and I loved the role they were interested in me for. When he offered to walk me out, I didn't think anything of it until he suddenly hugged me as we were saying goodbye. Now, I'm sure he staged the whole thing.'

'You think he set you up? To what end?'

She couldn't blame Nick for sounding sceptical; hell, even Dennis thought it was a stretch, even though they'd been unable to come up with an explanation as to why Chad Logan hadn't refuted the rumours. But that gut instinct of hers, the one that had tried to balk at the embrace, the one that had kept her up all night haunted by bad memories, was blaring a full five-alarm alert.

Her breath gusted out on a sigh. 'I don't know, it's just a feeling I have, that's all.' Plus Chad and Melissa's totally weird disappearing act. Whether it was accidental or planned, it still added up to the same thing. Her reputation was being trashed all over the internet, and she wouldn't be surprised if the tabloids would be the next to pick it up. It seemed like half their stories these days originated on Twitter. 'I need to take control of the narrative.'

'Take control of the narrative?' Nick's laugh echoed down the phone. 'You sound like Alex did when all that nonsense came out about his book.'

'Who's Alex?' She hadn't met many people in the few weeks she'd been sneaking around in the Point, and the name didn't ring a bell.

'He's a friend of mine; you wouldn't know him, though, because he only moved here in the spring.'

She felt a sudden pang of sadness for all the many things she didn't know about Nick. He'd told her a bit about his family, talked about his life in the small village and some of the frustrations and limitations. She'd sensed a restlessness in him, but she hadn't dug too deeply. Hadn't wanted to dig too deeply, if she was completely honest with herself, because she'd already been too involved with him. And yet here she was about to potentially expose herself to all those muddled feelings again. When Dennis had suggested the idea, she'd dismissed it out of hand, but the more they'd talked the more she'd realised it might be her only chance to salvage the tatters of the career she loved more than anything else in the world. 'Perhaps I could meet him, and some of your other friends too...'

4

'This is mad, you do understand that?' Laurie asked him for the tenth time in as many minutes. She'd been quiet the night before when he'd gathered his friends and family for an emergency meeting following his conversation with Aurora. Several people, including his mother, had voiced their protest over the plan he and Aurora had cobbled together. To Nick's surprise, it had been his father who'd stepped in and said in a firm voice that whatever Nick wanted to do, they would support him. It was rare for his easy-going dad to put his foot down and it had been enough to bring everyone else onside. Once the protests had died down, everyone had stepped forward to offer whatever help they could. Ivy had gone so far as to say Aurora could use her flat. It was a genius suggestion because it would mean the two of them would be staying in the same building, if not quite under the same roof.

He looked at his sister, who was bundled up against the freezing wind that whipped across the water and swirled around the harbour, determined to seek out every nook and cranny it could poke its frigid fingers into. The huge, knitted bobble on her wine-bottle-green hat jiggled in time with her shaking head, a comic counterpoint to the fierce expression on her reddening face. Clearly, she wasn't quite as in agreement as she'd made out last night.

'So you've said.' Nick continued to check the emergency travelling kit he kept in the boot of his car. Snow was forecast and he had a long drive ahead. He pulled back the elasticated cuff on his navy padded jacket and cast a pointed look at his watch. 'Don't you have a café to open?'

Laurie huffed. 'I'm just trying to look out for you, that's all! I can't bear the thought of you letting her hurt you again.'

Resisting the urge to slam the boot and deny he'd been hurt in the first place, he let it down gently, pressing the hatchback down to make sure it was properly secured. Leaning against the side of the car, he folded his arms and met his sister's concerned gaze. 'It won't be like last time because I'm walking into this with my eyes wide open. I'm doing her a favour, that's all. It'll be a couple of weeks, a month tops.'

'A couple of weeks pretending to be in love with the only woman I know who's been able to get close enough to you to break your heart,' Laurie scoffed. 'And at Christmas to boot! It sounds like a bloody *brilliant* idea.' She shook her head, the bobble bouncing around once more. 'What if it doesn't work? What then?'

He shrugged. 'That's not my problem, is it?' His sister's only response was a word that might have earned her an encounter with a bar of soap if their mother had been there to hear it. Nick sighed and resisted the urge to check his watch again because he really didn't have time to argue if he was going to make it to the airport in time. He knew Laurie only worried about him because she cared – knew she and their little gang of friends had probably set up a WhatsApp group behind his back so they could discuss how stupid they thought he was being. It didn't even matter that they were probably right. Fate had given him a chance to see Aurora again and he wasn't going to pass it up. 'I'll be careful,' he promised Laurie.

She tugged her bottom lip between her teeth as though to prevent more words of warning from spilling out. After a long moment she gave him a resigned nod and reached into the messenger-style bag she was wearing across her body. 'Here.' She thrust a large flask and a wrapped bundle into his hands. 'I guessed you probably haven't had time for any breakfast so this should keep you going.'

'Thank you.' Warmed by the simple act of love, Nick leaned down to place the food and drink carefully on the passenger seat before straightening up and opening his arms to his sister. 'Thank you,' he said again, letting his gratitude for this lovely woman he was lucky enough to call a part of his family warm his voice. 'You're the best sister I've got.'

She laughed. 'Don't you forget it!' She reached back inside her messenger bag and withdrew a second flask and package.

'What's this?' Nick asked.

'It's for Aurora. I thought she might need a bit of something comforting after everything she's been through the past couple of days. She must be exhausted from the stress of it all.'

'You didn't have to do that.' Nick was touched. For all her words of warning, Laurie really did try to do her best for everyone. He placed the little peace offering in the car.

Laurie rested a hand on his door to keep it open. 'If you're sure this is really what you want to do then I'll support you. I'll keep my opinions to myself and make sure Aurora feels welcome here for however long she remains in the Point. I'll make sure everyone else is onside too.'

Nick sighed with relief. Aurora's crazy plan had no chance of succeeding if his friends and family weren't on board as well. 'I think you'll really like her once you get to know her a little.' A disconcerting thought occurred to him. 'What about Jake?'

Hiding his journalistic credentials, Jake had come to the Point to investigate the mermaid sightings Nick had helped Aurora to stage. He'd almost blown her cover, forcing Aurora to 'leak' the story to the press before she was ready. Jake had lost his scoop, and jeopardised his relationship with Laurie in the process.

Laurie shrugged. 'He thinks she'll leave you in the lurch again, just like last time.'

'Well, if he hadn't been sniffing around for a story, things might not have played out the way they did. At least Aurora never lied to me.' As soon as the words were out, Nick wished he'd kept his mouth shut. He needed things to go smoothly and going over old ground wasn't going to help Aurora fit into their tight-knit group. 'I'm sorry, that was uncalled for.' The way Laurie wrapped her arms around herself as she looked away told him how much his thoughtless words had hurt her. Closing the short distance between them, Nick wrapped her in a tight hug.

She resisted for a moment before her arms curled around his shoulders. 'That was mean,' she muttered against his chest.

'I know.' Nick pressed a kiss to the top of her head. 'I really am sorry. The last thing I want is for me and you to fall out, especially over a situation neither of us had any control over.'

Laurie nodded against his shoulder then stepped back to offer him a small smile. 'If there's a conversation to be had then the two of them can sort it out. It's nearly Christmas, and I don't want anything spoiling it.'

'Agreed.' Nick did give in to the urge to check his watch this time. He hesitated, wanting to make sure Laurie really was okay, but also worried about getting caught up in traffic. 'I need to go.'

Laurie flapped her hands, shooing him towards the car. 'Go! Text me when you get there, okay?'

'I will.'

* * *

Thankfully the traffic was pretty quiet on the drive up. He'd timed his departure to avoid the worst of the rush hour around the Bristol area and he was well along his journey on the M4 before he pulled over and enjoyed a cup of coffee and a couple of the teacakes Laurie had wrapped up for him. He double-checked the flight details on his phone and found a parking spot in the short-stay car park and tried not to flinch at the cost. Hoping Aurora wouldn't be held up too long in passport control and the baggage lounge, he entered the terminal and looked for a strategic place to wait for her. There were people *everywhere*, which he supposed was a good thing given that the plan he and Aurora had hatched involved a very public greeting, which with any luck would be noticed and filmed by someone and posted online. He'd been a bit reluctant at first, but had eventually conceded there was no point in pretending to be Aurora's boyfriend if no one knew about it. Luck was with him and he managed to snag a table on the edge of the Costa café seating area. He'd purchased an extra-large cappuccino he didn't really want, but that would provide an excuse to sit down. He sent a text to Aurora letting her know where he was. Her plane had touched down about twenty minutes ago so, fingers crossed, she'd be through anytime.

An hour later he was trying not to think about the cost of the car park ticking up, or the way the sky had darkened visibly in the past few minutes. He checked his phone but there was nothing other than a double blue tick to say she'd seen his message. Where the hell was she? What if there was more than one Costa in the terminal? He was fiddling around on his phone, trying to find a map of the arrivals area when the sound of voices calling out over the general hubbub drew his attention. Like many around him, Nick turned to look, and his breath caught in his throat.

Even though they'd agreed to try to get noticed, he'd expected Aurora to arrive somewhat incognito. Most of those candid snaps people posted online when they spotted someone famous showed them with their face shrouded in a hoodie and big glasses as they did their best to go unnoticed. Instead, Aurora was in full glamour mode, her long legs clad in impossibly tight jeans that tapered into high-heeled boots. She'd finished off her outfit with a fire-engine-red jumper that managed to fall off one shoulder in a completely-casual-but-perfectly-staged way. Her short blonde hair gleamed as though freshly washed and framed an immaculately made-up face, her lips glossed the same vibrant red as her jumper. Even without that ineffable something that marked her out as a star, she would've stood out amongst the travel-weary passengers making their way around her.

A light flashed and Nick realised the voices he'd heard came from a small group of photographers hogging space near the doors that separated the secure arrivals area from the waiting zone. *What a way to earn a living.* The idle thought barely registered as Nick found himself rising from his seat and walking towards where Aurora had paused to smile for the cameras. He heard someone shout a question about Chad Logan and had to admire the way she didn't even flinch at the mention of the man at the heart of the scandal. She had one hell of a poker face. Not sure what to do, Nick stopped. He might have agreed to a random selfie or two being posted online, but he hadn't expected to have to contend with the paparazzi. Aurora's gaze turned from the cameras to do a quick sweep over the gathering crowd who'd stopped to gawk at the spectacle. When she spotted him, her smile seemed to brighten before Nick noticed a tightness around her eyes as though she wasn't sure of his reaction to this change in their plans.

He could walk away, he realised. Turn on his heel and slip out the door and no one would be any the wiser. He didn't need to get tangled up in this mess – and it would be a mess, he understood now, the reality of what he'd agreed to do crashing around him. It wasn't as if he owed Aurora anything. Hell, if this scandal hadn't blown up, what were the odds that he'd have ever heard from her again? Even knowing the answer, his feet remained rooted to the spot as he drank her in. She was back in his life; what if he could somehow persuade her to stay?

Clamping down on the crazy idea before it could take root, Nick took a deep breath and raised his hand to wave at Aurora. If he'd thought her smile beautiful before, the one she flashed him now was brighter than the midsummer sun beaming down over the Point. 'Nico!' Pushing his way past the people who'd turned to see who she'd called out to, Nick just had time to brace himself before Aurora flung herself into his arms. The familiar scent of her perfume enclosed him in a cloud of seductive memories and he tightened his arms around her, pulling her into him like he never wanted to let her go. 'Thank you. Oh God, Nico, thank you,' she whispered against his ear before pulling back to look up at him.

For a moment he was able to forget about everything other than how good it felt to be holding her again. 'You look beautiful,' he murmured, raising a hand to cup her cheek.

Though she leaned her face into his hold like she'd craved his touch since the moment they'd last parted, there was a cheeky glint in her eye. 'Perks of the first-class lounge.'

He laughed, reminded again that there were many things beyond her looks that had made him fall in love with her. And he was still in love with her, there was no denying it. 'Who's your friend?' The intrusive shout followed by an almost blinding camera flash just inches from his face brought him back to the absurdity of the moment.

It's all just pretend, remember?

Nick lowered his forehead to Aurora's as though they were in a private space and not in the middle of a media scrum. 'Should I kiss you?' he whispered, their lips almost but not quite touching. In answer, Aurora slid her hand into the back of his overlong hair and closed the gap between them. Her lip gloss tasted sweet and fruity – strawberry, perhaps? He barely registered the thought before her mouth was gone and she was leaning back against his hold. Taking his cue, Nick released her. 'Shall we get out of here?'

'Yes, please.' It took a couple of moments for Nick to locate and retrieve her designer suitcase. Thankfully, the press were more interested in yelling questions at Aurora than pestering him. 'We're old friends,' she was saying as he rolled the luggage up next to her.

'What's your name, mate?' one of the cameramen asked him.

'I'm not your mate, mate,' Nick retorted before turning his back, deliberately positioning both his body and the large suitcase as a barrier between the handful of men and Aurora. 'Ready?' Without replying, she hooked her arm through his and they started walking with purpose. Nick didn't stop until they'd almost reached the terminal exit and he spotted the sleety snow outside. 'Can you grab the case for a sec?'

'Sure.' As soon as Aurora unhooked his arm and took control of the luggage, Nick whipped off his thick, padded coat and swung it around her shoulders, taking the handle of the bag back under his control so she could wiggle her arms inside the sleeves. 'What about you?' she asked as she flipped the deep hood up over her hair.

'It's only a short walk; I'll be fine.' Mirroring her action, Nick tugged up the hood of the sweatshirt he'd been wearing under his jacket and braced himself as the automatic doors hissed open, letting in a blast of freezing air. 'Over there on the right.'

Aurora hesitated for a moment, head swinging as she tried to take everything in at once. 'Got it,' she said, and he could tell by the determined way she moved in the right direction that she'd spotted the bright yellow sign indicating the short-stay parking. He glanced back and was surprised but relieved to find no one had followed them out. Maybe the awful weather had been enough to put the photographers off – or perhaps they were busy uploading their photos already. The thought of it made him feel a bit sick and he wondered how Aurora dealt with the constant intrusion. By the time they hurried into the shelter of the car park, the only people around seemed more interested in finding their cars than who they might be. Nick led the way to the lift, finger jabbing on the 'close door' button as soon as they were both clear. He pressed the buttons for all four floors of the parking. 'Just in case,' he said with a shrug when Aurora raised an eyebrow at him.

'No, it's a good idea, thanks.' She shook back the hood. 'The weather's a bit different from Vegas, that's for sure.'

When the lift reached the second floor, Nick held his hand out to keep the door open. 'It's the red hatchback over in the far-left corner. I'll be there in a minute. I need to pay for the parking.'

'Oh, let me.'

He waved off her attempt before she could open the front pocket of the small bag at the top of her luggage stack. 'I've got this. You can pay for lunch, if you like?'

'Deal.' The clack of Aurora's heels echoed off the concrete as she rolled her luggage in the direction of the car, and Nick found himself glancing around more than once to make sure the noise didn't attract attention. Satisfied the level remained deserted, he jogged after her, using the key to unlock the car as she neared it. He caught up just as she reached the rear of the vehicle.

'I need my bag off the top,' she said, unhooking the matching Louis Vuitton holdall from the top of the stack while Nick gathered the blankets and other things he'd stowed in the small boot. They'd have to go on the back seat for the trip back. 'Oh, can I borrow that for a moment?' Aurora took a blanket from the top of the pile and draped it over the front two seats before shrugging out of his big coat and crawling into the back seat with her bag. 'Can you keep watch for a minute?' she asked, reaching for the button on her jeans.

Realising she intended to get changed, Nick spun on his heel, almost dropping the box he'd filled with his emergency car kit in his haste to offer her privacy. Something thudded on the ground next to him and he glanced down to see it was one of Aurora's discarded boots. The other joined it a few moments later. There was a lot of rustling behind him, followed by a soft grunt. 'Everything okay?' he asked without turning around.

'Bloody jeans,' was all she said, giving another breathless grunt. 'That's better.' The offending item landed on top of the boots. A few moments later, he felt a soft touch against the back of his leg. 'I'm decent.'

Nick moved out of the way, unable to stifle a laugh as he turned around and took in Aurora's new look. 'If only those photographers could see you now.' She'd changed into a pair of dark grey leggings and a huge, fluffy cream hoodie that covered her to mid-thigh and looked large enough that he could've climbed inside with her and there'd still be room to spare. Her feet were tucked into black Ugg boots. 'You look like a cuddly snowman.'

She grinned. 'I wanted to be comfortable for the drive.' She gathered up her discarded clothing and stuffed it into the holdall before zipping up the top. She pulled a small packet out of a side pocket then shoved the bag across the back seat to make room for him to put down the box and extra blanket.

'All set?' When she nodded, Nick unhooked the blanket she'd draped over the seats and folded it quickly while Aurora crossed around to the front passenger side.

'Oh, what's this?' Aurora leaned down and retrieved the flask and package he'd left on her seat.

'Something from my sister, Laurie. She thought you might need a pick-me-up.'

Aurora's beautiful smile all but stole his breath as she settled on the seat beside him, setting the flask gently between her knees. 'How kind of her.' She fastened her belt before unscrewing the top and the sweet smell of hot chocolate filled the interior. 'Oh, what a treat!' She secured the lid then set the flask at her feet next to where he'd set his own flask of coffee. 'I'll have some in a bit. Shall we get going?'

5

The sleet was still falling, melting the moment it hit the ground. Aurora heard Nick mutter something about hoping it would stay that way. She hoped so too, because she was already deep in debt to him for enduring that circus back in the terminal. Luckily, the woman at passport control had recognised her name and mentioned that the vultures who hung around the airport terminals looking for stories to fill the tabloid gossip pages had been spotted outside. Knowing there was no way to escape it, Aurora had diverted into the first-class lounge to take a shower and get changed. If she was going to have her face plastered across the papers, she'd be damned if they had any excuse to speculate on her looking tired, or suggest she was creeping around like she was trying to hide. She still had her doubts about whether she and Nick could pull off this plan to pretend they were a couple, but she had to admit he'd done a damn sight better than she'd had any right to expect in the face of the cameras.

Casting a glance at the sky through the front window, she thought their hopes about the weather might be in vain as they were driving directly towards where the clouds were darkest. What she wouldn't give for the Range Rover her production company had hired for the summer when she'd last been in Mermaids Point. Oh well, she would just have to put her trust in Nick and his little red hatchback. If things got too bad, there were plenty of places to pull off once they got onto the motorway. Turning her attention from the road, Aurora pulled a wet wipe out of the packet she'd retrieved from her bag and began to remove the thick mask of make-up she'd applied to hide any hint of tiredness after the overnight flight.

When Nick halted at a red light just before their exit onto the motorway slip road, she felt his eyes upon her and turned to offer him a smile. 'I couldn't wait to take all this muck off,' she said, showing him the tan foundation stain on the wet wipe.

'You always look better without,' he said. A horn blared behind them, and they both jumped. Scrambling to put the car in gear, Nick lurched away from the now green light and sped towards the slip road. 'Not that my opinion matters, of course,' he mumbled, keeping his face turned away as he watched his mirror and then over his shoulder for a gap to pull into the fast-moving traffic. 'Your body, your business and all that.' He was looking forwards now, but there was no missing the hint of red on his cheek.

'It's okay,' she assured him with a laugh. 'I swear having to wear so much make-up is one of the worst things about being in the public eye.' She didn't *have* to wear it, but those paparazzi cameras were unforgiving of even the slightest blemish as the rather cruel 'look at the state of that' pages in the lower-end fashion magazines loved to point out. She glanced around for somewhere to put the dirty wipes, spotting an empty paper bag on the floor beside the flasks. Which reminded her... A few moments later she took her first sip of the heavenly smelling hot chocolate and couldn't hold back a sigh of pleasure. 'Oh, that's really good.'

Nick flicked her the tiniest of sideways glances before fixing his eyes back on the road ahead. 'Wait until you try one of the pastries Laurie packed for you.' Though he didn't say anything, she couldn't help but notice he'd slowed down and pulled over into the inside lane until she'd finished her drink and snack. The Belgian bun had been every bit as delicious as he'd promised, the sweet icing contrasting perfectly with the zesty tang of the lemon curd coating the inner swirl of the fluffy treat.

'That was amazing. Remind me to thank your sister when I see her.' As she screwed the top back on the flask and tidied up the few crumbs that had escaped, a thought occurred to Aurora. 'Is your family okay with all this?' The last thing she wanted was to barge in and turn their whole Christmas upside down. 'We could book a last-minute holiday and leave them in peace, if you want?' Dennis would be able to sort them out a nice villa somewhere with a couple of bedrooms. In fact, that might be a better solution as they'd only have to be snapped again at the airport ready to jet away and stage a few loved-up photos for her Instagram account. She reached in her pocket for her phone to start looking at options.

'My family is fine with it.' There was a long pause. 'Mostly.'

Damn! How could she have been so thoughtless? She could blame the blind panic of potentially losing the career she'd worked so hard for, but that still didn't excuse what she was doing. Even expecting him to drop everything and jet off to a beach somewhere was unreasonable. 'It's too much. I'm asking too much of you and your family.' She spotted the sign for the next exit. 'Turn off here. You can drop me off at the nearest railway station and I'll make my way back into London. Dennis and Hetty can put me up until I sort myself out.'

'What are you talking about?' Nick said with a laugh as he ignored her instruction and, rather than indicating for the junction, he pulled into the middle lane to pass the lorry that was sending up a spray of water in its wake.

'Me gate-crashing your family Christmas like this!' she exclaimed with a touch of exasperation. 'None of this is your problem and it's totally selfish of me to drag you into my mess.'

'You didn't drag me,' Nick said in an even, reasonable tone. 'You asked me for my help, and I agreed.'

'It's still too much,' she muttered, feeling her face flame with embarrassment as the realisation of what she was putting him through finally hit home.

He fumbled for her hand without looking, giving her fingers a quick squeeze before returning his grip to the steering wheel. 'It's okay. We talked about it last night and everyone is on board.' That touch of hesitation was there again, though.

'Not everyone, from the sounds of it.'

Nick sighed. 'My sister's still dating Jake Smith – you know, the journalist who uncovered what we were up to?'

She remembered, all right. That would've been another PR disaster if Nick hadn't warned her that Jake was about to blow her cover. 'I didn't realise they were a serious item.' It was hard to keep the frost out of her voice.

'They've been living together pretty much ever since. Hey, you do know that he'd already changed his mind about publishing the story, don't you?' Nick paused for a second. 'No, you probably don't because we never talked after that, did we?'

Another stab of guilt jabbed at Aurora. Really, the way she'd treated Nick after their lovely time together was nothing short of appalling. 'It meant a lot to me when I got your text last Christmas,' she said softly.

'Not enough to answer, though.'

True. Well, not strictly true. She would have to be careful how she negotiated her way through the next few minutes. She'd already hurt Nick a lot, that much was crystal clear, but it was important to be honest too. 'I knew I was leaving the next morning and I had no idea when I would be coming back. If...'

'If this thing with Chad Logan hadn't blown up, you'd still be over there, right?' There was no resentment in his words, just simple resignation.

'Right.' She shifted in her seat, but it wasn't the cushions that were making her uncomfortable. 'The time we spent together was precious to me. I'd forgotten what it was like to be myself and being with you, it was...' She scrambled around for the right words to explain what she'd felt. *Safe.* No, not that because it would bring up too many questions. *Free.* 'It was like I could breathe properly for the first time in years, like there was no pressure to be special, to put on a show.'

'I felt the same way,' Nick said, his eyes still on the road. The sleet was still falling, but so far the windscreen wipers were coping and the road was quiet enough he could keep a good distance from the rest of the traffic. He gave a soft chuckle. 'Once I got over the fact that Aurora bloody Storm had kissed me.'

Her cheeks heated at the reminder that she'd been the one to make the first move. They'd had a long day out on the boat, and she'd been tired and cold from getting in and out of the water, but she hadn't been ready to go back. Nick had wrapped her in a pile of blankets and taken her for a quiet trip around the bay to where the lighthouse watched over the rocks at the end of the Point. He'd turned off the motor and they'd drifted quietly, sharing a bottle of beer as they watched the sun set. He'd looked so handsome in the soft golden light, his hair a tangled mess from the wind, a smile on his face as he'd pointed out a group of seabirds making their way towards their evening roost on one of the islands. When he'd turned to look at her, she'd wanted to capture the expression of simple joy on his face and before she'd known what she was doing she'd leaned over and pressed her mouth against his. She shoved the memory away, trying to ignore the languid feeling that was stirring in her middle. 'Most men never get over it, and the ones that do always seem a bit disappointed in the reality.'

'Most men are idiots, then.'

She laughed. 'I could say the same thing about most women because someone should've snapped you up a long time ago.'

'When you grow up somewhere like Mermaids Point you soon run out of options when it comes to relationships.'

Intrigued in spite of the little voice in her head telling her she should steer the conversation away from such intimate things, Aurora loosened her seat belt just enough so she could turn a little and face him. 'There's never been anyone special?'

His shoulder lifted in a half-shrug. 'I was a bit of an arrogant fool in my youth, always worried about what I might be missing out on rather than concentrating on the woman I was with. When I finally grew up enough to realise it, I'd either burned my bridges or the other girls were wise to my schemes and wouldn't give me the time of day. There was one girl I always had a soft spot for, but she was Laurie's best friend and so kind of fell into the little sister category.'

There was a wistfulness in the way he spoke about this mystery woman and Aurora felt a pang of what she rather suspected was jealousy. 'What happened to her?' she asked, doing her best to keep her voice neutral.

Nick shot her a quick glance and Aurora knew she'd done a bad job of keeping her question casual. 'Ivy's still around; she lives with a good friend of mine, actually. His older brother is marrying my aunt on Christmas Eve so you'll get to meet them both then, although I'm sure we'll bump into them before that.'

It was bad enough that she was gate-crashing Christmas, but a family wedding! 'I can't possibly go to your aunt's wedding!' Aurora protested.

'If you want anyone to believe you and I have been a secret item for the past eighteen months then you'll have to be there.'

She couldn't refute the logic of his statement, but she was struck once again just how much she was putting on him, and his family. 'It's not too late to turn back.'

Nick grunted. 'You're like a broken record. I've said I'm happy to help you sort this out, and I meant it.' A bullet-sharp flurry of hail hit the windscreen in a sharp rat-tat-tat, making them both jump. 'Bloody hell!' There was a silent pause other than the swish of the wipers and then another volley of hail struck, only this time it didn't stop. Nick checked his mirrors, instinctively slowing as the visibility dropped sharply.

Twisting around, Aurora checked the inside lane beside her. 'Clear if you want to pull in.'

'Thanks.' With a sigh, Nick steered the car over and eased his speed. 'Looks like it's going to take us a while to get home.'

'I'm not in any rush,' she assured him. 'Getting there in one piece is all that matters. Shall I put the radio on so we can listen out for the latest forecast?'

'Good idea.'

Once she'd switched it on and found a rolling news and weather station, she settled back in her seat, and let the silence fall between them once again. Nick needed to concentrate, and they'd have plenty of time to sort out some proper boundaries once they were safely back in the Point. They hadn't even talked about their living arrangements, other than Nick saying he had access to somewhere for her. She'd been so relieved that he'd agreed to help, it'd never occurred to her to question him further. It was on the tip of her tongue to ask, but she forced herself to stay quiet and keep her eyes on the road ahead. She turned her attention to her phone instead, having a quick look at social media to see if there was anything posted about the show she and Nick had put on for the cameras back at the airport. She didn't even need to open her apps; the number of notifications flagged was huge. It was tempting to shove her phone back in her pocket, but this was what she'd come back for, to try to counter the damage. Taking a deep breath, she opened Instagram. 'Well, we certainly got ourselves noticed,' she murmured half to herself as she scrolled through the dozens of posts she'd been tagged in. Most were copies of shots she'd posed for, but there were plenty of candid ones snapped and shared by members of the public along with various hashtags and speculative comments. There were a few trolls, of course; it was par for the course and one of the reasons she had high filters set on her direct messages. Every couple of weeks, one of the PRs who worked for Dennis had the unfortunate task of wading through the abuse, dick pics and solicitations for her to represent this or that dodgy brand. Anything that was a genuine offer was screenshotted and sent to her and Dennis for consideration. Satisfied that the vast majority of what she saw was more positive than negative, Aurora closed the app and put away her phone. 'You've got your own hashtag.' She knew Nick needed to concentrate, but she couldn't resist telling him.

'I don't want to know, do I?' He sounded half-amused, half-resigned.

'Probably not, Hashtag Mystery Hottie.' She coughed as she said the last three words as though trying to disguise them.

'Bloody hell, I'll never live that down,' he groaned. 'Maybe we can get lost in a snowdrift or something and with any luck it'll take them years to find our frozen bodies.'

She laughed. 'Knowing the way these things work, you'll have been forgotten before the end of today's news cycle.'

'I bloody well hope so.' Aurora might have let the guilt take over again, but he was smiling as he said it and what was done was done. It was too late to turn back now.

The next couple of hours passed in near silence as they made their way along at a steady pace. Aurora found herself holding her breath each time the weather and traffic reports came through the speakers. Each update added a list of accidents and road closures, but nothing on their planned route apart from a lorry getting a tyre changed, forcing the closure of one lane. Aurora winced and sent up a little thought for all the emergency services who would be turning out trying to help in such awful conditions.

A break in the weather allowed Nick to put on a spurt of speed and get them the other side of Bristol. The coffee, hot chocolate and food Laurie had provided had kept them going, but they were going to have to stop for petrol at some point. 'Let's push on to the next one,' he decided as they checked the details on the services sign. 'I'd like to make the most of the dry weather and the daylight.'

'Fine with me.' He was the one doing all the hard work, after all. They made it another half an hour before their luck ran out. The sky darkened and the snow began to fall. It was a sleety mix at first but soon turned into huge, fat flakes that reminded Aurora of fluffy cotton wool. With the head-lights on, the view ahead was quite disconcerting, like they were driving into a tunnel of lights. The traffic around them slowed and Nick decided to stick behind an articulated lorry as it offered a slight shield from the falling snow.

'That doesn't look good,' Nick murmured as a warning sign flashed ahead. Moments later the traffic reporter on the radio was talking about reports of an accident a couple of miles ahead, blocking two lanes. A siren screamed in warning as a traffic officer 4x4 flew past them along the hard shoulder, followed a few minutes later by a police car. By the time an ambulance passed, they'd slowed to a crawl. Nick drummed his fingers on the steering wheel, his jaw a tense line. 'I should've stopped earlier.'

'The next services are less than two miles away; you weren't to know. It was a good idea to try and push on while the weather was holding.' Aurora laid her hand on his thigh in a quick, reassuring gesture. 'We're still moving and should see the sign for the slip road soon. I just hope everyone is okay.'

'Yeah. I wouldn't want to be one of those poor emergency workers right now,' Nick said, echoing her earlier thought. He leaned forward to study the dark sky overhead as though he could see anything beyond the steadily falling snow. 'Let's hope the accident isn't blocking the services.' Retrieving his phone from where it was sitting in the cupholder space in the console, he opened the map. 'If this is accurate, the problem is about a mile the other side so we should be able to get off. There's a motel as well as a petrol station. I think we should fill up, eat a hot meal and then see how conditions are before we decide whether to keep going.'

'I think we should just stop. This doesn't look like it's going to get any better, does it? Give me the details and I'll see if they have any rooms left.' The 4G signal wasn't great but Aurora eventually found a website for the motel. She quickly tapped in her details and did an availability check; they had a few rooms left but given how many others were going to be looking for shelter, she hesitated over taking up two rooms. 'There's a family room that has two beds in it, so I'll book that if you don't mind sharing?' she asked, already clicking through to the checkout before Nick had a chance to respond. The little hamster wheel on the screen went around and around. 'Come on,' she murmured, hoping the website didn't time out or crash before she got her booking confirmed. 'Got it!'

By the time they'd inched their way into the services parking area, the road had disappeared under a compacted trail of snow. The car park itself was a free-for-all, the white lines demarking the spaces also hidden so people had stopped anywhere and everywhere. Nick spotted a gap just large enough for the hatchback to squeeze into and indicated. 'You'd better jump out.'

Aurora did as she was told, grateful for the deep hood on her fleecy top and the big square pocket on the front, which she shoved her hands into. Nick edged out of the car and opened the boot. He pulled out a rucksack and hooked it onto his back. 'Can you manage with your smaller bag?'

'Of course. Just let me sort it out.' She did a quick reorganisation, leaving only clean underwear, one set of clean clothing and her wash kit in the holdall. She checked the complimentary bits and pieces they'd given her on the plane. 'There's a spare toothbrush,' she said, tossing it into the holdall.

'I've got everything I need.' Nick half-turned to show her the rucksack. 'When I saw the forecast, I thought I'd better chuck in an overnight bag just to be on the safe side.' He reached across her to lift up her holdall and hooked the long strap over one shoulder. 'Stick my coat on.'

She wanted to argue at his bossy tone, but also knew any discussion about it would only delay them getting across the car park and back in the warm and dry. 'Thank you,' she forced herself to say as she pulled it on over her thick top. She stepped back to give him room to close the boot when a noise distracted her. 'What was that?'

'What was what?' Nick locked the car with the fob, the hazard lights turning the floating snow an eerie orange as they flashed twice. 'Come on, let's get inside.'

'Hang on a minute.' Turning sideways, Aurora squeezed down the gap between the cars and peered out into the shadowy patch of trees that separated the car park from the crawling traffic on the motorway beyond. *There it was again.* 'There's something here.'

'Probably a fox or something, come on before we both catch our death.' Even as he said it, Nick was holding the bag high over his head as he edged between the cars to join her.

A flash of something pale caught Aurora's eye, followed by that low, whiny sound she'd heard before. 'Oh, I think it's a dog.' The snow was a lot thinner beneath the trees and Aurora shoved back her hood as she crouched down and held out her hand to the little grey shadow huddled beneath one of the trees. 'Hello,' she said, keeping her voice soft and coaxing. 'It's all right, it's okay.' The dog whined but didn't move. Moving slowly, Aurora edged closer until she could hold out her hand within sniffing distance of the dog. 'You poor thing,' she crooned. 'Are you lost?' The dog whined again, but this time it was the one that moved. Aurora held still, keeping her hand out, muttering all sorts of soothing encouragement until the dog crept close enough to nudge at her hand with his head. She gave it a quick stroke, noticing how wet its fur was. 'He's been here a while.' She raised her voice enough for Nick to hear her. 'He's soaked through, poor little soul.' It was hard to tell exactly what breed it was, some sort of terrier from the size and shape. 'We can't leave him out here,' she said to Nick as he crouched down beside her.

'No, I suppose not. With any luck we'll find the owner once we get him inside. Hang on a sec.' He reappeared a few moments later with one of the blankets from the back of the car. Moving slowly, Nick draped the blanket around the shivering dog and when it didn't move, he scooped the animal up into his arms. Aurora couldn't help but notice the way he stood straight up, even with the awkward weight of the dog. He wasn't built like one of those action hero superstars from the screen, but there was a lean hardness to him. The physique of someone honed by hard, physical work rather than endless repetitions in the gym weight room.

The service centre building was packed with people like themselves trying to wait out the weather, or the accident, or both. Once inside the door, Nick set the dog down and gave him a rub with the blanket to dry him off and warm him up. The little terrier stood patiently and let Nick take care of him, his black button eyes bright and curious. 'He's thin,' Nick said, his voice terse. 'It's hard to tell under all that fur, but I definitely felt more of his ribs than can be healthy.'

'No collar,' Aurora pointed out, getting a sinking feeling in her stomach.

'Well, let's see if we can find his owner.'

They stopped the first member of staff they saw, asking if anyone had reported a lost dog. 'No, mate,' the young lad said. 'We've got some bowls in the back, I'll fill one up if you like?' He was back in moments, and the way the dog lapped desperately at the water sent Aurora's concern for the poor thing spiralling higher.

'Why don't you wait here, and I'll do a quick ask around?' Nick suggested.

Aurora watched as he moved with purpose through the crowded tables, asking repeatedly if anyone had lost a dog. The head shakes, glances around and general murmurs of denial told their own tale. By the time Nick made it back to her side a few minutes later, there was no mistaking the dismay in his eyes. 'No one's missing a dog,' he said, confirming her worst fears. 'I've left my mobile number with the staff in the shop, and behind the counter at Starbucks. They've promised to call if anyone comes looking.' Crouching back down, he pulled a sandwich out of the bag he was now carrying and removed several slices of ham from between the bread. The dog wolfed it down then pressed his nose into the bag, seeking more. 'Hold your horses,' Nick said, voice full of affection as he repeated the process with several more sandwiches. Once he'd sated the dog's initial hunger he straightened up and showed Aurora the rest of the contents of the bag. 'I grabbed a mix of things. I know I said about having a hot meal, but there's only burgers or paninis and the queue for both is a nightmare.'

'I'm happy with anything. Let's go and find the motel, and check in. Maybe the dog's owners are there.' Nick gave her a sceptical look, which echoed her own opinion, but didn't say anything. Using the blanket, he picked the dog back up and they ducked out into the still-falling snow to walk the hundred or so metres to the motel. They had to wait a few minutes while the harassed reception staff tried to find space for those wanting a room.

'It's the last one we have, I'm afraid,' the receptionist told the couple ahead of them with three children. The woman was trying to hold a crying baby in one arm and hang on to a toddler with the other. A boy of around five was zooming around the reception area driving the toy car he had in his hand over every available surface – the walls, the floor, up and over the holdall Aurora had dropped at her feet, making loud revving noises as he did.

'Stop that, Nicholas!' the man snapped in an exasperated tone as he shot Aurora an apologetic look.

'Must be something about the name,' Aurora murmured to Nick and his eyes widened in mock outrage.

'Are you sure there's nothing bigger?' The man had turned back to the reception and was asking in a plaintive tone.

'I'm so sorry, but as I'm sure you can understand we're absolutely maxed out because of the weather and all the family rooms are gone. All we have left is a small double.'

Aurora exchanged a guilty look with Nick. She'd booked them a family room so they'd have separate beds. He gave her a shrug as though saying it was up to her. It wasn't as if they'd never shared a bed before, even if it was under very different circumstances. With any luck there'd be some spare bedding and one of them could bunk down on the floor. It might be a bit awkward, but she couldn't bear to see this poor family try to manage with three small children and one bed between them. She gave Nick a nod and watched as he stepped forward. 'Hi. Sorry to interrupt but we have a family room reserved and we don't mind swapping...'

She wasn't sure who looked more grateful, the couple or the reception-ist, but in short order the switch had been made. Thankfully, they were so distracted by Nick's natural friendly demeanour and their sympathy for the plight of the dog, hardly anyone gave Aurora a second glance. As they'd suspected, no one there had reported a missing dog either. The staff were fine about them having a dog in their room and were even able to provide a water bowl and a sachet of dog food.

'You'd be amazed at what we've got out the back,' the receptionist said with a smile as she reached out to pet the terrier, who was basking happily in all the positive attention. 'What a little angel you are; I can't believe no one is missing you.'

'I'm sure someone will claim him soon,' Nick said as he tucked the dog closer against his chest and bent to pick up Aurora's bag, his own still on his back.

The family were still in reception trying to corral their kids long enough to gather their luggage. They stopped what they were doing to launch into another embarrassing round of thank yous, but the adrenaline crash after the scene at the airport had combined with a dollop of jet lag and the after-effects of the stressful drive and suddenly all Aurora wanted to do was fall into bed and sleep for a year. When they finally escaped to find their room, she leaned against the wall while he fiddled with the key card. Why did they never work the first time? 'Just leave me here,' she mumbled when Nick held the door open for her. 'I'll be fine.'

'Hold on,' he said with a soft chuckle before disappearing into the room and letting the door close behind him. She thought for a second he might have taken her at her word, and honestly, it was fine because she could just close her eyes and... The door swung back open and Nick returned minus the dog and their bags to help her into the room. 'Sit down.' He steered her to the edge of the bed, which, contrary to the description of a small double, was actually a decent size.

Unable to do anything else, Aurora plopped down and let him fuss around her, first removing his coat from around her shoulders, then her wet boots, which he carried over to sit underneath the radiator next to his own shoes. Her big hoodie was next, leaving her in a long-sleeved T-shirt, her comfy leggings and socks. 'I need to clean my teeth.' She wasn't sure at first if she'd said it out loud or just thought it, but Nick unzipped her holdall and retrieved her wash kit. When he leaned over her as though he meant to help her up, Aurora rallied enough to wave him off. 'I can manage.' She stood up and was immediately light-headed. 'Oops,' she said as he caught her before she could fall back on the bed, his expression a mix of amusement and mild exasperation. Once inside the bathroom, Aurora was able to splash water on her face, clean her teeth and wiggle her way out of her bra, because there was no way she wanted to sleep in it.

She returned to the bedroom to find Nick settling the dog on a temporary bed he'd made with a spare duvet and the blanket next to the radiator. 'He's such a sweet-natured boy,' Aurora said, sitting on the end of the bed to watch them. 'I can't believe someone has just abandoned him.'

'Me neither, but it's starting to look that way.' Nick settled back on his knees, his attention still all on the dog. 'If no one claims him, I reckon we should just take him home and see if the local vet can find an ID chip.' He reached out to play with the terrier's ears. 'Such a good dog, aren't you?'

'We can't just call him "dog".' Aurora barely got the words out around a massive yawn that felt like it might dislocate her jaw. She crawled up the bed and scooted under the cover, lying on one side as she watched Nick continue to pet the dog. The comment the receptionist had made about him being such an angel came to mind. 'We should call him Gabriel.' Nick's amused smile as he glanced across the room at her was the last thing she saw before her eyelids fluttered shut and everything went dark.

6

Did the Aurora Storm fan club know she snored? Nick glanced down at the sleeping woman beside him, his attention momentarily distracted from an old movie he'd found on one of the TV's free-to-air channels. He'd seen it loads of times, but it was an easy watch and although Aurora had crashed and burned, it was still too early for him to try to sleep. Reaching out, he tugged gently on her pillow – just enough for her to shift her head – and the room fell blessedly silent. With a grin, Nick turned his attention back to the film while he finished his makeshift dinner of a sandwich, a bag of crisps that claimed it was large enough to share – like that was going to happen – and a bar of chocolate. It wasn't the most nutritious meal, but it would fill the gap and stop him from waking up starving in the middle of the night. He'd left the food he'd got for Aurora on the bedside table in case she woke up at some point, though she'd not stirred in the past couple of hours, during which he'd taken a shower, taken the dog out for a quick pee and switched on the TV. He'd checked his phone only long enough to post a V-sign emoji in the family WhatsApp group in response to all the 'mystery hottie' comments. After a series of crying-laughing emojis had popped up in response, he'd let them know that he and Aurora wouldn't be home until sometime in the morning, then put his notifications on mute.

He cast a quick glance over to where the dog, Gabriel – he grinned at the silly, festive name – was dozing on his blanket. Someone had looked after him enough to train him at some point because the terrier had trotted over to stand by the door when he'd needed to go out. Who would abandon a dog, and in weather like this, for God's sake? The thought sent his blood boiling again and he forced himself to pay attention to the film until the white-hot rage inside him calmed a little. Even if someone came forward to claim Gabriel, Nick wasn't sure he'd be prepared to let him go given the state they'd found him in. When he took him to the vet, he was going to ask for a full condition check. And then what? Distracted from the movie once more, Nick looked down at Aurora, who was still dead to the world beside him. He seemed to be collecting waifs and strays at the moment.

Not that Aurora was going to let him keep her, no matter how much he might want to. He studied the deep shadows beneath her long lashes. She didn't look like anyone had been taking proper care of her either. She'd been slender when they'd met eighteen months previously, but there was a hollowness to her cheeks and her collarbones were visible through the thin material of her top. Appearing onstage night after night for weeks on end must have been gruelling, and not just physically. Well, that could be his mission over the next couple of weeks, to spoil her a bit and help her enjoy this unexpected bit of downtime as much as possible. When he turned back to the film it was to find the credits were rolling. He found the remote and flicked idly for a couple of minutes, but nothing captured his attention. He checked his watch to find it was only nine o'clock and sleep seemed a long way off.

Perhaps a bit of fresh air would help? He could check the car was okay and maybe grab a hot drink from Starbucks if things had quietened down in the food court. There was a small kettle and the makings on a tray on a shelf in the wardrobe, but he knew from experience those kettles could make an awful racket and he didn't want to disturb Aurora. When he got up, Gabriel raised his head briefly from his paws but didn't show any signs of wanting to move, so Nick decided he'd be fine for a few minutes. He would take him out for a final pee later. Finding a notepad and a pen – it amazed him when these budget hotels were cutting costs that they still provided stationery in a mostly digital age – he scribbled a quick note and tucked it under the food on Aurora's nightstand.

The snow had stopped, leaving a soft hush over everything. The white blanket managed to make the tired-looking buildings and concrete expanse of the car park look almost pretty – almost. There were tyre tracks everywhere and less than half the cars that had been parked when they'd arrived remained, as people had taken advantage of the end of the storm to try to continue on with their journeys. Rather them than him, Nick thought as he made his way carefully across the compacted snow to where he'd left the car. There was plenty of room closer to the buildings and he decided it would be worth the hassle of defrosting the car and clearing the snow to park it under one of the large spotlights rather than leave it in a shadowy corner over by the trees. He doubted anyone would have much enthusiasm for breaking in on a night like this, but why risk it?

Fifteen minutes later, he'd shifted the car and collected the flasks Laurie had given him that morning from the passenger footwell. The food court area was much quieter, although there wasn't much room to sit as people who'd been unable to find better accommodation were sprawled across the benches and curled up on chairs, trying to snatch whatever rest they could. He wove through a couple of families who'd resorted to the floor and approached the coffee counter. A brief chat with the man behind the counter got the flasks rinsed and returned to him. 'I can't refill them direct from the machine,' the server said, sounding apologetic.

'It's fine,' Nick assured him. 'More than fine; I appreciate the fact you were able to wash them up. Can I get an extra-large decaf cappuccino and the same size hot chocolate, please?' He studied what was left on the cake counter, which wasn't much. 'And a couple of chocolate brownies, please.' He thought about the receptionist who'd been so helpful back at the motel. 'Add another cappuccino to that order, will you please?'

With his order delivered and the drinks for himself and Aurora decanted into the flasks to keep them warm, Nick slipped the man a fiver in thanks and made his way back across towards the motel. It was freezing fast and the snow beneath his boots crackled with each step, his breath condensing into huge white clouds. Using his back, he pushed open the door to the reception in time to catch the girl behind the counter in the middle of a huge yawn. 'Oh, forgive me!' she said, her cheeks heating.

'Looks like this is a timely delivery.' Nick placed the cappuccino on the counter and slid it towards her. 'To say thanks for the bits for the dog.'

The rosy glow kicked up a notch as her smile widened. 'That's so thoughtful of you.'

Nick lifted one shoulder in a dismissive shrug. 'Not a problem; I hope you have a quiet rest of the night.'

He'd just opened the corridor door when she called to him in a hesitant voice. 'Do I know you from somewhere? I know I probably shouldn't ask, but you look very familiar.'

Damn. In all the drama with the weather and the traffic, Nick hadn't given the farcical scenes back at the airport more than half a thought. He recalled the hilarity in the family WhatsApp about his new nickname and offered the receptionist a weak smile. 'It's the hair, probably. Reminds some people of that bloke who was in *Poldark*.'

'Oh right, that must be it.' She didn't sound convinced, but thankfully was too polite to push it.

'Enjoy your coffee,' Nick said, letting the door swing shut behind him as he beat a hasty retreat back to his room.

He crept in as quietly as possible, only to find Aurora sitting cross-legged on the bed munching on one of the sandwiches he'd left for her. Gabriel was curled up on the bed beside her, his head resting on her knee as though he was staking a claim to her. 'How are you feeling?' Nick asked, as he bent to take off his wet boots and pop them back under the radiator to dry.

'A bit groggy, but okay. Sorry for crashing out like that.' She contemplated the second half of the sandwiches before ripping open a bag of crisps. 'Salt and vinegar, you remembered.' She said the last with a soft smile that sent little sparks of awareness through him. Her hair was pressed flat on one side and pushed up a little on the crown and she still had a crease across her cheek from her pillow. One of the things he'd always liked about her was that she never seemed to care what she looked like, or perhaps, more accurately, she was comfortable enough around him that she didn't feel like she had to put on a show. He took it as a compliment, a sign of trust in him. He remembered what she'd said in the car earlier about most men being disappointed in the reality of her and he wondered how on earth that could be true.

'Hot chocolate or decaf cappuccino?' he said, lifting the two flasks he'd brought back with him.

Her eyes lit up. 'How about a chococcino?' She eased her leg from under the dog's head, earning a grumble from Gabriel, but he was obviously too comfortable with his backside planted right in the centre of Nick's pillow to follow her off the bed. Making a mental note to swap the pillow for one of the spares in the wardrobe before he went to bed, Nick surrendered the flasks to Aurora when she held out her hands for them. He took a seat on the end of the bed while she retrieved a couple of mugs and filled each with a blend of the hot chocolate and cappuccino. 'Try it,' she urged when he gave the mug she offered him a dubious glance.

Taking a tentative sip, he closed his eyes as the taste sensation hit him. 'It's like drinking tiramisu.'

'Right!' Sounding delighted at his enjoyment, Aurora sat down beside him and clinked her mug against his. 'I discovered it in my favourite little diner back in Vegas.' A wistful look crossed her face.

'You really liked being out there, didn't you?'

She half-shrugged, half-nodded. 'There were aspects of it I loved – the wide-open spaces, the friendliness of the people. They seemed a lot less cynical, as long as you didn't get onto politics.'

Nick laughed. 'That's a given wherever you are these days.' He took another sip of his chococcino – it really was fantastic – then remembered the takeout bag in his coat pocket. 'I've got the perfect accompaniment to go with this.' He fetched the brownies and offered one to Aurora, who took it with a grin and dipped one corner into her drink before biting it off with glee. Well, at least the loss of weight he'd noted wasn't down to a faddy diet. Which reminded him of something. 'My dad messaged earlier and said he's booked a table in the pub for tomorrow evening so we won't have to worry about dinner when we get home.'

Aurora gave him a startled look. 'Us?'

Nick gave her leg a sympathetic pat. 'Consider my family like the Borg from *Star Trek*.' Her look of incomprehension made him sigh at her sad lack of education when it came to the best sci-fi show ever. 'They're an alien race who assimilate every being they encounter. "Resistance is futile" is their motto.'

Aurora threw her head back and laughed. 'I need to stop worrying about gate-crashing, is that what you're saying?'

'Exactly. And if we want to make people believe we've been together all this time, we need to be seen out and about. Having my folks there will help to back up our story.' He adored his family, but they could be a bit much. 'But I don't want you to feel like you have to join in with everything, I just want to make it clear that you are very welcome. If you'd rather have your own space then you only have to say.'

'I haven't had a family Christmas in a while.' There was that wistful tone again.

'It must be hard to get home when you're travelling all the time.' She'd never mentioned her own family, and he was curious as to why she'd been so happy to come to Mermaids Point rather than have him join her elsewhere.

There was a long pause while Aurora drained her mug, and Nick wondered if she was focusing on her drink in the hopes he'd forget this conversation. 'Things are a bit strained between me and my parents. They've never understood the fame thing and they got a lot of hassle when I took that career break.'

Career break. More like vanished off the face of the earth, from what Nick could remember of the fuss the press had made around that time. He filed it away for now. It was obviously hard for her to talk about her family. 'If it was anything like that circus earlier at the airport, it's understandable if they don't want a repeat of it.'

She looked a little lost for a moment before giving herself a decided shake and sitting upright. 'I hope your parents won't mind the attention, although hopefully there won't be a repeat of the fuss that came to the Point after the mermaid sightings.'

'They're used to dealing with people, and honestly, if a few people come down to gawk once they find out you're in Mermaids Point then let them come! The local businesses will be glad of the extra income. Speaking of which, I've promised to help Alex and Ivy out on Saturday in their bookshop. They're putting on a special day for the kids with a visit from Santa, that kind of thing.'

Aurora's face lit up. 'That sounds like fun. I'd love to lend a hand.'

Nick was surprised, but delighted at her willingness to pitch in. 'Fantastic. Ivy's going to meet us when we get back to let you in so you can have a chat with her about it then.'

'Let me in?'

It was only then that Nick realised he hadn't told her about Ivy's offer. 'She owns one of the other flats in the warehouse. She's all but living with Alex in their place above the bookshop so you can use her flat for the duration of your stay. We share the same entrance so we can come and go at the same time and no one need be any the wiser that you're not actually staying at my place.'

Aurora shook her head. 'Considering I dropped this on you with almost no notice, you've managed to organise so much.' She rose and refilled her mug with the cappuccino and chocolate mix. 'Do you want some more?'

Nick shook his head. It had been delicious but combined with the brownie was probably more of a sugar hit than he needed before trying to sleep. When he said as much, Aurora grinned as she carried her mug around to her side of the bed and settled back against her pillows. 'There's never enough sugar to keep me awake. The only time I struggle to sleep is after a show – the adrenaline is like nothing else I've ever experienced.'

Interested in this insight into her career, Nick settled on his side, head propped on his hand as he watched her sip her drink. 'What's it like, being onstage in front of a big crowd?'

She regarded him thoughtfully over the top of her mug. 'How did you feel today, having people watch you at the airport?'

He paused, really giving himself time to think about it. It had all passed in a bit of blur and then with the driving conditions he hadn't had time to think about it much. 'Weird. Incredibly self-conscious, perhaps even a bit scared at being the centre of attention.'

She nodded. 'Sounds about right, only amp it up about a hundred times.'

Nick found himself shuddering at the thought of it. 'Then why do you do it?'

Aurora set her mug back down and drew her knees up under her chin. 'There's something inside me that craves it. From when I was a little girl I loved to sing and put on little shows in the living room. At school I guess I was considered a bit of a show-off, but I didn't mean to be. There's just something that happens when I sing, a connection to the music, to the way it makes people feel good when they hear me.' She gave a little laugh. 'I'm sure the psychologists would have a field day with me.'

Nick thought about how good it felt at the end of a successful day trip out on his boat. It couldn't possibly be in the same league as what Aurora was talking about, but there was a real sense of satisfaction watching a group he'd taken out laughing and joking, or swapping stories of things they'd seen and showing each other the photos they'd taken. It felt good to make people happy. But what about the flipside, though? He'd had some pretty miserable times too, when the weather wasn't good or someone was seasick or left a horrible review for the pettiest of reasons. But the odd negative comment on Tripadvisor was worlds apart from the endless judgement people like Aurora must have to deal with. 'I've always considered myself a pretty confident person, but I'm not sure my ego could survive the constant scrutiny you must be under.'

She gave him a sad smile. 'There's definitely a downside to this business.'

'Is that why you disappeared off the scene for a while?'

Her face froze, then a strange, icy blankness settled over her expression. She got up, not looking at him as she circled around the bottom of the bed. 'I'm going to have a shower.'

Shit. Nick had no idea what had just happened, other than the fact he'd obviously stuck both feet in it. He stared at the closed bathroom door for a long moment, wondering what to do for the best. Deciding to give Aurora some space, he put his coat back on and signalled to the dog. He paused outside the bathroom door and when he couldn't hear the shower, he knocked lightly. 'I'm going to take Gabriel out for a walk.' When there was nothing but silence from inside, he looked down at the dog, who was waiting patiently as his side. 'Let's get out of here, eh?' Gabriel gave a soft woof of agreement and they headed outside.

Obviously feeling better now he was warm, dry and fed, Gabriel was almost bouncing with energy, in marked contrast to when they'd popped out earlier and he'd barely been able to coax the dog more than a couple of feet from the motel entrance. The stars shone overhead in a sparkling blanket, the storm clouds having blown through. Nick's ears ached within a minute or two and he pulled up his hood as he watched Gabriel dashing this way and that across the pristine white snow. He seemed determined to leave no inch of it unmarked by paw prints. Every few minutes he would stop mid-frolic to sniff at some delicious scent or other that captured his attention. Once he'd satisfied that olfactory desire, Gabriel would look towards Nick as though to make sure he was still there before bouncing off again. Nick made sure to stay in the light so the dog never had to search for him, amazed at how quickly they'd become attached to each other. He hadn't considered himself a pet person before. He loved his aunt's dog, Toby, and even had a soft spot for the grumpy old cat who had refused to leave the bookshop and now belonged to Ivy and Alex. With his parents working full-time in their shop, it had never been practical to have a pet when they'd been growing up. Now he had his own place, though, there was nothing to stop Nick having a dog... Unless Aurora was thinking of keeping Gabriel? But that didn't seem likely as she'd no doubt be back on the road again if she managed to weather the negative publicity around her and Chad Logan.

Calling Gabriel to his side, Nick made his way slowly back towards the motel, thinking again about the way Aurora seemed to have been set up. He believed her version of events, but what he couldn't get his head around was the motivation behind the leak. Everything pointed to it coming from Chad Logan and his team, but to what end? He was still puzzling over that as he let himself and Gabriel back into their room.

The TV was off, the only light from the bedside lamp on Nick's side of the bed. Aurora was little more than a lump burrowed under the duvet. Nick settled the dog as quietly as he could, cleaned his teeth and changed out of his jeans into a pair of pyjama bottoms in the bathroom. Eyeing the unoccupied side of the bed, he decided the room was warm enough to sleep on top of the cover. He and Aurora had avoided the subject of them sharing the bed and now he didn't want to presume and make her feel uncomfortable. He tossed the extra pillow on the floor and turned out the light, his eyes making an inventory of all the unfamiliar light sources in the room – the bright red standby light on the TV, the pale wash seeping under the door from the corridor, an occasional green flash from somewhere on the ceiling that was probably the smoke detector. He closed his eyes and rolled onto his side, listening to the soft inhale and exhale of Aurora's breathing, unconsciously matching his own to the slow, steady pace. He had all but drifted off when he felt the bed dip and shift as she rolled over. The rhythm of her breath changed, and he found he was holding his, awake again and aware, so aware of her just a few inches away.

'I'm sorry,' she whispered. 'I'll tell you about it sometime.'

'Sleep now,' he murmured. The covers rustled and her hand brushed his arm in the dark, moved upwards until she settled the back of her hand against the palm of his. He entwined their fingers lightly, letting himself start to dream about the possibility of a future where they did this every night, a future where they shared not only a bed but trusted each other with their darkest secrets and their brightest hopes and dreams.

Thankfully, the gritters had been out overnight and the rest of their drive to Mermaids Point was uneventful. As they crested the top of the hill, Aurora found herself straining forward against her seat belt, eager to catch her first glimpse of the sea. It was a crisp day, the sky the kind of pale blue that spoke of the coldness of the air. A few high wisps of white were a marked difference to the glowering dark cloudbanks of the previous day. To her surprise, there was little evidence of the snow that had stopped them in their tracks, not much more than a dusting on the grassy banks. 'Looks like the weather wasn't as bad here.'

Nick nodded as he steered the hatchback through the backstreets towards the little harbour at the far end of the village. 'We had a bit last year, but it rarely snows heavily enough to settle. Mum and Dad have got a picture somewhere of Laurie and me in the garden one Christmas. The snow is up to my waist and Laurie was only a toddler so it's just her head and shoulders sticking out. I can't have been much more than four or five and it's not something I really remember. They bring that year up every time it snows for more than five minutes at a time.' He laughed. 'It's one of those weird events where everyone older remembers it clearly, but my only image from that day is the photo and the stories they've told me. Do you know what I mean?'

Aurora nodded. She had a few of that kind of memory herself. 'My parents have a photo of me in a red and white dress. I think I'm probably around three years old. The bottom half of the dress is velvety and the top is white with big red polka dots on it. I'm wearing white tights and the shiniest pair of black Clark's shoes. My hair is in lopsided pigtails.' She found herself grinning at the image in her head. 'I think it was for a family wedding. Sometimes I imagine I can remember the feel of that velvety skirt under my fingers, but it's probably just because I've seen that photo a million times sitting on the sideboard in the living room.' Head full of memories of home, she turned to look out of the window. Christmas had well and truly come to Mermaids Point. Some of the houses had a single string of lights around the downstairs window or framing an outside porch. Others had little trees in pots sitting on the doorstep. A few had gone all out, every inch of the front of their houses covered in lights, climbing Santas and dancing snowmen. One even had a full sleigh including miniature reindeer on its roof. She wondered if her parents still got the scraggly fake tree down from the loft or if they'd splashed out on a new one. Thinking about them made her stomach ache. She would have to call and let them know she was back in the country, and that her plans for the holidays had changed. It would be one hell of a trek to their house, even more so than if she'd been staying in London. Unless the media scrum died down, the likelihood of them wanting her to visit and risk bringing attention to them was very small indeed. *Worry about that later.* She turned back to Nick. 'So where do you stand on the Christmas decorations front?'

'See for yourself.' He indicated right and steered the car onto a familiar road that led down to the old harbour.

Aurora didn't remember much about it other than the dock area where Nick and his uncle launched their boat trips from. There were still a few trawler ships tied up on the nearside as they drove slowly down the slope, together with huge coils of industrial rope in shades of orange and blue and clumps of nets here and there. They passed a row of warehouses, most looking worse for wear with peeling paint and rusted panels of corrugated iron. The last one in the row, the one nearest to the little white wooden hut from where they sold day-trip tickets, stood in complete contrast to the others. The wooden boards had been stripped, treated and varnished and the roof replaced with solid-looking dark slates. A bright garland of light bulbs decorated the roof's overhanging edge, a splash of joyful primary colours against the pale wood and dark slate. Beneath the lights, two long, narrow Juliet-style balconies protected a pair of enormous picture windows. Directly beneath the balconies, two double sets of patio doors had been installed into the lower half of the warehouse, the smoked glass opaque even though a soft glow shone behind the left-hand set. A long row of planters decorated the herringbone-tiled area in front of the warehouse, filled with miniature Christmas trees decorated with white lights. Aurora guessed the planting could be switched out to suit the seasons. 'Is that one-way glass?' she asked as Nick inched past the building. He turned right, and drove around to the rear where a large carport with space for half a dozen cars jutted out. He pulled into the furthest space and turned off the engine.

'Yes. It was a slightly higher spec than I originally planned for, but I wanted to offer maximum privacy to ensure the downstairs units were an attractive option. In the end, I had it installed in all the windows as it offers really good thermal regulation and helped to boost the overall environmental rating. Come on, I'll give the full tour.'

They'd got out of the car and Nick was just lifting her suitcases out of the boot when a pretty woman swathed in a black woollen cloak, a red knitted beret covering short red curls a few shades darker and her denim clad legs tucked into shiny red wellies, approached them with a wave. 'Great timing!' Nick said, pausing to kiss the new arrival on the cheek. He turned to Aurora with a smile. 'This is Ivy.'

Aurora cast an admiring glance over the other woman's eclectic outfit. She clearly had an innate sense of style, something it had taken Aurora many hours of consultations with stylists from some of the top fashion brands to try to achieve. 'I love your cloak, where did you get it?'

'It's Dior,' Ivy said, twisting from side to side with her arms held out to show the swish of the beautifully structured cloak.

'Dior!' Aurora looked from Ivy to Nick and back again, not able to disguise the surprise in her voice. When she'd last been in the Point, parts of the village had been looking a little rundown. She didn't want to come across as a snob, but it surprised her that someone owning a local business could afford designer clothes.

'I found it in a charity shop,' Ivy said, clearly able to read Aurora's mind.

She felt her face flush. 'Sorry, I didn't mean to imply...'

Ivy laughed. 'Imply away! If an outfit costs me more than ten pounds, I consider it a failure.'

'Ivy either makes or upcycles all the clothes she sells in her shop,' Nick said, the pride in his friend obvious.

Aurora tried to ignore the little twinge of – *something* – as she watched the obvious affection he felt for this attractive woman. 'Wait... I thought you ran a bookshop.'

'I do! Well, Alex handles the bookshop side of things mostly and I sell all sorts of everything else – clothes, bits of furniture, decorative nick-nacks, cushions – you name it, really!'

'Well, you look stunning. I'm definitely going to have to make time for a shopping trip while I'm here.'

Ivy's cheeks glowed in obvious pleasure. 'You'd be welcome, any time. You can come after hours if you want, you know, if you'd rather not be bothered by people.'

Her kindness and consideration warmed Aurora from the inside out. 'That's really very sweet of you, but I don't want any special treatment. I want people to see me out and about.' She looked towards Nick. 'To see us out and about.'

'That's the plan.' Nick hoisted the last bag out of the boot. 'Come on, let's get inside and you two can chat fashion to your hearts' content.'

Ivy rolled her eyes then hooked her arm through Aurora's. 'You really couldn't find anyone better than Nick to be your fake boyfriend?'

'Hey!' Nick protested as both Ivy and Aurora burst out laughing.

'Let me introduce you to the real man in my life.' Aurora led Ivy round to the side of the car and opened the door. Gabriel jumped down, his stiff little tail sticking straight up like an aerial, wagging a mile a minute.

'Oh my goodness, who's this gorgeous boy?' Unhooking their arms, Ivy dropped to her knees to give Gabriel a pat. He propped his front paws on her chest and swiped a lick on her cheek.

'Get down.' Aurora crouched to gently push Gabriel down onto all four paws. 'Sorry, I don't want him jumping up on anyone.' She scratched the dog behind the ears, making a big fuss so he would know he wasn't in any trouble. 'He seems mostly well trained, but we don't know anything about him.' At Ivy's puzzled glance, Aurora explained about finding the dog the previous night. 'We couldn't just leave him out there on his own.'

'Of course not!' Ivy exclaimed. 'Poor boy. Well, you are welcome to have him in the apartment, though I'm not sure what he'll make of Lucifer's scent.'

'Lucifer?'

Ivy grinned. 'He's my devil cat and lives up to his name. He used to belong to the previous owner of the bookshop and kind of never left. He spends most of his time over there, but he comes and stays with me on the odd night I sleep here.'

'I'm sure Gabriel won't mind, and if he does he can stay at my place,' Nick said, towing the luggage towards a large steel door set in the middle of the rear wall. 'We might only have him for a few days, anyway. I need to take him in to see Jim at the surgery and get him checked out, see if he's chipped and whatnot.'

Ivy made a choked sound. 'Gabriel?'

Aurora frowned at her for a second before a broad smile tugged at her cheeks. 'And Lucifer!' She started to giggle. 'The receptionist at the motel described him as an angel and with it being nearly Christmas, the name seemed to fit.'

'Well, I hope he lives up to his name as much as Lucifer lives down to his. Come on, let's get in the warm and get you settled in.'

They entered a plain-looking hallway with doors to the right and left and a wide staircase leading to the first floor. A set of four postboxes had been fixed to the wall beside the front door and Aurora noticed only three of the four had name labels. 'We're still waiting to complete the purchase on the final ground-floor apartment,' Nick said as he led them towards the stairs. 'There's been a bit of a setback as Louise, one of the buyers, hasn't been very well, so we've put everything on hold while she recovers.'

'Her mum was in yesterday,' Ivy said as she grabbed one of the bags without being asked and started to climb. 'Sounds like she's feeling a lot better so with any luck they'll be able to proceed early in the new year.'

'Ah, thanks for the update. I was wondering how she was but I didn't like to text in case they thought I was hassling them.' Nick was carrying the largest case as though it weighed nothing.

'Isn't it costing you money, not being able to complete the sale?' Aurora asked as they rounded the half-landing and completed the climb to the first floor.

Nick shrugged. 'I've made enough to pay back the bank loan, which was the most pressing issue. Besides, some things are more important than money.'

It was such a Nick thing to say, Aurora thought. Not flippant or careless about his finances, more that his priorities were elsewhere. 'You'll never become a ruthless business tycoon with that marshmallow heart.'

He laughed. 'Thank God for that, because I can't imagine anything worse. I've got my eye on another project, but it's very early days. If I'm not in a position to make an offer on it before someone else snaps it up, something else will come along, no doubt.'

It was on the tip of Aurora's tongue to say she could help him out with financing if he needed it, but she changed her mind. She didn't want to risk offending him by suggesting he needed her help. Not that it would be charity, more an investment opportunity. What she'd seen so far of the warehouse conversion impressed her, but she'd have a better idea once she'd settled in and had time to check out the quality of the finishes inside the apartments. Perhaps she could get Nick to show her the property he had in mind for his next project. She filed the thought away as Ivy unlocked the door on the right and pushed it open. 'Here we are.'

Though the floor was wood, Aurora made a point of removing her boots before she stepped inside. Light. That was the first word that came to mind as she got her first glimpse of the interior of Ivy's place. It flooded in not only from the huge front window, but from the row of high, narrow ones lining the side wall. A soft rug the colour of burnished wheat covered the floor in front of a long, dark green leather sofa that looked as though it ought to be in the smoking room of a gentlemen's club. Bookcases lined one wall, spilling over with not just books, but rocks, shells and bits of driftwood, which had obviously been picked up on the beach. Plants were everywhere – from spider plants and ivy dangling tendrils over the edges of shelves to a pair of large cheese plants framing either side of the front window. 'It's beautiful.'

The sound of claws on wood caught her attention and Aurora crouched to loop a gentle arm around Gabriel's neck before he got it into his head to explore the place. 'You need a bath, fella, before you're getting near any of the furniture,' she told the dog.

With a laugh, Ivy stepped past her and tugged a dark green and red checked blanket from the arm of the sofa and shook it out flat over the rug. 'Here, he'll be fine on this for now.' She patted the soft wool and Gabriel glanced from her to Aurora before trotting over to settle in the middle of it.

'I'll make sure to have it dry-cleaned,' Aurora assured her, before wondering whether Mermaids Point even had a dry-cleaner's.

'Don't worry about it. Pretty much everything is second – or likely third – hand. You must make yourself at home while you're here.' Ivy scratched Gabriel between the ears. 'Both of you.' She straightened up. 'Come on, I'll show you the rest.'

The living room area flowed into an open-plan kitchen, a chest-height partition cleverly dividing the two spaces without blocking any of the light. The appliances were sleek and modern, the stainless steel a nice contrast to the polished granite work surfaces. Ivy gave her a quick tour of everything, opening cupboards to show where the crockery, pans and utensils were all stored. She tugged open the door to the fridge to display a vast array of fresh vegetables, meat, cheese and staples. 'To get you started,' she said to Aurora with a smile. 'I wasn't sure what you liked so I got a bit of everything. If there's anything you don't want, let me know and I'll take it back to the flat with me.'

Aurora pressed a hand to her stomach before it could give an appreciative rumble; breakfast had been a quick panini bolted down so they could get on the road early. 'You shouldn't have gone to any trouble, but I'm so glad that you did. Will you stay for lunch?'

Ivy shook her head. 'I have to get back to the shop as I've left Alex fending for himself. We'll catch up this evening, though, for dinner.'

'You guys are joining us at the pub?' Nick asked as he finished his self-appointed task of carrying Aurora's luggage into a room that she assumed must be the bedroom.

Ivy grinned. 'Your dad issued a three-line whip to all the Morgans and the Nelsons; everybody will be there.'

Aurora tried to ignore the flutter of nerves in her stomach, wondering just how many people this 'everybody' constituted. 'Well, that'll be something to look forward to,' she said, with a bright smile. 'It'll give me a chance to get to meet the whole family.' She hesitated, looking between Ivy and Nick. 'They all know what's going on?'

Ivy reached out to pat her arm. 'Everyone has been fully briefed so you'll have plenty of back-up, don't worry.' She checked her watch. 'Look, I must dash, Nick can sort out the rest of the tour. I'll see you later.'

On impulse, Aurora reached out and gave this lovely, kind woman a quick hug. 'Thank you so much for lending me this place. I promise to take good care of it.'

'You're very welcome!' Ivy gave her a quick squeeze in return and when she stepped back, Aurora could see there was a genuine warmth in her gaze. She watched as Ivy gave Nick a hug then headed for the door with a cheery wave. If they had more time, Aurora could imagine the two of them becoming friends. It was a melancholy thought because she couldn't remember the last time she'd made a new friend. Perhaps if things went well over the next couple of weeks, she could think about making regular trips to the Point. And what? Expect Nick to keep playing along as her pretend boyfriend every time she condescended to visit? God, she really hadn't thought any of this through properly, had she? She'd have to have a proper talk with Nick before they met up with everyone later so they both knew exactly where they stood – and most importantly, how things were going to end so he wasn't left in the lurch once the holidays were over.

'Hey, what's wrong?'

Startled, Aurora glanced up to see Nick regarding her with a frown of concern creasing his dark brows. 'I was just thinking about how we rushed into all of this without thinking about the longer-term consequences.' With a sigh, she wandered across to the sofa and sank down on the butter-soft leather. Close up, she could see the material was cracked with age, but someone – Ivy no doubt – had treated and buffed the aged leather to a high shine. She pulled up her feet beside her, leaving room for Nick to sit down.

'We definitely need to set some ground rules,' he said as he slung one arm along the back of the sofa, turning his body so he was nestled in the opposite corner and facing towards her. 'We'll have to hold hands and stuff, to make the story believable, but we don't have to go in for a load of big PDAs like we did at the airport.'

Aurora nodded. 'I don't want to make you uncomfortable, and I definitely don't want you to feel used the way you probably did last time.'

Nick laughed. 'I didn't feel used. What happened between us was a mutual choice. I'll admit to being disappointed with the way things ended so abruptly, but I understand why you did what you did.'

She met his rueful smile with one of her own. 'I won't say I haven't thought about whether things might have turned out differently for us now and again.'

Nick's expression turned serious. 'And?'

She sighed and shook her head. 'It was clear even from those few weeks that our lives are just far too different. You have your friends and your family, a really special community you are a part of. I'm always on the road, living out of suitcases and in hotel rooms and I couldn't have expected you to give up everything and traipse around after me.'

'You could've given me that option.'

Aurora sighed. 'No, I couldn't. Not then, because I had to devote every single moment of my energy towards making sure my comeback was a success. I barely had time to sleep those first couple of months after the truth about the mermaid videos came out. My single dropped the next day, and then it was an endless round of interviews and appearances. When the song hit number one, Dennis decided to push the album out to maximise exposure and organised a last-minute tour. I never knew where I was going to be from one day to the next. I just did a show, fell asleep in an anonymous hotel, got put on a bus the next morning and did the same thing the next night and the next. I was living on adrenaline and junk food.' She'd forgotten how hard being back on the road was and it had taken a few weeks to settle into a more sensible routine. 'Then the single gained traction in the States and it was too good an opportunity to pass up.' She took a deep breath and said the words that she knew would reveal the very selfish core of her. 'I didn't have time for you, Nick.'

He stared at her for a long moment. 'And now?'

Of all the things she'd expected him to say, that was the very last one. 'Now?'

'Yes.' He slid across the sofa until their knees were touching. 'Do you have time for me now?'

Heat flared inside her, the passion she'd always felt for him stirring like a beast waking from a long slumber. 'What are you saying?'

He cupped her cheek, one long thumb stroking against her temple. He'd held her just like that when they'd lain together in the quiet moments after... A flush of remembered sensation rose up her chest, her throat, higher still until she was sure her face must be on fire. 'I'm saying we don't have to pretend, if you don't want to. We've got two weeks together. Give me the chance to show you how good things can be between us.'

He didn't need to show her; the memories flooding through her head were showing her in very vivid detail how good things between them had already been. He leaned forward until their lips were an inch apart. 'Tell me what you want, Aurora.'

The temptation to give in to the promise not only in his words but in his eyes was almost overwhelming. '*Nick*.'

'Tell me.' He whispered the words over her mouth like the sweetest caress.

'I... I need time to think.' She wasn't sure which of them was more disappointed when he sat back, running a hand through his tangled curls. 'Right.' A red spot glowed on his cheek, and she wondered what it had cost him to put his heart on the line for her again. How many more times would he be willing to reach out only for her to let him down? She suspected this might be the last. 'I really will think about it.'

A rough smile quirked his lips. 'Sure.' He pushed up from the sofa. 'Dad's booked the table for seven thirty so I'll give you a knock around seven, okay?' He clicked his tongue at the dog and Gabriel immediately came to his side. 'I'll take him for a walk and sort out a few essentials, try and speak to the vet and what have you.' Nick said all that without looking at her, his voice bland and completely lacking in emotion.

'Fine.' Gabriel turned at the single word and if doggy looks could talk, the one he was giving her was one of equal parts disappointment and disapproval. She didn't blame him. She was pretty bloody disappointed in herself too. She wanted to grab Nick's hand, to find a match to the courage he'd shown and give him the chance he'd asked for. Instead, she watched him let himself out of the flat, the quiet click of the door behind him somehow more of a statement than if he'd slammed it. With a sigh, she heaved up from the sofa and trudged into the bedroom. Her body clock was still all over the place from travelling and if she didn't try to have a nap, she'd be absolutely useless later.

* * *

To her surprise, Aurora managed to sleep for a solid three hours. It might have been longer if her bladder hadn't woken her. Trying to shake off her grogginess, she padded out of the bedroom in the T-shirt and her underwear and opened the door to a small storage cupboard before opening the one next to it and entering a bathroom that wouldn't have looked out of place in a posh hotel. The walls were sleek, shiny, white tiles, the floor a deep midnight blue with tiny flecks of gold. A double-length shower cubicle filled the entire wall to her right. At the sight of it, she caught her breath, forgetting all about why she'd come into the bathroom in the first place. Unable to tear her eyes away, she slid back the cubicle door and stepped inside, raising her fingers to trace the vivid ribbon of green that seemed to shimmer and dance. Beneath the bright green were shades of pink and purple fading into a starlit sky that echoed the floor tiles. She didn't know how it was possible, but the entire panel was a photo-realistic image of the northern lights, the aurora borealis, after which her solid, sensible mother had inexplicably named her. Was this a sign of Ivy's creative soul, or was it something Nick had suggested for her? Either way, Aurora found herself completely entranced by it. Her body urgently reminded her why she'd woken up and with that taken care of, she decided to try out the spectacular shower and retrieved her wash kit from the bedroom.

As the first drops of hot water pattered down, she closed her eyes and did what she'd promised Nick she would do – she thought about him, thought about them and the next two weeks. What did it mean? Did he want another fling like before, or something more meaningful? She had the feeling it was the latter, but what could they really find out about each other in such a short space of time? Even if they decided to really be together rather than faking it, there was no guarantee she would be able to shake off the rumours and unpleasantness of the story about her and Chad. Once something was on the internet it took on a life of its own and she knew she would be asked about it long after the initial buzz of scandal had burnt itself out.

And if the story faded away and her career was still salvageable, what then? She couldn't manage her career from a little village so far from London. Even if she didn't go back to America, and damn it, she'd been *so* close to breaking out there she could still taste the anticipation of it on the back of her tongue, she'd still have to spend most of her time away from whatever home she and Nick might try to make here. How long could she expect him to wait around for her? He was such a family-oriented person, she couldn't imagine him wanting to leave everything behind and follow her.

Family.

God, what if they somehow managed to make a go of things and decided they wanted kids? What then? Would he stay at home and look after them while she flitted in and out of their lives when she had the time? No. That didn't seem fair. The image of Nick holding a smiling, chubby baby with a headful of the same wild curls as his filled her mind and for a single, burning second it was something she wanted so badly the need of it all but doubled her over.

She'd always sworn she'd never be forced to give up on her dreams, not after the way Julian had tried to control her, but whatever Nick was, he was nothing like Julian. To even put the two men in the same bracket felt the height of disloyalty. Nick hadn't suggested she be the one to compromise; he'd only asked for her to give him a chance to prove he could fit into her life. *What life*? What was she still chasing that she hadn't already achieved? She'd hit the top of the charts, toured successfully and made enough money to secure her future as long as she continued to be sensible. For all her fame, she was still her father's daughter, still held those same engrained beliefs of living within one's means. Even if her means were a lot bigger than her parents' these days. If somehow things worked out and she had a chance to go back to the States, what was she hoping to achieve? She'd never wanted to be an actress until the opportunity had come along. Did she really want to spend the next few years pretending to be someone else? When would it be enough? When would she finally feel like *she* was enough?

She reached for her shampoo and began to scrub a generous handful onto her scalp, humming as she did so. When she realised the tune was 'I'm Gonna Wash That Man Right Outa My Hair', she couldn't help but laugh at her subconscious. If only it was that easy. Several months of intensive therapy had got her over the worst of what had happened with Julian, but the scars of him would always be with her. He'd wanted the star, not the woman inside. Wanted to catch her and keep her locked in a gilded cage where only he got to enjoy her. And when he'd trapped her, he still hadn't been satisfied.

But Julian had never tried to get to know the real person behind the sparkle. Nick, on the other hand, had met her at her very lowest ebb and never been anything other than delighted in the time they'd spent together. Her fear of the past repeating itself was not enough of an excuse to let life continue to pass her by. Julian was gone. Forever. If she was going to make a go of things with Nick, it had to be for the right reasons only. Forget the wrongs of the past, forget even about what it would mean for her career. This was all about her chance to find happiness. If she let it slip through her fingers now, she might regret it for the rest of her life.

Wrapped in a soft white dressing gown she'd found on the back of the bathroom door, Aurora padded into the kitchen and made herself a cup of tea and a couple of slices of toast, which she spread with a thick layer of peanut butter she'd found in one of the cupboards. Even with a table booked for seven, it would likely be closer to eight before they got any food. As she chewed, she scrolled through her phonebook to find the number she wanted and pressed the video call button.

'Aurora, darling!' Hetty Rouse's affectionate voice as much as her lovely smile warmed Aurora right down to her toes. 'How are you? All recovered from that awful drive?'

'All good, thanks. One of Nick's friends has lent me her beautiful apartment so I'm feeling very much at home already.'

'Ooh, do give me a tour!'

Aurora flipped the camera on her phone and took Hetty for a virtual walk around the apartment, saving the gorgeous bathroom for the last.

'My goodness, that shower is something else! Your Nick must be a very clever chap to come up with a design like that.'

Your Nick. The way Hetty said it unlocked something inside Aurora. He was hers; whether she'd given herself permission to think about him or not, he'd crept into her mind so many times over the previous year. There was a reason why it was his name that had sprung to her lips when Dennis had suggested staging a distraction to the negative press. Dennis had argued with her at first; his plan had been for her to work with one of the actors also signed to the agency, someone who was used to the attention and wouldn't be fazed by it. Someone who would treat it like any other acting job and be content to walk away at the end of it. But there was only one person Aurora had felt she could trust – or at least that's what she'd told herself. Perhaps that had been an excuse, though. Perhaps she'd been looking for a way for her and Nick to be together again and everything else was simply window dressing.

'You've gone very quiet,' Hetty said, drawing Aurora from her reverie. 'Is everything okay?'

Flipping the camera back so she could meet Hetty's worried gaze, Aurora gave her a reassuring smile. 'Yes. For the first time in a long time, I think it is.'

They chatted for another ten minutes, going over plans for the coming days. 'I'm so sorry I won't be able to spend Christmas with you and Dennis as planned.'

Hetty waved her off, but there was regret in her eyes too. 'We can do it another time.'

'Ask her about the concert!' Dennis called from somewhere in the background.

'Oh, yes! Are you still on for the charity do at the Albert Hall? Dennis put some feelers out and they are happy to have you. Their demographic aren't the type to follow the gossip columns, and it's not as if you are the headline act.'

Aurora had forgotten all about it. 'It's the twenty-eighth, right?'

'That's right, a week on Sunday. You could stay with us for a night or two if you have the time. Will you be bringing Nick with you? It would be a nice touch to show him off on the red-carpet walk. I must say he did a marvellous job at the airport!'

The concert was being televised so there was an expectation that both the performers and the specially invited guests would be filmed arriving. 'I'll ask him. We're having dinner with his family in a bit so I'll get a proper idea of what their plans are and then I'll let you know.'

'No rush, darling. It won't take much effort to make up the extra spare room.'

Aurora ignored that and quickly made her excuses. If things went according to plan, there would be no need for the extra bed. 'I must go and get changed for dinner. I'll call you tomorrow or Saturday at the latest. Love to you both!'

'Okay, darling, take care!'

After ending the call, Aurora made her way to the bedroom with renewed determination. She needed exactly the right outfit, something dressy enough to impress without looking out of place in a local village pub. She heaved her case up onto the bed and unzipped it, surveying the contents. Nick might think it was a friendly get-together, and Ivy might have claimed it was a rallying of the troops, but Aurora knew better. She would be under the microscope tonight and if Nick's friends and family found her wanting, the next couple of weeks would be very difficult indeed.

Especially now she'd decided to take Nick up on his challenge.

8

'Nearly done,' Nick told the little terrier as he towelled him off. Gabriel withstood the indignity of having his short fur rubbed damp-dry but the moment Nick raised the brush he'd bought, along with half the contents of the pet superstore he'd ventured to that afternoon, the dog gave him a baleful look and sat back on his haunches. 'No brush?' Nick asked him and Gabriel whined in response. 'Fair enough.' Accepting the reprieve, the terrier trotted past him and out into the living area, which was a mirror layout to the one next door. Nick surveyed the chaos of the bathroom and sighed. 'What was I thinking?' As he gathered the mess of towels and mopped up the water that had escaped the shower cubicle, he pretended his comment had been about his bright idea to try to bath a wriggly dog when he didn't possess a bath. With the tiles mostly dry, Nick carried the soaking towels out into the kitchen and shoved them straight into the washing machine before he fetched a fresh set from the airing cupboard ready for his own shower. A squeak came from the large dog basket that had also made its way into his shopping trolley, together with a rubber chicken that was being slowly murdered by the happy dog. He'd managed to get an appointment with the vet for the morning so he might well have spent several hundred pounds for nothing. He looked at the way Gabriel was sprawled across the fleece-covered cushion in his basket and shook his head. No. Even if they found his owners and he was back with them in a couple of days, Nick wouldn't regret a penny spent on bringing a little comfort into the animal's life.

He wandered back into the bathroom and caught a glimpse of his reflection. He shook his head again. What the hell had he been thinking? He hadn't been thinking, and that was the problem. All the way home he'd kept remembering the way her hand had felt nestled in his, the scent and feel of her body pressed into his back with only the quilt separating them. Then, when she'd turned the conversation to boundaries, he'd lost his head and blown right through them and out the other side. 'Should've kept your big mouth shut,' he admonished his reflection before stripping off his soaked shirt and climbing into the shower.

Forty minutes later, he was dressed and changed and locking his apartment when he heard the door open behind him. 'Oh, look at you! Don't you look gorgeous.' Nick knew better than to flatter himself that Aurora was talking to him and, sure enough, when he turned around she was crouching down to admire Gabriel, who was wearing the little tartan dog jacket that had also somehow found its way into Nick's trolley.

'I didn't want him to get cold,' Nick said, knowing he sounded defensive. Aurora looked up at him and his breath caught. Her face had that effortlessly no-make-up look that he knew from watching his sister took a hell of a lot of work to pull off. Her long lashes framed eyes as blue as the summer skies, her lips a delicate shade of coral like the inside of a seashell.

'You don't look so bad yourself,' she said, giving him a grin as she braced her hands on her knees and pushed herself upright. She was back in the high-heeled boots she'd worn at the airport, laced up over a pair of skin-tight black leather trousers, which she'd teamed with a soft cream jumper with a wide, floppy roll-neck. Her pale hair was artfully mussed, and when she lifted her hand to smooth the collar of his shirt, an armful of bracelets rattled and jingled together. She finished fiddling with his collar, then rested her hand on his chest, her fingers stroking against the soft cotton of the thin polo neck he was wearing under his shirt. 'I've had a think...'

He dropped his gaze to where her hand rested, then lifted it to meet her eyes. 'And?' He barely managed to rasp out the word from a throat turned suddenly dry.

'And,' she said, a wicked smile playing around her lips, 'I want my not-fake boyfriend to give me a kiss.'

Relief and desire flooded through him as he hooked a hand around her waist and jerked her up against him. The sudden move shocked a bright giggle from her, but she was already raising her hand to curl it around his neck as he lowered his mouth to meet hers. Sweet. She tasted so sweet, that same fruitiness that had haunted him since he'd kissed her at the airport the day before. Was that when it was? It felt like an age had passed since then. Her other hand snaked into his hair to join the first and she arched her body into his, her mouth opening in a welcome invitation to extend their kiss, make it deeper, take them higher. He stroked the pliable leather of her trousers, his hand curling over her hip, down and underneath her thigh until he was half lifting her up against him. She broke their kiss, turning her face to press it into his shoulder as her breath came in little pants. 'Dinner,' she gasped.

'What? Oh! Oh, hell.' With sheer force of will he released his grip on her leg and shifted instead to hold her hips, making a little space between them. 'I'm sorry. I got carried away.'

She laughed, a soft husky sound that was more than half moan. 'You weren't the only one.' She raised a hand to her cheek. 'How do I look?'

'Thoroughly kissed.'

She slapped his chest. 'Not helpful! I'd better go and fix my make-up.' She turned back towards her still open door.

'Leave it.' He caught her hand and pulled her back towards him. 'By the time we get to the pub, I'll only have kissed it all off again.'

'Oh, really?' She popped up on tiptoe to press a quick kiss against his lips before she wriggled free of his hold. 'Let me get my coat and then you can make good on that.'

They arrived at the pub a few minutes after seven. They might have been on time if Nick hadn't tugged Aurora into the darkened doorway of his parents' shop and kept her there until they were both ready to forget all about dinner and run back to his apartment. It was only after Gabriel started to whine that Nick got a hold of himself enough to remove his hands, which had stolen under both her coat and jumper. Laughing like a pair of guilty teenagers, they straightened their clothing and Nick took a quick stroll up and down the street until his body had calmed down enough that he could think straight. 'Ready,' he said, hand braced on the door of the pub.

Aurora sucked in a deep breath and straightened her spine. It was a subtle shift but all of a sudden it was like another woman stood beside him. Which he supposed in a way she was. This was Aurora Storm, the pop star, the public face. She held out her hand to him. 'Ready.'

He pulled open the door, letting out a wave of hot, stale air and noise. Laughter, the sound of a dozen conversations and the instantly recognisable tune of Paul McCartney having a 'Wonderful Christmastime'.

The conversation at the nearest table stopped as their arrival was noted, then the next and the next until half the pub had turned around to have a good gawp at them. A deep voice boomed out across the room. 'Well, well, if it isn't world-famous pop star Aurora Storm and her Mystery Hottie.' Cheers and laughter rose up and Nick wasn't sure whether he would hug his father for breaking the ice, or throttle him for reminding everyone about his embarrassing new nickname.

'Your dad?' Aurora asked, giving him a wry grin.

'For my sins. Come on, let's get you settled.' It took longer than expected to make their way across to where his friends and family had commandeered several tables. At first it was a few shy smiles and hellos, but then someone asked Aurora if they could have a quick photo to show their granddaughter and it was like the floodgates opening. If Aurora was bothered by the attention, she hid it very well, stopping to pose and chat to everyone who called to her. She asked them questions and listened to the responses, even pulled out a spare chair at one point to sit down with Luca and Maria, who ran the local deli, so she could tap the details of their niece into her phone. The little girl hadn't been very well, apparently, and was a big fan. 'I'm completely unprepared for Christmas,' Aurora said, giving them both an apologetic smile. 'But first thing tomorrow I'll go out and buy some Christmas cards and I'll send her one.'

'Oh, that's so kind of you,' Maria said, reaching out to clasp Aurora's hand, completely forgetting how starstruck she'd been a few moments before. 'It will mean the world to her.'

'It's my pleasure.' Aurora squeezed the woman's hand, then stood. 'If I don't catch up with you before, I hope you have a wonderful Christmas.'

More than a few people had overheard the exchange and Nick could sense there wouldn't be enough Christmas cards in the village to meet demand unless he nipped things in the bud. He slid an arm around Aurora's waist and put himself between her and the next table. 'Come on, folks, give her a break. Aurora's here on holiday; she's not a sideshow. There'll be plenty of time to say hello another day.'

Apologies rippled around the nearest tables and several people made a point of turning away to strike up their conversations once again. 'Thank you,' Aurora murmured as they made their way to the back of the room without any further interruptions.

'Here you are at last!' Nick's mum, Sylvia, swept around the table and held out her hands to Aurora. 'It's so good to finally meet you. FaceTime is all well and good, but nothing like the real thing.' She leaned forward and pecked a kiss on Aurora's cheek before leading her around to the space she'd saved between her and Nick's dad.

'What about me?' Nick protested with a good-natured laugh.

'Oh, there's room for you over there,' his mum said, with a dismissive wave towards the only empty chair between Jake and his aunt, Nerissa.

'Yes, come here,' his aunt called, patting the chair. 'And introduce us to your handsome new friend.'

Nick bent to pick up Gabriel, not wanting him to get overwhelmed by all the new faces, and sat down. 'This is Gabriel,' he said, turning in his seat to face Nerissa. 'He's very good with people, but be gentle with him.' He hadn't needed to say anything, really, because his aunt was one of the kindest souls he knew and she had an instinctive empathy, which was one of the reasons she was so good in her role as the receptionist at the doctor's surgery.

'Hello, Gabriel.' Nerissa held out her hand for the dog to sniff, not moving to stroke his head until Gabriel had given the tips of her fingers a little lick.

'Where's Toby?' Nick asked, twisting his head to glance under the table, looking for his aunt's retriever.

'He's up the other end with Max and Em.' Nerissa pointed to where her fiancé's teenage children were sitting with Ivy and their uncle, Alex. Max was chatting a mile a minute to Aurora, while his older sister kept giving her shy glances before ducking her head to tap furiously on her phone.

'Emily's friends will be green with envy,' Nick observed with a grin.

Nerissa laughed. 'Wait until she plucks up some courage because she's already asked me if I think Aurora will do some TikTok dance with her.'

'I can't make any promises on her behalf, but she might.' He watched Aurora wriggle past his mum to duck down beside Emily and pose for a selfie with her. 'Looks like she's finding that courage just fine.'

'How is everything?' His aunt gave him a searching look. 'Are you sure about all this?' She tilted her head in Aurora's direction.

Nick nodded. 'We've decided not to fake anything.'

Nerissa's expression changed from concern to confusion to wide-eyed comprehension. '*Really?*'

'Really.' He found his gaze wandering back to Aurora, like there was a string drawing him back to her time and again. She was back between his parents now, holding the single-page menu the pub offered and laughing about something his dad was saying. She looked like she'd been a part of their group forever.

'Who's this?'

Nick turned to his left at Jake's words to find his friend staring at him, rather than at the dog in his lap. 'This is Gabriel. Aurora found him abandoned at the motorway services.' When his friend's gaze didn't shift from his face, Nick wondered what the problem was. 'How are you, Jake?'

'All right.' He did an admirable job of not looking in Aurora's direction. 'Did I hear you right?'

'Yeah, you heard.' Nick couldn't keep the note of challenge out of his voice. Of all the people here, he expected the strongest pushback from Jake. His background as an investigative journalist made him naturally suspicious of everyone and everything – or perhaps it was the difficult time he'd had with his dad when he was growing up that made it hard for him to trust. His dad had died the same time the story about Aurora had broken so perhaps that had something to do with it as well. It had been a really tough time for Jake and Nick could only imagine how all those emotions could get tangled up with each other. He offered his friend a conciliatory smile. 'It's a good thing.'

Jake stared at him for a long moment before finally giving him a nod. 'If you're happy, I'm happy for you.' He looked down at the terrier perched on Nick's lap. 'Now then, fella, what's your name?'

That was the last Nick saw of Gabriel for a while as Jake and his sister commandeered the dog. With some effort, his father called them to some semblance of order and food and drink selections were made. A list of everyone's choice was jotted down on a scrap of paper torn out of a notebook his mum had found in her handbag, and Nick agreed to accompany his dad to the bar. He managed to squeeze into a spot at the crowded bar and greeted the landlord and his sometime boss, Pete, with a grin. 'I hope you're ready for this,' he joked as he handed over the list.

Pete rolled his eyes and gestured to the waiting patrons who were standing two or three deep along the bar. 'It's a madhouse in here tonight. I was going to give you a call earlier, but I didn't think it would be fair to interrupt your family dinner.' He cast a scowl at Andrew Morgan, who'd managed to wiggle in next to Nick. 'Trust you to arrange a get-together and monopolise two of my best staff!' Jake's mum, Linda, did much more regular shifts in the pub than Nick and, like everyone else who came within his parents' orbit, had become a part of their wider family.

'I'll give you a hand.' Nick turned to his dad. 'You don't mind, do you?'

'Of course not. I'll fetch Tom and he can help me ferry the drinks instead.'

Ignoring the landlord's call of protest, Nick persuaded a couple of regulars to step aside so he could lift the bar hatch and let himself through. He continued into the kitchen where he tore off the food order from the bottom of his mum's list and handed it to the chef. Turning to the huge stainless-steel sink, he folded back his sleeves and washed his hands and forearms. Returning to the bar, he sorted out his family's order first, his dad and Tom forming a little chain gang to ferry the drinks back to the tables. There was a polite scuffle between the pair once Nick put everything through the till and they both tried to pay for it. 'Just split it,' Nick said with an exasperated sigh as he snatched both debit cards and tapped them in turn on the payment terminal. 'Don't worry, Dad, I made sure you covered my hefty tip,' he said with a grin as he handed the cards back.

'Cheeky so-and-so.' Andrew tucked his card back in his wallet. 'Don't let your beer get warm, now.'

'I'll just help Pete clear this lot and I'll be back. Look after Aurora, yeah?'

His dad beamed at him. 'She's holding her own, son, don't worry about that.'

It only took Nick ten minutes to help Pete clear the rush at the bar, and he returned to the tables with a promise to lend a hand after they'd eaten if needs be. Aurora had moved from her spot between his parents and was now chatting to Ivy and Alex. Determined not to let the family monopolise her for the whole evening, he made everyone scoot around so he could make room for himself between her and Alex. 'You're a man of hidden talents,' Aurora said with a smile as he slung a casual arm around the back of her chair. He let his fingers rest on her back just below the nape of her neck. Nothing intrusive, just a small point of connection, which she leaned back into for a moment before turning her attention back to Ivy. 'So what can I do on Saturday that would be of most help?'

'You really don't have to,' Ivy protested, which received a quick hush from Alex.

'If she wants to help, let her help,' he said, turning the full wattage of his charming smile on Aurora. If he kept grinning at her like that, Nick might have to have a quiet word with him.

'Alex,' Ivy chided. 'Aurora's here for a break, not to perform like some dancing monkey at everyone's beck and call.' She turned a horrified look on Aurora. 'Not that I'm comparing you to a monkey, oh my God, I can't believe I said that.'

Laughing, Aurora reached out to pat her hand. 'It's exactly what I feel like sometimes, but honestly, I'm more than happy to pitch in. I could pop in tomorrow and we could take some publicity photos and I'll stick them on my Instagram and let people know I'll be helping out. It might bring a few more people in.'

'Brilliant!' Alex interjected before Ivy could object again. 'Dad's going to be Santa so perhaps you could help him with that? Do a few selfies with the kids after they get their gift boxes?'

'Sounds perfect. Do you want me to wear a costume, or anything? I can dress as an elf, or a character from a children's book even.' She touched a hand to her short crop of blonde hair. 'I could be Tinkerbell!' Aurora sounded genuinely excited about it and Nick wondered again about how much Christmas fun she must've missed out on over the years.

It wasn't his sort of thing at all, but if it made her eyes shine like that, then what the hell. 'I'll dress up too if you like. Though I'm not being Peter bloody Pan,' he added hastily.

'I hadn't thought about it, but that sounds like a fabulous idea!' Ivy grabbed Aurora's hand. 'I've got of the perfect bolt of green fabric at the shop so if you let me take some measurements tomorrow I can run up a dress for you, no problems.'

'It's Friday tomorrow,' Alex said in a gentle voice as though he didn't want to dim his girlfriend's enthusiasm.

'It'll be fine!' She eyed Nick thoughtfully. 'Do you have any black boots?'

He frowned. 'I've got some black wellies I wear on the boat.'

'Perfect! I've got an old nightshirt somewhere that I can easily turn into a shirt. Dark trousers, a bandana for your hair and a sash for round your waist and you can be a pirate.'

'Do I get an eye patch?' Nick said, screwing up one eye.

'If you want one. Hmm, I wonder if I'll have time to knock up a toy parrot for your shoulder...' Ivy leaned her elbow on the table and called across to Alex's mother. 'Mimi, can you give me a hand tomorrow to run up a few things on the machine? I'm going to make a few extra costumes for Saturday.' Mimi was the nickname Philippa Nelson had adopted when Tom's children were small, refusing to be called anything like Granny, which she said made her sound ancient.

The older woman smiled. 'Of course, darling. Archie's sloping off to the golf course with his pals so I'm free all morning.'

'You know the physio said I need to walk lots to keep my leg going.' Archie said it like going to play a round of golf was a great sacrifice and not his favourite pastime. The presence of a championship-level links course just along the coast had been almost as much of a reason for him to agree to move to the Point as getting to spend more time with his sons and grandchildren.

Mimi rolled her eyes. 'It's such a hardship for you, my dear. How very brave you are.' Every word dripped with gentle sarcasm. 'How many costumes are we talking about?' she asked, turning her attention back to Ivy.

'Depends how far we get, but probably four?'

'Four?' Alex shot her a suspicious look.

Ivy's smile was all sweetness and light. 'We can't expect our friends to get dressed up and not join in.'

'No. No bloody way.' Alex shook his head vigorously but there was an air of defeat to his words.

Nick gave him his best suck-it-up-mate grin. 'Come on, Alex, where's your Christmas spirit?'

Alex glared daggers at him. 'In the bottom of a bloody whisky bottle if I have to dress up like an elf.'

'Not an elf,' Ivy said as she rose from her chair to settle herself on Alex's lap. 'I was thinking something more along the lines of the nutcracker soldier.' She kissed him before he could give voice to any more protests.

'Well, if you put it like that,' Alex said, sounding marginally less grumpy. 'We can continue this discussion later.'

* * *

Nick was well into his second stint behind the bar when Pete caught his elbow in passing. 'You didn't have to do this, you know.'

He shrugged. 'It's fine, really. Besides, it gives Aurora a chance to get to know everyone without me hovering over her.'

The barman followed his gaze towards where the Morgans and the Nelsons were sitting. Their plates had been cleared and the tables spread apart a little to make room as the group had expanded. Tony, Nick's uncle on his mother's side, hadn't been able to make it to dinner but had arrived with his girlfriend for a late drink. A couple he recognised as friends of

Linda had also joined them and Doc Gadd – Tom's predecessor at the surgery – had his hands resting on the back of the chair occupied by his partner, Barbara Mitchell, who was a lovely woman but never one to shy away from the opportunity of a good gossip. Food service had stopped an hour before but there was no sign of the crowded tables thinning out. 'Well, you can stop by with her anytime,' Pete said, giving Nick a nudge and a grin. 'She's very good for business.'

'I'll send you a bill later.' Nick's laugh was cut off by someone waving an empty pint glass in his direction. He'd just finished serving the man when the background music switched to a song Nick immediately recognised. He spun towards Pete with a suspicious glare, but the landlord was oblivious, deep in conversation, one hand resting on the tap of a local brewery ale. A hush fell over the room as the first haunting strains of a crystal-clear voice drifted from the speakers. It was 'Home Again', Aurora's number-one hit from the previous Christmas. Heads popped up and swivelled with the inquisitive eagerness of a mob of meerkats, all eyes fixed on one person.

'Give us a song, love,' a voice called from somewhere over near the door.

'Oh, yes, Aurora, sing for us, please!' another called, followed by a quick round of applause.

Helpless, Nick could only watch as Aurora glanced around at his family before rising to her feet and holding up a hand when the applause started up again.

The first verse of the song swelled to its climax, and as it switched into the chorus, Aurora opened her mouth and began to sing along. '*No matter how far, no matter how long we are apart, I'll hold tight to the dream of you, until I'm home again*'. Her eyes caught Nick's, and for a moment he let himself dream she was singing those words for him alone. By the time she finished there were more than one or two damp-looking eyes around the room. A huge round of applause broke out and Aurora grinned and took an exaggerated bow, flourishing one hand as she bent at the waist. When she straightened up, her cheeks were flushed and Nick could tell how much she fed from the energy in the room. When the playlist rolled into the next song – something from a nineties boy band he couldn't remember the name of – Aurora went to sit down.

'More!'

'Please, Aurora!'

With everyone distracted, the pressure at the bar had eased so Nick let himself out through the hatch and began to push his way through the people who'd stood up and were looking like they might crowd around the table. Before he could intervene, his mum came to the rescue. Standing, she tugged Nerissa to her feet. 'This is our era,' she said to Aurora with a wink. 'Have a seat and let the professionals show you how it's done.' The next moment she started singing along with the song with more enthusiasm than proper regard for the key of the tune. A laughing Nerissa tried to pull her hand free and back away, but then Tom jumped up and hooked an arm around her waist and started singing too. His deep baritone wasn't bad at all and earned him a few cheers and whistles. Surrendering to the inevitable, Nerissa joined in and they soon had anyone old enough to know the words to the song joining in.

Nick edged around them to claim the empty seat next to Aurora, who was clapping along. 'All right?' he asked.

'Oh, Nico, your family are the best!' She flung her arms around his neck and pulled him close. 'You're so lucky.' As he watched his mum in all her glory waving people nearby to their feet and encouraging them to join in the impromptu singalong, he found himself agreeing wholeheartedly.

9

By the time they spilled out onto the pavement with the landlord's impassioned pleas to 'Get lost, the lot of you, before I call the police,' Aurora was half-hoarse from too much talking, laughing and singing. Though the busy pub had thinned out a bit, plenty had stayed until last orders and beyond for what had turned into an impromptu Christmas party. They stood around on the pavement, buttoning up coats, tying scarves and identifying friends and neighbours to walk home with. Aurora was tucked into Nick's side, Gabriel nestled against her chest so she could keep him safe from the crush of bodies all trying to leave the pub at the same time.

Once the crowd started to thin out, she set the terrier on his feet, his lead hooked loosely in her free hand. Nick tugged her against him again as soon as she straightened up and she rested her head contentedly against his chest as their group slowly splintered. Laurie and Jake headed off first. They lived up on the top of the Point, according to Nick, so had the furthest to go. Alex and Ivy and Andrew and Sylvia went next, turning down a side street that would take them away from the seafront and into the village proper. Everyone else was heading in the same direction as her and Nick so they started a slow meander along the street. Aurora had been too distracted by Nick's kisses on their way down to pay much attention, but now she had time to take in the shopfronts with their pretty lights and festive window displays. It was tempting to pause and study each one, but Max wasn't the only one stifling a yawn so she kept pace with Nick towards the rear of the group. A gleam of blonde hair a few shades darker than her own flashed in the glow of a street light as Emily turned her head, as though checking they were behind them. Aurora gave her a smile when their eyes met. She was a sweet girl, a little shy at first but she'd grown more confident as the evening had progressed.

They reached the end of the row of shops and paused in front of a sprawling white building set back somewhat and surrounded by a low stone wall. 'Here we are,' Tom said, pushing open the wrought-iron gate and ushering the family towards what Aurora supposed must be the surgery.

'Thank you for a wonderful evening,' Aurora said, trying to take everyone in at once with her smile. Max broke from the group and surprised her with a hug. Untangling herself from Nick's arm, Aurora returned the embrace and pecked a quick kiss on Max's cheek, making his face flame even in the gloom.

'Come on, you, stop stalling on bedtime.' Nerissa tugged Max away with a laugh, then turned back to Aurora. 'You will come on Wednesday, won't you?' she asked, repeating the invitation to her and Tom's wedding she'd extended earlier in the evening.

'If you're sure it's not too late to add another guest, then I'd love to.'

'Of course I'm sure! It's all very casual. Sylvia, Laurie and the other ladies are gathering here to help me get ready before we walk up to the church, so come and join us. The reception is in the pub and it's open to everyone in the village. I'll see you before then, most likely, so we can chat a bit more if you have any questions.' Nerissa glanced behind her to where the rest of the Nelsons were disappearing into the open door of the surgery. 'Look, I must go because it'll be ages before we can get everyone settled and Tom has an early start in the morning. Nick has my number so send me a text, okay?'

'Okay. Goodnight!'

'Come on,' Nick said, settling his arm around her once more. 'Let's get you home.'

Home. She liked the way that sounded on his lips, and with a little tug on Gabriel's lead to get him moving they made their way up the hill that shielded the harbour from the rest of the seafront.

By the time they'd climbed the stairs to the first floor, Aurora was in full post-adrenaline crash. She might be used to performing in front of thousands of people, but standing up and singing in The Sailor's Rest had almost been more nerve-racking because it mattered *more*. Not that she didn't put everything into each show she did, but the audience was an amorphous entity rather than individuals who mattered to Nick, and now to her. These were potential friends, people she would pass in the street, threads of the fabric that had been woven into a pattern of community. She wanted them to like her – it scared her a little how much she wanted it. After her third yawn in quick succession, Nick paused in the act of unlocking the door to his flat and smiled down at her. 'We don't have to do this right now. Why don't you go to bed?'

She stifled another yawn as her sleepy brain tried to fathom what he was saying. 'I thought we were planning on going to bed anyway?'

He dropped a kiss to the top of her head. 'I meant you could go to your own bed rather than...' He trailed off, but there was no mistaking the banked heat in his eyes. 'There's no expectation on my part, is what I'm saying.'

Even though her legs could barely hold her up and doing as he suggested was probably the sensible option, Aurora gripped the front of his coat and pulled him down to her for a kiss. 'I,' she said on a little breathy gasp when they broke for air, 'on the other hand, have many, many expectations.'

His surprised laugh was quickly swallowed by another kiss and then they were all hands, tugging at zips, fumbling with buttons all while Nick tried to turn the key in his lock without looking. They half-fell through the door into his apartment, Aurora hopping on one leg as she tried to tug off her left boot with one hand and untangle her coat, which was dangling from the other. Nick was clutching at the unbuttoned fly of his jeans to stop them from falling down while he urged Gabriel into his basket and toed off his boots. His coat and shirt were still on the floor in the hallway and Aurora dragged them inside with her now-bare foot and shut the door.

She leaned back against it, partly for balance as she wrestled with her other boot, partly because of the need sweeping through her as she watched Nick strip off his polo neck, leaving him bare-chested and curl-tangled in the most delicious way. 'Come here.'

Kicking aside her boot, Aurora reached for her jumper and yanked it over her head so by the time they met in the middle of the living room there was only the thin wisps of her lace bra separating the top half of their bodies. Nick's arms swept under her bottom as her arms curled around his neck and then he was carrying her towards the bedroom, her feet locking behind his hips as she pressed kisses to every available inch of his skin she could reach. Everything was so familiar, the sweet-salt taste beneath her tongue, the heat of his hands cupping and squeezing and yet it was different, too. Last time had been a bit of fun, a summer fling that somehow neither of them had quite got over. The stakes were higher now, the potential for heartbreak much more real.

Nick laid her down in the centre of his bed and she got a vague impression of dark walls and white wood, but it was all peripheral as she only had eyes for him. He pushed aside his jeans and underwear without a shred of insecurity – not that he had any need of it because he was strong and beautiful and exactly the way she remembered him. 'Wait,' she said as he propped one knee on the bed, ready to cover her body with his.

He froze. 'You've changed your mind? It's okay if you have.' The pained expression on his face almost made her want to laugh as much as the trust in her heart made tears itch at the back of her eyes.

'It's not that.' She gestured down at her skin-tight leather trousers, which had seemed like such a great choice when she'd posed in front of the full-length bedroom mirror earlier. 'You're going to need to peel me first.' Nick's laughter rang out as she closed her eyes for a long moment, feeling her cheeks heat with embarrassment before her own giggles started.

By the time she'd huffed and grunted and wriggled her way out of the trousers while Nick tugged and swore and declared the bloody things were going straight in the bin as he tried to pull them from the other end, it was impossible to do anything but collapse side by side in a fit of giggles. 'I'm bloody worn out now,' Nick grumbled as he rolled on his side to look down at her.

'Well, if you're too tired...' Aurora hooked her foot over his leg and ran a teasing stroke up and down his calf. He stole her laugh with his mouth, and she forgot everything other than relearning the physical angles and planes of him while he reminded her of all the secret spots of her body he could tease pleasure from.

* * *

Their stroll the next morning to the bookshop took longer than expected because so many people stopped to chat with them. If they weren't telling Aurora how much fun they'd had, they were lamenting the fact they'd missed out on the singalong and asking if she'd be popping into The Sailor's Rest again over the holidays. She tried desperately to file away the names of everyone, but it was an impossible task and she settled for studying their faces in the hopes she'd at least recognise them the next time they met and she'd be able to bluff her way from there. One person she did recognise was Barbara Mitchell. She'd made quite the impression when she and Doc Gadd had entertained them all with a rendition of 'Rockin' Around the Christmas Tree' complete with some very impressive jive moves. There was no sign of Doc this morning, but there were several ladies of a similar age in Barbara's wake as she approached them with a wave.

'Aurora!' Barbara said her name like they'd been friends forever and honestly, Aurora had to admire her confidence. 'I was hoping to catch you. Now, I'm assuming you know about the charity fete and shopping day on Sunday. I know it's rather short notice, but I was going to have a chat with Pete about borrowing his karaoke machine. Everyone had such fun singing with you last night, we might as well put your presence here to good use, especially when it's for such a good cause!'

'The RNLI do such a wonderful job, and it's almost entirely volunteers,' a plump, sweet-faced woman piped up at Barbara's shoulder. 'The communities around here would be lost without them.'

'I... they're very brave,' Aurora stuttered out, shooting a 'help me' look at Nick. Karaoke? What on earth were they expecting her to do with a karaoke machine?

'Yes, well, there's always plenty of folks that like to show off, aren't there?' The third woman in the group had the kind of deep-etched lines that said the disdainful frown she was throwing in Aurora's direction appeared to be her default expression. 'Might as well make them pay for the privilege.'

Aurora shot a dead-eyed stare at the woman. It didn't come naturally to her, but she could give good bitch-face when she needed to. 'Some people just find it easier to enjoy themselves, I suppose.'

The plump woman stifled a giggle with a cough, while Nick decided the most important thing he needed to do was scratch his nose. *Oh, Aurora, you and your big mouth.* She was about to apologise when Barbara steamrollered back into the conversation. 'Yes, exactly. So, you'll do it then? It'll only be a couple of hours and you can do a stint in the afternoon for the children, and one in the evening for the grown-ups. Lovely! I'll speak to Pete now. See you on Sunday!' And with that, Barbara swept off up the street like a mother duck with her little bobbing ducklings in tow.

'What the hell just happened?' Aurora asked, hands on hips as she watched them disappear into the café with a jaunty jingle of the overhead bell.

'You were just bested by the knitting circle,' Nick said, throwing a sympathetic arm around her shoulders. 'Remember that scene in *Jurassic Park* with the velociraptors? While one distracts you, the other delivers the killing strike.'

Aurora settled against his side with an exaggerated sigh. 'Looks like I have plans for Sunday.'

Nick nuzzled a kiss to her temple before they started walking again. 'If it's any consolation, I was roped in months ago. I'm on the set-up crew, but I have no doubts Barbara has a very long list of jobs that will keep me running around all day.'

Of course he would be helping out. Just like last night when he'd gone behind the bar when Pete needed a hand, just like the way he'd dropped everything to drive to London and rescue her from a mess entirely of her own making. She stopped him so she could loop her arms around his waist and give him a tight hug. 'You know what, Nick Morgan?'

'What?' He was all smiles and sweetness with a hint of wickedness gleaming in his eyes as though he was already thinking about what he planned to do with her later.

Her insides turned hot and liquid. She had a list of her own, which hopefully would match his. 'You're pretty bloody special, that's what.' Going up on tiptoes, she pressed a kiss to his mouth.

His hands rose to cup her cheeks as he held her in place and turned one kiss into five, into a dozen. 'You're not bad yourself, Aurora Storm,' he replied, when he finally let her go.

They parted at the door to the bookshop with more kisses until Alex yanked the door open and told them to behave themselves as they were bothering his customers. With a furtive rude gesture to his friend and another quick kiss for Aurora, Nick headed off with Gabriel to meet the vet. Aurora knew she wasn't the only one hoping his owner couldn't be traced, but they would cross that bridge later. 'Ivy's out the back,' Alex said, ushering her inside the delightfully charming shop. 'You can go straight through.'

Aurora nodded, but took her time, wanting to take everything in. Racks of colourful clothing filled the left-hand side of the shop and with one sweeping glance Aurora spotted at least half a dozen things she immediately wanted to try on. The rest of the layout was more in keeping with an actual bookshop, but the shelves were an eclectic mix of toys, nick-nacks, games and soft furnishings in amongst row upon row of paperbacks. Promising herself time to have a good nose around afterwards, Aurora headed in the direction Alex had pointed. The whir of a sewing machine guided her until she found herself standing in the doorway of a large workroom. Shelves along the back wall were full of bolts of cloth; a long rail held a mish-mash of clothes along another wall. A jumble of furniture, most of it looking very the worse for wear, was stacked up in another corner. In the centre sat a large bench, the kind of thing Aurora remembered from science classes at school, behind which sat Ivy and Philippa, heads bent over the sewing machine. 'Hello.'

They both looked up, matching smiles of welcome on their faces. 'Oh, you're here nice and early!' Ivy moved away from the machine to circle the bench and greet her with a quick hug. 'Thank you again for agreeing to this.'

'It's my pleasure, honestly, I'm really looking forward to it,' Aurora assured her as she watched Philippa take Ivy's seat and handle the heavy red material with a sure, steady action. 'Is that for Archie's Santa costume?'

Ivy shook her head. 'No, that's done and dusted. I had enough material left over that it'll be perfect for the soldier's jacket I'm making for Alex.' She led Aurora over to the rack of garments. It looked like something one might find in a charity shop, which was probably where most of it had come from given what Ivy had told her last night.

'Look, this is the nightshirt thing I can adapt for Nick.' She held up a long off-white cotton shift with flouncy sleeves. 'I think it'll work, don't you?'

'I can barely thread a needle, but I trust your skills entirely. Did you make everything that's on display out the front?' Aurora let her admiration shine in her voice.

'Yes,' Ivy replied with a pleased little smile. 'I've always loved making things and fixing things.'

'We all have our talents,' Philippa said as she worked the fabric free from the sewing machine. 'And with that beautiful voice of yours, you don't need anything else.' It was clear she meant it as a compliment, but it stung at something deep inside. What would she be if she didn't have her voice? Aurora hadn't been joking about not being able to sew – she had very few practical skills like that. She'd never shown much of an aptitude for school. She wasn't stupid, or lazy, she just hadn't found anything that gave her the same kind of joy as singing. Still, she needed to face facts. She was lucky to have been given a second chance at her career; what were the odds on her being given a third? Taste was so transitory these days and the power of social media could knock the wind out of the sails of the most solid-looking career in a matter of moments.

Aurora forced a smile to her lips and focused on what the day was about. 'And what about for me? You said you thought you had some green material that would suit for a Tinkerbell dress.'

Ivy scrunched up her nose. 'Look, I know we agreed that Tinkerbell and a pirate would go well together, but as you were leaving last night I had another idea.' Moving to the bolts of material at the back, Ivy took down a roll of pale blue and white gingham. 'I bought this to do some girls' summer dresses, but then I realised they'd probably end up looking like school pinafores and would be the last thing they'd want to wear on holiday. It would make a very good Dorothy dress, though.'

'Dorothy? As in *The Wizard of Oz*?' Aurora had liked the Tinkerbell idea because she wouldn't have to do anything with her hair.

Ivy nodded. 'I saw little Gabriel trotting at your heels, and he looked just like Toto and that's what gave me the idea.'

'Aw, that's so cute. I actually love it if you think we can pull it off.' She ran a quick inventory of what she had in her luggage at home. There were all sorts of hairpieces and wigs in her stage costume bag. 'I'm sure I have a wig we can plait; I might struggle with the ruby slippers, though.'

Ivy deflated for a second, then brightened as she rummaged in a set of plastic storage boxes under the bench. She produced a pot of bright red sequins and set it on the table with a grin of triumph. 'Anything is possible when you've got a glue gun and a bit of imagination!'

10

When Nick returned to the bookshop with Gabriel trotting at his heels, it was to find Aurora by herself perched on a stool in Ivy's workshop sticking sequins to a pair of white shoes. She was so intent on her task, it took her a while to notice he was even there. 'Oh, you're back! How did you get on?' Setting down her tools, she rounded the bench to give him a quick kiss before she bent and scooped Gabriel up into her arms. 'And how's our boy? Everything okay?' She nuzzled the dog, but her eyes were fixed on Nick, and there was no mistaking the worry there.

'He's fine. A little underweight, but no other signs of mistreatment. The vet scanned him from top to toe but he couldn't find a chip. Either he never had one fitted, which is illegal, or he had one and it was removed for some reason. There's no sign of a recent scar, though it's hard to tell under all that fur, but he reckoned it was more likely whoever used to own him never had him chipped in the first place.'

'Used to own him?' Ah, so she hadn't missed that.

'He's mine now – ours if you like, but I thought it would be easier to register him in my name as I'm the one with a permanent address here. I've booked an appointment for the new year to get him chipped and the vet will probably vaccinate him as we've no records of what he has and hasn't had done in the past.'

Aurora's face lit up in a huge smile. 'That's the best news! And of course it makes sense for you to register him, but you must let me pay for the bills.'

Nick rolled his eyes. 'We'll talk about that later. Now, what's with the shoes?'

Before she could explain, Ivy's voice came from the corridor. 'Mimi's giving Alex's jacket a steam; I think it's turned out really well.' She entered carrying two mugs and stopped dead at the sight of Nick. 'I didn't realise you were back; do you want a drink as well?'

Nick shook his head. 'I nipped in to see Laurie and my folks on my way back so I had a coffee in the café.' He turned back to Aurora. 'I checked with Dad about their plans and we've agreed that what with the wedding on Christmas Eve, we'll all have a quiet Christmas Day and then it'll be everyone round to my folks' for Dad's traditional monster buffet.'

'Oh, you're going to love it!' Ivy said as she set down the mugs in order to clutch her stomach. 'Andrew does the most amazing spread – I'm hungry just thinking about it.'

'Sounds great. Honestly, I'm just happy to fit in with whatever everyone else is doing for the most part. I will have to pop up to London for a couple of days between Christmas and New Year, though. I've got a concert at the Albert Hall.'

Nick remembered the big advert he'd seen for it in his dad's Sunday paper a few weeks previously. 'It's a charity carols by candlelight thing, right?'

Aurora nodded. 'I spoke to my agent and his wife yesterday about it. I was supposed to be staying with them for the holidays before, well, you know.' She reached out a hand and placed it on his arm. 'They've been amazing to me, almost surrogate parents, and I hate that I've let them down when I know they were looking forward to having me around for a bit.'

'Then you must go.' It wasn't even up for debate. He couldn't imagine going a week without seeing his parents, though he wasn't always sure that was a good thing. Still, it was clear he wasn't the only one who'd been missing Aurora all these months. 'Take as long as you like with them.'

She squeezed his arm, a hint of colour on her cheeks. 'I was rather hoping you might like to come and stay with them as well.'

'Oh.' *Oh.* There was no way Aurora wasn't going to have been introduced to his family because what had started as a ruse to fool the public would never have been believed if he didn't have them onside to support them. This felt different, like Aurora was inviting him into a part of her life he knew nothing about. 'I'd love to.'

'Thank goodness! And will you come to the concert as well? I have guest tickets and there's a whole red carpet walk-in thing I have to do. It's never much fun if you have to do it on your own.'

'I guess.' The fuss everyone had made over Aurora the previous evening hadn't bothered Nick because he knew those people, trusted his community. Being shoved in front of a load of cameras was a different prospect entirely. But it was part of Aurora's job to deal with the press and if he really wanted to make a go of things with her then it couldn't be purely on his terms. If he was going to be a part of her life, he needed to be part of all of it – even the bits that made him uncomfortable. He couldn't make himself lie, but he could give her a more enthusiastic response than 'I guess'. 'I'd love to see you onstage.' He didn't need to do an inventory of his wardrobe to know he didn't have anything suitable to wear. 'I'll need to try and get a DJ or whatever, somehow.'

Her relieved smile was worth any amount of discomfort. 'Leave that to me! I'll speak to Hetty later and as long as you let me know your size, she'll be able to sort something out.' When Nick gave her a puzzled glance, Aurora laughed. 'It's what she does. She's the agency's fixer. She's going to find something for me to wear on the red carpet and an outfit for the actual concert. It won't be any problem to sort you out some black tie. They're coming to the concert, too, so you won't have to worry about sitting on your own, either.'

'Well, it sounds like it's all sorted, then.' At least he'd have a few days to get used to the idea, and as Aurora had said, he wouldn't be alone in the crowd. He was about to give her a kiss to seal the deal – because, honestly, any excuse, right? – and then he remembered something very important. 'There's a slight flaw in our plan.' He nodded towards Gabriel, who was still nestled in Aurora's arms and looking content to stay there for the rest of the day.

'We can take him,' Ivy butted in. Nick turned in surprise, having forgotten she was there. She gave him a knowing little smile that said she knew, and that she didn't mind in the least. 'He's such a sweet boy, I'm sure he'll be no trouble at all.'

'That's very kind of you, but aren't you forgetting about a certain very territorial cat?' Nick glanced around. 'Where is Lucifer, anyway?'

Ivy laughed. 'He's upstairs in his favourite spot – Alex's pillow.' Though they'd had something of a rapprochement in the past few months, Lucifer still seemed to enjoy tormenting Alex. 'We will have to introduce them, of course, to make sure they get on.'

'Introduce who?' Philippa said, returning to the workroom. 'The jacket has come up a treat,' she continued. 'All it needs is a few gold buttons and perhaps a bit of braid for the shoulders.'

'There's loads of buttons in that box over there.' Ivy pointed it out. 'Aurora and Nick are going to London for a couple of days between Christmas and New Year and so I said we would look after Gabriel, but we'll need to make sure he and Lucifer get on first.'

'Oh, that sounds lovely,' Philippa said with a wistful sigh as she pulled out the box and began rummaging. 'Don't get me wrong,' she said hastily. 'I don't regret for one second that we moved here to the Point, but there's something about Covent Garden when it's all dressed up for Christmas.' She held up a couple of bright round gold buttons. 'These will be perfect.' She smiled over at Nick and Aurora. 'And don't worry about Gabriel; Archie and I will take him for as long as you need. It'll be a good excuse to get Archie out walking without a golf club in his hand for once!'

After a quick fitting for his costume, Nick waited outside while Aurora stripped down so Ivy could take a set of measurements for her dress. With that done, and Ivy's assurances that she had everything in hand, they said goodbye to Alex and promised they'd be back by seven thirty the next morning for any last-minute fittings and to help get the shop ready before opening. The weather was still clear, the vast expanse of blue sky making it hard to believe there'd been such a massive storm just a couple of days ago. Aurora wanted to see more of the village so they took a roundabout route via the high street, up towards the church and then along the top of the village until they dropped down at the opposite end of the seafront, at the base of the hill that led up to the top of the Point. 'Which way now?' Nick asked her, content to wander or head back towards the warehouse, whichever Aurora pleased.

'Let's head back, but can we walk along the beach?'

'Sure.' He led them down the stone steps then bent to unclip Gabriel's lead. The dog trotted off, stopping every few paces to look back as though checking they were still there before setting off once more on his explorations. Nick wondered again how anyone could've dumped such a sweet-natured animal. Not that any dog deserved that kind of treatment, but Gabriel was such a loving and loyal little thing, it was incomprehensible. The dog trotted up with a stick in his mouth and soon they were engaged in a game of tug-of-war, which ended up with Nick flat on his back with Gabriel standing on his chest, barking his victory. Aurora was laughing and when Nick looked her way, she had her phone out and was taking photos of the pair of them.

Reaching out, he snagged the ankle of her jeans and tugged, sending Aurora off balance. He caught her as she fell, the three of them a laughing, sprawling heap on the pebbles. 'Come here.' Nick claimed a kiss, only to be thwarted when Gabriel wriggled between the two of them, not willing to be shut out. Aurora lifted her phone and took a series of photos, culminating with one of the three of them grinning into the lens. Aurora had a smudge on her cheek, and Nick's hair was a wild tangle from the wind. They looked carefree and silly and perfect. 'Send me that one, will you?' He wanted it for his lock screen, wanted to remember how he felt in this moment. Bored with posing, Gabriel retrieved his stick and scampered away, clutching it in his jaws like a trophy.

They helped each other up, Nick rubbing at the mark on Aurora's cheek with his thumb. 'Do I look a mess?' she asked him, raising a hand to her mussed hair.

'You look beautiful.' And she did. She looked a million miles away from the made-up mannequin at the airport – younger, carefree and happy.

'You say all the right things,' she said with a laugh and kissed him before claiming his hand and they headed off after the little terrier, who was still waving his stick about like he was conducting an orchestra.

There were a few people strolling along the strip of sand that separated the pebbles from the water's edge, enjoying the sunshine. Being on the coast, conditions could change in a matter of hours, so the community had learned to make the most of any decent spell of weather. The forecast was set to be fair for the rest of the weekend but looked a bit changeable after that. 'Are you sure you don't mind getting roped into the fete on Sunday?' Nick asked Aurora as they followed the dog on his meandering route over the stones.

She tucked her arm through his and leaned against him a little. It had been less than twenty-four hours and yet it felt like that weight of her against him had been part of his life forever. 'I'm happy to help in whatever way I can. It'll be a nice way to repay everyone for all the disruption I caused after the mermaid videos went viral.'

Nick snorted. 'If you give people a chance, they'd probably give you a civic award in thanks. We needed a busy summer after a couple of very lean years and you helped put Mermaids Point firmly back on the map. No one with any sense would be anything other than grateful that you chose our village as your location.' No one more than him, that was for sure.

'Still, it'll be nice to give something back. I'm rather looking forward to it and it'll be good to keep my voice in use before the concert. I've got a lot of stamina built up after the shows I did in Vegas, but it doesn't take long to get rusty. I'll have to start my vocal exercises again this afternoon because it's not good to go into it cold like I did last night.'

It hadn't occurred to him that she'd need to train, but he'd never had much time for singing. Other than school assemblies and the odd foray into church on special occasions, his entire musical experience could be summed up as 'sing along in the car when no one else can hear you'. It made sense now he thought about it. 'When we get back, I'll leave you in peace, so you concentrate on your exercises. I can make us something for dinner if you like and we can have a quiet night in.'

'I'd like that.'

11

Aurora hunted through the kitchen cupboards as she waited for the kettle to boil. Hiding behind a box of normal teabags, she found a smaller box of chamomile ones and a quick scan of another cupboard produced a bottle of squeezy honey. Her practice had gone well, but she didn't want to take any chances. With a bit of effort, she managed to turn an armchair around so it was facing out the window and curled up in it with a blanket over her knees and the cup of soothing tea in one hand. In her other she held her phone. She'd been putting it off, but she needed to check her social media and gauge the lie of the land.

Before she did that, she scrolled through the photos she'd taken earlier on the beach. She sent Nick the one he'd asked for with a message saying she was looking forward to seeing him later, and chose another one of him laughing while Gabriel licked his chin and set it as her phone background. There was another one of her and Nick pulling silly faces that she thought would be fun for her Instagram, and she opened the app. She posted them together with a few scenic shots of the beautiful landscape around the Point. She contemplated what text to add before deciding that whatever she said, someone would find a way to twist her words. So instead she settled for adding a load of generic feelgood hashtags about relaxing and recharging, getting back to nature, taking time out, love and friendship.

Within seconds of posting, the replies started. At first there were lots of positive responses, hearts, 'love this', 'you are so beautiful', 'who's the lucky guy?' She hearted a few, recognising the account names as long-time fans of hers. They were swiftly followed by the endless bots urging her to share her posts on some random account or another. She ignored those. Someone on the PR team would go through and delete and block them on her behalf. It was a thankless task, like playing that whack-a-mole game, because as many as they squashed, another one popped right back up. Aurora didn't understand the point of them, but she was sure there had to be one because why else would people go to the trouble of setting up these fake accounts? And then the trolls arrived. 'Such a fake'. 'Who cares?', 'whore', 'talentless'. With a sigh, Aurora closed the app and tossed her phone aside. What was she doing? Why was she serving up even more of her life for people to dissect? A sick feeling grew in her middle. Her walk on the beach this morning with Nick and the dog had been so special and now she'd tainted it forever. She reached for her phone, intending to delete her post, when it started ringing.

'Hello, pet!' Dennis boomed over the speakerphone. 'I just saw your Insta post and wanted to say how great it looks. Exactly the sort of thing you need to be sharing.'

'Why? So I can keep feeding the trolls?' she snapped, knowing she was angry at herself, at the situation rather than at him.

'Ignore them; it's not them we're interested in. This is all about keeping your fanbase onside, remember? We're pushing out an alternative narrative, assuring them that they're right to support you.'

'It feels so manipulative, though.'

He laughed. 'That's because it is. Love it or hate it, image is as important as the music these days.'

'Well, I hate it.' Aurora knew she sounded like a sulky brat, but God she was just so tired of it all.

'I know it's difficult, but you are doing all the right things. You don't have to post every day, just drip-feed a few more photos of you and Nick together. He's a good-looking lad and far more age appropriate for you. Chad Logan's old enough to be your father. Most people will look at those candid shots of the two of you enjoying yourselves and believe your side of the story, because why would you chase after a has-been like Logan when you've got a gorgeous boyfriend on your arm? I have to say the pair of you really look loved up. Tell Nick if he wants to explore an acting career then I'd be happy to represent him.' His big booming laugh made Aurora cringe into herself. She was going to have to confess the truth.

'He... umm, we, we're not acting exactly. We had a chat and we've decided to make a go of things for real.'

'Are you having a laugh?' Aurora squirmed at the disbelief in Dennis's voice. 'What the hell is going on down there?'

'Surely it's better this way? At least we're not lying to anyone!' Aurora hated feeling like she had to defend herself, especially to Dennis of all people. 'I really like him, Dennis. Can't you be happy for me?'

There was a long silence before Dennis heaved a sigh. 'It would've been a lot easier if you were faking it, because we'd be able to control when the two of you break up.'

'Who says we're going to break up?' Aurora retorted, feeling angry and upset all at once. 'Don't you have any faith in me?'

'It's not about having faith in you, sweetheart, it's more me having seen this kind of thing a million times before. Are you going to give up your career for him?'

'Of course not!' She might have been secretly thinking how nice it might be not to be on the road all the time, but plenty of people managed long-distance relationships. She said as much to Dennis.

'That's true, but how many of those are relationships where it's the man who waits around for the woman?'

'God, Dennis! When did you turn into such a dinosaur? Nick doesn't expect me to stay at home and wash his bloody socks for him! He knows who I am, knows how important my career is to me and what being with me means.'

'You're right, you're right, I'm sorry. Don't tell Hetty what I just said or she'll have my guts, and quite right too.' He gave a rueful chuckle. 'I'll have to put myself on an equality training course in the new year.'

Aurora laughed in spite of herself. 'I'm still telling Hetty.'

Dennis groaned. 'I'll tell her myself. Look, petal, I'm really sorry if I upset you. I only want what's best for you. That's all I've ever wanted.

You've been on your own for a long time; it's about time you had someone special in your life.'

A wave of relief washed over her. She owed Dennis and Hetty both so much, the last thing she wanted was to fall out with either of them. 'Thank you.'

'Mind you, if I meet him next week and decide he's not good enough for you, we'll be having words.'

'You have nothing to worry about on that score. Promise not to growl at him too much.'

'We'll see.'

'I know you're only being grumpy because you love me,' Aurora teased.

'You know we do. Tell Nick to bring an appetite with him because Hetty's been baking non-stop. I've told her you'll only be here for a couple of nights, but she's gone full mother hen.'

'We can probably stay a couple of extra nights. I'd have to check with Nick, but I don't think he's got anything planned with his family after Boxing Day until New Year's Eve.'

'Hetty would love that.' There was a gruff note in his voice, and Aurora felt her heart swell for this man who would defend her through anything, even if he sometimes went about it the wrong way. When he spoke again, his tone was gentle. 'What about your parents? Any plans to see them?'

Aurora swallowed a sudden lump in her throat. 'I haven't heard back from them yet.'

'Why don't you give them a ring? If it's too much to travel up there, maybe you could get them to come to town? We've enough tickets for them to attend the concert. I'll have a word with Hetty. There's that nice boutique hotel we use sometimes for clients near Piccadilly Circus. If they wanted to visit the sales, or go and see a musical we can help put together a package for them.'

It would make a lovely present for them, which was something Aurora always struggled with. Whenever she'd tried to give them nice things in the past, they'd said they didn't need anything, so she'd ended up donating to places like the local working men's club her dad was a member of, and helping the local school fund its breakfast and after-school clubs. 'I'm not sure it's their cup of tea, but I'll ask them, thanks, Dennis.' They chatted for a few minutes more until Aurora knew she was only making small talk to avoid calling her parents and she said her goodbyes. She stared at her phone for a long minute. Putting it off wasn't going to make things any easier, and if by some miracle they did want to come, she needed to give them at least a bit of notice. Mind made up, she scrolled through her phonebook.

It rang for a long time and she was just about to give up when her dad answered. 'Hello?' He sounded irritated and she wondered if he'd been upstairs or out in the garden and she'd disturbed him. It wasn't an auspicious start.

'Hi, Dad, it's me.'

'Oh.' Ross Powell huffed out a breath. 'Hello, Aurora. I thought it was another one of those blasted reporters.' She'd originally adopted Storm as her stage surname in an effort to preserve her parent's anonymity, but it hadn't taken the press long to track them down.

Her heart sank. 'I'm so sorry, Dad, have they been hassling you a lot?' She'd urged her parents to change their phone number, but her dad could be stubborn about silly things like that.

'We've had a few calls from the usual suspects trying to find out if you were here or not. What have you been up to now?' The accusation in his tone stung.

'I didn't do anything, it's all a big misunderstanding. I've made it known where I am now, so you shouldn't get any more trouble.'

'There's always a misunderstanding when it comes to you and men, isn't there?' Her father sighed. 'That's what you get for living your life in the spotlight, I suppose. It's just a shame for the rest of us who get caught up in it.'

It was a familiar refrain. Her parents had never understood why she couldn't settle down and enjoy the quiet kind of life that had always been enough for them. There was no point in trying to defend herself because they'd go round in circles, each getting progressively more annoyed with the other. She decided to deflect instead. 'How's Mum?'

'She's fine. Had to put up with Audrey giving her the third degree down the Co-op yesterday about whether you'd be showing your face around here now you're back in the country.'

'I thought, given everything, you'd probably prefer it if I stayed away.' Even though she knew it was likely true, a little part of her still hoped he'd deny it and tell her that of course they wanted her to visit, that they couldn't wait to see her.

'Well, it might be for the best, until things calm down at your end.'

Aurora pressed a hand to her chest as though the pain of those words was a physical rather than an emotional one. 'You could always come to me for a few days. Not down to Mermaids Point because I know that's a bit of a trek, but I'll be in London next weekend to do a concert at the Royal Albert Hall. I thought perhaps I could treat you and Mum to a nice mini-break in the city and tickets to come and see me sing.' When he didn't say anything, Aurora found herself babbling. 'I know a lovely hotel in the heart of the West End, but it's in a lovely little mews so very private too. You could have a look around the sales, or visit a museum. If there's a show you wanted to see I could try and get you some tickets, take you out for lunch, or dinner. We could go up the Shard, or take a boat trip on the Thames. Whatever you like...' She petered off into the silence.

'It's all a bit sudden, love.'

'I know it's short notice, but you wouldn't have to do anything other than pack a case. I'll take care of everything.'

'Still, it's a bit much to expect us to drop everything at the last minute.'

'Because you're so busy, eh, Dad? What else would you be doing other than going down the club?' She couldn't keep the edge of hurt out of her voice, even though she should be used to his rejection by now.

'Don't take that tone with me, young lady. You've clearly been spending too much time swanning around like a spoiled brat. There's nothing wrong with the club, nothing wrong with people who work hard for a living. You should have more respect for your roots.'

She closed her eyes and wished she'd never listened to Dennis. Did her father honestly believe she had no idea what hard work was? She might not be standing in a factory, or in an office doing the same thing every day, but she'd put in the effort and earned everything she'd achieved. There was no use saying any of that, though. 'I'm sorry. I was just hoping to see you both. It's been a long time.'

'Yes, well, that's hardly our fault, now, is it?'

'I didn't say it was anybody's fault, it's just the way things have turned out. Look, forget about it, Dad, okay? I thought it would be a nice treat for us all to get together, but it's selfish of me to drop this on you at the last minute.'

'It was good of you to think of us, love, but your mum's got her heart set on going to the caravan for a few days. There's a few of us heading to the site for a bit of a get-together after Christmas.' They had a static caravan on the coast about an hour from where they lived. Aurora had spent many a wet, miserable weekend on the same campsite growing up because her parents had never seen the point in going abroad when all the people who went on package holidays did was lie about in the sun and get burnt.

'I'm sorry,' she said again, and meant it this time. 'I shouldn't have expected you to drop everything to fit in with me. Perhaps when things have settled down, I can come up and spend a few days with you.'

'Yes, that's a good idea.' God, he didn't have to sound quite so relieved. 'Besides, you don't want to go wasting your money on fancy hotels and the like. It's not our sort of thing.'

Her heart felt like it might break. It might be their sort of thing if they'd only give it a try. 'Dad, there is nothing that would give me greater pleasure than to see you both, and there's no one I would rather spend my money on than you two. Is there something else I can get you for Christmas?'

'That's nice of you to say, love, but we have everything we need.' She knew he really believed that, but it still hurt that they wouldn't accept anything from her. 'As you say, let's wait for this latest fuss to settle down and then we can see about you coming for a visit.'

'Okay.' There didn't seem much else to say. 'Give Mum my love, and I'll give you both a call on Christmas Day, if that's all right?'

'That'll be just the ticket.' He hesitated. 'Look, are you sure everything is all right with you? This nonsense in the papers isn't anything we need to be worried about, like last time?'

Her heart ached. They might not have the easiest relationship, but he really did care about her. 'No. It's nothing like last time, I promise.'

'That's good because I'm not sure your mother's heart could take it. Not sure mine could either.' He sounded so sad and Aurora wanted to cry at the pain in his voice. Guilt surged through her even though the stress they'd all been put through had been Julian's fault, not hers. They'd never said it out loud, but she wondered sometimes if her parents blamed her. After all, if she'd stayed at home and been content with the life they'd wanted her to lead then she would never have come to the attention of Julian Knox-Cavendish, never put her parents through the emotional trauma of almost losing their only child. It was all Aurora could do to swallow back her tears as she said, 'I'm safe and I'm happy, Dad. There's nothing for you to worry about. I'll give you a call next week, okay?'

'Okay, love. Be good now.' It was what he always said to her instead of goodbye and for a moment she was a little girl sitting at the kitchen table eating a bowl of cornflakes as he kissed her on the head before heading off to work.

'I will. Bye, Dad.' She managed a smile as the tears began to trickle down her cheeks.

12

Nick was still making the sauce for the spaghetti bolognese he'd settled on for dinner when he heard a knock on the door. Given no one had buzzed to be let in downstairs, it could only be one person. 'You're early,' he said, opening the door with a grin. 'Not that I'm complaining.' As he took in Aurora's red-rimmed eyes, his smile faltered. 'Hey, what's wrong?'

'It's nothing, just family stuff.' She bent to give Gabriel a hug and Nick couldn't help but think it was an avoidance tactic. His instinct was to push, to find out what the problem was so he could fix it, but he held his tongue. He didn't know much about her family set-up, other than the hints she'd dropped about not being very close with her parents.

Deciding it was enough that she'd come to him rather than be on her own, Nick held the door open in welcome. 'Give me a few minutes to finish up and then I'm all yours.'

There was no mistaking the relief in her wan smile. 'Smells good.'

'Spag bol. I won't be earning any Michelin stars, but no one leaves Andrew Morgan's house without knowing how to cook a decent meal or two.'

She followed him towards the kitchen area. 'Your dad likes to cook, then?'

'Loves it, though some of his recipes are a bit more experimental than mine. I'm not sure I'll ever fully recover from the beef and banana curry.'

'And he's in charge of the buffet on Boxing Day? Should I be worried?' Nick was pleased to see Aurora was smiling and that a little more colour had returned to her pale cheeks.

'Mum will keep an eye on him, don't worry. There's some wine in the fridge if you want a drink?' He didn't like to say she looked like she could use one, but bloody hell, she looked like she could use one.

'Thanks. Do you want one?'

He raised the half-full glass of red he'd left beside the hob. 'I thought I'd better check it was all right before I put any in the sauce. Quality control and all that.'

Aurora laughed and some of the strain melted away from around her eyes. 'But of course. And it would be rude of me to make you drink alone.'

Reaching a glass down from the cupboard, Nick set it in front of her. 'Exactly.' He claimed a quick kiss then turned his attention back to the half-made sauce.

The kitchen was silent apart from the rhythmic tap of the spoon against the side of the pan as he brought the mix of tomatoes and herbs to the boil then turned it down to a low simmer. He sent a quick glance towards Aurora, who was leaning against the counter watching him. She was holding her wine glass, but hadn't taken more than a sip or two. 'You're welcome to put the TV on if you like.'

'I'm happy here,' she assured him. 'I was going to ask if there was anything I can do, but you seem to be very well prepared.' She nodded at the neat row of dishes containing chopped onions, minced garlic and the mince. He liked to have everything organised before he started, something he'd learned from his mum.

The family kitchen had always been in the heart of their home. After a busy day in the shop, his parents didn't have time to mess around. One would supervise homework, sort out whatever kit or uniform they needed for the next day, while the other cooked. His dad had been a whirlwind of chaos, flying between the fridge and the cooker, tugging open this cupboard or that, demanding to know where the pan he needed was. It was all a pinch of this, an extra teaspoon of that. Chuck it all in and see what happens. When it was his mum's turn to cook it was an altogether different affair. Everything was done to the exact specifications of the recipe, all the utensils and pans laid out on the counter in advance. Laurie was more like their dad, instinctive and unafraid to try new things, whereas Nick liked to know the outcome before he started. Digging out a large frying pan, he quickly browned the garlic, onions and mince, then whacked up the heat as he added a generous glug of the red wine and let the heat burn off the alcohol while retaining the flavour. Once everything was combined in the big sauce pot, Nick slid it onto a low shelf in the oven.

He gathered his half-full glass, held out an arm to Aurora and ushered her over to the sofa. It was a sprawling L-shape, a bit too big for the room but he liked the way it helped to divide the open-plan space. He settled in his favourite spot, the corner where the short side extended so he could prop his feet up. Aurora nestled against him with a sigh, her back to his side so she could stretch out as well, her feet at a ninety-degree angle to his. 'Do you want to talk about it?' he asked.

'Not really.'

He'd made the offer, but there wasn't much else he could do other than give her time and space and his company. He reached for the remote and passed it to her. 'Why don't you find us something to watch?'

After ten minutes of her endlessly scrolling through the menus of his various subscription services, Nick was seriously regretting giving her the choice. When she finally pressed play on *Pacific Rim*, he was surprised as he hadn't thought giant robots fighting off an alien invasion would be her sort of thing. He'd also watched it a couple of weeks previously, but he'd sit through it again if it meant an end to her infernal scrolling. They hadn't made it to the end of the opening monologue when she spoke. 'I invited my parents to come to London when we're up there, but Dad turned me down flat.'

'I'm sorry.' He waited for her to continue, but her eyes were fixed on the screen while they watched the pilots of the first enormous robot get suited up and ready for battle.

'The press have been bothering them again. I told them to change their number after last time, but he didn't see why he should have to.'

Nick watched the action on the screen, barely registering the enormous pointed-headed alien creature that rose from the depths as he absorbed what she'd said. One thing snagged in his brain. 'Last time?'

'With Julian.' In a macabre counterpoint to the almost cartoon violence playing out in front of them, Aurora began to speak. In a low, halting voice she sketched out the slow decline of a promising relationship, the way her ex had morphed from a fun-loving party guy to a demanding control freak who needed to know where she was every second of the day. 'Things came to a head when I was booked to go on tour. He told me to cancel it. Told me!' There was no mistaking the outrage in her voice.

'What did you do?' He had a mental list drawn up of all the things he would've liked to have done to this entitled creep.

'I broke up with him.' She half-turned to look at him for the first time since she'd sat down. 'He was so shocked. I honestly believe he'd never been rejected before. His parents were wealthy, more than wealthy. His dad had a title of some sort. He took me home to meet them, and they lived in a bloody castle! Can you imagine what it was like for me to step into that world? Fame had opened plenty of doors for me, but this was a whole different level of privilege.' She looked away, watching the film again, although he doubted she was taking any of it in. 'I've never been ashamed of where I came from, regardless of what my parents might think. They took good care of me, there was always plenty of food on the table, plenty of laughter and love under the roof of that little two-up, two-down terraced house. I just wanted something different.'

Nick curled his arm around the front of her chest and drew her back against him. 'There's nothing wrong with following your dreams, Aurora.'

She snuggled against him. 'You seem to be one of the few people I know who believes that. At first Julian seemed delighted to have me on his arm.' A bitter laugh escaped her lips. 'I was like a pet to him, a new toy for him to show off.'

'He sounds like a prick,' Nick growled, unable to keep his growing anger and unease inside.

'You're a better judge of character than I am because I fancied myself in love with him.' She was quiet again for a long time.

Nick wondered if he should change the subject. He could join the dots well enough to know what she was leaving unsaid wasn't going to be good.

Had he pressured her into quitting? 'Is he the reason you took a break from your career?'

'He showed up the next day with armfuls of flowers, a bottle of champagne and a diamond ring the size of a small bird's egg. It was a family heirloom.' He felt her shrug against him. 'He was so full of apologies and promises and I was desperate to believe him. It's hard to make a lasting connection when you are on the road all the time; I convinced myself it would all be okay.' Her voice shook a little and he tightened his arm around her until the shuddering stopped.

'You don't have to tell me, if you don't want to.'

She sighed. 'He convinced me to take a break before the tour started. Dennis was furious because I should've been in rehearsals, but I thought I could find a way to keep everyone happy so I told him I'd practise while I was away, but that we needed some time alone first. Julian took me home, only when we got there the place was closed up. I found out afterwards his parents had decamped for the summer to their villa in the South of France and taken the staff with them. Julian told me it would be more fun having the place to ourselves. He smashed my mobile phone on the first night.'

She'd said enough. He didn't need her to relive it. He wanted to pull her closer but forced himself to loosen his grip so she would know she was free to move away if she wanted to. 'How did you escape?'

'Dennis. I'd told him I needed a week off and he'd respected that. When that week passed, he thought I was having a bit of a rebellion and decided to give me a couple more days. His wife's birthday was coming up and he knew I'd never miss it. When I didn't so much as text Hetty to wish her a happy birthday, he knew something was wrong. He jumped straight in his car and drove down to Surrey. The gates were locked tight. He put in a call to Julian's father's office and told them his next two phone calls would be to the press and the police, in that order. Five minutes later, Julian's father called him and gave him the security code. By the time Dennis reached the door, Julian had dragged me downstairs and dumped me in the hall. I don't know what his father said to him; I don't really care.'

'How the hell has none of this ever been made public?' Nick recalled the headlines and the speculation around Aurora's disappearance, but the press would've had a field day with a scandal of these proportions.

'Dennis struck a deal with Julian's father. He did it for me, not for them. They paid for my treatment in a private facility. I was there for nearly six months.'

It didn't seem like enough of a price to pay, not nearly enough. 'And what about him?' He couldn't even bring himself to say the monster's name. 'He got away with it?'

Instead of answering, Aurora reached for her phone. She fiddled with it for a moment before handing it to him. It was open on an old newspaper article. *Peer's son dies in tragic hunting accident.* He didn't bother reading any further than the date. 'Do you know what actually happened?'

She shook her head. 'He's gone and that's all that matters. Or at least that's what I keep telling myself.' Aurora rose from the sofa and walked towards the balcony door. He watched in silence as she pressed her finger-tips to the glass, eyes fixed on the far horizon. 'Days pass, sometimes weeks when I don't think about him, but the nightmares always come back.'

Nick wanted to go to her, to wrap her tight in his arms and promise her that nothing and no one would ever hurt her again. It wouldn't be to comfort her, he realised, but himself. He clenched his fists and forced himself to sit tight. Aurora didn't need rescuing; he was years too late for that. And he could make her all the promises in the world about her future, but they'd be nothing more than hot air. She was healing, not healed, and she'd got this far without him. 'Did the stress over this stupid thing with Chad Logan make things worse?'

She nodded. 'At first I was going to give it all up. Even after I left the clinic and was living on my own again, I had no desire to sing. I found a cottage in Ireland and stayed there for a while. It was hard not seeing my parents, but I knew I'd be recognised if I visited. I didn't know how bad things had been with the press until after it had all died down. They called me every few days when I was in the clinic and never said a word. Dennis did his best to help them, but I think they've always held him responsible for what happened.'

Nick shook his head in disbelief. 'How did they work that out?'

She turned from the window and gave him a sad smile. 'He's been with me from the start. If he'd sent me home when I knocked on his office door instead of indulging my foolishness then I'd have gone back home with my tail between my legs and settled down to live a normal life. That's how my dad sees it anyway.'

'Don't they feel any pride in what you've achieved?' Nick pictured how his dad would be if either he or Laurie had an ounce of the talent Aurora had. He'd have taken them to London himself, knocked on every agent's door if he'd had to.

'It's not that they're not proud so much as they just don't understand why I feel the need to do it. When I told Mum I was working on a new album, I thought her heart would break with the worry of it. I tried to explain it to her, but I don't think she'll ever really forgive me for making a comeback.' She turned back to the window and pressed her forehead to the glass. 'I'm not sure I'll ever forgive myself for putting them through it all again, but I had to.'

Nick couldn't bear to hear the pain in her voice. Crossing the room, he placed his hands on her shoulders, offering her what support he could. 'You couldn't let him win.'

She turned to look up at him. 'Stupid, isn't it? He's not going to know either way so what difference did it make?'

'You knew.'

Her eyes closed, her lips stretching into a smile of relief as she nodded. 'You understand.'

He slid his arms around her. 'All the success you've achieved is down to you, no one else. Your talent, your strength, your hard work. He doesn't own one single bit of you. Not one.' Whatever misgivings he might have harboured about putting himself in the public eye, they were gone now. One selfish bastard had tried to steal her dreams, and Nick would do whatever it took to make sure another one couldn't do the same.

He would never hold her back, even if that meant having to let her go.

13

Aurora woke the next morning with a smile on her face and Nick's words still ringing in her ears. *He doesn't own one single bit of you. Not one.* It was like he'd found the missing piece to complete the puzzle. She'd known it for herself, she'd just never let herself believe it – until now. There was nothing to prove, no reason to do anything other than because it was what she wanted to do. The compulsion was gone.

Her good mood carried her through the early morning rush of showers and breakfast and a brisk walk to the bookshop – well, as brisk as they could manage on the icy pavements. A heavy frost had turned everything white, giving almost the illusion of snow up on the hills behind the village. There were still a few stars lingering overhead when they'd left the warehouse. On any other day, Aurora would've liked to linger on the dock and watch the sun come up over the sea.

They made it to the bookshop just after quarter past seven, but they'd still been beaten to it by both Alex's parents and Linda, who had agreed to come in and help mind the tills while the rest of them managed the children's party. She let them in the front door when they knocked and told them to go straight upstairs while she returned to the workroom where she and Philippa were putting the finishing touches to a huge pile of shiny gift bags. Aurora followed Nick up the stairs where they were met with a cry of welcome by Ivy, who was looking utterly adorable in a pink gown covered in shiny crystals. The short skirt stood out from her waist thanks to layers of thick netting like a ballerina's tutu. She waved the little wand in her hand. 'I'm the Sugar Plum Fairy, or at least I will be once someone helps me get my wings on.'

'Your wings will have to wait,' Alex said, poking his head out from a nearby bedroom. 'Dad's sat on my hat and squashed the bloody thing!' He waved a crumpled-looking bit of black vinyl that had definitely seen better days.

'Oh hell!' Ivy gave them an apologetic smile. 'Your costumes are in the other room. Can you sort yourselves out while I try and fix this?'

'Of course we can,' Aurora assured her, though she thought it might take more than a miracle to salvage the hat. 'I've brought my make-up kit with me. It's proper stage stuff so it'll stay on all day.' She held up the bag she'd slung over her shoulder that had her make-up, her wig and a couple of spare pairs of tights.

'Fantastic! Give me a shout when you're ready and I'll come and do any last-minute adjustments.' Ivy disappeared into the other room in a swirl of pink.

'I'm exhausted already,' Nick grumbled, though he was grinning as he said it. 'And don't think you're putting any make-up on me.'

'Not even a dash of black eyeliner? I think it'll really suit you.'

'I'm going to be wearing an eyepatch, remember?' He closed one eye and gave her an exaggerated wink.

'A scar, then? Or a skull-and-crossbones tattoo?'

'Now that sounds more like it!'

Aurora was laughing as they entered the bedroom Ivy had indicated, but she stopped short at the sight of the biggest cat she'd ever seen sprawled across the pretty floral duvet cover. 'What the hell is that, a mini-panther?'

'That's Lucifer. Don't mind him, he only bites Alex.'

The cat gave them both a disdainful look before leaping onto all four paws, back arched, teeth bared as he hissed in fury. He wasn't looking at them now, his gaze trained instead on Gabriel, who Aurora was ashamed to admit she'd forgotten all about for a second. She was about to scoop

him up out of harm's way but the terrier wriggled past and propped his
front paws on the edge of the bed, little stub of a tail wagging as though he
was greeting a long-lost friend rather than ten pounds of spitting black
rage.

'I'll grab the cat, you grab Gabriel,' Nick urged as he edged around the
side of the bed ready to make a lunge for it. Lucifer's head swung around,
sending a warning hiss in his direction before turning his attention back to
the dog.

Gabriel woofed, tail still going a mile a minute and Aurora pulled her
sleeves down over her hands as she prepared to grab the dog and pull him
out of harm's way. The cat twitched and Aurora was ready to move when
she noticed the arch of Lucifer's back had lowered a fraction. 'Wait,' she
murmured to Nick, who was edging once more along the side of the bed.
Lucifer sent a half-hearted hiss towards the dog, seeming nonplussed at
the failure in his intimidation tactics. Gabriel wiggled forward until he
could rest his muzzle on the bed and woofed again, softer this time. The
cat stared at him for a long moment before all the tension melted from his
frame and he settled back down on the bed, his nose an inch away from
Gabriel's. The dog licked him then scrambled up to sprawl next to the cat.
Moments later they'd both closed their eyes and were breathing in
harmony.

'What the hell just happened?' Nick said, shaking his head as he
retreated back to her side.

'Call it a Christmas miracle.'

* * *

Alex's hat had proven beyond rescue, but with minimal grumbling he
allowed Aurora to add a couple of red circles to his cheeks to match the
brilliant red of his nutcracker soldier's tunic. 'I look like an idiot.'

'Hush, you look great and the kids will love it,' Aurora told him as she
added a kohl line around his eyes.

'Easy for you to say,' he said, grabbing the end of one her pigtails and
giving it a gentle tug. 'You're used to all this dressing up. Don't you worry
about making a fool of yourself?'

She settled back on her heels to survey her handiwork. 'I did a bit in the beginning, especially when I had to do all those dance routines because that was what was expected. But then I realised the people who were watching weren't really looking at me, they were looking at Aurora Storm.'

Alex gave her a puzzled frown. 'But you *are* Aurora Storm.'

'Not really. It's hard to explain. She's a part of me, but she isn't all that I am. She's a performance, a costume if you like, that I can put on and off.' Reaching out, she brushed a crease from the shoulder of Alex's tunic. 'When you go downstairs, you're not Alex, you're a fairy-tale character that's come to life. You're a toy soldier and the children will want to play with you.'

* * *

Alex certainly took her advice to heart. Within a couple of minutes of the doors opening, he had the excited children formed up in a little troop and marching around the shop. He wove in and out of the shelves, did a figure of eight around two mannequins, made each of them salute as they passed his laughing mother, who was behind the till, and generally caused chaos until he finally led them to the children's corner where he collapsed on top of the big pile of cushions laid out in the centre of the carpet. The giggling children flopped down in a big heap on top of him and refused to let him up as he pretended to struggle. 'Don't you think you'd better go and rescue him?' Aurora asked Nick, as she tried and failed to hold in her own laughter.

'He's not doing too badly,' Nick said with a wicked grin. 'Look, he's almost got one arm free.'

'Nico!'

'Oh, all right.' Nick headed towards the cushions; the toy parrot Ivy had fashioned from a few scraps of felt and a bit of stuffing bounced on his shoulder with every step, making Aurora giggle harder. 'Avast, me hearties!' Nick cried with a yell as he jumped in front of the children. 'What have ye caught 'ere then?' His slight West-Country accent had gone full-on pirate's drawl. 'Why, it's me ole pal Nutty the Nutcracker!' If looks could kill, the glare Alex shot him for that nickname would've felled a full-grown bull elephant.

'Oh dear,' Aurora sighed, trying not to start laughing again as the children took up a chant of 'Nutty, Nutty' as Alex finally scrambled free from the wriggling pile of bodies. She lifted Gabriel up into her arms and turned the little dog to face her. 'I think we'd better intervene before there's a full-scale riot.' Gabriel licked the underside of her chin as though in agreement. Taking a deep breath, Aurora set her shoulders back and fixed an exaggerated smile on her lips as she hurried towards the cushions. 'Hello! Who's here to see Father Christmas?' As she'd hoped, a dozen hands shot up into the air and all eyes were turned on her, leaving Alex free to make his escape. Aurora lifted Gabriel up to her ear and frowned as though she was listening to the dog whisper something. 'What's that, Toto? Father Christmas will only come out for people who've been very good?'

'I've been good!' yelled a little boy as he scrambled up on his knees.

'Me too!'

'I've been good all year!' The little girl who said that made it sound like it was the hardest thing she'd ever had to do in her life.

'Is there anyone here who hasn't been good?' Aurora asked. Everyone shook their heads, including Nick and Alex. 'Are you sure?' She turned a suspicious look towards Nick. 'No looting?' He shook his head. 'No pillaging?' Shake. 'No making anyone walk the plank?' He pulled a face like he had to think about it before shaking his head. 'Not even any stealing of treasure?'

Nick sighed and threw up his hands. 'Okay, you got me with that one.' Reaching into the bag he had over his arm, he pulled out a handful of chocolate coins and tossed them onto the cushions. The children shrieked in delight and scrambled to gather the little treats.

While Aurora and Nick settled down with the children and asked them questions about what they wanted for Christmas, Ivy and Alex laid out paper, pencils and crayons on a set of low tables. For all their boisterousness, the children were delightfully gentle with Gabriel. He lapped up the attention, sprawling across the cushions like some Roman emperor accepting the adulation of his citizens. Aurora kept a close eye and warned one little boy who looked like he might offer the terrier one of his precious gold coins, 'Chocolate isn't good for his tummy. He has some special treats of his own, which he can have later.' The boy tucked his chocolate back in his pocket.

Soon the children were sitting around the tables, making pictures to show Father Christmas. Aurora didn't have an artistic bone in her body, but Ivy was as gifted with a pencil as she was with her sewing machine and was busy drawing outlines of Christmas trees and reindeer for the smaller children to colour in. The children didn't seem to mind when Aurora didn't join in; they were happy to answer her questions and explain what they were drawing and chatter about anything and everything. When she glanced up it was to see a little girl with a mop of blonde hair standing in front of Nick. She was fascinated with his eye patch, giggling wildly every time she lifted it up and he winked at her. Aurora thought she might melt into a puddle right then and there at the sight of it. She'd never thought of herself as particularly maternal, but in that moment her ovaries were doing a tango at the thought of how Nick might look with a little girl with a mess of brown curls the same as his. *Too soon.* It was way too soon to even be thinking about something like that, but still she filed the sensation of it safely away in the corner of her mind and turned her attention back to the boy beside her who was painstakingly colouring in a dinosaur with only minimal attention to the lines.

Pictures complete, they returned to the cushions for a game of pass the parcel, which only resulted in one round of tears. Given the party had been going for over an hour, Aurora thought that was pretty good going. She scooped up the little girl and carried her over to a quieter corner. Setting the girl down, she handed her a tissue from the pocket in her pinafore dress and waited for her shoulders to stop heaving. 'Better now?'

The little girl shook her head. 'Damien snatched it when it was my turn to unwrap. He's a cheater.'

Aurora bit back a sigh. 'Not everyone plays by the rules, unfortunately. Never mind, I'll have a word with Father Christmas and let him know what a big, brave girl you are.'

A harassed-looking woman hurried over, crouching down next to them. 'Sorry, I was distracted at the other end of the shop. What happened, Sophia?' She stroked the little girl's hair, which prompted another half-hearted smattering of tears.

'Sophia missed out during pass the parcel,' Aurora explained. 'I was just telling her I was going to tell Father Christmas how brave she's been.' As she'd hoped, the mention of being brave was enough to quell the smattering of tears once more.

'Well, thank you for looking after her.' The woman took the tissue from Sophia and wiped her cheeks. She glanced at Aurora then did a double-take so comical it was like something out of a *Looney Tunes* cartoon. 'You're—'

'Dorothy,' Aurora cut in quickly, 'and this is my dog, Toto.' She patted Gabriel, who was curled at her feet.

'Oh, of course!' the woman said with a conspiratorial smile. 'It's lovely to meet you, *Dorothy*. Come along, Sophia.'

As Sophia's mother led her away with the promise of looking for a new book, another woman sidled up to Aurora. 'Well, this is all very nice, isn't it?'

Not liking her conspiratorial tone nor the way she'd positioned herself just a shade too close, Aurora took a small step to the right as she offered the woman a neutral smile. 'The children are certainly enjoying themselves.'

'And what about you? Are you enjoying yourself?'

Startled at the bluntness of the question, Aurora turned and took the woman in properly for the first time. She looked like everyone else in the shop, dressed for the weather in jeans and a jumper, but there was something about her that didn't sit right. 'Which one is yours?' Aurora tried to deflect the woman's attention away from her by pointing towards where the children were finishing up their drawings.

The woman's eyes barely followed the motion of Aurora's gesture before they locked back on her face. 'How long have you known Nick Morgan? The two of you looked very cosy at the airport, but when I asked around no one seems to have seen the two of you together before, well, not until this week.'

Aurora took another step backwards. 'Who are you?'

The woman extended a hand. 'Carly King.'

Aurora's stomach turned queasy as she recognised the name. Carly was the showbiz reporter for one of the national tabloids and had never let the truth get in the way of a good headline. 'I've got nothing to say to you.'

Carly left her hand extended for a moment longer before letting it drop. 'There's no need to be like that, now, is there? How about the two of us get together after this and you can put your side of the story. Everyone is dying to know what happened between you and Chad Logan.'

'How about you get lost and leave her alone?' Aurora had never heard Nick speak in such a harsh tone before, and if looks could kill...

'Carly was just leaving,' Aurora said, keeping her tone and her smile just the right side of polite. She slid her arm through Nick's and turned her back on the reporter, hoping she would take the hint. Bitter experience should've taught her better by now. You didn't get on in a job like Carly's without developing a hide like a rhino.

With a flick of her over-highlighted hair and a laugh as fake as her nails, Carly stepped in front of them, blocking their view of the children. 'Nick, isn't it? How did the two of you meet, then? I was just saying to Aurora how strange it is that no one I've spoken to in the village had even the slightest clue about the two of you. It's all a bit mysterious.' She said the last with a conspiratorial wink.

'Is everything all right?' It was Sophia's mother, who'd returned from settling her daughter with the rest of the children. She'd spoken loud enough to draw attention from some of the other parents and Aurora was conscious of a number of heads turning in their direction.

'What's the problem?' It was Maria from the deli, who'd brought her son to the party.

Aurora shook her head, feeling a bit desperate now. She should've known the press would track her down, she just hadn't expected it to be quite so soon. 'It's fine, I'm sorry if we are disturbing things.' Aurora turned to Carly. 'Let's take this outside and leave everyone in peace.'

'No,' Nick said in a voice that brooked no argument. 'She can leave, no one else.' He turned to look at Maria. 'Bloody journalist harassing Aurora, just like they did when I went to pick her up at the airport.'

Maria turned to glare at Carly. 'Why can't you people leave her alone?

Fancy showing up and trying to ruin a children's Christmas party. You ought to be ashamed of yourself!'

'Quite right,' Sophia's mother agreed, shooting her own glare towards Carly, whose fake smile was fading rapidly. 'I don't know how people like you sleep at night, sticking your nose into people's private lives.'

'I'm just doing my job.' Carly sounded defensive as a faint hint of red began to stain her cheeks. Perhaps she did know some level of shame after all.

'Not in here, you're not.' It was Alex, managing to look intimidating even dressed as he was in his silly nutcracker uniform. 'This is my shop and you're not welcome.' He pointed towards the door.

'And not just in the shop, either,' a man who'd been standing close by and watching everything chipped in. 'If I were you, I'd make myself scarce and sharpish. Troublemakers like you aren't welcome in the Point.' A murmur of agreement rose at that and Aurora had to hide a grin. They'd have the pitchforks and torches out at this rate.

'All right, all right.' Carly held her hands up as though in surrender. 'I'm going.' She pushed herself deliberately between Nick and Aurora, hard enough that Aurora stumbled back a few paces. 'You can't hide down here forever,' Carly snapped at her. 'The truth will get out eventually.'

'Well, it won't be in your column, love, will it?' one of the other parents observed with a wry grin. 'Off you pop.'

Aurora held her breath as Carly stalked across the shop. It wasn't until the door slammed shut behind her that she let herself sag against Nick in relief for a few seconds. His arm closed around her waist, offering her his strength until she was able to snap herself back into performance mode. 'I'm so sorry about that,' Aurora said with a smile of apology as she looked around the concerned faces watching her.

'You've nothing to be sorry about,' Maria assured her.

'Of course you haven't.' Alex stepped up to her other side and gave her a quick squeeze before he addressed the crowd. 'Let's get this party re-started, shall we?'

'I think it's time for a snack!' Ivy announced from over by the tables, which had been carefully cleared of the drawings while they'd all been distracted.

'I'll help you!' Aurora hurried over, hoping for a couple of moments in the back to recompose herself. There was no chance of that, however, because a small army of volunteers joined them. Everyone had either a kind word or a simple touch for Aurora as they bustled around ferrying the items Ivy had prepared earlier over to the tables. Plastic jugs of squash were set out together with apple slices, mini cheese crackers and little boxes of raisins Aurora hadn't seen since she was a child herself. While the parents supervised snack time, Ivy took Aurora to one side. 'Are you okay?'

'I'm fine,' Aurora reassured her with a smile and found to her surprise that it was true. The residents had taken the fuss caused by Carly in their stride and the only looks that were cast her way were ones of encouragement or concern. 'Everyone's been very kind.'

'The Point looks after its own,' Ivy said. 'Word will go out and that awful woman will get short shrift wherever she goes. Try to forget about it if you can.'

'I'll try.' Aurora wished she felt as confident as Ivy sounded. Even if Carly didn't show her face again, it was naïve to think she'd be the only one sniffing around. Not wanting to talk about it any more, Aurora cast a look over the party. 'It's going well, don't you think?'

Taking her cue, Ivy nodded. 'It's going brilliantly. Everyone seems to be having a good time.'

Grateful for her new friend's tact, Aurora set her shoulders straight. 'Right, what's left to do?'

'We're going to do story time next, and then Archie will do his turn as Father Christmas. Alex and Nick have gone to fetch the rocking chair that Archie will use, and we've got a couple of stools to go next to it for the children. If you don't mind supervising the queue from one end, I'll handle giving out the gift bags at the other.'

'Are you sure you want them to queue? I know there's only a dozen or so kids, but they might get restless.'

Ivy shrugged. 'I was wondering about doing it while story time is going on, but then they'll be up and down and disrupting the flow every few minutes. If you've got any better ideas, then I'm all ears.'

'I can do some singing with them if you like?' It seemed like the least she could do, given she'd almost ruined the party just by being there. 'A few little Christmas carols they can join in with.'

Ivy reached out and hugged her tight. 'That would be amazing. I was going to ask you yesterday, but then I thought you must get fed up of it.'

Aurora hugged her back then straightened up with a smile. 'I never get fed up of singing.'

'In that case…' Ivy swallowed and Aurora could see her eyes turn damp. 'As you're dressed for the part, do you think you could sing 'Over the Rainbow'? It was Mum's favourite. We listened to the Eva Cassidy version a lot last year.'

'It would be my pleasure.' Nick had told her about Ivy's mum dying after a long illness. She hesitated, then decided Ivy wouldn't have brought it up if she didn't want to talk about it. 'You must miss her a lot.'

Ivy nodded. 'She would've loved today.' She sucked in a tremulous breath. 'Right, then. Let's get story time started.'

Aurora watched in admiration as Ivy set her shoulders and waded back into the throng of the party. Whatever distance there was with her own parents, at least she still had them to be annoyed with, to worry about, to care about. With a promise to herself that she wouldn't wait until Christmas Day to call them again, Aurora started ushering the children towards the cushions.

Alex and Ivy handled story time like a couple of pros. They'd chosen *The Gruffalo* as the children would be familiar enough with the book to follow along. The couple took it in turns to read, doing lots of different voices. The children were so absorbed they even managed to smuggle Archie out of the back and through the shop without being spotted. He looked fabulous with a little extra padding under his jacket to round out his tummy and a luxurious white beard that covered the lower part of his face and halfway down his chest.

'Ho! Ho! Ho!' he cried, the moment Alex closed the storybook, setting off screams of excited delight. He fielded a barrage of hugs, patting heads and promising each child he had received their lists and that his elves were working hard on finishing everyone's presents. It took a bit of effort to settle the children again, but he eventually escaped to his rocking chair. Alex held up a bag with numbers written on squares of paper and each child chose a lot. It had felt like the fairest way to decide who would see Father Christmas first.

'They're brilliant at this,' Aurora said as she watched Alex and Ivy organise the children.

Nick nodded as he slung an arm around her shoulders and pulled her close. 'They've been doing regular story sessions on Saturday mornings and really taken to it. I'm glad they revived the tradition.' When she glanced up at him, Nick pointed to the rocking chair that Archie now occupied. 'Old Mr Cavendish who owned the shop before them used to tell us stories when we were kids. He always used that chair. Ivy found it in the back with a load of other junk and restored it. Most of the parents with kids here today will have sat on the carpet at his feet just like we did.'

'What a lovely tradition.' Aurora cuddled close to him, thinking about how nice it was that communities like the one at Mermaids Point maintained their connection with the past. It wasn't that different to where she'd grown up, either. The club her parents frequented hosted a Christmas party for the local children. It had been one of the highlights of the year and was one of the reasons Aurora had chosen to fund the refurbishment of their events room a few years previously. It was funny how she'd struggled so hard to get away from the claustrophobic atmosphere of her childhood and yet those same things she'd rebelled against – living on top of each other, everyone knowing everyone's business – felt different in retrospect. Then it had felt like she'd been spied upon, that she couldn't do anything without someone or other running the tale back to her mother. Now she could see it was about taking care, a busy community who were stretched thin working extra jobs to make ends meet looking out for their friends, their neighbours.

'What's with the sigh?' Nick asked. 'You're not still worried about that bloody reporter, are you?'

Aurora shook her head. 'It's not that. Do you ever feel like you don't really know your family at all?'

He pressed a quick kiss to her lips. 'Chance'd be a fine thing.' When she didn't smile back, he touched a finger to her cheek. 'Hey, are you okay?'

She nodded. 'Ivy asked me to sing a song her mum loved, and it's made me reflect on a few things, that's all.'

'Ah.' It was Nick's turn to sigh. 'Jen was an amazing woman. She was my mum's best friend from when they were little.'

'I'll do my best to do her memory proud.'

As Alex led the first child over for his visit, Aurora took her place at the front of the cushions and clapped her hands together. She settled in amongst the children and started off easy with carols such as 'O Little Town of Bethlehem' and 'Away in a Manger'. Lots of people joined in, not just the children and their parents, but people who'd popped into the shop for a browse. As she'd expected, there were a few swivelling heads towards where Archie was sitting but with the help of the parents, the children remained engaged enough until it was their turn to sit with Santa.

Only once every child was settled back on the cushions with a shiny gift bag nestled protectively in their laps did Aurora stand and move a few steps away from the cushions. She tapped her thigh, calling Gabriel to her side, and he trotted over to rest his head against her leg. 'I want to thank you all for coming today, and I hope you've had as much fun as I have. First off, I think we should all say thank you to Alex and Ivy for working so hard.' Applause and cheers rose up and Aurora quickly raised her hands to quieten the room. 'And extra-special thanks go to Father Christmas for taking time out of his very busy schedule to visit us today.'

Louder cheers and a few shouts of 'Thank you, Santa!', 'Thank you, Father Christmas!' came next.

'And finally, I want to say thank you to you all for letting me share such a special day; your support earlier means more than I can say.' To her surprise, Aurora found she had to swallow around a lump in her throat before she could continue. 'I want to wish you all a very merry Christmas and a peaceful and prosperous new year. If you'll indulge me for just a little longer, I've got one more song to sing. This is for Jen, who I know many of you knew and loved.' Drawing on all her years of practice and experience, Aurora managed to squash down the swirl of emotion threatening to rise again. She caught Ivy's eye and began to sing.

As the last note faded, there was a loud sniffle followed by the sound of someone blowing their nose. Several people laughed and the spell Aurora had cast over the room was broken. Customers clapped and cheered and crowded around her, but she only had eyes for one person. Ivy stood across the room, tears streaming, but with the most beautiful smile on her face. It was all the acknowledgement Aurora needed.

She'd done what she was born to do, brought someone comfort in the only way she knew how. As people continued to thank her for making the day so special, Aurora realised there were many different ways for her to use the gifts she'd been given.

14

They were up early again on Sunday morning, but Aurora was surprised to find she didn't mind. Though she'd told herself she wasn't going to worry about the encounter with Carly King, she still found herself checking the tabloid's website for a story and wasn't sure whether it was a good or a bad thing when there was no mention of her. Though Nick tried to persuade her to stay in bed and take a couple of hours to herself, she preferred to keep busy rather than dwell on it further. 'There must be something I can do to help out with the preparations,' she said as she rinsed her breakfast bowl under the tap. 'Unless you think I'd just be getting in the way?'

'I'm sure Mum will find you a hundred and one jobs; I just want to make sure you don't feel obligated to join in with everything. This is your Christmas, too, and you've been working non-stop all year. Give yourself a break.'

She dried her hands on the tea towel then came to put her arms around his waist. 'I had so much fun yesterday – well, apart from you-know-who showing up – I swear I'm still buzzing from it. I can rest tomorrow, unless there's something else on the schedule I don't know about?'

Nick shook his head. 'We've got tomorrow and Tuesday all to ourselves, and we've already agreed to a lazy Christmas Day.' He dropped a kiss on her upturned mouth. 'I'm glad you want to join in with stuff and you're not going to let that reporter's nonsense spoil your time here. I've got your back, and so has everyone else.'

Aurora nodded, deciding not to mention what Carly had implied about some people in the village being willing to gossip about them. She'd probably said it just to try to get a rise out of Aurora. Deciding she'd given the matter more than enough of her time, she tilted her face up towards Nick. 'Kiss me again.'

He might have done more than that had his mobile not started ringing. 'It's Dad,' he said with a disappointed sigh. 'I could ignore it.'

'Answer it.' Aurora gave his chest a playful shove. 'Work now, play later.'

'I'll hold you to that,' he promised as he answered the phone. 'Hey, Dad, we're on our way.'

'I'm glad I caught you, son. Can you bring your electric drill with you? The battery on mine is completely flat because *someone* unplugged it last night.'

The barbed comment must have been aimed at his mum because moments later Sylvia Morgan's cheerful voice was speaking in his ear. 'That's because *someone* knows better than to leave things plugged in overnight. Ignore him, darling, he's in a grump because I told him he can't have a bacon sandwich.'

Nick laughed. 'Tell Dad I'll bring my drill. We'll be there in ten minutes; we just need to call in to the surgery and drop Gabriel off for the morning.' Tom's teenagers had volunteered to dog-sit. Nick's parents were still bickering in the background so he ended the call. They'd be like that all day, teasing each other over one thing or another. Nick didn't like to think about it too closely, but he was sure it was their version of flirting because it always ended with a kiss at some point.

As he'd suspected, his mum was only too pleased of an extra pair of hands and Nick soon found himself being shooed away while his mum hooked an arm through Aurora's and led her towards the café, which the ladies from the organising committee were using as their base of operations. He left them to it, heading to the other end of the road with his dad to start setting out the tables and chairs that would be used by the various shopkeepers whose businesses didn't line the seafront. They worked their way along on the road, the tables filling up behind them almost as soon as they'd finished setting them up, everyone chattering and buzzing with excitement about what they all hoped would be a successful day ahead. The space either side of the giant Christmas tree was reserved for the volunteers from the RNLI. They had a pop-up stand with information boards and leaflets as well as a display showing the kit they wore when going on a call-out and were planning to run some drill demonstrations on the beach.

The tree was the same design they'd introduced the previous year, a huge pyramid of lobster pots wrapped in green fishing nets, with colourful buoys instead of baubles. Nick thought it was a nice reminder to people of where they'd come from. The village had been built on the back of the once-thriving fishing industry and even if there were many fewer trawlers tied up in the harbour, there was still a strong sense of pride in the men and women who'd founded the Point. Nick's own family on both sides had roots going back to the very first days and he'd done a few years on his uncle's trawler before he'd decided to sell up and switch to the tourist side of things. The only fishing he was involved with now was when he took enthusiasts out for a day with their rods and reels. He knew which he preferred.

When he finally caught up with Aurora, she was up on her tiptoes trying to hang white labels on the upper branches of a pretty, traditional Christmas tree outside his parents' gift shop. 'Need a hand?'

'Oh, yes please.' She handed him the half-dozen labels still to be hung from the lengths of red ribbon tied through them. He turned the first one over. *New books for the primary school library* had been printed on the label in neat black letters. 'What's this?'

'It's a wishing tree. The organising committee invited local groups to submit wishes for things they need.' Aurora pointed to a stack of small brown envelopes and a wooden donation box on the table beside the tree. 'People can donate in cash or scan the QR code, which will take them to a GoFundMe page for the event. They can make a general donation or choose a specific cause they want to support.'

'That's a really good idea.' Nick hung the label and looked at the next one. A request from the local care home for some new games and puzzles for their recreation room. The third was details of a sponsored trek some of the pupils at the nearby sixth-form college were planning the following summer. Pulling out his phone, Nick scanned the QR code and book-marked the donation page. 'I'll have a proper look later.' He placed the last of the labels on the branches Aurora pointed to, then stepped back to admire the tree. They'd kept the decorations simple, just a few lights and some red tinsel draped between the branches to ensure the labels were the primary focus. 'Looks good. Hey, I'm on a ten-minute break if you've got some time free?'

'I'm promised to Laurie for washing-up duty when she's finished in the kitchen, but I've got time for a coffee.'

Thankfully the committee were just about wrapping up so they managed to sneak past the eagle eyes of the knitting circle ladies and take refuge in the back of the café. Laurie and Jake were busy at the big stain-less-steel table in the middle of the room packing a selection of Laurie's homemade cakes into takeaway boxes. 'Don't you dare,' his sister warned as Nick's hand hovered over a rack of millionaire's shortbread. 'Everything here is already allocated so don't go messing up my system.'

'Busted,' Aurora admonished him with a laugh.

'Come on, Laurie,' Nick wheedled. 'Spare a morsel for a hardworking man.'

Jake picked up a stack of the white boxes and carried them over to where a load of others were already waiting to be carried outside. 'She won't even let me have anything, so you've got no chance, mate.'

'Harsh. Can I at least get a coffee to go?'

'Only if you make it yourself,' Laurie muttered, her focus on the check-list in front of her. 'I think we're almost there.'

'Thank God,' Jake said beneath his breath, but not quite low enough for Laurie to miss it.

'Did you say something?'

'Only what a pleasure it is to work with you when you are in such a good mood, my love.'

Laurie glared at him for a second before she started giggling. 'I'm sorry, I've been a tyrant, haven't I?'

'You've been under the most extreme provocation,' Jake said, rolling his eyes as someone called Laurie's name from the front of the café. 'I'll sort it out.' He pointed at Nick as he walked past. 'You get on the cappuccinos.'

Five minutes later and Jake had herded the last of the organising committee out of the front door and pulled the blind down to block out the ladies from the knitting circle who were still chattering on the doorstep. The four of them settled around one of the tables where Nick had laid out four steaming mugs of coffee and a collective sigh went up. 'I told you not to let them in here,' Jake said, casting a baleful eye around the room. 'Look at the state of this place.' Dirty cups littered the tables and Nick spotted a pile of used napkins on the floor where someone must've spilt a drink and made a half-hearted attempt at mopping it up.

'I know, but mine is the most central property along the road and the one with the most space. It won't take long to tidy up and at least we're only doing takeaway drinks so no one will be coming inside.' Like everyone else, Laurie would be operating from a couple of tables set out the front. The idea was to keep people circulating between the stalls as much as possible rather than hunkering down in the café for long periods of time.

'I'm not scheduled to do my first karaoke session until twelve thirty so I can stick around for as long as you need me to,' Ivy offered.

Nick's heart swelled as he watched his sister and his – did he dare think it – girlfriend share a smile. His phone beeped and he grabbed for his half-finished coffee with one hand while he checked his messages. 'I'm being summoned again,' he said before he gulped down the rest of his drink. 'I'll be back by eleven, though, to help out with what will hopefully be a rush of customers.'

As he stood, the others joined him, finishing up their drinks. He caught Aurora's hand and held her back as Laurie and Jake headed back into the kitchen. 'You sure you're all right here? Things are okay between you and Jake?'

She nodded. 'He's been lovely. I was a bit wary because of what happened but he seems content to let the past stay in the past and so am I. Besides, it's been nice to hang out with your sister and get to know her a bit better. It was hard to chat in the pub with everyone around, you know?' She glanced around the room. 'I love what she's done with this place and it's been fascinating to hear how she got the whole thing up and running from scratch, the same way you did with the warehouse conversion.'

He shrugged. 'There's not a whole lot of opportunities in a place like this unless you make them for yourself. Laurie never wanted to leave the Point so she had to carve out a future for herself.'

Aurora reached out and took his hands in hers. 'What about you? Did you ever think of leaving?'

'I think most people contemplate leaving where they grew up, especially when they come from a small community like I do.' He loved his family and was happy working with his uncle, but the Point was too dependent on seasonal visitors to comfortably support them both in the lean years. It had been easier when Nick had lived at home, but who the hell still wanted to be living with their parents at twenty-eight? Not him, that was for damn sure, no matter how much he loved them. The warehouse project had been make or break for him. He needed a home of his own and with properties in the village rarer than hen's teeth, it had been either build one for himself or face the prospect of moving into one of the big towns like so many of his school friends had been forced to do. Once their connection with Mermaids Point had been broken, they'd inevitably drifted away. Living elsewhere gave them better job prospects, which led to new friends, new partners and less reason to make the drive back home, especially when the summer visitors descended and took over the place.

It was a difficult balance for a village like theirs, finding a way to maintain its identity, keeping a community tied together when so many of the threads of their unique pattern were snapped by circumstances beyond the control of most of them. There was another reason he'd seriously contemplated leaving, but he wouldn't put that on her shoulders. Meeting Aurora, falling head over heels in love for the first time in his life and losing her again in a matter of weeks had only highlighted to him what he was missing out on. There was no one in the village for him, no one he'd felt even came close to the connection they had. Both Laurie and Ivy had been lucky to fall in love with people who were willing to settle in the Point. In both Jake and Alex's cases it had been a positive decision to relocate. They'd made big changes in their lives for sure, but they'd both had more than their relationships to build upon. What future was there for

Aurora here beyond being with him? They'd have to cross that bridge at some point, and probably sooner rather than later. For now, he wanted her to enjoy herself, to see the Point at its best. To rest and relax and not have to worry about anything. 'I need to go and finish with the setting-up; I'll be back in a bit.' After a quick kiss, he headed for the door and tried to convince himself he was avoiding the difficult conversations for Aurora's sake, and not his own selfish desires.

It didn't work.

* * *

'She was born to be onstage, wasn't she?' Laurie said as she and Nick stood side by side in front of the small platform that had been erected in front of The Sailor's Rest. Aurora had nipped home to change before her first round of karaoke and was wearing a glittering silver top over her black leather trousers and boots. The sequins or whatever they were covering her top had some sort of coating on them that flashed rainbow sparks every time she was caught in the beam of the stage lights. The temperature had dropped close to freezing since the sun had set, but Aurora had shrugged off her thick jacket before stepping onto the stage and was showing no effects from the cold other than the odd mist of her breath as she sang.

'Okay, who's next?' she said into her microphone, sounding excited even though she'd been up there for the past forty minutes. A teenager gave her a shy wave. 'Hey! Come on up.'

Nick watched the way Aurora noticed the girl's obvious nerves and led her to the limited privacy at the back of the stage where a volunteer was operating the karaoke machine. Aurora turned the girl back to the gathered crowd, her arm going around the girl's shoulders as they studied the menu. They chatted – well, it looked as if Aurora did most of the talking – until the girl finally nodded and gave her a bright smile. Only then did Aurora take her by the hand and lead her forwards. 'Everyone, I want you to meet my new friend, Janey.' Nick and Laurie clapped and stamped their feet along with everyone else. 'Now, we've had everything this evening from country and western to heavy metal...'

'Whoo, yeah!' yelled a voice from somewhere behind Nick. He suspected it was the middle-aged man who'd requested Guns N' Roses and rocked out like he'd been living his best life. Nick thought the mulled wine Pete had been dispensing a bit too freely with his big ladle had more than a bit to do with the man's performance, but at least he hadn't fallen off the stage.

Aurora wasn't the only one who laughed at the enthusiastic shout. 'Anyway, Janey is going to help me get you all in the proper spirit of the season.' She turned and nodded to the man at the back of the stage to cue him in. A rhythmic drumbeat came through the speakers, the rat-a-tat-tat of a marching band. Nick frowned, trying to place it, but all became clear the moment Aurora and Janey began to sing the opening lines of *Little Drummer Boy* in perfect harmony. Aurora had pitched her voice an octave lower and to Nick's surprise it was young Janey who took the more complicated peace on earth counterpoint made famous in the David Bowie and Bing Crosby duet. Her voice was soft, a little hesitant until Aurora gave her a smile and an approving nod and then she soared along the top notes, sending a shiver through Nick and he was sure many others. Where they'd clapped and cheered and sung along with most of the previous efforts, this time the crowd remained silent, spellbound until the final note faded away.

'Gosh that was beautiful,' Laurie choked beside him, raising a hand to catch a tear before she began to applaud and cheer. Nick could only nod around the lump in his own throat as he raised his hands high over his head and clapped as hard as he could. Aurora took a step to the side, her own hands raised to applaud as Janey beamed out over everyone. She looked completely transformed by the experience and Nick wondered if this was what it had been like for Aurora as a young girl. He hoped she'd had someone like herself to guide her through that first performance, to encourage her and acknowledge how special she was.

Laurie leaned against his shoulder. 'I never really understood what people meant when they talked about star quality, but I do now.'

Nick could only nod, unable to tear his eyes away as Aurora helped Janey off the stage and welcomed the next person. His performance could best be described as enthusiastic, but if his off-key singing bothered

Aurora, she gave not one hint as they belted their way through 'Summer Nights'. She rested one hand on the man's shoulder and set his opposite one on her hip so they could shake and shimmy like Danny and Sandy had in the classic film. The crowd joined in, singing the T-Birds' and Pink Ladies' chorus parts.

'Nick?' Laurie tugged on his arm. When he looked down there was something about her expression, a sense of concern so he didn't resist when she led him towards the back to a quieter spot.

'What is it?' He watched his sister as she glanced away, swallowed and then looked back at him. Laurie was very rarely lost for words, but she looked like she was wrestling with something now. 'Tell me.'

Laurie sighed. 'I'm worried about you.' She shot a quick look towards the stage. 'About both of you. I think you're rushing into things.'

Nick felt himself bristle, but tried to keep his cool. 'We've not made any massive commitments; we've just decided to enjoy this time together and see where things lead.'

'I hope you're doing a better job of convincing yourself that it's all very casual between you two, because I'm not buying it.' When he opened his mouth to protest, Laurie held up her hand. 'Anyone with eyes can see you're head over heels in love with her. Hell, you've been gone for her since the summer Jake and I met!'

'So what if I am?' The words burst out before he could stop them. 'She's the most amazing woman I've ever met, and if I want to be with her, what's wrong with that?'

Laurie reached for his hand, hanging on when he would have shaken her off. 'I want you to be happy, Nick, that's all. I like Aurora, I really do, but I think the pair of you are playing a very dangerous game.' Her next words pulled him up short. 'Did you know she's talking about chucking it all in?'

Nick shook his head. 'You've got it all wrong. She's using the Chad Logan thing to take a break, that's all. Once the fuss has died down and she's had a proper rest, she'll be back on the road again.'

His sister's look was sceptical. 'When we were chatting in the café earlier, she wasn't talking like a woman in any hurry to leave. She wanted to know all about how I'd got myself set up, how Jake was getting on with his freelance stuff, could I think of something the village was missing, where I went shopping.'

'Maybe she was just trying to get to know you a bit better,' Nick pointed out.

'Or maybe she was trying to work out where she might fit in here,' Laurie countered. 'I tried asking her about America, but she brushed it off. Said it wasn't all it was cracked up to be and she was tired of living out of a suitcase.'

'She's said the same kind of things to me, too, but there's a lot of stuff going on that you don't know about. With a bit of time and space to work through it, I'm sure she'll find her enthusiasm again.' He wished he felt as confident as he made himself sound. He should have been thrilled that Aurora seemed to be paying serious consideration to whether she could make Mermaids Point her home. After all, it was what he'd thought he wanted when he'd agreed to help her. But what happened in three months, or six months or even twelve months down the line? How could he possibly fill the gap in her life that performing occupied? It didn't seem possible. He'd almost rather lose her now than wake up one morning and find out his quiet, simple life wasn't enough for her.

'And where does that leave you?'

Nick shrugged. 'Pretty much in the same place I am right now. Look, I appreciate your concern, but this is stuff Aurora and I need to sort out between us.'

Laurie nodded, though he could tell it was with some reluctance. He loved his family, but they didn't always understand the line between caring and interfering. As though determined to prove his point, Laurie asked the million-dollar question. 'Will you leave if she asks you to?'

Ah, so this was the heart of it. Laurie wasn't worried about whether Aurora was planning to stay in the Point in the long term; she was worried that if she decided that she couldn't, then Nick would leave with her. 'Maybe.'

Laurie looked so sad that all Nick could do was gather her into a big hug. 'You're worrying about stuff that isn't even on the table yet. Please don't say anything to Mum and Dad, okay? I promise I won't make any big decisions without talking to you guys first, but you need to give me some space right now.'

Her arms closed tight around his back. 'I know, but I can't help thinking about it. One of you will have to give up everything. It's horribly selfish of me, Nick, but I don't want it to be you.'

Easing from her embrace, Nick turned his sister so they were facing the stage. Somehow, Aurora had persuaded Barbara, Kitty and the rest of the knitting circle ladies to join her and they were belting out a very risqué version of 'Lady Marmalade'. 'Look at her, Laurie. I won't do anything that diminishes that light inside her. I'd never forgive myself.'

15

Aurora woke the next morning to sunlight streaming through the bedroom curtains and the smell of freshly brewed coffee. She reached out instinctively, even though the evidence told her what she would find. Not only was the bed beside her empty, Nick had been up long enough for the sheets to have cooled. Sitting up, she reached for her phone to check the time but the bedside table was empty apart from a glass of water she'd poured the night before and not touched. There must be something about the sea air because that was the second night she'd slept straight through. She pushed aside the quilt and smiled at the sight of Nick's dressing gown draped over the end of the bed where he'd clearly left it for her. Or perhaps he was the secret ingredient to a good night's sleep.

Having used the bathroom and cleaned her teeth, Aurora shuffled into the kitchen. The dressing gown dwarfed her small frame and she'd had to roll back the cuffs a couple of times because the sleeves were so long but she hoped Nick wasn't in a hurry to get it back. Maybe she'd let him borrow it now and again to refresh the clean scent of his shower gel that was always a part of him. She'd had a good sniff of everything in his bathroom already to identify it and was going to buy him a lifetime's supply of it. He was sitting at the table, a half-eaten slice of toast on a plate beside him, which Gabriel was eyeing up from his seat in Nick's lap. 'You should've woken me,' Aurora said as she circled the table to give Nick a kiss before stealing the toast from his plate and taking a bite. 'What time is it? I'm starving.'

'It's just after nine,' Nick said with a smile as he set the whining dog on the floor and went to drop a couple more slices of bread in the toaster. 'Ignore him, he's already had his breakfast.'

Aurora waited until he'd turned away to pour her a coffee before breaking off a corner of the toast and dropping it on the floor. Gabriel hoovered it up and popped his head straight back up, clearly expecting another bite. 'No more,' she told the terrier. With a sigh he wandered out of the kitchen to flop down in his basket, with the absolute air of being hard done by. 'Thanks,' she said when Nick set the mug of coffee on the counter beside her. 'Hey, if I ask you something, do you promise not to get mad?'

Nick's eyebrows raised in surprise. 'Do I strike you as the kind of person who easily loses their temper?'

Realising she'd gaffed when she'd intended to make a light-hearted joke, Aurora set aside the remains of her toast and curled her arms around his neck. 'You are one of the calmest people I know. It's one of the many things I love about you.' The words had slipped out so easily and she knew them to be true.

His hands captured her waist. 'Love, is it? Whatever it is you've got to ask me really must be terrible.'

She wanted to correct him, but decided to let it go. There was no need to make things heavy between them. 'Laurie told me about the out-of-town shopping centre; will you take me? I'll wear a bit of a disguise so we shouldn't get hassled. There's just a few things I need.'

* * *

'I can't believe I let you talk me into this,' Nick grumbled for the third, or perhaps fourth time since they'd got in the car. As they crawled around the multistorey car park attached to the shopping centre, Aurora was starting to wonder if perhaps it'd been a mistake, even if she'd had a lot of fun persuading Nick in the shower earlier. The long dark wig she'd put on was already starting to make her head itch, not helped by the woollen hat she'd tugged down on top of it to keep it in place. They'd decided to leave Gabriel where he was, and a quick call to Nerissa had resulted in a very happy Emily showing up at the apartment. Delighted at the prospect of having access to Nick's Netflix password and not having to fight with her younger brother over what to watch, she told them to take their time as she'd flopped on the sofa.

'There's one.' She pointed towards a space near the end of the row. When they got there, it was as unusable as the other two they'd found thanks to the inconsiderate parking of other shoppers. 'Sorry, this was a really bad idea, wasn't it?'

Nick manoeuvred the car out of the partial turn he'd made towards the space and trundled up to the next level. 'I can think of other things I'd rather be doing, but it's fine. I think it's very sweet that you want to buy gifts for my family.'

When she'd told him why she wanted to go to the shops, he'd told her she could just add her name to his gifts, but she wanted to show her appreciation to the Morgans for their hospitality. 'We won't be long, I promise. I've already got an idea of what I want to get.' There was also the matter of having nothing suitable to wear for Tom and Nerissa's wedding. Thankfully there was plenty of room on the next floor up and they were soon parked and heading down in the lift. 'You still haven't given me any ideas about what I can get for you,' she reminded Nick as the doors opened onto what looked like Dante's fourth circle of hell, but with more tinsel and a tinny backing track of Christmas carols.

'If you change your mind about this shopping trip, that might be the greatest gift you ever give me,' Nick said in a wry tone as they walked a wide circle around a small child who was lying on his back screaming absolute bloody murder.

'That'll be you in a couple of hours,' Aurora joked, giving his hand a squeeze as she led him over to the large display board that detailed all the different retail outlets and their locations.

'More like twenty minutes,' Nick grumbled as a woman accidentally sideswiped him with a bundle of shopping bags. 'No, no, it was my fault,' he assured the woman, voice dripping with sarcasm when she turned around and glared at him.

'Oh God, let's get you somewhere out of the way.'

By some miracle, there was an empty table outside Starbucks so Aurora left Nick there with a large cappuccino and a slice of cake. He could look after the bags as she accumulated them, and she wouldn't have to listen to him moan every five minutes. It was a win-win for them both. She started in the big Waterstones a few doors down, buying a cookbook for Andrew full of comfort food recipes and a large Moleskine notebook for Jake that was so tactile she couldn't stop stroking the cover as she queued to pay for her purchases. With the first bag deposited with Nick, she headed for the escalator to the first floor where there was a L'Occitane store. She loaded up on luxury hand cream for Laurie, who spent so much time washing her hands at the café, and a toiletries selection in their best-selling verbena range for Linda. She hadn't had much of a chance to get to know her yet, but felt it was important to include everyone who was considered a part of the Morgans' extended family group. She was heading back towards the escalator when a black fedora caught her eye in the window of a men's outfitters. With a grin, she nipped in and bought it for Alex, to replace the hat his father had unceremoniously squashed when he'd sat on it.

A visit to the large Waitrose food hall at the far end of the complex was worth the walk as it garnered a bottle of vintage champagne for Tom and Nerissa to help them celebrate their impending nuptials, and a luxury hamper of breakfast treats for Archie and Philippa. 'Are you planning on buying the whole mall?' Nick asked as he poked his nose in the latest round of bags she dropped off with him. He'd finished his coffee and had moved on to some sort of iced confection. 'Want a sip?' He offered the straw to her and she took a slurp – well, as much of a slurp as she could suck up of the heavily frozen mix. 'Oh, that's lovely, what is it?'

'It's a toasted white chocolate mocha frappuccino.' Nick pulled out the seat beside him. 'Sit down for five minutes.'

'I've still got loads to do.' She hadn't quite managed to surrender the drink back to him, though.

'Sit. I'll get another one.' He was back five minutes later with another frappuccino and a huge round biscuit that had been frosted to look like a bauble.

After resuming his seat, he reached a hand out to touch a strand of her dark wig. 'I can't get over how different you look in this.'

Aurora barely resisted the urge to reach up and scratch her scalp. 'It's driving me mad. I should've thought about how hot it would be in here.'

'You could probably take it off if you wanted. Look at this place.' He gestured around them. 'Everyone is too busy trying to get what they need and get out of here.'

'You're probably right. If it gets any worse, I'll duck into one of the bathrooms and take it off.' As she worked her way through the delicious drink, including an obligatory bout of brain freeze when she drank too much too quickly, Aurora did a mental inventory of what she'd bought so far and what was left to get. 'I've no idea what to get for the kids.'

'Vouchers,' Nick replied without hesitation.

'Doesn't that seem a bit impersonal?'

'They're teenagers. Cash or vouchers will be fine. If you want to personalise them a bit then Max is addicted to his PlayStation so you can get him a voucher from the game store over there.'

He nodded behind her and Aurora turned to see. Given the number of teenage boys hanging around both inside and outside it, he was probably right. 'What about for Em? If I get her one that's accepted in all the shops she'll be able to please herself, I suppose.'

'I think they sell them at the information point, which is next to the pay machine for the car park so you can pick one up on the way out. What else do you need?'

Aurora closed her eyes to think for a second. 'Just something for your mum, but I've got an idea for that and something for Ivy. Oh, and you.' She shot him a meaningful look.

Reaching out, Nick grasped the seat of her chair and pulled her close. 'I've got you. That's all my Christmases come true.' She wasn't sure what made her heart beat faster, his words, the look in his eyes as he said them or the swift, hot kiss he laid on her afterwards. A lethal combination. 'Does that mean you haven't got me anything?' she teased when she'd finally caught her breath.

Nick laughed and held a finger to his lips. 'That would be telling.'

She rolled her eyes. 'Just tell me yes or no.'

'I'm working on something, but you might have to wait for it.'

Well, that was delightful and infuriating in equal measures, which was no doubt exactly what he intended. At least it took the pressure off and gave her a bit of time to think about what she could get for him. She had one idea, but she needed a bit more information before she could make a final decision. 'I'd better get cracking,' she said. 'Are you staying here?'

Nick shook his head. 'I'm going to dump these bags in the boot and stretch my legs. Send me a text when you're ready and I'll meet you by the information desk, okay?'

'Okay.' Aurora adjusted her knitted hat and stood up. She really needed to ditch this blasted wig before she boiled to death. 'I'll be as quick as I can.'

Her first stop after a quick trip to the bathroom was the game shop, where she queued for what seemed like forever before she finally reached the till. She'd stuffed the wig in her bag but kept the hat on as it covered the bright blonde of her hair. As Nick had suggested, no one gave her so much as a second glance. Still racking her brain for what she could get for Ivy, she headed towards the department store at the opposite end of the complex from the food hall. She found a gorgeous silk scarf for Sylvia, a rich swirl of colours from the deep dark green of the winter ocean to the pale icy blue of the winter sky. Making her way towards the outlet of one of her favourite designers, a display of handbags caught Aurora's eye and she stopped to take a closer look. The bag designs were quirky and amusing, the kind of thing she thought would suit Ivy's unique sense of style. She picked up one that had poodles marching in formation along the bottom, their snooty little noses poking high in the air along with their little cotton-ball tails. When she spotted the one that had been half-hidden behind it, she set the poodles aside with a grin, knowing she'd found the perfect gift. It was a school satchel design, with paintbrushes, pots of paint and all sorts of other art materials cleverly picked out in bright colours.

Hooking the bag over her arm beside the silk scarf, Aurora hurried towards the clothing section.

* * *

'Are you sure it's suitable for a wedding?' she asked the shop assistant as she turned to survey her reflection from the back. Though she'd gone looking for a dress, she hadn't been able to resist the crimson satin jumpsuit. It was a simple design cuffed at ankles and wrists and cinched in at the waist.

'I think it's stunning on you, and the colour is dark enough, especially if you team it with a jacket for the ceremony itself. Will you be in a church?' Aurora nodded. 'I think I've got just the thing, give me one second.' The assistant returned with a black, crushed-velvet blazer. 'Try this.'

Aurora slipped it on and surveyed her reflection once more. The jacket muted the bold splash of colour of the jumpsuit, which was what she'd been worried about. She wanted to look good for the wedding, but she also wanted to fit in with everyone else. It was Nerissa's day and all eyes should be fixed on the bride. 'I think that works.'

'Very classy.' The woman edged closer. 'It'll look good in *Hello!* or one of those other celebrity magazines,' she said to Aurora in a conspiratorial whisper.

Aurora swallowed a sigh; she really should've stuck with the wig. At least they were alone in the relative privacy of the curtained dressing room. 'It's a very private affair, a close family friend.'

'Ah, I see.' The woman looked a trifle embarrassed, as though worried she'd overstepped the mark.

Feeling sorry for her, Aurora reached out and touched her arm. 'I really appreciate your help today; you've been a godsend.'

'All part of the service,' the woman said, brightening. 'Do you need any accessories, or are you all set?'

'This is perfect, thank you.'

'Well, you take your time getting changed and I'll be over by the till when you're ready. Shall I take these and wrap them for you?' She pointed to the bag and scarf, which Aurora had placed on the chair in the corner of the fitting room.

'That would be so kind of you.'

The gift wrapping was so beautiful that Aurora ended up giving the woman a huge tip, waving off her protests and wishing her a merry Christmas. No one worked harder than retail staff at this time of year and she'd seen for herself the way many had been spoken to already that morning. She understood that people were in a rush, that they had their own pressures and worries, but she'd been raised to believe that kindness cost nothing and was worth its weight in gold and it was something she'd tried to carry through her life. It was hard sometimes. She'd found the fawning behaviour of some people in the industry painful to the point of embarrassing, until she'd understood they were only behaving that way because they were afraid of losing their jobs. She'd seen one of the other Divas live up to her name with a full-scale backstage meltdown because she'd been given a bottle of water that was cold rather than room temperature. The poor kid who'd messed up had been left in tears and hadn't been seen around after that. Respect was a two-way street as far as Aurora was concerned.

Worried the rest of her presents would look shabby in comparison, she found a card shop and started looking for pretty paper, ribbons and gift bags. She spotted a gorgeous bag with what looked like a replica of a Victorian Christmas-card scene of a couple skating on a pond. It would be perfect for Sylvia's scarf. As she reached for it, she touched hands with someone. 'Oh, I'm so sorry!'

'It's fine,' the older woman said with a smile. 'You take it, I can find something else.'

Aurora pulled the bag forward on its rack, hoping to see another one behind it, but it appeared to be the only one like it. 'No, honestly, you take it,' she assured the woman, hoping she would indeed just take it or they might be there all day apologising to each other.

The woman smiled gratefully then gave her a quizzical look. 'Do I know you?'

Damn. Aurora flashed her a quick smile. 'I don't think we've met, no.' It wasn't a lie. 'Well, I've got lots to do.' She turned away, pretending to study a selection of gift tags.

'No, I'm sure... *Oh*. I know you.' There was something brittle and ugly in the way the stranger said those last three words. Whatever was coming next, it wasn't going to be good. Aurora was still debating whether to drop the stuff she'd picked out and walk away when she felt a sharp poke between her shoulder blades.

She spun around, taking several steps back to make sure she was well out of range of another poke from the woman's accusing finger. 'Please don't touch me.'

'It is you.' The woman's generous smile was gone, her mouth an ugly twist of disgust. 'Women like you give the rest of us a bad name! After all the good the #metoo movement has done and there you are trying to use it to get a decent man's career ruined!'

Aurora didn't even bother to argue with her; she just did what she should have done straight away and headed for the exit, dumping the cards and rolls of wrapping paper in her hands on a display stand as she hurried past. *Head down. Keep your head down.* It was tempting to run, to get away as fast as she could, but that would only draw attention to herself. There was an escalator to her right, but she didn't want to risk getting trapped on it if the woman decided to follow her so she ducked into the staircase on the left. The moment the heavy fire door closed behind her, she grabbed the handrail and ran as fast as she could, the weight of her shopping bags banging against her leg with every step. She didn't stop until she was on the ground floor and merged with the crowd.

She tapped into her phone with a shaking finger:

Where are you?

In New Balance looking for a new pair of trainers. You ready to go?

Yes. I'll be by the parking machine.

She wanted to tell him to hurry, but that would only lead to more questions and she just wanted to get out of there. Weaving through the crowd, she found a spot against the wall where she could keep an eye on who approached, without being too close to the machine that people would hesitate to use it.

It seemed like an age before she spotted Nick cutting through the crowds. His bright smile of greeting faded to a frown before he'd reached her. 'What's wrong?'

'I'll tell you in the car,' Aurora muttered, plastering a fake smile on. 'Just get the ticket, please, and let's go.'

'Okay.'

The moment they were in the lift, Aurora pressed the button to close the doors and kept her finger on it until they were safely cocooned inside. She yanked off her hat and rested her sweat-damp head back against the cool metal of the wall with a sigh. 'What's wrong?' Nick asked again.

'Oh nothing. I ran into a member of the Chad Logan fan club, that's all.' She tried to smile, tried not to let her upset over the encounter show, but it was hard. She was glad when the lift announced their floor and the doors eased open, letting in a blast of cold air from the car park.

Nick swore low under his breath, but he didn't say anything, just took Aurora's hand firmly in his and walked her back to the car. There were cars everywhere and it was impossible to tell who was queuing to find a space and who was desperate to try to escape. 'Hey!' a voice called behind them and Aurora flinched, but it was only someone wanting to know if they were leaving and where they were parked. She knew she was being silly, but she pushed the lock doors button on the car's central console as soon as they were both inside.

'The woman must've said something awful to have you spooked like this,' Nick said as he reached for her hand again.

'It was nothing, really.' But there was something about the woman's words that nagged in her brain. A horn beeped and they scrambled to put on their belts. At least the person wanting their space meant they were able to reverse out into the queue, but then they were stuck like everyone else inching along until the lane finally split into an up ramp and a down exit. Aurora opened her phone, but the thick concrete and metal construction of the car park made it impossible to get any kind of a signal so all she got on her Twitter app was a 'tweets aren't loading right now' message. It was the same for the rest of her social media, which was probably a good thing. She was just about to close Instagram when they emerged out into the sunshine and Aurora found herself momentarily blinded after the gloomy depths of the car park. She tilted her screen so she could see it and gasped at the number of notifications. Feeling suddenly anxious, she clicked them open and felt her stomach lurch at the first post. She'd been tagged in the comments section below a teaser trailer for a TV show along with a string of abusive hashtags, the politest of which labelled her a whore. The second tag was just her name and a long line of snake emojis. What the hell was going on?

When she clicked play on the original video, she was greeted with the sight of Chad Logan and his wife, Melissa, sitting on a minimalist set. Behind their plain pair of armchairs was a white backdrop with the words 'The Big Conversation' emblazoned upon it. They were dressed in sombre clothing, hands clasped tightly. A large silver crucifix shone bright against her black top as Melissa stared up adoringly at Chad. 'I've made mistakes,' he said, straight into the camera. 'Unforgivable mistakes.' He choked just the right amount as he glanced down at Melissa, who was shaking her head.

'So you admit there was something behind that photo of you and Aurora Storm embracing?' the disembodied voice of whoever was interviewing them asked.

'No there bloody wasn't!' Aurora shouted at the screen. 'Oh my God, what is this crap?' Realising she'd missed what they said next, she jabbed the pause button on the video and turned to Nick in a panic. 'What the hell are they playing at?'

'Hang on a minute, let me park up.' He flicked his indicator and steered into an unloading zone. He switched on his hazard lights and turned in his seat to face her. 'Show me the rest of it.'

Feeling sick, Aurora restarted the clip.

'She... I...' Chad looked to Melissa, who patted his hand the way she might a small child.

'All we have to say on the matter is that it's a sad indictment of this industry that young women still feel the need to do whatever they think it'll take to get ahead.'

As though prompted by her words, Chad began to nod. 'I am a man with the same weaknesses as any other and though nothing untoward happened, it was enough to realise I'd been tempted. We've always been honest with each other, even if it means hurting the other person.' He raised Melissa's hand to his mouth and kissed it. 'I'm blessed to be married to this incredible woman and to have the strength of my faith to help me.'

Melissa turned her big blue eyes to the camera, sooty lashes blinking rapidly against non-existent tears. 'Forgiveness is a part of any marriage, especially when you've been together as long as Chad and I have. Temptation comes in many forms and none of us are immune to it.'

'Even Adam and Eve found themselves tested by the serpent in the garden of Eden,' the interviewer intoned, sounding like one of those televangelist preachers.

The clip came to an end and all Aurora could do was stare at Nick in horror and disbelief. 'Is Chad seriously implying I made a pass at him to try and get the part?'

'That's what it sounds like, although I didn't catch the first part of the interview. Is there any more, or is that it?' He took the phone from her unresisting hands.

While he scrolled back and forth, Aurora leaned her head back against her seat and closed her eyes. Leaking a photo he'd obviously staged had never made any sense to her because it would damage his reputation as much as it would hers. In fact, given his A-list status and how long Chad had been at the top of his game, he had way more of a reputation to lose than her.

'That's the only clip I can find. Well, versions of it,' Nick said after a few minutes. 'I'm still trying to find the original post as I don't recognise the channel logo on the bottom left of the screen.'

Aurora had been too stunned to notice anything other than Chad's insincere tone and Melissa's wildly fluttering eyelashes. Had they always been such hammy actors and she'd been too overawed by their celebrity to notice? 'Doesn't matter who it is,' she said. 'Once something like that goes viral, the networks all pick it up and play it, even when they are pretending to condemn whatever it is.' It was the reality of today's media; the constant drive for clickbait and content meant even the most serious news networks felt required to report on whatever had social media in a tizz on any given day.

She felt a gentle touch on her cheek and opened her eyes to meet Nick's look of concern. 'What can I do?' he asked.

'Nothing. Just take me home.'

16

They didn't speak for the rest of the drive. Nick didn't know what to say, if he was being honest; it was all so far out of his realm of expertise. The few words that came to mind sounded so trite and clichéd in his head, he decided it was probably for the best to keep them to himself. The traffic was awful, so he pushed his worry for Aurora to the back of his mind and concentrated on doing what she'd asked him to do – get her home.

When they reached the first floor of the warehouse, Nick set down the pile of shopping bags to find his keys but Aurora had already taken out her key for Ivy's apartment and was unlocking. 'I need to lie down for a bit.'

He wanted to point out there was a perfectly good bed in his place, but then he remembered Emily was dog-sitting. He gathered up the pile of bags and followed Aurora inside, where he set them down on the sofa. 'Okay. I'll see what Em's been up to while we were out and take Gabriel for a walk. Why don't you send me a text later once you've had a rest and we'll take it from there?'

Aurora stared at the pile of shopping bags for a long moment before pulling out the bottle of champagne. 'Will you give that to Nerissa and Tom and give them all my best wishes for the wedding?'

Nick made no move to take the bottle. 'What are you talking about? You can give it to them yourself on Wednesday.'

Shaking her head, she thrust the bottle towards him again. 'I don't think I should go, not with everything that's going on; it wouldn't be fair.'

He took the champagne from her then immediately set it down on the coffee table. 'Look, I understand you're upset about the clip, but don't make any hasty decisions. No one cares what a few muppets on social media have to say.'

He'd meant it to be reassuring, but he knew he'd made things worse by the way her eyes flared wide. 'Those muppets are the people who make or break careers, Nico. You might not care what they have to say, but I do! I have to because it's part of my job whether I like it or not! And you seem to have forgotten about Carly King. What if she's still hanging around and decides to try and gatecrash the wedding? I'd never forgive myself!'

'I'm sorry.' About so many things. He wanted to help her but he had no idea where to start. His instinct was to pull out his phone and start replying to all the trolls who'd upset her but he knew from witnessing other online dramas that reacting like that was a one-way ticket to disaster. Lashing out might make him feel a bit better, but it would do nothing to help Aurora and everything to harm her. He'd promised to support her in whatever way she needed him to and if that meant giving her some space while she decided what to do next, then so be it. It did not extend to her shutting herself away like she was the one in the wrong, however. The wedding wasn't for another forty-eight hours so there was time for her to deal with this latest setback and to understand she had nothing to hide from or be embarrassed about.

The little smile she gave him was full of defeat. 'I'm sorry too. I'll text you later, okay?'

Wishing he didn't feel quite so useless, Nick nodded and headed back to his own apartment.

Though he was worried about Aurora, he couldn't help but grin when he opened his front door to a riot of noise and colour. Music was blaring from the television, a Harry Styles concert by the looks of it. Emily was sitting on the sofa with one foot propped on his coffee table, painting her nails and video-chatting to a couple of friends on her iPad, which was propped on a stand beside her foot. She appeared oblivious to his arrival, even when Gabriel climbed out of his basket and trotted towards Nick, stubby tail wagging. He had a red ribbon tied around his neck and a tiny ponytail sticking up from the top of his head.

'Making yourself at home, I see?' he called to Emily over the racket.

'Oh my God!' she shrieked and he almost felt guilty when she smeared the varnish she was applying all over her big toe.

'Who's that?' one of the voices said from her iPad.

'He's well leng,' said another, which sent them all into a fit of giggles. Nick had no idea what it meant and wasn't sure he wanted to either.

'Ew, Ruby, he's ancient!' Emily said, sounding appalled. 'Look, I've got to go, talk later.' She ended the chat then beamed up at Nick like she hadn't eviscerated his ego in the way only a teenage girl could. 'I wasn't expecting you back yet! Where's Aurora?' She glanced around as though expecting Aurora to pop up from behind the sofa.

'She's having a lie-down next door.'

Emily's face fell. 'Oh. I was hoping she'd do my TikTok video with me.'

He was a bit surprised at that; maybe he'd been right after all and this thing with Chad Logan wasn't such a big deal. Or perhaps Emily hadn't heard about the latest drama. Knowing he'd need to tread carefully, Nick reached for the remote and muted the TV before sitting down on the sofa next to her. 'Someone recognised her when we were out shopping, and they weren't very nice.'

Looking up from where she was trying to wipe the mess off her toe, Emily's face was the very picture of confusion. 'But she's so cool. Why would anyone be mean to her?'

Nick sighed. 'It's all to do with this misunderstanding over her meeting with Chad Logan.'

Emily stuck her tongue out like she'd just tasted something disgusting. 'He's so gross! No one's going to believe him over Aurora.'

Her loyalty was touchingly sweet. 'Unfortunately, there are plenty of people who believe whatever they read, or just like to spread gossip because they think it's funny. We know better, but it's going to take a little bit of time for Aurora to sort things out. All we can do is be here for her and make sure she knows she has people who care about her.'

Her face fell and Nick couldn't bear to see it. 'Hey, don't worry about it. Aurora's stronger than all those haters.'

Emily nodded. 'People can be really mean sometimes.' She sounded so young, a throwback to the shy girl he'd met the previous summer and not the gregarious young woman he'd become used to talking to. *Damn*. Emily had got caught up in a dare at her old school that had involved girls sharing inappropriate photos. It was one of the main reasons her father had decided to try to adjust his workload and ended up bringing the children to Mermaids Point where they could have a fresh start.

He could pretend he didn't know what she was thinking about, or he could treat her like the sensible, mature person he knew her to be. 'I didn't mean to stir up any bad memories, Em. You know better than most people how upsetting it can be when people talk behind your back. You also know the kind of people who do it aren't worth a single second of your time.'

As he'd hoped, she straightened up at his words and a frown of determination chased the sadness from her eyes. 'Tell Aurora it'll be okay.'

He nodded. 'I will. Come on, get your stuff together and I'll walk you back to the surgery.' When she rolled her eyes as though to say she wasn't a child that needed walking anywhere, Nick held his hands up. 'I'm going that way anyway.'

As he hefted Emily's bag onto one shoulder, Nick wondered what on earth she had in the bottom of it. Bricks from the weight of it, maybe a bowling ball. Gabriel was still wearing his red ribbon, which looked rather fetching with his tartan walking coat. Nick wasn't sure about the little topknot but he hadn't wanted to hurt Emily's feelings by taking it out. He was just locking up when the door opposite opened and Aurora appeared. She'd changed into her fleece leggings, Ugg boots and cosy hoody. 'Oh, I just caught you in time,' she said, giving Emily a quick hug of greeting.

'I thought you were going to have a lie-down.'

Aurora lifted one shoulder in a half-shrug. 'A sulk, you mean? Dennis gave me a pep talk and here I am.' She made 'pep talk' sound more like an arse-kicking but she was smiling as she said it.

'Don't let the bastards grind you down,' Emily said, hooking her arm through Aurora's. It was on the tip of Nick's tongue to tell her off for her language, but then he remembered she was nearly seventeen and he wasn't her father so really it wasn't any of his business. Besides, he wholeheartedly agreed with the sentiment and had used much coarser language in his head about the trolls who hounded Aurora.

He let the two of them walk ahead of him a bit, content to keep at Gabriel's pace, which involved stopping every few steps so he could sniff at whatever had captured his attention. When he realised Aurora and Emily had crested the hill leading down into town and were out of sight, Nick encouraged the terrier to move a bit quicker. By the time he spotted them again, the two women had stopped by the surgery gate and Nick watched as Emily pulled the tie off the end of her messy braid and started shaking out her hair. Aurora combed her fingers through it, then picked up a section and started twisting it into a complicated design. She did the same with a matching piece from the other side and then wrapped both sections around Emily's head like a plaited crown. He caught up in time to hear Emily say, 'Are you sure you don't mind?'

'Of course I don't.' She raised a hand to her short crop and ruffled it with a laugh. 'It's not like it takes me a long time to do my hair, after all. I can help you with your make-up as well, if you want?'

Emily squealed and hugged her. 'Ruby is going to die when I tell her!' She grabbed her bag from Nick with a quick word of thanks and dashed up the path. 'See you on Wednesday!' she called over her shoulder.

'Well, you've made someone's day, possibly her year,' Nick said with a grin as he slung an arm around Aurora's shoulder. 'Shame poor Ruby's not going to survive long enough to see Christmas, though.'

Aurora laughed. 'She's a sweetheart, isn't she? She told me not to worry about stupid trolls and that Instagram is over anyway so no one cares what happens on there.'

'I think Instagram is for ancient people like us, even if we are leng.'

She glanced up at him with a puzzled smile. 'We're leng?'

Nick grinned. 'Well, I am according to Ruby. I think it must mean "devastatingly handsome".'

Laughing, Aurora gave him a shove before tucking herself back under his arm. 'In your dreams, Nico.' Her voice turned serious. 'Anyway, it sounds like Emily had a rough time of it before she came here, and I wanted to do something nice for her. She's so excited about the wedding and being a bridesmaid for the first time.'

'You've changed your mind about the wedding, then?' Nick couldn't keep the relief out of his voice.

'A wise man once told me that no one owns a single bit of me.' He couldn't help but smile as he recognised the words. He'd said them to her about Julian, but she was right, they applied equally to the rest of the world. 'I forgot that for a moment,' she continued. 'But it won't happen again. Dennis has put me on a social media ban and made me delete all my apps while we were talking.' She laughed, but he could still sense the lingering upset behind it.

Nick stopped her on the path and pulled her against his chest. 'What happened today must've have been horrible,' he murmured against her hair. 'It's bad enough when it's online, but to have someone have a go at you in public?' He shook his head.

'I dropped my guard.' The fact she was making it sound like she was even remotely to blame infuriated him and he pulled back to look at her. Before he could say anything, she held up a hand. 'No lectures. I've already had enough of that from Dennis. I know I haven't done anything wrong. He's sure there's something fishy going on so he's going to do some digging and I've promised him I'll try and forget all about it.'

'No lectures,' Nick promised. The sweet smile she gave him followed by an even sweeter kiss made it that much easier to swallow his anger down. It wasn't helpful so he wouldn't let it spoil any more of the day. 'Do you want to head back?'

She shook her head. 'I didn't get a chance to get wrapping paper and a few other things so I wouldn't mind a wander around if you can face more shopping?'

Nick flung his hand to his forehead and staggered a few paces. 'Must I?'

'Well, who else is going to carry my bags? I am a famous pop star, you know!' With a toss of her head, she turned and marched off up the street. It must've been hard to put that much sass into her walk when she was wearing scruffy boots and an oversized fuzzy hoodie, but he had to admire her effort.

When she paused on the doorstep of his parents' gift shop and shot him a superior look over her shoulder, Nick reached up and tugged at his forelock. 'Yes, Ms Storm. Sorry, Ms Storm. I'll make sure I stay three paces behind you at all times, Ms Storm.' She laughed so hard she all but fell over the threshold into the shop.

'Glad to see someone's having fun!' his dad called from behind the counter. 'To what do we owe this pleasure?'

'I'm looking for some nice wrapping paper and a few decorations,' Aurora said. 'And I'm told you've got the best taste in Mermaids Point.'

If Andrew Morgan was a light bulb, he couldn't have glowed much more under that compliment. 'Ah, I think you've mistaken me for my lovely wife. She's the one with all the taste.'

'That's why she married you, right?' Aurora said, making Andrew roar with laughter.

'Tell me you're keeping her, son, because only a fool would let a treasure like this go.'

'I'm doing my best, Dad, believe me,' Nick assured him as he came to lean against the counter. 'Now if I can interrupt this mutual appreciation society, the lady has some urgent shopping to do.'

'Don't be jealous of how fabulous we are, son.' His dad shook his head in mock disappointment.

'Oh God.' Turning his back on his father, Nick pointed towards the middle of the shop. 'Gift wrapping is over there.' He watched Aurora head towards the section he'd indicated then turned back to face his dad, who was grinning at him like the Cheshire Cat. 'What?'

Andrew held up his hands. 'Nothing.'

'Well, that's all right then. Where's Mum?'

'She's popped next door to get us a bite to eat. It's been manic all morning so this is the first time we've had a chance to take a break.' It was easy sometimes to forget how hard his parents worked because they seemed to take everything in their stride. He noticed now there were dark shadows under his father's eyes.

'Is everything okay?'

Andrew nodded. 'It's just been a long few weeks. Don't get me wrong, I'm never going to complain about the shop being busy, but I won't be sorry when I turn the closed sign around tomorrow and we get to have a few days off.'

'You're not opening at all on Christmas Eve?'

'Nope. We talked about it, but your mum's right. It's Nerissa's special day and we've waited so long to see her happy and settled. We've had a good year, and the fete last Sunday brought in more than enough to make up for being closed for an extra half-day. Laurie's staying closed as well. She and Jake are going to come to us for a late breakfast; you'd both be welcome to join us.'

'Aurora's going to help Emily with her hair and make-up so let me check with her and see what time she's arranged to do that.'

His father beamed. 'That's nice of her. She's a lovely girl.'

'I think so too.' Master of the understatement, that was him.

'I've got you cheese and pickle on brown and a slice of rocky road. Oh, hello, darling!' Sylvia Morgan placed a pair of loaded plates on the counter then turned to give Nick a hug. 'Where's that gorgeous girl of yours?' She tilted her head as though Aurora might be hiding behind him.

'She's looking for some stuff to wrap the gifts she bought this morning.' He wondered about mentioning cutting their trip short, but knew neither of his parents would be incapable of making a fuss. Aurora had said she wanted to try to forget about it, so he would honour her wishes.

'Oh, she didn't need to bother with presents!' It was clear from the bright smile on his mother's face that she was delighted at Aurora's thoughtfulness. 'I'll just go and see if she needs a hand.'

'That's the last we'll see of either of them for a good half an hour,' his father observed as he picked up one half of his sandwich, then pushed the plate towards Nick. 'Might as well make yourself comfortable.'

Andrew Morgan's prediction wasn't far off the mark and by the time a grinning Aurora made her way back to the till with her arms loaded down with rolls of paper, gift bags and goodness knew what else, he and his dad had eaten both sets of sandwiches and the two slices of cake.

'I can't leave you unsupervised for a minute,' Sylvia said, pointing an accusing finger at the two plates, which were empty apart from a scattering of crumbs.

'I'll get you another one,' Nick promised, giving her a quick kiss on the cheek. 'Two minutes.'

Gathering the empty plates, he headed to the back of the shop and through the connecting archway into his sister's café. The worst of the lunch rush had passed, but a few people were lingering over cups of coffee. There was no sign of Laurie so he assumed she was out the back. As he carried the plates towards the counter, Nick noticed a familiar tree standing on one of the tables by the window. It was the wishing tree from the fete, the white labels still dangling from its branches. He'd forgotten all about it and was just scanning the QR code with his phone when Laurie came out of the kitchen, drying her hands on a tea towel. 'Hey, what are you up to?' She settled for leaning her head against his arm for a long moment because a hug would mean she'd be straight back in the kitchen washing her hands.

'Hey. I accidentally ate Mum's lunch so I came to get another sandwich and a piece of cake for her.'

'How do you accidentally eat someone else's lunch?' Laurie shook her head as she walked back behind the counter and pulled a couple of slices of wholemeal bread from a bag. 'Never mind, I forgot who I was talking to. Aurora not with you?'

'She's next door buying up half the shop.' Nick pointed to the wishing tree. 'How did you end up with this in here?'

Laurie rolled her eyes. 'I got knitting-circled.' They shared a laugh. 'It was only meant to be a temporary thing when we were clearing up after the fete but then I thought I might as well hang on to it in case anyone missed it on Sunday and wanted to donate.'

Nick held up his phone. 'It's a good job you did because I forgot all about it.' He opened the GoFundMe page and whistled when he saw the total. The fund was sitting at over 180 per cent of its target total. 'The people of this village never fail to surprise me at the levels of their generosity.'

'I think we might have our very own secret Santa to thank this year.' When Nick looked over at her, Laurie was grinning from ear to ear. 'Scroll down through the donations.'

He did as she suggested and stopped when he got about a third of the way down. There was an anonymous donation for the original total the fete committee had set of £2,000. 'Wow, that's amazing.'

'Isn't it? And I have it on good authority that the RNLI got a £10k donation, which is double the target they'd set for the event.'

Nick shot her a stunned look. 'Are you serious?'

Laurie nodded. She sliced the sandwich she'd made in half and popped it on a clean plate together with a piece of rocky road, then handed it to Nick. 'I think we both know who to thank, don't you?'

It suddenly dawned on him what she was hinting at. 'She never said anything.'

'And that's just another reason to like her.' Laurie grinned. 'Not that I think you need any more reasons to like her.'

He laughed. 'True. Still, I wonder why she didn't mention it?'

His sister shrugged. 'Maybe because she didn't want anyone making a fuss about it. Look, I don't have any proof that it was her, but I can't think of anyone else with that level of disposable income who has a vested interested in the village, can you?'

Nick had to admit Laurie had a point. Their friends and neighbours did what they could, but the lean times were never far behind when your economy was dependent on so many varying factors. 'Perhaps the old legends are true, and mermaids do bring good luck to the Point.'

'Aurora has certainly blessed a lot of us with good fortune.' Laurie reached beneath the counter and produced a sealed paper bag with little dog bones printed on it. 'Sorry to change the subject, but I'm trying something new and need some consumer research. Can you give these to Gabriel and see if he likes them?'

Nick held the package up and studied it. 'Dog biscuits?'

Laurie nodded. 'I'm trying to think of things that I can sell online to keep things ticking over for the next few months, especially when Easter is a late one next year.' Now the pre-Christmas rush was all but over, the next real opportunity to welcome a large volume of visitors would be the long Easter school holidays.

'At least the weather should be good with it being later.' Nick immediately crossed his fingers. The one thing that you didn't do in a coastal community was tempt fate by predicting the weather. 'I never said that.'

'I never heard a thing,' Laurie said, holding up her own crossed fingers. 'Hey, are you guys joining us at Mum and Dad's for breakfast on Wednesday?'

'Dad mentioned it, but Aurora has agreed to help Emily with her hair and make-up so I'm not sure what time she needs to be at the surgery.'

Laurie smiled. 'Mum, Ivy and I had already planned to help Nerissa and Emily so that will work out perfectly. Tom and Max are getting ready at Mum and Dad's so you can stay and hang out with them.'

'Sounds like a plan. Look, I'd better get this food back to Mum before she completely disowns me. We'll see you on Wednesday.'

17

Unlike the previous few mornings, Christmas Eve didn't so much dawn as creep out reluctantly from behind a thick blanket of cloud. The air hung heavy, the kind of dank cold that chilled you to the bone in minutes. Gabriel barely stuck his nose out of the front door long enough to take a pee before he scampered back in and straight up the stairs. Aurora couldn't say she blamed him and was starting to rethink the wisdom of sitting in a stone church on what felt like it might be the coldest day of the year in a silk jumpsuit. As she followed the dog back up to Nick's apartment, she did a mental inventory of her wardrobe and concluded that as neither leather trousers nor fleecy leggings were wedding-appropriate attire, she would just have to grin and bear it. She followed her nose all the way to the kitchen where Nick was brewing a huge pot of coffee and decided it was only fair to give him an update on the weather by shoving her cold hands up the back of his T-shirt and placing them on the small of his back. 'Bloody hell!' He reached behind him and tugged her arms away, but only long enough to turn around and pull her into his arms. 'You have a very mean streak, you know?' he grumbled as he bent to kiss her. He tasted like mint toothpaste and lazy mornings, and she wanted to start every day just like this.

'What time do we have to go?' She cast a glance over her shoulder towards the bedroom door, not even trying to be subtle about it.

'If we want to make breakfast then we need to be out of here in about forty-five minutes.'

Aurora heaved an exaggerated sigh of disappointment. They had spent most of the previous day in bed, but she'd never believed in the old adage that one could have too much of good thing. Laughing, Nick took her hand and led her not towards the bedroom, but towards the bathroom and its very large shower cubicle. 'The trouble with you,' he said as he stripped off both their pyjamas in between kisses, 'is that you need to think a little more creatively.'

Fifty minutes later, Aurora was still congratulating herself on what she thought had been some *very* creative thinking as she finished fastening Gabriel into the warmest of the little jackets Nick had bought for him. It was made of thick red fleece and decorated with white snowflakes, and had a little hood with cut-outs for his ears and tail to stick through. 'You look gorgeous,' she told the little terrier as she clipped on his lead.

'Why, thank you,' Nick quipped as he finished zipping up his padded coat and tugged on a pair of gloves. 'Are you sure you've got everything you need in here?' He indicated the wheeled suitcase into which she had packed her outfit, several different options of footwear and accessories and her full make-up and hair kit. 'I'm sure we could squeeze in the kitchen sink.'

'Stop moaning and start carrying,' she ordered. 'You know it's the only reason I keep you around.'

'Yes, ma'am.' Nick did that silly forelock tug and hefted the much smaller rucksack that contained his gear onto his back. Draping his thin suit-carrier over one arm, Aurora gave a reluctant Gabriel an encouraging click of her tongue and followed Nick out the front door.

The cold hit them like a wet slap the moment they set foot outside. Aurora wasn't sure if the mist had come up from the ground or the clouds had lowered to hang around their heads, but either way she wasn't a fan. She was grateful her trademark messy hairstyle meant wearing a hat wasn't a problem. A splash of water and a quick fiddle around with some gel would sort it out once she reached the surgery later. Clearly as keen to be back in the warm as quickly as possible, Nick set out at a brisk pace. They made it to the seafront before Gabriel began to whine. Bending down, Aurora pulled off her glove and touched the cold pavement before pulling back with a shiver. 'Poor boy. We should've got you some little boots to protect your paws.' She was just wondering how she could manage the suit-carrier and carry the dog when Nick solved the conundrum by scooping Gabriel up and tucking him inside the front of his coat. He zipped it back to just under the terrier's chin, leaving only his red-hooded face poking out. He looked so adorable Aurora couldn't resist whipping out her phone and taking a few photos. Her phone pinged, not for the first time that morning, and she flicked open the WhatsApp group Sylvia had created for the wedding. 'Your mum wants to know how much longer we're going to be.'

'Why don't you tell her the reason we're running late,' Nick teased. Trying to pretend it was the biting cold that was making her cheeks red, Aurora sent one of the photos she'd just taken of Gabriel and assured Sylvia they were on their way. Half a dozen heart-eyed emoji reactions sprang up on the corner of the photo before she had a chance to close the app. Nick took hold of the handle of the case and began towing it once more, his other arm tucked underneath the bulge in his jacket to make sure Gabriel didn't slip.

They were almost at the end of the street when a voice called out behind them and they turned to find a red-faced Barbara Mitchell hustling along the pavement towards them. 'I thought it was you!' she exclaimed as she came to stop just in front of them.

'Morning, Barbara,' Nick said. 'We're on our way to Mum's for breakfast before we get ready for the wedding.'

If he'd said it in the hope she would let them get on their way, it didn't work. Ignoring his comment, she turned to Aurora and placed a hand on her arm. 'I'm so sorry about that awful rubbish in the paper today. Honestly, when I find out who's been speaking out of turn they will get more than a damn flea in their ear, I can tell you!'

It took all of Aurora's stage training to keep her voice even as she said, 'I haven't seen the papers this morning. I'm on a self-imposed media and socials ban.'

'Oh, I don't blame you!' Barbara was still patting her arm. 'Honestly, it's all rubbish. Not even worth wrapping tomorrow's fish and chips in. Still, it's not right for them to imply the two of you are pretending to be together, or that you've somehow bribed the village into supporting you...' She shook her head as she trailed off.

Aurora exchanged a fearful look with Nick. What the hell was going on? 'Which paper are you talking about, Barbara?' Nick asked, his voice terse.

'It's in *The Daily Extra* – that awful Carly King who was hanging around the village, remember? It's her column.' Barely pausing to draw breath, Barbara turned back to Aurora. 'I mean we all *knew* it had to be you who'd made those very generous donations, but we wouldn't have dreamt of saying anything because you did it anonymously.'

'Oh.' Aurora closed her eyes for a long moment. She should've known better than to think she could get away with it, but she'd been so touched by the simplicity of the requests made on the wishing tree that she'd wanted to make sure all of them were met. It had also become clear to her just how vital the RNLI's work was to a seaside community like Mermaids Point so she'd wanted to do what she could to help them too.

'Here.' Nick handed her his phone, subtly positioning his body between Aurora and Barbara to give her some privacy. Taking a deep breath, Aurora scanned the gossip column.

A Storm in a Teacup, or Something Fishy?

After that photo and that kiss at the airport, I needed to know more about Aurora Storm and her Mystery Hottie. Thanks to a tip-off from one of you, I made a quick trip down to the remote seaside village of Mermaids Point. Aurora fans will no doubt remember it as the location where she staged her viral video comeback pretending to be a mermaid. Where did Ms Storm disappear off to, by the way? I'd love to know!

Anyway, it turns out that Aurora's convenient new boyfriend is Nick Morgan, a resident of the village and something of a ladies' man according to sources on the ground. I bumped into the pair of them at the most adorable Christmas party in the local bookshop, but they weren't keen to chat about their relationship. Locals apparently pride themselves on the warm welcome they offer to visitors, but sadly I found it to be in very short supply.

Was my frosty reception down to the weather, or is there something more to the eager way in which the residents defended their newest addition's privacy? I'm sure they are simply delighted that Aurora has found true love with one of their own and it's nothing at all to do with the very generous anonymous donations that were recently made to support the village's charity Christmas fete.

The column continued with another story, or should that be another hatchet job? Thankfully, Nick was still keeping Barbara occupied, giving Aurora precious moments to compose herself. It wasn't the first nasty article she'd had written about her, and she was damn certain it wouldn't be the last, especially with Chad and Melissa's antics still hanging over her. Still, this one hurt more because it wasn't only aimed at her. Nick didn't deserve to be dragged under the microscope, nor did the lovely residents of the Point. It was all so unfair. There was nothing she could do about it, other than put a brave face on things. Stepping up beside Nick, Aurora handed him back his phone before tucking her arm through his with a smile. 'Well, we knew something like that was coming, didn't we?' Before he could answer, Aurora turned to Barbara. 'I really appreciate you drawing this to my attention, Barbara. The press are a law unto themselves, unfortunately. I'm used to their tricks, but it's not fair that you and the rest of the committee have been sullied by these ugly insinuations. I only meant to do good with my donations, but I should've realised reporters would be poking around looking for gossip and found a more discreet way to do it.'

Barbara stiffened, the picture of indignation. 'You've got nothing to apologise for! No one worth their salt will give this rubbish any credence.' The look on her face made Aurora almost feel sorry for anyone who did give the story any merit.

Aurora glanced back at Nick. 'I think perhaps I should give the wedding a miss and go home. The last thing I want is to be a distraction on today of all days.'

'If you don't go then people will talk about the fact you aren't there,' he countered. 'The only thing to do is to ignore this just like we are ignoring everything else.'

'Nick has a point, dear,' Barbara said. 'You shouldn't let this derail your plans for the day, and I wouldn't worry too much about it spoiling Nerissa and Tom's wedding. Anyone who tries to cause trouble on that front will have the whole village to answer to! We've waited too long for Nerissa to find the happiness she deserves to let a bit of nasty gossip interfere.'

Feeling like she had no other option, Aurora reluctantly nodded. 'Okay.'

'Good girl.' Barbara gave her arm another one of those motherly pats. 'Now, I must be on my way. I'll see you both at the wedding.' With that she turned on her heel and marched off down the pavement like a woman on a mission.

Nick reached out and tucked Aurora against him, taking care not to squash Gabriel, who was still wedged inside the warmth of his jacket. 'I'm sorry I've dragged you into all this,' she sighed.

He pressed a kiss to the top of her head. 'I'm not.'

Aurora pulled back and shot him a look of disbelief. 'Surely you don't like having your name splashed all over the papers?'

'One bitchy gossip column is hardly a splash, now, is it? Besides, I wouldn't care if my name was plastered across the front page, because what's the alternative? I made a choice when I saw those photographers at the airport. I could've walked away then, but I didn't. I'll never walk away from you, Aurora. You're everything I've ever wanted and if being with you means I have to deal with crap like this now and then, it's a price I'm happy to pay.'

How did he always know just the right thing to say? 'I love you. You know that, don't you?'

'I do.' He leaned forward and captured her lips with his own. 'Feel free to tell me again, though.'

* * *

Though she was fit from the strenuous hours of training her stage routines required, the hill leading up to Nick's parents' house was still steep enough to make Aurora puff a little. 'Nearly there,' Nick assured her when she paused for a second to suck in a mouthful of the damp air.

She hadn't paid much attention to the properties they'd walked past so she took a quick look around and immediately spotted the For Sale sign in front of a faded double-fronted property. A gold-lettered plaque on the wall read 'Hillside B & B'. The tarmac parking area was cracked and in need of renewing and the whole building had a tired air about it, as if it was crying out for some serious maintenance. 'Needs a lick of paint,' she observed, adjusting the suit-carrier so it didn't catch on the ground.

'Needs more than a lick of paint,' Nick replied, with a shake of his head as he began to walk. 'It's like a seventies time warp inside.'

'You've been in it recently?' Aurora was intrigued by the idea.

Nick shook his head. 'Not exactly. Alun sent me the details as soon as it came on the market. He thinks it could be my next refurbishment project.'

Aurora turned to look backwards, her gaze roving over the tatty building. The roof had been converted at some point so it sprawled over three storeys and she could see from the slightly different shades in the pebble-dashed veneer that it had been two houses at some point. 'What would you do with it?' When Nick didn't answer, she turned again to see he was almost at the front door of a modern townhouse. Hurrying to catch up, she asked her question again.

Nick pressed the bell then immediately turned the handle of the door before answering her. 'Nothing until I can get the financing sorted, and that won't happen until the sale on the other downstairs apartment finally goes through.' He pushed open the door and entered to a chorus of greetings while Aurora found herself staring back down the hill. *I wonder...*

The Morgans' house was blessedly warm after their chilly walk and Aurora was soon swept inside on a tide of hugs while Jake took the suit-carrier from her arm and hung it up from the top of one of the door frames next to another one, which she assumed he'd brought with him. They'd barely finished stripping off their coats and hats when the doorbell rang again and Alex and Ivy arrived to add to the mayhem and milling bodies. With lots of laughing and arm waving, Andrew eventually got everyone into the dining room, where the table was laid with glasses full of orange juice and baskets of pastries. 'Dig in, everyone,' he urged before disappearing towards what Aurora assumed was the kitchen.

'I hope everyone remembered their Spanx,' Sylvia said with a grin as she appeared with a huge teapot and set it in the middle of the table. 'Andrew's been cooking up a storm.'

She wasn't kidding. The table was soon heaving with platters of bacon, sausages, cooked tomatoes and mushrooms. Aurora seemed to be the only one fazed by the amount of food, and by the fact Andrew disappeared into the kitchen once more to return with a massive stack of Scotch pancakes and a jug of syrup. 'Don't let it get cold,' he said as he finally took the remaining empty chair. 'We decided it was probably best to feed everyone up. You know what it's like at wedding buffets, everyone is too busy talking to eat properly.'

'Speak for yourself,' Nick said with a grin as he speared a couple of sausages and put one on his plate and the other on Aurora's. 'Some of us have our priorities right!' He helped himself to a couple of pancakes and doused them in syrup before offering the jug to Aurora.

She shook her head, opting for a couple of slices of toast so she could make herself a sausage sandwich. 'Has anyone spoken to Nerissa this morning?' Aurora couldn't help but wonder if she'd seen the newspaper column.

'She's fine,' Ivy said with a grin, before her face grew serious. 'I know what you're worried about and you can stop it, right now.' A murmur of agreement rippled around the table.

'You've all seen it, then?'

'And we're treating it with the contempt it deserves,' Sylvia said in a voice that said that was the end of the matter.

'As I was saying, Nerissa's fine,' Ivy said, picking up her earlier thread. 'It's Tom I'm worried about.' She turned to Alex. 'How many times has he panic-texted you this morning?'

'Seven, I think?' Alex tugged out his phone and checked the screen. 'No, make that eight. The flowers have just been delivered and he thinks the buttonholes are too big.' He set his phone down and picked up his knife and fork. 'I hope you've got some brandy to hand, Andrew.'

'Don't think my sister-in-law is going to marry your brother while he's stinking of booze,' Sylvia warned Alex, pointing her fork at him.

'The brandy is for me,' he deadpanned, and Aurora couldn't stop a loud snort of laughter.

All eyes turned towards her, and she wanted to shrink in embarrassment, but she forced herself to sit up straight. There was only one way to manage in a boisterous group like this and that was to hold your own, even if she wasn't naturally extroverted. People assumed because she loved being onstage, loved the energy from a crowd who were all having a great time because of her, that she was outgoing all the time. The first few times she'd had to perform in public she'd needed a bucket at the side of the stage. The Morgans were lovely people and they couldn't have made her feel more welcome, but they were also a lot to deal with when they all got together like this. 'It's my laugh, get used to it.' She took a large bite out of her sandwich to underline her point.

'It's certainly... something,' Laurie said, with a wink.

'Well, I like it,' Andrew said, reaching across the table to pat Aurora's hand. 'Pay this lot no mind, my lovely girl, and just carry on being yourself.'

The conversation turned to a discussion about timings for the wedding and Aurora sat back, happy to let it flow around her. She was still not quite sure of the dynamics of the group, but she was getting there. Jake was quiet like her, though when he did speak it was often to deliver a devastating takedown of Nick or Alex. Their friendship was clearly born from proximity and circumstance, but Aurora got the impression the three of them were a solid team. Any attempts at teasing from outside their triumvirate were staunchly defended against. The bond between Ivy and Laurie was softer and ran much deeper, their conversational cues the kind of shorthand that only came from years of friendship. They both made attempts to draw Aurora back into the chat, asking her opinion or addressing a particular observation to her. She wasn't sure if it was a conscious effort to include her, but she appreciated it nonetheless. She wasn't quite part of this group, not yet, but she could see a point where she would fit in as seamlessly as Jake and Alex now did. It surprised her how much she wanted to get to that point. Something shifted inside her as she watched

Sylvia pause in the act of gathering dirty plates to kiss her husband. She didn't just want to be a part of Nick's life; she wanted to be a part of this family.

Nick curled his arm around the back of her chair and leaned close. 'Everything all right?' he murmured against her ear.

Turning in her chair, Aurora smiled up at him. 'Everything is wonderful. I'm so glad I have the chance to share today with you all.'

His hand caressed her shoulder. 'I'm sorry for all the hassle you're going through right now, but I'm not sorry it's brought you back to me.'

'Me neither.' And for all the hurt and upset of the past few days, she wouldn't have changed a thing because there was nowhere in the world she'd rather be.

18

'If I'd had any sense I would've dropped this bloody suitcase off on the way to yours,' Aurora grumbled as they finally arrived at the surgery.

'At least it was downhill,' Sylvia observed as she adjusted the strap on the large holdall hooked over her shoulder. 'Come on, we'll go in round the back.' She led the four of them around the side of the large white building and down a path that opened out into a sizeable back garden, which was deserted apart from a plastic football goal that was tilted against the fence as though blown there by the wind. As Nick had done at their house, Sylvia announced herself with a knock and immediately opened the door. 'I'm looking for a beautiful bride!' she called out as she stepped inside.

'I'm afraid you'll have to put up with a handsome groom,' Tom said, rising from the kitchen table to give Sylvia a kiss on the cheek.

'Well, you look a lot calmer than I expected,' Sylvia said in her no-nonsense way. 'From Alex's reports I expected to find you climbing the walls by now.'

Tom rolled his eyes as he moved to give Ivy a kiss next. 'What's that idiot brother of mine been saying now?'

Laughing, Ivy draped the suit-carrier she'd been holding over the back of a chair and gave Tom a hug. 'You did wake him at 5 a.m. in a panic about the weather,' she chided him gently.

He cast a scowl towards the leaden sky outside. 'The forecast all week has said it was going to be bright and sunny, and now look at it.' He grabbed his phone from the kitchen table and thrust it under Ivy's nose. 'Look at it now. Bloody snow from lunchtime onwards!'

'There's only a 40 per cent chance,' Sylvia said in a soothing voice as she took his phone away and put it back down. 'You know how rare it is for us to catch it; I bet it blows right past us.'

'I still think we should've booked cars for the day.' He checked his watch. 'I suppose it's too late to think about that now.' He caught Aurora's eye and sent her an apologetic smile. 'Hello! Sorry, where are my manners. Please, make yourself at home.' He turned back to Sylvia. 'Nerissa's upstairs; I'll give her a shout.'

'No you won't.' His almost sister-in-law shook her head. 'You'll get your stuff and take yourself off to ours and leave us ladies in peace.'

Tom opened his mouth to protest, and Aurora had to hide a smile when Laurie placed a hand on his arm. 'Think how much quieter and calmer it'll be.'

'But it's quiet and cal—'

'Max!' Sylvia bellowed up the stairs. 'Put down that game controller and get yourself down here on the double.' Without waiting for a reply, she turned to point at Aurora, Laurie and Ivy. 'You girls head on up and see how Nerissa and Emily are getting on while I finish sorting Tom out.'

If she'd been a bit braver, the pleading look Tom shot in their direction might have made Aurora inclined to intervene on his behalf. Shooting him an apologetic grin, Aurora grabbed the handle of her case. At the same moment, a tall, lanky body came flying down the stairs and Max skidded to a stop on the kitchen tiles. He was still wearing his pyjamas. 'I thought I told you to have a shower an hour ago?' Tom said, sounding like he was about ready to give up on the day.

'Chill out, Dad. It'll take me five minutes, that's all.' One look at the matching expressions on Tom and Sylvia's faces had Aurora wincing behind the teenager's back.

'That's our cue,' Ivy said, giving Aurora a nudge. 'Let's get out of the way before all hell breaks loose.'

'I'm right behind you,' Laurie agreed, taking the suit-carrier Ivy had left on the chair in one hand and her own small suitcase in the other.

The scene upstairs wasn't any better than what they'd left behind. Nerissa was sitting on the end of a king size bed in her dressing gown, her head covered in a mass of huge rollers. She was staring forlornly at the nail on her ring finger, which was considerably shorter than the others. 'I knew it was too much to hope for,' she said, holding up her hand to display the jagged edge.

Now this *was* something Aurora could handle. 'Give me a couple of minutes to get set up and I'll soon have that fixed for you,' she promised Nerissa. She steered her case to the corner of the room, laid it down and flipped it open. The first thing she did was lift out her jacket and jumpsuit, which she'd folded carefully with sheets of packing paper to keep the creases out. She shook the jumpsuit and hooked it quickly on a hanger, glancing around for somewhere to hang it out of the way.

'Oh, what a gorgeous colour,' Nerissa exclaimed, her woes over her ruined manicure momentarily forgotten. 'I cleared a space in the wardrobe for everyone to hang their things.' Standing from the bed, she opened the door on a large pine wardrobe and held out her hand. Aurora hooked the black velvet jacket onto the same hanger and passed it over. Ivy laid her carrier on the bed and unzipped it to reveal an emerald-green fifties-style tea dress with a pleated skirt.

Aurora caught sight of the label and her admiration for Ivy's taste went even higher than before. 'You and I really need to go on a shopping trip one of these days.'

Ivy handed the dress to Nerissa, then offered Aurora a shy smile. 'I'd love that.'

'Count me in,' Laurie said as she opened her own case. Instead of a dress, she pulled out a pair of navy-blue wide-legged velvet trousers and a cream blouse. She hung both on separate hangers and added a shiny blue sash to the trousers. She was already wearing a long cream wool coat and a navy beret, which would look fabulous over the top of her outfit.

'I'll go and check on Em, shall I?' Laurie asked when they'd finished hanging everything up.

'She was having a bath last time I looked,' Nerissa said, then immediately checked the delicate gold watch on her wrist.

Reaching out, Ivy pushed her hand down with a gentle smile. 'There's plenty of time. Sit down and relax and let Aurora fix your nails.'

Aurora had just finished laying all her kit out on the top of the dressing table when there was a tap at the open door. 'I thought I heard voices.' It was Linda, Jake's mother. Dressed in a pair of leggings and a T-shirt, her hair was also up in rollers, but much smaller ones. She had a bottle of champagne in one hand and the stems of half a dozen flutes dangling from the fingers of the other. 'Is it too early to start celebrating?'

'Definitely not!' Ivy took the bottle from her and began twisting the wire collar free with an impressive amount of expertise.

'Ooh, bubbles!' Laurie said, returning to join them with a pink-cheeked Emily in tow. Ivy eased the cork free with a satisfying pop and they all oohed in appreciation.

'I sweet-talked Dave into letting me *borrow* a couple of the ones that he got in for the reception,' Linda said with a grin. 'The other one's upstairs in my fridge so it stays cold until we want it.'

'I've brought some champagne, too,' Aurora said, reaching into her bag to pull out the vintage bottle of Dom Perignon. 'But it's not for sharing, I'm afraid.' She handed it to Nerissa. 'It's for you and Tom, just a little token to say thank you for including me today.'

'That's so lovely of you,' Nerissa said, accepting the bottle with a smile. 'I'm going to hide it in the bottom of the wardrobe, so it doesn't get guzzled by accident.' She held out her free hand to Aurora. 'I'm sorry about that horrible column in the paper; are you okay?'

Taking her hand, Aurora squeezed it. 'I'm fine, just worried about casting a shadow over your special day.'

'Oh, don't even give that a second thought! Now let's have some bubbles and get this party started!'

'Hear, hear,' Linda said as she handed the first glass of straw-coloured liquid to Nerissa then a second to Laurie. 'Where's your mother got to?'

'Downstairs, helping Tom get sorted.' Laurie made a set of air quotes with her free hand as she said the word 'helping'.

'Oh dear, should I go and rescue him?' Nerissa asked, half-rising from the bed.

'You sit and relax,' Ivy ordered. 'I'll go and find out what's going on and fetch another glass.' She was back a few moments later, shooing Max before her. 'Just put anything on for now and you can have a shower when you get to Uncle Andrew's house.' She stood on the threshold, shaking her head. 'I think Tom and Sylvia are going to come to blows if someone doesn't intervene.'

Nerissa jumped up, almost spilling her champagne in the process. 'What on earth is going on?'

'Tom is arguing with her about trying to find a car to take you to the church. He also wants to say goodbye to you before he and Max head off but Sylvia's giving him all that "bad luck to see the bride before the wedding" stuff.'

'Oh, for goodness' sake! We woke up in the same bed this morning.' Nerissa thrust her glass at Aurora, who had no choice but to grab it, then tugged on the belt of her dressing gown to tighten it before marching from the room.

'I'm not missing this!' Laurie said with a grin and followed on her aunt's heels. The rest of them exchanged a look and scurried after them.

They reached the bottom of the stairs in time to see Nerissa plant her hands on her hips. 'Sylvia Morgan, will you please stop terrorising my future husband?' Her sister-in-law gaped like a fish and Aurora made a silent bet to herself that it was probably one of the few times Sylvia had been lost for words. Nerissa rounded on Tom and pointed a finger at him. 'You stop faffing about and get your act together. We are getting married today even if I have to wade to the church through a waist-deep snowdrift. I don't care how cold it is, I'm walking to the church like every other woman in my family has done since Mermaids Point was a handful of cottages and the church was a wooden hut.'

Tom stared at Nerissa, his stunned expression a picture-perfect match of Sylvia's, then he burst out laughing. 'God, I love you.'

'I love you too. Now come here and kiss me and then go away because my champagne is going flat.'

Two steps and Tom had Nerissa swept up in his arms and was kissing her like they were the only two people in the room. Sylvia gave a loud tut, but she was grinning as she came to join them at the foot of the stairs. 'Oh my,' someone murmured from behind Aurora and she was grateful for an excuse to turn away.

Her eyes met Linda's and they shared a grin. 'Oh my, indeed.' Aurora raised her free hand and fanned it in front of her face. She saw Linda's gaze stray beyond her shoulder and couldn't hold in a giggle. 'Are they still going?'

'Yup.' Linda took the glass of champagne from Aurora's hand and knocked back what was left in that. 'I'll tell you something,' she said in what Aurora assumed was a deliberately loud voice. 'Pete's really going to have to pick up his game.'

'Well, all I can say is some talents run in the family,' Ivy said in a satisfied voice.

Tom surfaced from the kiss long enough to send them a mock glare. 'Go away!'

Laughing like a bunch of schoolgirls, they hurried each other back up the stairs to find Max waiting at the top. He was dressed in jeans and a thick jumper, a rucksack on his back.

'I'd wait a few moments before you go downstairs,' his sister warned him as she handed him a bag with her overnight things in it. The children would be staying at Andrew and Sylvia's house after the reception.

'Are they at it again?' He groaned, ducking his head out of the way of his sister's fussing. 'Leave it, I need a shower anyway.'

Emily gave a loud sniff. 'You sure do.'

Max pulled a face then laughed. 'I walked right into that one, didn't I? Right, I'd better go and break it up. See you later.' He stomped his foot loudly on the first step. 'I'm coming down now!' he called out, then banged his other foot down on the next step. 'Here I come!' Stomp. 'On my way to the kitchen!' Stomp. 'Halfway down the stairs!' Stomp. 'I'm already traumatised enough as it is!' Stomp.

A very flush-cheeked Nerissa appeared at the bottom of the stairs. One of her rollers was dangling from the end of a loose section of her hair and she was hastily retying her dressing gown. 'Have you got everything you need?' she asked Max as they met on the stairs.

'Yeeeees.' He dragged the word out in an exaggerated sigh.

'Good boy.' Nerissa cupped his cheek. 'You'll look after your dad today for me, won't you?'

'Of course.' Max leaned in for a hug. 'I can't wait until you're my bonus mum.'

Aurora had to turn away again before the touching moment made her start crying. She shared a watery smile with Laurie. 'Remind me to put extra tissues in my bag; I think I'm going to need them.'

'Me too.' Laurie put an arm around her waist as they headed back into the bedroom to wait for Nerissa, and Aurora had to suck in a deep breath at the casual intimacy of the gesture. She really had a place here amongst these kind, funny people.

Thanks to the best stick-on nails Aurora had ever found courtesy of a make-up artist's tip, Nerissa's manicure was soon restored. While Sylvia and Laurie unwound the rollers from Nerissa's hair and fastened the rippling waves back, Aurora used her hot wand to transform Emily's ruler-straight hair into a series of soft waves. She wove the two side sections into braids and secured them around Emily's head like a crown. Rather than flowers, Emily had chosen some pretty spiral clips decorated with crystalline snowflakes and Aurora soon had them fixed into the braided crown. There wasn't much space in the bedroom so they took it in turns to get changed in one of the other rooms until only Emily and Nerissa were left to get into their dresses. Aurora went with Emily to help her into a beautiful ice-blue gown with elbow-length sleeves. The top half of the dress was an intricate lace cinched at the waist with a simple silk band and falling away in delicate layers of chiffon to the floor. 'You look so beautiful,' Aurora said, stepping back to admire the outfit.

'You really think so?' Emily's little smile said she knew it was true, and Aurora was delighted in her self-confidence. Too many young women worried about their appearance, hiding behind filters and heavy layers of make-up.

'One hundred per cent gorgeous.' Aurora lifted her phone. 'Shall I take some photos and I can send them to you?'

Emily stood still for a few sensible ones, then asked Aurora if they could take a selfie together. By the time they'd finished pulling goofy faces and striking ridiculous poses, they were both out of breath from laughing. 'Sit on the bed and I'll help you with your shoes,' Aurora said when they'd calmed down.

Emily sat and pulled up the hem of her dress to reveal her thick white tights. 'You think they'll be okay?'

Picking up one of the white Converse trainers that had been covered in lace and diamond sparkles – no doubt with the help of Ivy's glue gun – Aurora helped Emily slide her foot into it. 'I think they're fabulous. I'm going to buy a pair for myself and bling them up.'

'They're not too casual?' Emily stuck out her foot and twisted her ankle from side to side.

'Would you rather be wearing something with a wafer-thin sole and a spindly heel and have frostbite in your toes by the time we get to the church?' Aurora had already had the same thought when she'd realised they were all walking up together. 'If I can wear my Uggs, then you can wear these.' She rose from her crouch and shook out the legs of her jump-suit. 'Come on, let's get you into your coat and then we can see how Nerissa's getting on.'

Nerissa was just emerging from her bedroom and Aurora felt her breath catch in her throat at the sight of her. Her dress was off-white, almost café au lait, and covered in swirls of chiffon that looked like the entire thing was made of roses. The bodice was studded with crystals and ended in delicate cap sleeves. Behind her, a beaming Sylvia was carrying a coat over her arm that had soft faux-fur details at the sleeves and neck. 'Don't say anything nice to me,' Nerissa warned with a laugh. 'I've already had to do my make-up twice and if I go off again my nose will be redder than Rudolph's in all the photographs.'

Aurora laughed. 'I won't say a word, I promise!' Seeing that everyone else was ready to go, she hurried around them into Nerissa's bedroom to retrieve her jacket and boots. 'Where's the rest of my stuff?' She looked around the room, which had been tidied of all evidence of their prepara-tion party.

'We put everything upstairs in my flat,' Linda said, holding a small box in her hand. 'You can nip back later and take your stuff home or pick it up in a couple of days if there's nothing you desperately need. I'll be staying at the pub for the next few nights to give Nerissa and Tom a bit of privacy.' She opened the box and scattered a handful of red rose petals over the crisp white sheets. 'That should do it.'

Down in the kitchen, Aurora was presented with a wrist corsage made with white roses, rich, dark greenery and miniature pinecones that had been sprayed gold. It matched the two bouquets resting in a box on the table, a round posy for Emily and a more elaborate trailing one for Nerissa. 'I think we're all set,' Sylvia said as she reached for her sister-in-law's hand. 'Are you ready to become Mrs Nelson?'

Nerissa cast a long look over them all and nodded. 'I'm ready.'

The worst of the damp air had lifted, though the grey-tipped clouds hid all trace of the sun. Aurora tugged the collar of her velvet jacket a little higher and was grateful she'd chosen sense over style as they began to walk along the seafront. A small group of women were waiting on the corner next to the pub and as they drew nearer, Aurora recognised the ladies from the knitting circle amongst them. Nerissa paused to accept hugs, well wishes and a couple of horseshoes hanging from silk ribbons, which she hooked over her hand, so they dangled beside her bouquet. One or two cast a quick glance at Aurora, and when they caught her eye it was only to give her a reassuring smile. Barbara had clearly put the word out. As they moved on, Aurora was surprised to note the older ladies joined the back of their small group. They turned the corner and there were more women waiting along the road. Some greeted Nerissa as the knitting circle had with kisses and well wishes; others were content to swell the numbers of their group. On they walked through the village and on the women came. Aurora spotted one or two men waiting with their wives, but they walked on ahead as the bridal party approached. 'Do you do this for every wedding?' Aurora murmured to Laurie.

Laurie smiled. 'It depends. Incomers don't always understand or want it, but older families like mine are strong on tradition.'

'Well, I think it's beautiful.'

'I do, too,' Ivy said from her other side. 'When we had Mum's funeral at the beginning of the year, everyone came out and it made an awful day a little bit easier to bear. It's one of the things I love most about the Point: we stand by each other through the very best and the very worst of times.' Her voice hitched a little at the end and without thinking twice Aurora reached out and took her hand. Ivy gave her a little squeeze and they continued on like that.

The final stretch towards the church was uphill, but thankfully not as steep as the one the Morgans lived on. About halfway up, a woman was standing on her own. 'Oh God, it's Margot,' Laurie whispered, exchanging a stricken look with Ivy. Before Aurora could ask, Laurie continued. 'Nerissa was engaged to Margot's son, Gareth, when they were both in their late teens. He joined the army and was killed in a road traffic accident while on a peacekeeping mission in the Balkans.' Behind them, a low hum of chatter arose, and Aurora didn't need to hear what was being said because it was bound to be a variation of their own conversation. Everyone here would know all the ins and outs of the drama playing out before them.

'How awful. For both of them,' she murmured, more to herself than anything else. Aurora watched as Nerissa moved ahead of them and approached Margot. Sylvia took a couple of steps as though she would follow, then stopped.

Laurie nodded, her eyes fixed on her mum, a worried frown marring her brow. 'Things have been difficult between them ever since. I hope Margot isn't going to upset her on today of all days. I'm going to check on Mum.' She strode away to join Sylvia, taking her hand and bending her head close. Whatever she said, it seemed to relax her mother enough that Sylvia's tense shoulders slackened. She nodded in agreement and let Laurie lead her back to where the rest of them were waiting.

Ivy squeezed Aurora's fingers. 'I don't think we have anything to worry about; look, Margot is smiling.' They watched Margot lean forward to pin something on Nerissa's jacket before the two women embraced. As Nerissa walked back towards them, Margot turned and entered a nearby house, closing the door quietly behind her.

'Daffodils,' Nerissa said to Sylvia as she touched a finger to the little yellow brooch pinned to her jacket. 'She gave me daffodils.' Tears shone in her eyes, but her smile was bright and warm. Aurora didn't understand the significance of the moment, but that didn't matter. Nerissa's joy was all that counted today.

When they arrived at the church, Andrew was waiting beside the wooden lychgate, a broad, beaming smile on his face. 'Well, you look pretty as a picture,' he said, greeting his sister with a kiss on the cheek. The wedding party stood to one side and let the rest of the women who'd accompanied them on the walk move ahead to where Nick and Alex were flanking the church doors, together with a doggie guard of honour. Gabriel on one side in his little red jacket, Toby, Nerissa's golden retriever, wearing a black bow tie and a top hat on the other. Aurora gave Nick a quick wave and he blew her a kiss before offering his arm to Barbara and leading her and the rest of the knitting circle inside to their seats.

'Coats on or off?' Sylvia asked Nerissa, then turned to her husband. 'Have you been inside yet? Do you know how cold it is?'

Andrew rubbed his hands together. 'It's warmer in there than it is out here, for sure. Come on, let's get this show on the road.'

Feeling a little awkward, Aurora stood back and let the others help Nerissa and Emily remove their coats and fiddle around getting their dresses just right. A hand touched her back and she turned to find Nick smiling down at her. 'You look beautiful. I think my ushering duties are done; shall we make our way in?'

'Yes, please.' She'd had a wonderful morning with everyone, but this moment felt too intimate, and she worried she was intruding. It wasn't anything anyone had said or done; there was just a familiarity to their movements, an unwritten code in their body language that she had yet to decipher.

Whoever had decorated the church had done a wonderful job. Wreaths of holly and ivy hung at the end of each pew and thick white candles lined the stone window ledges, casting a warm, honey-coloured light against the stained glass. At the front of the church stood a pair of flower arrangements – white roses, gold pine cones and the same dark green foliage as Aurora's corsage and Nick's matching buttonhole. As they reached the front pew on the left, Aurora hesitated for a moment, but Nick encouraged her forward with a nudge. Jake was already seated and he stood to give her a kiss on the cheek. 'Do you want to swap seats so you can sit next to Laurie?' she asked before he could sit back down.

'Probably a good idea as I'm the official hanky provider,' he said with a laugh as he patted the top pocket of his suit jacket. It was a bit awkward trying to shuffle around in the narrow pew but they managed without anyone's toes being stepped on. Aurora sat and scooted her bottom into the corner of the hard wooden bench. Nick lifted Gabriel up and took the seat beside her, settling the terrier on his lap. Aurora glanced around, and tried to catch Tom's eye to offer him an encouraging smile, but he was preoccupied with something the vicar was saying to him and Max, who was obviously going to stand with Tom as his best man. She tilted her head towards the opposite pew and shared a little wave with Philippa and Archie, who had driven up to the church because Archie's leg was still giving him a bit of bother in the cold. A few minutes later, Laurie and Sylvia slid into their pew, and Alex and Ivy joined his parents on the groom's side, settling Toby on the floor beside him.

Reverend Steele nodded to Tom and they both turned to face the aisle. *Here we go*. The first sonorous notes of the organ sent a chill down Aurora's spine and she reached for Nick's hand as she turned to try to catch a glimpse of Nerissa. It was impossible to see much through the sea of turned heads and then Emily was there, smiling from ear to ear. Tom walked a few paces down to meet her, kissed her cheek and led her to her place in front of where they were sitting. Aurora caught her eye and gave her a discreet thumbs up before she turned again in time to see Nerissa arrive on Andrew's arm. The smile on Tom's face as he shook hands with Andrew was bright enough to power every Christmas light in the village and Aurora had to swallow the huge lump in her throat.

'Oh goodness,' Laurie hiccupped, drawing Aurora's attention away from the bride and groom just long enough to see Jake whip the hanky out of his top pocket and settle a supportive arm around Laurie's shoulders. She clung tighter to Nick's hand and willed her own eyes to stay dry.

The organ music faded and Reverend Steele raised his arms wide. 'A very warm welcome to you all on this most special of days. It's wonderful to see so many family and friends...'

There was a kerfuffle from the Nelson family pew and Aurora heard a hissed 'Toby, no!' from Alex as the retriever slipped past his grabbing hand and trotted up to nose his way between Nerissa and Tom. Laughter rippled around the church as the dog sat on his haunches, looking between the two of them as his tail beat a tattoo of happiness against the flagstone floor. Tom reached down and straightened Toby's top hat, which had been knocked slightly askew, then turned to nod at the vicar to continue.

Reverend Steele cleared his throat then picked up the thread of his opening speech. '...friends, family and *canine companions* here to help Tom and Nerissa celebrate their sacred commitment to each other.'

Aurora made it through the vows without crying, though not without Nick having to adjust her grip on his hand when she squeezed it tightly enough to leave nail indents in his skin. She started to slip when Tom bent his head to kiss Nerissa and she heard him whisper 'Hello, Mrs Nelson.' The thing that completely finished Aurora off was when Nerissa held out her left hand to Emily and Tom held out his right to Max and they drew the children in for a hug. A huge round of applause rang around the church as the four of them exited together, Toby leading the way.

Aurora managed to compose herself as she followed the rest of the family out of the pew. Hers weren't the only damp eyes, she noted, as they gathered around Nerissa and Tom just outside the door for hugs and kisses. An officious photographer appeared and began bossing everyone around, or trying to at least as he was roundly ignored until everyone had finished with their congratulations. Aurora waited her turn beside Nick, giving both bride and groom a hug and a kiss.

'Family members, *please!*' There was a note of desperation in the photographer's voice, but the Morgans and the Nelsons allowed themselves to be herded to a spot on the grass nearby. Aurora stood out of the way, happy to hold on to Gabriel's lead and spectate with everyone else.

'Aurora! Where's Aurora?' called Sylvia, looking around the family group then past them to catch her eye. 'Well, are you a part of this family or not?' the older woman asked.

Was she? She looked towards Nick, who was holding out his hand to her from the edge of the group. The corners of his mouth curled up in that lazy smile that never failed to send butterflies dancing inside her. 'Yes, yes I am.'

There were more tears after the photographs when Nerissa and Tom walked hand in hand to a quiet section of the graveyard and she bent to lay her bouquet in front of a simple white headstone. Understanding the grave must belong to her former fiancé, Aurora had to turn and bury her face in Nick's shoulder. His hand slid under her hair to rest on the nape of her neck, holding her against him for a long moment while she drew in a shuddering breath. When she was able to look up at him, it was to see tears shining in his eyes too. Something white drifted between them, settled on one of Nick's lashes then melted. He blinked and they both looked up. A drop of something cold hit Aurora's cheek, another speck of white settling on the brown tangle of curls on Nick's forehead, and then the sky was a mass of fluffy white flakes. 'It's snowing,' he said, letting out a delighted laugh.

'I bloody told you we should have had cars,' Tom grumbled as he helped Nerissa into her coat and turned up the fluffy collar to rest against her chin.

'Oh, hush,' Nerissa said, pressing a kiss to his lips. 'It's romantic.'

'It won't be romantic when I have to treat half the village for pneumonia next week,' he said, but he was smiling as he dropped a kiss on the end of her nose. 'Come on, Mrs Nelson, let's go and get slightly tipsy and then I can take advantage of you.'

'Gross, Dad, just gross,' Max exclaimed.

Tom hooked an arm around his son and pulled him in for a hug. 'Give it a few years and it'll be your turn.'

'I'm never getting married,' Max declared with all the bravado of a teenage boy yet to experience the reality of what hormones were about to wreak on his peaceful existence. 'Girls are boring.'

'That's because you haven't met the right girl,' Nick called to him as he put his arm around Aurora's waist and they started following the others who were making their way towards the lychgate. The snow was falling harder now, cotton wool flakes that were already sticking to the grass. As they passed beneath the shelter of the carved oak gate, Aurora glanced back at the church. Did she dare let herself believe that *she* was the right girl, and perhaps not the next time but in a time not too distant, she and Nick would pass through this lychgate as husband and wife?

19

The pub was packed to bursting, even with Pete opening up the function room at the rear. It felt like everyone had turned out to wish Tom and Nerissa well, or had decided their wedding was the perfect excuse to start their Christmas celebrations early. Even with plenty of champagne on offer and the extra bar staff Pete had recruited, it didn't take long before Linda was behind the taps trying to keep up with the demand. Nick had followed through on his strategy of positioning himself next to the buffet table and Alex and Jake had bowed to his wisdom and they'd formed a nice cordon around the mini pork pies and Yorkshire pudding bites. Everyone had crowded in earlier for Tom and Nerissa's first dance, but now the floor was deserted apart from a few kids who were more interested in doing knee slides than dancing.

Nick had lost sight of Aurora a while ago. She'd gone off to the ladies with Ivy, because it was a truth universally acknowledged that women were incapable of visiting a public restroom alone. He checked his watch, surprised to see it was nearly forty minutes since he'd last seen her. His pint glass was almost empty, so he decided to kill two birds with one stone. 'Another?' he asked his friends, pointing at their drinks.

Jake shook his head. 'I'm going to take a break, I think. I'll have a sparkling water.'

'Actually, that doesn't sound like a bad idea; I'll snag us one of the big bottles and we can share it.' He turned to Alex. 'What about you?'

'Sounds like a plan. I can't afford to be shabby tomorrow.'

Interesting. 'Big plans for the morning, eh?'

Alex stared down at the inch of beer left in his glass for a moment before he raised his eyes and gave them both a bashful grin. 'I'm going to ask Ivy to marry me.'

'That's amazing, mate!' Nick cried, then quickly lowered his voice when Alex gave him a furious glare as he shushed him. 'Sorry, I'm just really pleased for you both.' He wanted to hug his friend, but, wary of drawing more attention, he settled for clinking his glass instead.

'Can't let your big brother do anything without you, eh?' Jake teased, but he too was grinning. 'Seriously, though, I'm thrilled for you although I'm not so keen on the pressure it puts on me.'

Alex chuckled. 'What are you waiting for? Laurie's the best thing that's ever happened to you, and you know it.'

Jake nodded. 'I do know it, but there's still a few things we're ironing out.'

'Shit, have I put my foot in it?' Alex looked stricken at the idea.

Reaching out, Jake clapped him on the shoulder. 'Everything's good, I promise. You have to remember I didn't grow up with the same example as you guys did with your parents. I know that Laurie and I are a million miles from the kind of relationship my folks had, but when the time comes I want to make sure my head's in a place where I can be the kind of husband she deserves.'

Nick appreciated his friend's candour, but he also felt Jake could be a bit too introspective at times. 'You'll get there when you are both ready.'

Jake nodded. 'What about you?'

He shrugged. 'I know Aurora's the one. I've known it since the first day we met. How on earth we make it work is something we're both trying very hard not to think about at the moment.'

Alex's brow creased. 'You think she'll go back to the States when this Chad Logan thing blows over?'

'I've honestly no idea; she hasn't said much other than how nice it is not to be on the road. I'm not sure how much of that is her putting a brave face on things, though. The idea she might not perform again seems unthinkable to me. I don't think I could face her giving up her career just to live here with me.'

'You could go with her,' Jake said. 'I walked away and started again to be with Laurie, and I'd do it again in a heartbeat.' He drained the last of his drink. 'Then again, I didn't have much to give up. Now Mum's settled here, everyone and everything that matters to me is right here in the Point.'

'Same for me,' Alex agreed, his voice sombre. 'I love my family, hell, I've never had friends like you two either, but if Ivy wanted to leave, I'd pack my bags tomorrow.'

Nick nodded. 'That's kind of where I'm at, but it's still early doors. For now, I'm going to track down my gorgeous girlfriend and make the most of the time we have together.'

'Sounds like a plan,' Jake agreed. 'Don't worry about the water; I'm going to hunt down Laurie and see if she fancies a smooch on the dance floor.'

Alex reached down and snagged a sausage roll. 'I'm quite happy here, thanks. If you see Ivy, send her in my direction, won't you?' With a grin, he bit the savoury snack in half and began to chew with gusto.

'If you're going to stay here, will you keep an eye on Gabriel?' The terrier had settled himself under the buffet table safely away from careless feet but in prime position to snaffle any dropped snacks.

Alex lifted up the edge of the tablecloth and dropped the remains of his sausage roll into Gabriel's already open jaws. 'You'll be all right with me, won't you, Gabe?'

Nick did a full circuit of the pub, but there was no sign of Aurora. He found Ivy chatting to Philippa and Archie, but she said they'd gone their separate ways some time before when Aurora went to the bar for a drink. He tried his parents next, but they'd not seen her either. 'Is everything all right?' his mum asked, smoothing away a non-existent crease from his jacket.

'Yes, fine. There's just a lot of people here and I don't want anyone hassling her for selfies.' He bent to peck a kiss on her cheek. 'I'll track her down, don't worry.'

'Try giving her a call, maybe?' his dad suggested as he raised his head to scan over the crowded room.

'I'm going to check over by the bar and then I might just do that.' As he walked away, Nick pulled out his phone but there were no messages. Neither Pete nor Linda reported seeing Aurora so Nick ducked through the door that led towards the bathrooms. With the noise of the bar muffled, he pressed Aurora's number and raised the phone to his ear. It went straight to voicemail. He hung up without leaving a message, starting to feel really concerned.

The swing door opened, and his father appeared. 'There you are. I was asking around and someone saw Aurora step outside a few minutes ago; they thought maybe she was on the phone.'

Well, that would explain the voicemail just now. 'Cheers, Dad.'

'You know where your mum and I are if either of you need anything,' Andrew said, holding the door back so Nick could scoot past him.

The snow had stopped, but there was a good couple of inches accumulated on the pavement outside. There were lots of footprints and scuff marks but one set led across the road and Nick followed it with his gaze to a street light about thirty metres away. The yellowish glow illuminated Aurora's pale hair like a halo. She still had her phone up to her ear, but she spotted Nick and waved as he approached. 'No. No, that's fine, Dennis. Yes, I'm disappointed too, but you're right, it's probably for the best.' She paused and then continued. 'He's here now. Yes, I'll call you in the morning. Don't be silly, none of this is your fault. All right, all right. Love to Hetty.' She shoved the phone in her pocket, then raised her hands in an I-give-up gesture. 'The National Children's Foundation no longer believe I am a suitable ambassador for their charity and have cancelled my appearance at their fundraising concert next week.'

'Over a spiteful bit of nonsense in a gossip column? You must be joking!'

Aurora shook her head. 'I wish I was. And it's nothing to do with what Carly King wrote – well, I don't suppose that helped, but that's not the main reason. Apparently the full interview with Chad and Melissa was shown on American TV overnight and, well, let's just say Jezebel has nothing on me.' Her tone was light-hearted, but she was shivering, and Nick didn't think it was just from the cold.

'Come here.' He pulled her against his chest and wrapped his arms tight around her back. God, she was freezing. How long had she been out here? 'Let's go back inside and get you warmed up.'

He felt her shake her head against his chest. 'I can't face it. Dennis said it's trending on social media again and I can't bear the thought of someone saying something.' She lifted her head. 'It's Nerissa and Tom's special day, and I've already played with fire just by being here. With this on top of the newspaper thing, someone's bound to say something, especially after a few drinks.'

'But you haven't done anything wrong,' Nick gritted out, wishing like hell he could get his hands on Chad bloody Logan.

'That doesn't seem to matter these days,' Aurora sighed. 'Can we please just go home?'

'Hold on.' Keeping her against him with one arm, Nick pulled out his phone and called Jake. 'I need to take Aurora home so can you bring Gabriel outside?'

'Is everything okay?' Even with the noise of the disco in the background, he could hear the concern in his friend's voice.

'Not really. I'll explain in a minute.'

'I'm on my way.'

Aurora was still shivering against him, so Nick began to rub his hands up and down her back and arms to try to get her circulation working. His coat was buried beneath a pile of others somewhere in the pub and her velvet jacket wasn't doing a great job at keeping out the cold. 'How long were you out here?'

'I don't know, ten minutes maybe?' She tilted her head back to look up at him. 'I'll be all right once we get home in the warm.'

She didn't look all right, she looked completely wiped out, but he gave her an encouraging smile. 'I'll make you a chococcino and you can take it to bed with you.' She nodded and tucked herself back against his chest.

The door of The Sailor's Rest swung back, sending a rush of noisy laughter out into the quiet night. Jake appeared with Gabriel in his arms and was followed by not only Laurie, but his parents as well. 'Brace yourself, the cavalry's here,' Nick whispered to Aurora as he pressed a kiss to the top of her head.

'What's going on?' his mother called as she tiptoed her way across the snowy street towards them. 'Are you not feeling very well, darling?' She raised a hand to touch Aurora's forehead.

'I'm fine, Sylvia, just a little tired, that's all.'

'But we were just about to cut the cake. Can't you manage another few minutes?'

'Leave it, Mum, yeah?' Honestly, Nick adored his mum, but sometimes she didn't see what was under her nose.

His mum opened her mouth as though to argue, but thankfully his dad stepped in and placed one hand on her shoulder, the other holding out Nick's padded jacket. 'Here, I thought you might need this.'

'Thanks, Dad.' Nick swung the jacket around Aurora's shoulders, and she immediately huddled down inside it. 'Everyone, go back inside before we all freeze to death. I'll give you a ring in the morning, okay?'

'Nick's right,' Laurie said. 'Let's get back in.' She caught Nick's eye and gave the slightest nod towards Jake, who was frowning at his phone. Looks like they'd worked out what the problem was.

'I'm sorry to put a dampener on the evening,' Aurora said.

'Not at all,' his dad assured her. 'We'll see you both on Friday. I've got a new turkey curry recipe I'll be trying out, so bring your appetites.'

'Sounds good.' Nick reached out and gave his dad a grateful hug. 'Merry Christmas, Dad.'

Andrew kissed him on the cheek. 'Merry Christmas.'

Of course, no one was prepared to go back inside until they'd all had a chance to hug and kiss them both and exchange Christmas greetings for tomorrow. After assuring his mum that everything was fine (again), Nick turned to see Laurie and Aurora had moved a little to one side. His sister was talking intently, holding both of Aurora's hands in hers. When she finished whatever it was she had to say, the pair shared a tight hug and there was even a little smile on Aurora's face as they separated. At last, his family began to retreat towards the pub, calling a last few goodbyes, leaving only the three of them standing beneath the street light. 'Come on, let's go home,' Nick said, tucking Gabriel under one arm and holding his other hand out to Aurora.

'Home,' Aurora echoed. 'Yes, let's go home, Nico.'

By the time he let them into the apartment, his shoes were soaking wet and his toes had turned into blocks of ice. Even with his jacket, Aurora didn't seem to be faring much better and he urged her towards the bedroom to get changed into her pyjamas while he poured some milk into a pan to heat. She emerged looking much warmer, dressed not only in her pyjamas but an old sweater of his she must've found in his bottom drawer and a thick pair of knitted socks. 'Better?'

She nodded. 'Much. I'm sorry for dragging you away from the reception.'

Nick opened his arms and hugged her when she stepped into them. 'There's nothing to apologise for. Here, watch the milk for two minutes so I can get out of this suit and then we'll have a proper chat about everything, okay?'

When he returned, Aurora was adding hot chocolate mix to the milk and humming to herself. He smiled as he recognised one of the hymns from the wedding service earlier. She seemed to have rallied remarkably well from what must've been a terrible shock. As he filled the water tank for the coffee machine to make the cappuccino, he considered the impact such a high-profile cancellation might have on her career. Up to now, he'd privately dismissed the whole scandal as a bit of a flash in the pan. One of those things that blew up on social media then died away as the next bit of clickbait started trending. Now it was starting to have real-world consequences for Aurora, he realised it was going to be an uphill battle for her to prove her innocence. 'I still don't understand what Chad is hoping to achieve,' he mused aloud as he popped the first coffee pod into the machine and started it brewing.

'That's one of the things Dennis and I were trying to figure out earlier. He's been doing a bit of digging around in the background, chatted to a few contacts and he thinks Melissa might be the driving force behind it.'

Even more confused, Nick leaned back against the counter beside the hob and frowned. 'That makes even less sense.'

Aurora gave the hot chocolate one last stir, then turned off the gas burner beneath it before she came to stand between his feet and placed her hands on his hips. 'Rumour has it the ratings on her talk show have been struggling and the network was planning to let her go. He thinks she's trying to pivot in a new direction as the interview was with a cable network that has a strong evangelical theme.'

'It still sounds like an incredibly risky strategy to me. Any idea why they decided to pick on you?'

The laugh she gave held a bitter edge. 'Dear old Dennis is never one to beat about the bush and he reckons it's because I'm disposable. My album success and the Divas shows have given me enough profile to make my name and face recognisable to a lot of people, but I haven't established my career well enough to be able to stand up against their combined star power.'

'Ouch.' Nick knew Aurora put a lot of faith in her manager and that their relationship went back to the very start of her career, but surely he could've found a less brutal way to put it.

Aurora's smile was completely unfazed. 'Stop glaring like an angry bear. One of the reasons I've survived as long as I have in this crazy industry is because Dennis has never shied away from telling me how it is. I don't need someone to pat my hand and tell me how amazing I am. I need honesty and that's what I get from him.' Her smiled faded. 'He also said he thinks we should cancel our visit to see them, stay here and carry on as we have been.'

'You were really looking forward to spending some time with them, weren't you?'

She nodded. 'I told you before how much they mean to me. Honestly, I'm far more disappointed about that than the concert cancellation. It's funny, you know, when he first told me the charity didn't want me to perform, my overwhelming reaction was relief. I'm so tired of it all and think it's time to call it a day.'

Nick studied her face, searching for a hint of upset or uncertainty. She might have been shivering in his arms less than half an hour earlier, but the look she gave him was calm and clear. He wanted to protest, to tell her it was just a shock and that once she'd had some time to think about it, she would feel differently, but he held his tongue. It wasn't for him to tell her what to think and what to feel about the situation. He could try to be empathetic and put himself in her shoes, but he honestly didn't have any idea how she could possibly be feeling in that moment. She was likely still in shock and this reaction could be nothing more than a bit of self-preservation. If she feared her career was ruined, wouldn't it be better to feel like she could exercise some control over her life and decide she was quitting rather than being cancelled? As much as he longed to fix things, he was powerless to do so. All he could do was let things play out and find a way to support Aurora in her choices without making her overcommit to something she might regret later. 'You don't have to rush into anything now. Let it sit for a few days and if that's still what you decide is best for you, then you have my wholehearted support. Besides, I think Melissa and Chad have made a big mistake with their timing because come tomorrow the only thing that will be trending is people moaning about whatever crap films are on the telly and eating too many sprouts.'

Aurora wrinkled her nose. 'We're not having sprouts tomorrow, are we?'

He laughed. 'Nope, although I can't vouch for what might be in Dad's experimental turkey curry on Boxing Day.' He was pleased when she laughed and he decided it was probably for the best not to mention that he wasn't entirely joking. 'For now, I suggest we finish up these drinks and take them to bed. If we hurry, we can still catch the greatest Christmas movie of all time on the BBC.'

Aurora crossed her arms and gave him a fierce look. 'You'd better be talking about *Die Hard*, or I might have to rethink this whole relationship.'

Laughing, Nick gathered her into his arms for a swift, hot kiss. 'See, this is why you and I are the perfect match. Look, I can understand why Dennis thinks it's a good idea for you to avoid London, especially once the news gets out about the concert cancellation, but that doesn't mean you can't still see him and Hetty. The flat next door is basically free as you're spending most of your time here. We'd have to check with Ivy, but I'm sure she'd have no objections if you invited them down to visit you here in the Point instead.'

With a gasp of delight, Aurora flung her arms around his neck. 'That would be wonderful, thank you, Nico.'

20

Aurora must've fallen asleep at some point during the film because one minute she was cheering on Bruce Willis as he crawled through the air conditioning ducts of the Nakatomi Plaza on his way to defeat Alan Rickman and his dodgy crew of terrorists, and the next she was semi-conscious and wondering why her bottom was freezing cold. Raising her head from the pillow, she squinted down the bed to find she'd somehow managed to kick the covers off her lower half. She tried to tug the duvet back over her but it didn't move. She sat up and took a firmer grip on the quilt, pulled and received a grunt from the muffled form beside her, but that was it. 'Well, as long you're all right,' she grumbled at Nick's sleeping back. He didn't stir.

She was awake now so she might as well make a cup of tea to fortify herself for what looked likely to be a full-on wrestling match to reclaim her half of the covers. She was soon wrapped up in his dressing gown – really, it was hers now by default – and tiptoeing into the kitchen. Gabriel gave her a gentle woof of greeting from his basket but didn't move. Puttering around, Aurora filled the kettle and checked the dog's water bowl, then curled up in the corner of the sofa, her feet tucked up under her. She tapped the power button on her phone and blinked at the number of notifications on her lock screen. The top one was from

Dennis – always an early riser – wishing her a happy Christmas and saying if it was okay with her friend then he and Hetty would love to come and stay for a couple of days. The rest were from the family WhatsApp group and when she opened it, it was clear Laurie had told the rest of them the real reason Aurora had wanted to go home. She scrolled back to the top of the messages and began to read her way through them. The first dozen or so were addressed to her, sending love and telling her not to worry because they had her back, that they believed her 100 per cent and whatever she needed they would be there for her. Touched at the unwavering support in each and every one, Aurora knew the decision to quit she'd reached the previous evening was the right one. She had people here who cared about her, who would help her make what was bound to be a difficult transition. She was under no illusion that she would miss performing, but the rest was a weight she no longer wanted to carry.

As she continued to read, the conversation switched to what they ought to do about Chad and Melissa. Sylvia, in particular, had some very graphic suggestions that were equal parts eye-watering and amusing. She was still chuckling over one of them when a yawning Nick came shuffling out of the bedroom. 'How long have you been up?'

Setting her phone down, Aurora headed back into the kitchen to re-boil the kettle. 'Only a few minutes. Umm, while we're at your parents' tomorrow, it might be worth a quick search through the kitchen drawers and confiscating the garlic press.'

Nick paused in the middle of scratching his head to stare at her. 'I know I'm still half asleep but I'm pretty sure that sentence wouldn't make any sense after half a dozen cups of coffee.'

'Your mum's threatening to use it on the more intimate bits of Chad Logan's anatomy.'

He winced. 'Yikes. That's a mental image nobody needs. I take it that means they all know the latest developments.'

'They had to find out sooner or later and as Laurie told me last night, I have nothing to feel ashamed of.' Crossing the room, she curled her arms around his waist. 'And now we're going to forget all about it and enjoy ourselves.'

A soft smile spread over his lips as he pulled her close. 'Merry Christmas, my beautiful girlfriend.'

'Merry Christmas, Nico. I'm sorry but I never got around to getting you a present.'

He tugged at the belt on her dressing gown, pulling the bow she'd tied free in one long, slow motion. 'I'm already unwrapping the only thing I need.'

After a lazy breakfast, they wrapped up warm and ventured out for a walk. The oppressive grey of the previous day had given way to blue skies and a brisk wind off the sea. Though she felt calm in herself, Aurora wasn't much in the mood for any company other than Nick's so rather than head into the village for a walk along the beach, they went in the opposite direction to explore the rockier terrain on the other side of the harbour and on towards the lighthouse. An overnight frost had given the snow underfoot a crust that crunched beneath their boots. Gabriel was in his element, jumping around in the snow like a little puppy.

They didn't say much, content just to enjoy the fresh air and the spectacular views of the incoming tide crashing against the rocks below. The path meandered this way and that, following the uneven coastline that spoke of eons of erosion from the elements. As they followed a deep horseshoe cut out in the rocks, Nick paused and took her hand. 'I want to show you something, but mind where you step.' He led her slowly away from the path until they were close enough to the edge they could see over it. He pointed down at a sliver of sand below them. 'When the tide goes out there's a fabulous beach down there. Hardly anyone uses it because it's only accessible by boat and then only for a few hours. It's the perfect sun trap in the summer, though.'

Aurora stared down. There was so much about the Point she didn't know. So many little secrets like this she wanted to explore, and she wanted to do it with the man beside her as her guide. She wanted to see it in all weathers, experience every season, follow the ebb and flow of village life as the tourists came and went like the tides. There was much she could do here, she was sure of it, she just needed some time to understand the needs of the community better. Things like the wishing tree and the RNLI fundraiser had been easy, but she wanted to do more than throw money at causes and walk away. She wanted to participate, to be around to dress up for story time at the bookshop, to sing at karaoke nights in The Sailor's Rest, to be spectacularly terrible at one of the quiz nights she'd seen advertised on a poster in the pub window. She wanted to find out if the church had a choir and go back to where it had all started for her – singing for the pure love of it. Singing in celebration, singing to offer comfort, to offer hope to those in need. She wanted to invest in things, to help projects get off the ground and be around to watch them flourish. She thought about how Nick had not only built a home for himself but had been able to give some of his peers an affordable way to continue to live in the village. He was helping the community to survive and thrive. It was only a handful of flats now, but there was so much more he could, so much more *they* could do together. And she knew just where to start. 'I want to buy Hillside.' She hadn't meant to blurt it out but she was bubbling over with the excitement of it all.

Nick turned to stare at her. His hair was tangled from the wind, his cheeks flushed from the icy fingers of its bite, and he'd never looked more gorgeous. 'What are you talking about?'

'The bed and breakfast, the one near your mum and dad's. I want to buy it for you, Nico.' She could tell how hard she was grinning from the stretch in her cheeks. It was the perfect plan, and she couldn't wait for Nick to share her excitement.

He took a step back. 'I don't need your money, Aurora. I'm not some local charity shaking a bucket for donations or tying a label to the wishing tree begging for someone to come to my rescue.'

Oh God, she was doing a terrible job of explaining herself. 'That's the last thing I was thinking about! I love what you are trying to do to help the community and I just thought it would be a way of cutting through the red tape.' She placed a hesitant hand on his chest. 'I didn't mean to insult you, or imply you couldn't manage perfectly well on your own. It's certainly not something worth falling out over. Forget I said anything.'

She made to turn away, but Nick captured her hand and held it over his heart. 'No, wait. I'm the one who should be saying sorry. You just took me by surprise, that's all, and my stupid ego engaged before my brain had a chance to.'

'You're not mad at me?'

Nick threw his free arm around her and pulled her close. 'Not a bit.' He kissed her forehead, her cheek, using his lips to coax her to look up at him until he could press a soft kiss to her mouth. 'The only person I'm angry with is myself for jumping to such a stupid conclusion. Can you forget I said it?'

Aurora wanted to say yes, but it felt like something too important to brush under the carpet. 'I wasn't trying to buy my way into people's affections, or bribe the community into liking me.' Though she'd tried hard to put it behind her, the horrible insinuations from Carly King's article still rubbed raw. 'I saw a chance to help, so I took it. For the first time in as long as I can remember I felt at home somewhere. I felt accepted by people for who I am as a person, not because they've seen me on the TV or because they've heard my music on the radio.' She swiped a hand across her cheek, trying to stop the silly tears that had started to fall. 'Do you know why I made those donations? I was helping your mum write out those labels and there was one request to fund a school trip to a museum and I knew if they didn't get the money they needed, some of the children in this village were going to miss out. I know what it's like to not have much, to have parents who want to treat their kids but sometimes they can't because the electric bill needs paying. I just wanted the children to have a fun day out and for their parents not to have to worry about the cost for once. What's wrong with that?'

Nick held her close against his chest, rocking them both gently. 'There's nothing wrong with that. I think it's a wonderful thing to do.' He leaned back only far enough to look down at her. 'I think you're wonderful, but I don't care about your money.' He stopped himself and shook his head. 'No, that's not right. I do care about your money, especially now I understand why you want to help me. With your financial backing I can be more ambitious, really look at a long-term strategy rather than fiddling about doing piecemeal projects. But I also need you to know that I would love you as much as I do even if you didn't have a penny to your name. I love *you*, not what you might be able to do for me, or for anyone else.'

'I wasn't trying to buy you, Nico.' She blew out a deep breath. 'Perhaps

I was trying to buy a place for myself in this community, though. I love it here and I want so much to be a part of it.'

'You already are; my mum doesn't just let anyone in the family WhatsApp group, you know.'

Aurora laughed. 'Speaking of which, we'll have to calm her down before she goes ahead and takes out a hit on Chad and Melissa.'

Nick grinned and then his expression turned serious. 'There's a place here for you at the Point for as long as you want it. Forever, if I have anything to do with it. I'm going to do whatever it takes to prove it until you are ready to believe it for yourself.' This time she let him draw her into his arms and kiss her, grateful they seemed to have found a way to negotiate their way through the minefield of their first serious argument. 'I'll agree to the purchase of Hillview on one condition,' he said when they came up for air. 'You let me do exactly what I want with it.'

Aurora had no problem in agreeing to that. 'Of course. I didn't envisage my role as anything other than a silent partner. This is your dream, Nico, not mine.' She didn't know what her dream was any more now she'd decided to retire from the entertainment industry, but she was sure she'd find a new one.

In time.

21

Nick was still feeling a bit guilty for jumping to the wrong conclusion when they arrived at his parents' house the next day, loaded down with the presents both he and Aurora had bought for everyone. She was generous in heart and spirit, wanting only to share her good fortune with those around her and he'd come too close for comfort to hurting her. He didn't have time to brood over it as the house was already a zoo with everyone talking all over each other as they shared hugs and belated Christmas well wishes. He'd barely managed to get his coat off when the bell rang, announcing the arrival of Alex and Ivy. One look at the sparkling ring Ivy was flashing on her finger and his sister and Aurora broke into ear-piercing squeals of excitement as they rushed to embrace Ivy, then dragged her off towards the kitchen to show his mum. 'You talked her into it, then?' Nick joked, giving Alex a hug of congratulations.

'How could she say no? I mean, look at what I'm working with here.' Alex held his hands out as though inviting Nick to admire his physique.

Nick folded one arm across his chest and propped his chin on his other as he pretended to give Alex a good once-over. 'Hmm, I see what you mean. Ivy's always been good at restoring knackered old things.' Laughing, he ducked the mock-punch Alex threw at him. 'Seriously, mate, I'm really pleased for you both.'

Alex grinned like he'd won the lottery. 'Cheers. So how's things with you?' He cast a quick glance over to where the three women were still admiring the antique emerald-and-diamond-studded band on Ivy's finger. 'Aurora okay now?'

Nick made a so-so gesture. 'She says she's fine and seems really determined to turn her back on her career and settle down here.'

'Then maybe it's all for the best. Perhaps she was already fed up and this is giving her the excuse she needed to take a step back. It would certainly resolve your dilemma about whether or not to leave.'

'It sure would, but I still feel like there's a lot of unresolved stuff so I'm just trying to let her work it all out. Mind you, I almost cocked the whole thing up yesterday by acting like a total idiot.'

Alex frowned. 'I'm sure whatever it was, it's not that bad,' he protested. After Nick gave him a quick rundown of what he'd said to Aurora about not wanting her money, Alex shook his head. 'I can't believe you thought she was trying to buy your affection.'

Nick groaned. 'It was a split-second reaction; I honestly have no idea where it came from. Forget I even mentioned it.'

'Forget you even mentioned what?' Jake asked as he approached them, holding out a couple of bottles of beer.

Nick sighed, not really wanting to admit for the second time how close he'd come to hurting Aurora, and perhaps causing irreparable damage to their relationship. 'Not in here,' he said and led the two of them into the relative privacy of the hall. 'I took something Aurora said the wrong way yesterday.'

'Is that all?' Jake took a swig from his own beer. 'We all say and do stupid things from time to time. What matters is how we deal with it. Are things okay between the two of you now?'

Nick shrugged. 'Yeah, I think so. I just feel really bad because I can't bear the idea of hurting her. Everyone thinks she's got the world at her feet, but they don't see the person behind the facade who's as messed up and as vulnerable as the rest of us.'

'But you see the real her and that's what is important.' Jake reached out and slung a consoling arm around his shoulders. 'Relationships aren't easy even when you're both from similar worlds. Look at how hard I tried to stuff things up with Laurie because of all my stupid baggage with my dad.'

'And I almost blew it with Ivy because I'm the master of avoidance,' Alex added, as though that was in any way helpful.

'Jeez, guys, if this is your idea of a pep talk, I think I'll pass,' Nick grumbled.

Jake laughed. 'All we are saying is it takes a lot of work and we're not dating someone who is in the public eye.' His expression grew serious. 'I know you love Aurora, but I think you need to really think about how being with her is going to change your life.'

'You think I'm making a mistake?' Not that it would make a blind bit of difference to Nick because he wasn't going to give Aurora up for anything, not even his friends. The only way things weren't going to work out between them was if she changed her mind and went back to her old life. The possibility chilled him to the bone.

'I didn't say that, now, did I?' Jake shot him an exasperated look. 'You were the one who wanted to talk about this so don't go jumping down my throat. All I meant was that it's crazy to think Aurora can go from being famous to being a nobody overnight so there's going to be stuff like that hit piece from Carly King to contend with. You just need to make sure you are fully prepared for that and that you've got all your shit together so you can be there for her when it happens. I know therapy's not for everyone, but I've found talking about it to someone neutral has helped a lot. I thought building a wall around myself was the way to protect myself. It locked a lot of the bad stuff out, but it prevented all the good stuff from getting in too.' He pointed his bottle at Alex, who was lounging against the wall opposite. 'And take Prince Charming over there. He thought he could just keep walking away every time he encountered a problem he didn't want to deal with.'

'Harsh,' Alex protested, then nodded his head in agreement. 'But fair. I thought life kept dealing me a bad hand until I met Ivy and I realised I had no idea what real difficulties were. Look, I know my folks are amazing, but they spoiled me rotten when I was a kid and I became a bit too used to expecting things to come to me without putting much effort into it.'

Nick looked between the two of them. 'So if your parents were too harsh on you,' he said to Jake, 'and yours were too soft on you' – he pointed at Alex – 'what's my excuse? Mum and Dad have given me all the love I ever needed and more, but Laurie and I have always had to work for what we want. I'd say that's a pretty good balance.'

Jake scoffed. 'All right, Goldilocks. If your life was so perfect, why have you systematically sabotaged every relationship you've ever had? Laurie told me how you worked your way through pretty much all the eligible girls in the village. And the ones you didn't date you put in categories that made them untouchable, like you did with Ivy.'

'Hey, no one's touching Ivy but me,' Alex protested with a grin.

'Sure, sure,' Jake said with an impatient shake of his head. 'But on paper you have to admit that she and Nick are pretty well matched and could've made a good go of it if Nick hadn't decided she was like a second little sister to him.' He turned back to Nick. 'The only woman you let yourself fall in love with was the one who was completely unobtainable, until suddenly she wasn't.'

'So you think subconsciously I'm waiting for things to fall apart with Aurora? That doesn't make any sense when she's everything I've wanted.'

'Ah, but now you've got her, are you good enough to keep her?' Jake folded his arms across his chest and fixed him with an unwavering stare.

'I think I liked you better when you were the brooding, silent type,' Nick muttered.

Jake laughed. 'Look, I'm not the expert but once you start self-analysing it almost becomes a habit to turn it on the people around you and wonder what's going on inside their heads. Your parents have an amazing relationship, and I adore them both, but they're a lot to live up to.'

'I guess I never really thought of it like that.' It was true that his father had always been Nick's role model and whenever he'd thought about what kind of future he'd wanted for himself, it had always been a variation of what his parents had. People who didn't know them well would likely assume that Sylvia Morgan was the one who ran things because she was the more outgoing and outspoken of the two, but Nick knew better. His father was the steel core of their family. The anchor that held them all firm in the worst of life's storms. Was there a basic part of Nick that felt the need to emulate his father in that traditional provider/protector role in order to be successful? 'I think you'd better give me the number of whoever it is you've been talking to.'

'I'll text it to you,' Jake said. 'Now we've got you on the right track, it's time to do something about Aurora.'

Nick frowned. 'What do you mean?'

'She needs to start fighting back is what I mean. I can appreciate her reasons for not wanting to get drawn into a spat with Chad Logan but she's let them control the narrative for too long. It's getting to the point where no one will care what she has to say because they'll have already made up their minds. Now Carly King has muddied the waters, it's only going to get worse.'

He got Jake's point, but it was up to Aurora how she wanted to tackle things. She had Dennis and his team to advise her and they'd been in the business a long time. 'It's not for me to tell her what to do; she's got plenty of people doing that already.'

Jake frowned at him for a long moment before he conceded with a nod. 'Okay, but I'm going to make the offer to help her with a right-to-reply interview all the same. I won't put any pressure on her, but I kind of feel like I owe it to her to give her the chance. I'm still in touch with Mac, my old editor, and he's got the contacts to sell the story. She wouldn't have to speak to anyone other than me.'

'I'll leave it to you to have that conversation with her. My job is to support her in whatever way I can while she finds her way through this.'

* * *

'Did you have a nice time?' Nick asked Aurora as they strolled down the hill later that evening. He was stuffed to the gills with turkey curry and feeling lethargic after being shut inside with so many people. He raised his face to the cold wind, grateful for the salt-tinged slap to his senses. He'd seen her and Jake with their heads together when they'd been recruited by his dad to do the washing-up and he'd left them to it, but he couldn't deny he was curious to find out how she was feeling about what he assumed was Jake's offer to do an interview.

'It was great, but I don't think I need to eat again for about a week. I thought your dad was going to try and make us take some of the leftovers home with us.' Aurora gave a little moan as she pressed her hand to her belly.

Nick laughed. 'Don't think we've seen or heard the last of it. It'll all go in the freezer and be dished out to everyone in Tupperware boxes every time we see him for the next couple of weeks.'

'Don't say that. If I keep letting him feed me like that, I'll have to buy a whole new wardrobe. Well, that's another good thing about retiring: I can spend the rest of my life in trousers with elasticated waists.'

'Ah, now we're getting to the heart of it,' Nick teased. 'You don't want to maintain that punishing workout schedule.'

'I've hardly done a thing since I've been here,' Aurora said. 'I haven't been on the scales, but I'm bound to have put on a few pounds.'

Nick couldn't say he'd noticed, not that it would have bothered him in the slightest. 'I think you look beautiful, but you always do.'

'The perfect diplomatic answer,' she said as she skipped a little ahead of him and turned to face him with a grin.

'I wasn't being diplomatic; it's the truth. Your body is your business. If you want to do less exercise and put on a bit of weight as a consequence, it's not going to affect what I feel about you, or how attractive I find you. I always put a few pounds on over the winter because I'm doing less. Once the season starts and I'm back out on the boat, it soon comes off again.'

'So, what you're saying is I have to put up with this little pot belly of yours for the next few months.' She poked him in the tummy and Nick let out a pained grunt.

'I probably didn't need that third helping of curry. Come on, let's get home so we can lie around in our pants without worrying about what anyone else thinks of us.'

'Good idea. Speaking of which, I had a chat with Jake earlier.'

Nick wondered if he should pretend he didn't know what she was referring to, but he thought it was best to be honest. 'About doing an interview?'

She stopped walking and turned to face him. 'He spoke to you about it?'

'Yeah. I think he was sounding me out on the subject. I had a chat with him and Alex earlier about a few things and he mentioned it then.' He didn't go into detail about the rest of the conversation as there were still some things he wanted to work through first. He would talk to her, though, once this mess with Chad Logan had been resolved and they had time to focus on themselves and what the future might hold.

'And what do you think I should do?' It was hard to read her expression in the rapidly fading light, but she didn't sound annoyed they'd been talking about her, more curious.

'I think it has to be your choice. I mean, I'm as angry as anyone about the way those two are twisting things but I can also see how trying to put the record straight might easily backfire on you.'

She nodded. 'That's my biggest concern as well. I hate feeling power-less, but if I engage then I'll just be adding fuel to the fire.' She leaned her head against his chest and Nick raised a hand to cup the back of her neck, feeling the baby-soft ends of her hair tickling against his fingers. 'I just wish I knew *why* they are doing it because then I feel like I'd know better what to do.'

Shifting his hand around to tip up her chin, Nick met her worried gaze with what he hoped was a reassuring smile. 'Maybe Dennis will have more information when he and Hetty come down and that will help you make a decision.'

'I hope so,' she sighed. 'I just want it all to go away, you know?'

22

Her conversation with Nick had helped to solidify Aurora's feeling that she didn't have enough facts at hand to go ahead with the interview Jake had suggested. Though it was always there in the back of her mind, she did her best to relax and enjoy the next couple of days. In between long walks, she gradually transferred her things from the next-door apartment and gave the whole place a good clean so it would be ready for Dennis and Hetty's arrival. Though she hadn't bothered with decorations for herself, Aurora persuaded Nick to take her on a trip to a local garden centre where she found a lonely little tree in a bright red ceramic pot. A good watering and a profuse application of fairy lights and it was looking right at home in front of the large balcony window. When she turned it on after dark, the reflection back from the darkened glass gave the whole thing a glorious glow.

Dennis and Hetty arrived in time for lunch on the twenty-eighth with a boot loaded down with presents and even more food. At this rate, she and Nick wouldn't need to go food shopping for a month. She thought they'd be tired after the drive down, but Hetty couldn't wait to get out and about. 'It's been so long since I've been by the sea; can we at least have a quick walk along the beach?' she pleaded after they'd fortified themselves with sandwiches made with the thick homemade loaf Hetty had brought with her and a cup of tea.

'Of course. I'll show you a few of the sights.' She turned to Nick, who, having cleared the kitchen table, was spreading out his notebooks and the plans he'd been sketching for Hillside. He hadn't let her look at what he was doing and having pored over the photographs on the estate agent's details she was dying with curiosity. The agent was closed until the new year but Nick had promised he would follow up with Alun as soon as the office reopened and arrange for a viewing of Hillside. 'Are you coming with us?'

He glanced up and gave her a distracted smile. 'Unless you want me to, I was going to carry on with this for a bit. Besides, it's been months since you've seen each other so I thought the three of you might like some time alone.'

Gabriel didn't so much as raise his head when she unhooked his lead from beside the front door and shook it. 'Well, it really is just the three of us, then,' Aurora said as she hung the lead back up and opened the front door.

As they descended the stairs, Hetty hooked her arm through Aurora's. 'I do like your young man, but I'm glad we get a bit of time to ourselves. Tell us all about what you've been up to. How was the wedding?'

They chatted a mile a minute, Hetty stopping every few moments to point out this or that thing she'd spotted, seemingly delighted with everything. They did a circuit of the harbour first before Aurora led them to the top of the crest and stopped to allow them to take in their first proper view of the Point in all its glory. The shingle beach with its thin stretch of pale sand stretched out before them like a silver ribbon, leading the eye all the way to the impressive promontory of land that gave the village its name. 'Nick's sister and her other half live in a little cottage right on the top,' Aurora said, pointing to the faint cluster of buildings. 'It's part of a working farm and was originally a holiday rental but the owners seem happy to let them have it on a long-term basis.' It was proof perfect to her of the need for more affordable housing and only served to underline how important what Nick was trying to achieve would be for the community.

'And that's the surgery.' She drew their attention to the large white building just below them that marked the beginning of the buildings that lined the seafront. 'There's the gift shop, with Laurie's café attached, and beyond that is The Sailor's Rest.'

'That'll definitely need a bit of closer inspection,' Dennis said, turning up the collar of his camel-coloured wool coat. 'Let's keep moving before we freeze to death.'

'It'll be a bit better once we're down on the beach, especially if we stick close to the wall,' Aurora promised as she led them down the hill towards the steps.

'You seem very at home here,' Hetty remarked as they wandered along the beach. Dennis had moved a bit ahead of them and kept stopping to pick up stones and shells that caught his eye. He'd be brushing sand out of his coat pockets for a week at the rate he was going, Aurora thought with a grin.

'It feels like I've been here forever, rather than less than two weeks,' she admitted to Hetty.

'And everyone is making you feel welcome?' There was no missing the hint of concern in her voice and Aurora knew Dennis would've told her about her run-in with the woman at the shopping centre.

'Everyone's been lovely, I promise.' Aurora had stuck to her guns and kept her phone free of social media apps, but she'd be lying if she said she wasn't worried about what was being said. 'What's the latest from the wilder corners of the internet?'

Hetty sighed. 'Things have settled down a bit and there haven't been any more statements since the interview. We've got alerts set up, of course, and Chad and Melissa were filmed glad-handing the congregation at a big evangelical church service on Christmas Day. It's been hard to dig around because everyone's been off for the holidays. Dennis is going to make a few more calls, because honestly it stinks worse than last week's fish.' She patted Aurora's hand. 'It'll all come out in the wash, just give us a few more days.'

Well, now was as good a time as any, she supposed. 'Whether it does or not doesn't really matter in the grand scheme of things, because I'm not going back.'

'Not going back where?' Dennis said, making her jump. She'd been so caught up in her conversation with Hetty that she hadn't noticed his return.

'Anywhere, to any of it. I've had enough of the whole bloody business. I did what I needed to do and proved I still had it in me after everything that happened with Julian. I've got nothing left to prove to anyone, least of all myself.'

Dennis's face turned a rather alarming shade of red. 'So you're going to let another man dictate what happens to your career? How the hell is this any different from what that maniac did to you?'

Aurora took a step back, surprised at the vehemence in his tone. 'It makes a world of difference! Bloody hell, Dennis, you were there! You know what he did to me, and this is nothing in comparison.'

'He didn't mean it like that, did you?' Hetty intervened, always the peacemaker.

Dennis threw up his hands. 'No, of course I didn't. The two things aren't even in the same stratosphere, but you can't honestly tell me you'd given even a passing thought to retiring until all this nonsense happened.' He shoved his hands in his pockets and turned away, marching a few angry steps along the beach, the shingle slipping and sliding beneath him. He got half a dozen paces away before he turned and marched back. 'I blame myself, you know! I should've known there was something dodgy about that audition, the way Logan just happened to be in Las Vegas at the same time as you. Thirty bloody years I've been in this game, and I should know how to spot a wrong 'un by now.'

'It's not your fault,' Aurora said, hating to see how upset he was. 'You are right that I hadn't thought about giving it up, but I haven't stopped to think about anything much for the past eighteen months because I've been too busy to breathe half the time. I said yes to everything that came my way because I was so desperate to make a point. To show a dead man that he hadn't taken anything from me. I was the one that was pushing for acting roles, remember, so you were only doing what a good agent does when a chance like that gets put on the table. No one could've foreseen the outcome – hell, let's be honest here, none of us understands what they hope to achieve, but it doesn't matter. I'm ready to take my life in a new direction. I want a proper home, a family of my own, right here in Mermaids Point. It's time to let go of the past and focus on the future.'

'Oh, lovey.' Hetty looked close to tears as she held out her arms. Aurora stepped into them, but to give rather than receive comfort. She'd already been through it all in her head and she knew the answer.

'I'll never be free of what happened with Julian, not really, and that's okay. It's not something I have to escape any more; it's something I have to learn to live with and being with Nick is helping me to do that.'

'What are you saying, then? That this is it?' Dennis asked, shaking his head.

Stepping away from Hetty, Aurora held out a hand to him, waiting until he took it before she offered her other one to Hetty. 'I'm saying that the loneliest place on earth is standing on a stage in front of thousands of people and I don't want to be lonely any more. I've got new dreams now, ones full of hope and happiness and love and family.' She squeezed both their hands. 'And I need you to know that you're both a really important part of that new future. I love you both and I'll always be grateful for everything you've done for me, but I don't want you to be my agents, I want you to be my family.'

Hetty was crying openly, one hand fumbling in the pocket of her coat for a tissue. Releasing Dennis's hand, Aurora put her arms around the woman who had in recent years been more of a mother to her than anyone else. 'I'm sorry if you're disappointed, but please don't think of this as me quitting; I'm just choosing something else for me, something better.'

The older woman pulled back to beam at her through her tears. 'Oh, you silly girl, I'm not disappointed in you. I could *never* be disappointed in you. All I've ever wanted—' She reached for her husband and pulled him into their embrace. 'All we've ever wanted is for you to be happy.'

'Amen to that,' Dennis said in a voice even more gravelly than usual. 'Now that we've got that out of the way, can we please go the pub because it's brass monkeys out here.'

Aurora threw back her head and laughed, mostly in relief rather than anything else. Relief that they understood, relief that they supported her decision, relief at the ever-growing certainty that she was doing the right thing.

By the time they sat down to dinner, it was almost nine o'clock and Aurora was more than ready to eat. After a fortifying double Scotch to warm himself up, Dennis had kept the celebratory mood going when they'd got back to the apartment by cracking open one of the bottles of champagne he and Hetty had brought with them to help see in the New Year in style. Though both she and Nick had tried to protest it should be them taking care of their guests, Hetty had dug out an apron from one of the many bags she'd brought with her and had set about making beef Wellington from scratch, though she apologised for cheating by using shop-bought pastry. Aurora had done her best to help, but had been shooed from the kitchen for getting in the way and in the end had settled for sneaking in to wash up anything Hetty placed in the sink and to make sure her glass was topped up. Dennis was in his absolute element, holding court as he regaled Nick with scandalous tales from his thirty years in the business. By the time they were settled around the kitchen table, Aurora's sides were aching from laughing.

'And you've got photographic proof of this?' Nick asked, his face a picture of disbelief as Dennis finished off a story about a former national treasure who had apparently had a fetish for dressing up like a baby.

Dennis winked at him as he poured them each a glass of rich, red burgundy. 'You'd be amazed at the things I've got stuffed in the back of the safe. Time was you could reach a gentleman's agreement over things like that – well, get bloody fleeced by whoever managed to sneak in a camera. Now, everyone's a paparazzi with their camera phones and live streams so it's impossible to keep things quiet. I never covered up anything illegal or dangerous, just tried to save a few clients from their own stupidity.' He paused in what he was saying to offer an appreciative smile to his wife as she set a loaded plate in front of him. 'This looks wonderful, pet, thank you.'

'It really does,' Nick agreed as he thanked Hetty for his food. 'I'm putting my foot down tomorrow, though, and neither of you are doing a thing.'

Taking her seat opposite Aurora, Hetty shook out a napkin and laid it across her lap. 'That's very sweet of you, but it's only what I'd already planned to make before your trip to London got cancelled. Cooking is my passion; before I met Dennis, I was all set to go off to culinary school and become a chef.'

'But you gave it all up for a good man,' Dennis said with a wink as he reached for her hand and placed a kiss on the back of it.

'For a very bad man, you mean,' Hetty teased with a roll of her eyes. 'And I didn't give it up, I just realigned my priorities. Building the agency with you has been a wonderful experience and if I had my time over, I'd make the same decision in a heartbeat. I still get to do the thing I love, but as a hobby instead. Besides, I don't think I have the temperament to have made it in a high-pressure kitchen environment. I'm very content to potter around and be the mistress of my own domain.' She sent a soft smile across the table towards Aurora. 'The only thing certain about life is the uncertainty of it. All we can do is play the cards we are holding at any one time.'

'I'll drink to that,' Dennis said, raising his glass.

'You'll drink to anything,' Hetty said, her voice as dry as the ruby-red wine. 'Make the most of it while you can because we're doing Dry January, and I'll be extending it into February if you carry on like this.'

They were sitting around waiting for the coffee to brew when Nick stood up. 'I'll be back in a minute; I just want to check on Gabriel.' When he returned a few minutes later he was carrying a tell-tale stack of papers.

'Oh, is that what I think it is?' Aurora turned to Dennis with a grin. 'Nick's been working on the plans for his next conversion project, but it's all been top secret.'

She turned avid eyes to the first A1 sheet of paper he laid out in the middle of the table. It took her a moment to understand she was looking at the ground floor layout. 'You're going to keep it as a single building? I thought you'd at least split it back into two separate houses or convert it into several flats.'

'That's what I was originally going to do, but then something else came up.' When she tilted her head to give him a quizzical look, he leaned forward and kissed the tip of her nose. 'You.'

Oh. Looking at the plans with fresh eyes, she pointed to a long room that ran the length of the back of the building. He'd sketched in the outline of what looked like kitchen units and appliances at one end and a large dining room table and chairs in the centre. The far end had a long rectangle and a couple of squares. 'Kitchen, diner and...?' She tapped the squares.

'An entertainment space, maybe, or a play area.' When her eyes widened, he grinned. 'For the dogs.'

She laughed. 'Dogs, plural?'

'Gabriel needs at least one friend, I reckon, don't you?'

A buzzy feeling started in her head and she didn't think it was the after-effects of too much champagne. He'd been thinking about them, about what their future might look like and was designing a home that would accommodate those plans. 'And what's this?' She pointed to another room at the front of the house.

'That's the sitting room, with a nice open fire for getting cosy in the winter.'

She could almost hear the wood crackling in the grate. 'And this?'

'An office space for you.' He hesitated. 'Or a music room, if you'd prefer, somewhere you can be creative on your own terms.'

Heat stung the back of her eyes and she had to blink to try to stop a sudden rush of tears. 'On my own terms,' she whispered.

He gave her a shy smile. 'Retiring doesn't mean you have to give up music. Even if you don't want to perform any more, you might find the urge to do a bit of songwriting.' He shrugged. 'I don't know, I just thought it's something I should accommodate.'

She laid a hand over his. 'It's perfect. I love that you thought of it. I love everything about this.' She held his gaze, heart too full to find the right words.

'Stop making cow eyes at each other and show us the rest,' Hetty said with a laugh. 'I'm particularly interested in where the guest room is going to be.'

Nick took them through the plans for the second floor. The left-hand side of the property had a master suite complete with a changing room and an en suite shower at the back. The rest of the plan was less defined. 'I'm still working on how many rooms we might need, but we can talk about that later.' He slid a final sheet of paper on the top. It was the dormer attic space and he'd marked one room as an office for himself and the other as a gym. 'It's just a suggestion of what we might do with it. Once we're sure we want to go ahead, I can speak to the architect, and he'll work up a proper set of plans.'

'It's the perfect location,' Aurora mused, thinking about his earlier reference to a playroom. 'Your mum and dad will be practically on the doorstep when we need them for babysitting duties.'

Nick grinned. 'That's a very good point.'

Aurora all but floated around the kitchen as she helped Hetty tidy up and make a pot of coffee. Her head was full up to bursting with images of her and Nick nestled on a huge sofa with Gabriel and maybe a rescue greyhound sprawled on a rug in front of a blazing fire. Of Nick grinning at her on the patio as he and his dad stood guard over the barbeque and the kitchen was filled with noise and laughter. Of them, Alex and Ivy and Laurie and Jake sitting around the dining table long into the night as they drank one too many bottles of wine and put the world to rights. Of walking into a sun-filled nursery and picking up a smiling, chubby baby with a riotous head of curls just like her father's.

'Penny for them,' Hetty said, giving her a gentle nudge and a knowing smile.

'It'd cost you more than a penny,' Aurora said, letting the daydreams go for now as she concentrated on brewing the coffee. There wasn't enough money in the world to buy them because they were priceless to her.

They were back around the table soon after, and Aurora was regretting Hetty's suggestion of 'Just a bite or two of cheese' to go with the coffee when Dennis's phone started to ring. 'Damn, I thought I'd switched that thing off,' he said, jumping up from the table to go to where he'd left his phone resting on the arm of the sofa. He sent it to voicemail and flicked the silent mode key on the side of the handset. 'Sorry about that.' The phone began to vibrate in his hand and then there was a chorus of muffled pings from the handbag Hetty had left on the sideboard near the front door.

'Whoever that is they can wait. We told everyone we're on holiday and we meant it,' Hetty said with a scowl, before she smiled and reached for the cheese knife. 'Now, who's going to try a bite of this Camembert? How about you, Nick?'

He held up his hands in surrender. 'I couldn't manage another bite, Hetty, thanks.'

The phone was still pinging away in the background and Dennis hadn't returned to the table, his eyes glued to his phone. Aurora sighed. 'I think whatever it is, you need to check it out,' she said gently to Hetty. 'If that was me on the other end of the phone, you wouldn't hesitate to answer it.' Whatever time of the day or night, they'd been there when she needed them. There was no such thing as office hours or holidays when it came to the entertainment business. 'Nick and I can clear up.'

'I think you might want to stay sitting down for this,' Dennis interrupted as he slid back down into his own chair, his eyes still fixed on his screen.

Aurora's stomach clenched, the spike of adrenaline at Dennis's words sending all that food and wine churning in an unhappy mass. Nick was already reaching for her hand and she fumbled towards his, the reassuring grip of his fingers an anchor she could only cling to as she asked, 'What's happened?'

The smile on Dennis's face when he looked up could only be described as triumphant. 'Looks like Chad and Melissa's little scheme has backfired in a rather spectacular fashion. At least three different actresses who've worked with him in the past have made statements to a journalist at the *New York Times* accusing him of inappropriate behaviour on set.'

'You're kidding me?' Reaching out, Aurora took Dennis's phone and began to read for herself. It was one of those long Twitter threads with extracts from a longer article but the salient points were all there. The allegations were unpleasant, and one of the actresses claimed she'd reported it to a producer who'd then had her summarily removed from the project and she claimed to have found it difficult to get more work afterwards.

'There's more,' Hetty said, having gone to retrieve her phone to check her alerts. 'Something about a junior staffer on Melissa's talk show.'

Aurora snapped her head up at that. 'My God, do you think she knew?'

'Sounds like she might have.' Lowering the phone, Hetty reached out a hand to Aurora. 'Thinking it about, she must've known because why else would she have been there in Las Vegas?'

'I'd forgotten all about that.' In all the fuss, the image of Melissa sitting in the back seat of the limo that had come to collect Chad at the hotel had completely slipped her mind. She closed her eyes, trying to picture it, trying to analyse the way they'd smiled and waved at her as they'd driven off. It had been a matter of seconds and she'd been thrown off guard by her reaction to that overly long hug from Chad as he'd said goodbye.

'So why do you think they involved you in all this?' Nick asked her as he leaned over her shoulder to try to read what she'd been looking at. 'If they were expecting something to leak, then why not turn the tables on one of his actual victims and accuse them?'

'I have no idea...' Aurora thought about it for a long moment. 'Unless it's because I couldn't come back with any kind of counterclaim other than a denial that anything untoward happened. Chad was the perfect gentleman throughout the whole meeting. The only physical contact we had was when we shook hands at the start and when he grabbed me on the pavement outside. He only did that to stage the photograph, though, and there was nothing sexual about it.' She shuddered as she realised how different things might have been.

'It's still a hell of a gamble,' Dennis muttered. 'He must've known someone was going to go digging around.'

'Perhaps they're hoping to muddy the waters,' Hetty mused as she continued to scroll through her phone. 'His defence is either going to be denial or something along the lines of the story he told about Aurora, that it was a consensual moment of weakness.'

Feeling sad and sick to her stomach, Aurora let Dennis's phone drop to the table. 'Those poor women.'

'There's not a lot we can do for them, but we need to get our ducks in a row and figure out what your response is going to be,' Dennis said as he got up from the table. 'Hetty, love, where's my laptop?'

Stunned at his seeming lack of concern, Aurora could only watch as Dennis started hunting around the lounge for his laptop. 'What are you doing? Don't you care about what he's done to them?' she demanded when he settled back in his chair and began pushing Nick's plans aside to make room.

He frowned at her. 'Of course I care, but they're not my clients and therefore not my immediate concern. They'll have their own agents and advisors to support them. We need to get the word out that you've been an unwitting dupe in all of this. If we get this right, then all this rubbish goes away. Who knows, we might even be able to get you reinstated for the concert tomorrow night.'

Aurora shot a pleading look towards Hetty while Nick began to gather the house plans before they could get creased. 'Can you speak to him, please?'

'He might have a point, darling. I know you said you want to quit, but wouldn't it be better to go out on a high, so to speak? One final appearance for people to remember rather than just fading away?'

Frustration coursed through Aurora. Only hours ago, they'd told her they respected her decision, that they were happy for her and yet here they were trying to shove her back under the spotlight.

'Stop it.'

Hetty must've read something on her face because she closed her eyes and nodded. Dennis continued to type, oblivious to anything other than the plans whirring in his head. Reaching out, Aurora pushed the back of his laptop screen down until he had no choice other than to remove his hands from the keys. He looked up, giving her a distracted frown as he tried to push her hands away and open his screen back up. 'What are you doing? I need to get this email out to the concert promoter asap.'

'I'm not doing it. I won't use those poor women's misery as a way to salvage a career I don't even want any more.' Leaving the truth of that to sit with Dennis for a minute, Aurora glanced up at Nick, who had been silent throughout. 'It's not right.'

Nick crouched down beside her chair, taking both her hands in his. 'No one would think you were taking advantage of them. You might not have gone through the same thing they have, but you're still a victim in all this.'

'But I've already made up my mind about retiring. I don't need to take a final bow.'

'You're allowed to change your mind.' When she opened her mouth, he pressed a finger to her lips. 'I'm not telling you what to do, I'm just saying that it doesn't change anything. If after the dust settles on all this and you find yourself missing it, then you mustn't be afraid to speak up. The house will still be here, *I'll* still be here. Your home will be here for as long as you want it to be.'

His hand cupped her cheek. She loved the feel of it against her skin, the calluses that spoke of all those hard hours out on the boat, so unlike the pampered, manicured softness of Chad Logan's hand when he'd shaken hers and started all of this. 'I want it to be my home forever. I want you to be my home forever.'

He stroked the ball of his thumb across her cheek. 'Then it's all yours. I'm all yours.'

EPILOGUE
EIGHTEEN MONTHS LATER

'So, what do you think?' Nick asked as he led Aurora into one of upstairs rooms of what had previously been the Hillside Bed and Breakfast. Even though the contractors were packing up for the day, he'd made her put a hard hat on at the front door and checked for hazards before he let her into each room. After months haggling back and forth with the council, and moments when they'd both been ready to throw in the towel, Nick's plans had finally been approved. Now they were full steam ahead and he had been throwing everything he had at the project to get it finished in record time.

Aurora touched a hand to the freshly plastered wall and smiled. 'I didn't realise how light and airy it would feel in here once that awful wood panelling came down.'

Nick curled an arm around her waist and pressed a kiss to her cheek, knocking her hard hat askew in the process. 'What did I tell you?' he teased as he removed her hat and set it on top of a dustsheet-covered table that was standing in the middle of the room.

'That I should trust you.' She slid her arms around his neck and went up on tiptoe to kiss him.

'Exactly.' His hands came to settle on either side of her waist, and she smiled to herself. He'd always liked to hold her like that, but now even more so since they'd received the surprising news just before Easter that had expedited the conversion works. She wondered if he even realised he was doing it, forming a protective cage around her still-flat belly.

'I had lunch with your mum today, and I thought for a minute she'd worked out what was going on because I had to put my sandwich down after only a couple of bites.'

Nick raised a hand to her brow and then shifted it to cup her cheek. 'Still feeling peaky?'

She leaned her face into his palm. 'I had a lie-down afterwards and I feel fine now.'

'Still, it's something we should talk about with the doctor tomorrow when we go for the scan.'

She curled her arms around his waist and clung to him. 'It'll be all right, won't it?' She'd asked him that a thousand and one times since she'd made him sit in the hall outside the bathroom of their apartment and pass her the half a dozen different pregnancy tests that he'd snuck to the big out-of-town supermarket to buy after she'd missed her first period.

'It'll be fine,' he promised her. 'Do you still want to tell everyone on Sunday?' His parents were throwing a barbeque in their back garden, the last one before the full onslaught of the summer season started and everyone would be working late nights and weekends.

'We said we'd wait until after the first scan and it's been lovely having time to get used to the idea ourselves, but I'm ready to let them know our family is going to be five instead of four.'

'Come on, let's get you back home so you can put your feet up.' He was equally as cautious as he led her downstairs to where they'd left Gabriel and Dolly, the white and tan greyhound they'd fallen in love with when they'd popped into a local rescue shelter, only meaning to put their names down on the waiting list.

When they reached the bottom of the hill, the glorious sight of the sea called to her like a siren's song. 'Can we go for a paddle?'

Nick laughed. 'It'll be freezing.'

'Just for a minute?' she pleaded, holding his gaze until she'd coaxed the lopsided smile she loved so much from him.

'You know I can't resist you when you look at me like that.'

Reaching up, Aurora slid a hand into the messy curls at the nape of his neck and drew him down for a kiss. 'The feeling is entirely mutual,' she whispered against his lips.

ACKNOWLEDGMENTS

It's our final visit to Mermaids Point...

I feel a bit choked up writing that because I have had the most wonderful time in the Point with the Morgans and the Nelsons. I hope you have enjoyed getting to know them as much as I have. I know many of you have been waiting for Nick's story since he first popped up in *Summer Kisses* so thank you for being patient! I have known he and Aurora would end up together right from the very start but the timing needed to be right – and what better time than surrounded by the magic of Christmas?

Thanks to Becca Allen (Copy Editor) and David Boxell (Proof Reader) for catching my mistakes. It takes a team to bring a book to life.

Much love and gratitude goes to everyone at Boldwood Books for making the past two years such a wonderful experience. I am so looking forward to working with you all again very soon!

Thanks to Alice Moore for the most beautiful cover, you really have brought the spirit of Mermaids Point to life.

#TeamBoldwood! As always just the most wonderful group of writers to be a part of x

Special thanks to Karen Stephens who came up with Gabriel's name. I think it suits him perfectly!

Writing can be a lonely business, so I am blessed with the most wonderful friends who help me through the bad times and are always the first to celebrate the good times. Jules Wake, Bella Osborne, Philippa Ashley, Rachel Griffiths, Rachel Burton and Jessica Redland. You are simply the best x

Last but never least, all my love and thanks go to my husband who is always on my side x

I'm very excited to start work on a new series of books, and I hope you will join me for lots of love, laughter (and maybe a few tears) with the new friends who will be waiting to greet you in *Juniper Meadows*.

MORE FROM SARAH BENNETT

We hope you enjoyed reading *Happy Endings at Mermaids Point*. If you did, please leave a review.

If you'd like to gift a copy, this book is also available as an ebook, digital audio download and audiobook CD.

Sign up to Sarah Bennett's mailing list for news, competitions and updates on future books.

https://bit.ly/SarahBennettNewsletter

Summer Kisses at Mermaids Point, another warm, escapist, feel-good story from Sarah Bennett, is available now.

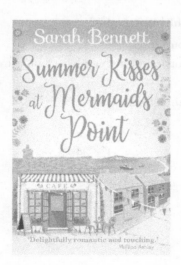

ABOUT THE AUTHOR

Sarah Bennett is the bestselling author of several romantic fiction trilogies including those set in *Butterfly Cove* and *Lavender Bay*. Born and raised in a military family she is happily married to her own Officer and when not reading or writing enjoys sailing the high seas.

Visit Sarah's website: https://sarahbennettauthor.wordpress.com/

Follow Sarah on social media:

- facebook.com/SarahBennettAuthor
- twitter.com/Sarahlou_writes
- bookbub.com/authors/sarah-bennett-b4a48ebb-a5c3-4c39-b59a-09aa9idc7cfa
- instagram.com/sarahlbennettauthor

Boldw∞d

Boldwood Books is an award-winning fiction publishing company seeking out the best stories from around the world.

Find out more at www.boldwoodbooks.com

Join our reader community for brilliant books, competitions and offers!

Follow us
@BoldwoodBooks
@BookandTonic

Sign up to our weekly deals newsletter

https://bit.ly/BoldwoodBNewsletter

Lightning Source UK Ltd.
Milton Keynes UK
UKHW041038030123
414752UK00002B/6